KU-611-319

Praise for *Edith & Oliver*

'The novel tells a painfully sad tale, but Forbes imbues it with such **wit and tenderness** for her damaged characters that it remains **a pleasure to read**'   **A** *Sunday Times Culture* **Must Read**

'**Engaging** ... [Forbes] is an award-winning theatre, television and film actor, and her insight into the world of performance and talent – particularly wasted talent turned rancid – is astute. Oliver's hubris – his downfall – is striking in his increasingly wretched attempts at stardom'   *Irish Times*

'**Forbes writes beautifully** on the hard, peripatetic reality of theatre life behind the greasepaint and glamour. She is also particularly **insightful** on the internal torment of a man brought down by the slow growth of self-deception ... **shimmering**'   *Daily Mail*

'A **finely written love story** ... lyrical and evocative'

Belfast Telegraph

'The long gone vaudeville word is engagingly brought to life ... Forbes's debut novel *Ghost Moth* was highly praised. This **atmospheric** follow-up by the Belfast-born author deserves to be equally well regarded'   *Sunday Business Post*

'*Edith & Oliver* brilliantly evokes the seedy ambience of the old music halls and the tantalising promise of glamour and fame that keeps its performers going ... It is an often heartbreaking story but Michèle Forbes invests it with **wit, grace and tender understanding**'

BBC History magazine

'A **heart-wrenching** follow-up to the well-praised *Ghost Moth*'

Irish Country Magazine

Praise for *Ghost Moth*

'**Clever, unpredictable, beautifully written and crafted** – *Ghost Moth* stayed with me for a long time after I'd finished reading the final, sad, wonderful page' Roddy Doyle

'**Deeply – sometimes erotically – charged.** The writing soaks up the world, and thrills to the beauty of it . . . Katherine Bedford – so ordinary and so passionate – is a heroine to treasure'

Anne Enright

'Delicate and unusual . . . **outstanding**' *Guardian*

'A bountiful river of **lovely images, fresh and perfect,** a triumphant story both familiar and strange. A **stellar** debut'

Sebastian Barry

'An **impressive debut** by a writer who is not afraid to address the so-called ordinary lives of real human beings' John Banville

'This beautifully written first novel is about the kind of love that can never be blotted out . . . **a tender, heart-breaking story**'

The Times

'**Mesmerising** . . . this haunting novel will linger in your mind'

Sunday Mirror

Born in Belfast, Northern Ireland, Michèle Forbes is an award-winning theatre, television and film actress. Her first novel, *Ghost Moth*, was published in 2013 to great critical acclaim and Forbes was shortlisted for Newcomer of the Year at the Irish Book Awards. She lives in Dalkey, Dublin.

www.micheleforbesauthor.com

Also by Michèle Forbes
Ghost Moth

MICHÈLE FORBES

WEIDENFELD & NICOLSON

A W&N PAPERBACK

First published in Great Britain in 2017 by Weidenfeld & Nicolson
This paperback edition published in 2018 by Weidenfeld & Nicolson
an imprint of The Orion Publishing Group Ltd
Carmelite House, 50 Victoria Embankment
London EC4Y 0DZ

An Hachette UK Company

1 3 5 7 9 10 8 6 4 2

Copyright © Michèle Forbes 2017

The moral right of Michèle Forbes to be identified as the author of this work has been
asserted in accordance with the Copyright, Designs and Patents Act of 1988.

'The Man Watching/Der Schauende' from

A TRANSL. POEMS ... ...OBERT BLY.
Copyright © ...98... by Robert Bly. Rep... ...ns Publishers

Al ... ...the part of ... ...ed,
s... ...ed in a retrieval system, or ... ...ny
mea... ... ...wise,
w... ...then the prior ...rmission... ...the

A ... ...ce
... the characters in this book ... ...
In actu... factions, uning... ...
A CIP catalogue ...

**Coventry
City Council**

CEN*

3 8002 02359 506 1	
Askews & Holts	Jan-2018
	£8.99

ISBN (mass market paperback) 978 1 4746 0469 7
ISBN (eBook) 978 1 4746 0470 3

Typeset by Input Data Services Ltd, Somerset

Printed in Great Britain by Clays Ltd, St Ives plc

www.orionbooks.co.uk

For Owen, Megan and Ethan
with love and gratitude

'*This is how he grows: by being defeated, decisively by constantly greater beings.*'

'The Man Watching'
Rainer Maria Rilke, 1901
Translation by Robert Bly

I

fire And wood

One

Dublin, 1922

Starlings quiver on the black trees as Edith removes her hat. She wants to feel the wind about her head, the pure stoke of it, whipping her hair up all out of order. She wants to sense the briny sting of the sea against her brow, the pluck and tug of it upon her lips and cheeks. The spring sun has turned the water white, as though there is a vast field of snow stretching before her towards Howth, not sea.

She stands on Carlisle Pier, brittle, twig-like. Her silhouette against the milky sky as dark as the starlings on the black trees beyond. Her hair is a riot, wild strands of it waving Dun Laoghaire goodbye, waving *him* goodbye, rising and spiking like flickering black flames against the white. In her left hand she holds a soft leather bag and now her hat. In her right a suitcase, one of its clasps secured with string. Slung over her shoulder by a loop of rope is a small wooden box, her daughter's portable garden: alpines, nubbles of limestone, miniature ferns, tiny narcissi. As light as a bag of apples.

She leans into the wind as razorbills strain to hover overhead, her eyes following the contours of a landscape she will never see again. In the distance the elegant purple hills, below them the esplanade, closer still the black trees. She can hear the sound of the church bell rising from the town, then the calls from the porters. The mailboat is to depart for Holyhead, its funnels already spewing rills of black smoke into the early morning sky.

'Let's go,' her daughter says to her.

She does not move. She cannot bear to leave him.

'Let's go,' her daughter says again.

Setting down her luggage for a moment, she gathers her hair. She puts on her hat, tugs the rim of it down to shade her eyes. Before she boards the boat she wipes away the tears that are now running down her face and tells her daughter they are only caused by the wind.

Two

Belfast, 1906

O liver has no idea where he is, or why he is where he is. There's a dense fog in his brain. His head feels as though it has been split in two. His throat is sore, his tongue leaden, and his lips feel as though they are sutured together like barnacle to rock. He opens his eyes slowly, can make out only dark irregular shapes in the room, whatever room it is he's in.

He shudders, looks down at himself. He is dressed only in his underpants, a white cotton blur in the gloom. A sharp worry creases his brain. Try as he might he cannot latch on to any detail which will help him explain why he is on the floor in such a state of undress. He squints as he looks around him. Eventually a shape takes form on the other side of the room. A face? He holds his focus as best he can. It's a face all right, but it's the pale face of a clock, its large hands signalling seven – in the morning, he assumes by the weak light inching round the window frame, but what morning? And why is he slouched against someone else's furniture and not in his own bed? Then he remembers. *Jesus, the party, Fred Felix's party! Last night – after the 8.45 – I'm in Felix's dressing room – must be?*

He hears a gentle snore close to him. *God!* There's someone else in the room with him, and him practically buck-naked. Then another thought – maybe they're just as naked as he is. Struggling to turn on to his knees; he feels an icy pain like a knife in his head. His back aches. He grabs on to the corner of the chaise longue against which he is slouched. As he pushes himself up on to his feet he feels something hard in his right hand. He opens it to find a small, white object. A stone? He looks closer. Sees its irregular shape. A charm from a bracelet, perhaps? He walks stiffly over to the window, pulls at the limp curtains. A spill of innocent morning light pours into the room. The air now furry with dust.

Oliver looks down at his open hand. He's holding a large molar, bloodied at its root, a sinewy fragment of vein and flesh attached to it and a cloud of blood on his skin. The fingertips of his other hand are covered in blood. Oliver immediately checks his mouth, stuffing his fingers in to feel his teeth and gums. Nothing is missing. *Whose tooth am I holding, then?* He looks at the molar with alarm and disgust. *What in God's name happened last night? And where are my clothes?*

He walks unsteadily over to a figure lying on the floor. As he bends over to get a closer look his head buzzes, his stomach goes into spasm, feels as though it's being folded a thousand times over. Slowly the figure takes form and he realises it's a woman sprawled out on top of his clothes. One part of her skirt is hitched up to her waist and his Prussian blue cravat, which he doesn't even remember wearing at the party last night, is tied around her thigh. She is sleeping soundly. There is blood around her mouth. He draws back, worried. Is it *her* tooth he's holding in his hand?

He pushes her shoulder gently but she does not stir. He hears another snore, but this time from the other side of the room. He turns towards the sound, approaches it cautiously. The shape he finds huddled in the corner turns out to be Fred Felix, the host of last night's party, dressed in the blue chiffon evening dress which Oliver now vaguely remembers the young barrel jumper Elsie Smart wearing when she arrived. Felix's legs and feet are bare. His hairpiece – *damn it, I knew it was a bloody wig* – has been removed. Across his pasty bald head someone has written the words 'Go to Hell' in bright red lipstick. Oliver turns back to the woman. He bends down and tugs at his clothes. The woman doesn't move. He places the bloodied tooth on the table beside him, which is littered with empty beer bottles and plates, and wipes his hand on his underpants. Then he pulls hard at his clothes, freeing his shirt and trousers. The woman rolls over on to her front. He searches for his socks – somehow he'd feel less vulnerable with his socks on. He finds them and slips one on his right foot with great difficulty, then the other on his left. Slowly he dresses himself but it seems as though he is getting colder the more clothes he puts on, not warmer. Shivers run through every muscle in his body.

He moves slowly across the room, realising now that he's in the kitchen of the Empire Theatre and not in Fred Felix's dressing room. At what stage of the evening's proceedings did they migrate to the kitchen? He needs something hot to drink. *Tea, yes, tea would help – no, maybe something cold, water, just water – no, tea would be better.* He gradually makes it to the sink near the window and fills a small kettle with water. He turns on the gas of the two-ringed stove. As he places the kettle on the ring he lifts his head to the mirror on the wall in front of him. A ghostly face stares back. *Oh Jesus, Mary and sweet Saint Joseph* – this is certainly the worst hangover he has ever had. How much in God's name did he drink? He looks closer at his face in the mirror. There is blood around his lips. He splashes water on his face and wipes the blood away with the back of his hand. He stands clutching on to the edge of the sink waiting for the kettle to boil. It feels as though it is taking an interminably long time. Finally it whistles feebly, a screeching inside his brain. He empties the green metal teapot and puts two large spoonfuls of tea into it, then pours in the boiling water. He waits this time for the tea to draw. Again, it feels torturous. He might as well make a cup of tea for the woman, at least then he'll be able to ask for his Prussian blue cravat – too much of a liberty to untie it from her thigh while she's asleep. If she woke up while he was retrieving it, how would he explain himself? He pours out two cups of tea, and brings one over to the woman. He pulls her body round and shakes her. She doesn't respond. He shakes her again. She opens her eyes and immediately flinches at the light, dropping her chin to her chest.

'Hello . . . em . . . how are you?' he asks.

The woman eventually lifts her head and with bleary eyes stares at his mouth as though wondering what it is.

'How am I . . . or . . . who am I?' she replies, her voice croaking.

'How are you? Are you all right?'

'I don't know.'

'I made you some tea.'

'Oh . . . thank you.'

The woman pushes herself up into a sitting position with some difficulty and takes the cup of tea from Oliver. He looks at her face. Blood is crusted around her mouth, a ring of stale ale visible on her upper lip. She has the beginnings of a black eye.

'Oh . . . thank you,' she groans.

'Sorry,' he says tentatively.

'Shorry?'

'Yes, I'm sorry,' Oliver continues politely, 'but I think I've removed one of your molars.' He lifts the tooth from the table and shows it to her.

The woman looks puzzled. 'Did I ashk you? I musht have ashked you. That tooth wash giving me sho much bother.'

Oliver meekly hands it back to her. They both stare at it in her palm. There is an embarrassed silence. If neither of them remember him ramming his hand into her mouth and wrenching out her molar, what other heightened intimate encounter do they not remember?

The woman looks up at Oliver.

'And, come to think of it – who *are* you?' Oliver says.

'I'm Edith.' The woman meekly reaches out her hand to him.

He shakes it. 'Pleased to meet you, Edith.'

'Edith Foshter. Pleashed to meet you too. You're Oliver Fleck – the Illushionist.'

'I am.'

'A wonderful performance lasht night,' she says flatly, then rubs her head.

A beat while Oliver contemplates what she might be referring to. 'Oh,' he says realising. 'Thank you. Yes, I had a new illusion which seemed to go down well ...' He sighs audibly with the effort of speaking.

Edith attempts to stand and Oliver helps her to her feet. Holding on to his arm, she sways from side to side. She is an odd little thing, he thinks, tipping thirty perhaps, and for a small woman has a tall woman's nose. Even though she's smiling – a strange, placatory crumpled smile – the natural fall of her face gives her a serious look, almost angry. Her skin is delicate and creamy. Her dark green eyes are peppered with violet (echoed now by the rising violet bruise on the right side of her face). Her eyebrows have a noble arc to them, he notes, and although most of her cinnamon brown hair is gathered at the back of her head in a loose bun like a bird's nest, one long thick strand of it falls across her shoulder. She wears a plainly fashioned dress of black merino with a thin cream stripe along the skirt. He stares at her moustache of stale ale, at the trim of dried blood around her mouth.

He wants to ask her for his cravat back as it is still tied around her thigh but for some reason, which he is unable to fathom, he cannot bring himself to. He feels a flush of self-consciousness, which is most unlike him.

They stand in the kitchen holding on to one another as though on the deck of a sea-tossed ship. If not for the scratching at the door they would happily have stayed like that – one a fulcrum for the other – for quite some time, for as long as it took for their world to stop turning.

Oliver slowly breaks away from Edith and opens the door. Fred Felix's dog Minty races in, dashes straight over to Felix and begins licking his bald head. Oliver decides to make his exit before Felix comes around, offering a ridiculous little flutter of his fingers to Edith as he goes. She flutters her fingers back at him, still smiling. He cringes as he closes the door. *Let's forget about all that, better to forget the whole damn thing!*

Three

His matinee performance that afternoon at the Empire is a disaster. Apart from the fact that every move Oliver makes feels excruciating to him and that big drum is still banging in his head, what's worse is that he has learned that Edith, the woman whose molar he removed at the party, has been hired at the last minute to replace the resident pianist Arthur Sullivan for the matinee. Worse still, the orchestra have been hired to play for the evening performances only and so Edith will be providing the only musical accompaniment.

Edith sits at the piano now with a huge bandage around her head, her black eye shining. She has taken laudanum for the atrocious pain in her jaw and downed two whiskies and she cannot find the keys. 'The Sparkling Songsters Wilson & Welsh' wait patiently for their intro for 'She Got away with Murder', which never arrives, then sing unaccompanied regardless, feigning cockiness, only to have Edith join in with them halfway through playing a completely different tune. When Mlle Sabine arrives on stage, stocky and low-bosomed in her sky blue paduasoy, ready with her flock of performing cockatoos, Edith's sudden and over-enthusiastic flurry on the keys startles

11

the birds so much they panic and squawk and will not stay on their perch. Then 'The Famous Foot Controller', Gordon McGregor, finds it all but impossible to keep in time with Edith's alternating tempo, first he has to drag his legs like ancient stones across the boards then high kick at such an agonising speed it nearly kills him.

When it is Oliver's turn he carries on the best he can but the entire performance is a shambles. During his 'The Appearing Woman' illusion he signals frantically at Edith – who, having now found the piano keys, appears completely baffled as to the order in which she should play them – to cease her musical accompaniment as he is finding it impossible to concentrate. After his 'Medusa' illusion, he bows stiffly as Edith attempts to play him off the stage, now punching the piano keyboard with her fists as though she is deflating a long and unwieldy slab of dough.

Oliver feels sickened. He has always been meticulous in his preparation and professional in his performance. Always has and always is. He can never bear to be mediocre. He had, after all, learnt from the greatest illusionists and hypnotists of the day, men who performed at the Alhambra Theatre when he worked there first as a call boy and then as assistant to the house manager. When The Great Bandini appeared for the first time, he remembers, he had stood enthralled in the wings. He had watched Bandini – in his signature golden turban – at every matinee and evening show until he knew the performance by heart. When Bandini's assistant had fallen ill one evening, Oliver, then almost nineteen, had offered to take his place. At first he was laughed at – traditionally it was always a woman the illusionist made disappear – but when he talked through the performance moment by moment, Bandini was so impressed by his knowledge he agreed. The new partnership made the illusion an even greater success and, after the run at the Alhambra, Bandini asked Oliver to work with him on his upcoming British tour. He worked with Bandini for the next five years. A wonderful time, he remembers fondly. Bandini had become like a father to him.

Determined to redeem himself after the afternoon's fiasco – he must, for he still has two Saturday evening shows ahead of him – he sends his button-fly collared shirt out to Patterson's Dyers & Cleaners on Castle Street to be starched. He grabs a quick and rather fevered nap in his dressing room then asks the management for a full rehearsal with Sullivan and the orchestra before the 6.45 p.m. In the midst of organising the finer details of next week's programme, the management half-heartedly agree.

At six o'clock Oliver heads for the stage.

'Can we please get the rehearsal started!' he shouts out into the auditorium. Silence. 'Please can we – can we start from the top!'

A female voice rises from the dark of the orchestra pit. 'He'sh gone. They're all gone.'

Oliver spreads his hand flat out in front of him to block the glare from the footlight. 'Who's that?' he asks curtly.

'There'sh only me.'

Oliver's heart sinks. He recognises the voice. It's her again, Edith 'Foshter'. 'Where's Sullivan? I was told he would be back. Do we have house lights?' he throws out to the wings.

'Shullivan's gone acrossh Telfair's Entry to The Kitchen Bar, shaid he won't be back for the evening shows, or ever.'

Oliver steps forward, a spool of darkness eclipses him enough to aid his vision. He frowns and squeezes his eyelids together in order to get a better view of the woman seated at the piano, her face a milky blister in the murk. His eyes adjust slowly. Yes, it's Edith all right, still sporting a black eye but without the bandage around her head this time.

'What on earth do you mean – he's gone?' Oliver arches his back in disbelief.

'What I mean by "gone" ish – he ish no longer here.' Edith strikes one brisk chord on the piano as though to say *and that's as much information as you're going to get out of me.*

Oliver looks at her. 'And what about the orchestra? Where's the conductor?'

'Dunno,' she shouts up to the stage. 'From the top, then?'

'Sullivan can't walk out like that!' Oliver leans back on his heels, turns to check each side of the stage as though expecting Sullivan to return.

'Well he jusht did – he'sh quit,' Edith pipes up. 'Shaid the whole thing ish nothing but a damn dingy circus.'

'He said that about my performance?'

'I think the dingy circush he wash referring to wash life in general. I wouldn't take it too pershonally. Don't worry, I'm only booked for tonight, then you'll be free of me. From the top, then?' she asks brightly.

Oliver rubs his hand across his chest as if to calm a rising temper. 'Eh, yes . . . from the top, but this time perhaps "Intermezzo" in A by Brahms,' he mutters.

Edith immediately thrashes out the opening chords of a raucously jolly tune.

'What the hell is that?' Oliver shouts.

'Didn't you shay "The Prehishtoric Man"?'

'No, I said' – *is she doing this on purpose?* – 'I said "Intermezzo" in A, by *Brahms*!'

'You should shpeak more clearly then.'

Oliver does a double take, but says nothing.

Edith starts playing.

'Wait!' Oliver roars at her. Edith stops. 'I need to time my entrance.'

Edith sighs audibly and Oliver can feel his jaw tighten at the sound. *Who the hell does this woman think she is?*

A clattering of heels and Millie Evans, Oliver's assistant for 'The Appearing Woman' illusion, appears on stage. She wears a glittery frock, which balloons from her robust waist. Her hair is set in tight curls.

'It's too cold down there,' she complains.

'Tough,' says Oliver. 'We're just about to start. Wear a blanket until Maclagan winds you up. Maclagan – you ready?' Oliver hollers at the floor.

'He's gone for a keek.' Millie rubs her bare arms with her hands to warm them.

Oliver winces at the sound of the word coming out of such a pretty mouth. 'Jesus, in that case we'll never get started.'

He has one more week here at the Empire before he heads off on the Ernie Talbot Circuit for a six-month tour: Derry, Dublin, Edinburgh and a whole cluster of venues in the North of England. Tonight, as on the rest of the tour, Oliver will perform at the end of the first half despite his best efforts to secure the prime spot of closing the show. He knows at this stage in his career, with his reputation, he deserves that billing. But Sydney Brown, the theatre manager, has booked The Ted Lennard Five, a troupe of trampolinists, to close the show at the Empire tonight. Got to give the crowds what they want, Sydney Brown had said, got to keep up with the times. Well you've certainly struck fucking gold there, Sydney, Oliver thinks as he waits for Hughie Maclagan, his mechanical assistant. Up with the times! *Hope they end up going through the fucking roof!*

Maclagan pokes his head in from the wings. 'Sorry. Nature called.'

'You took your time,' Millie shivers and scowls at him.

'Well,' Maclagan answers calmly, 'as my mother always used to say – a man should never bolt a shite.'

A 'ta-da' resounds from the piano.

Maclagan extends a hand in the direction of the orchestra pit in appreciation.

'Let's get on with this,' Oliver growls.

He is finding her distracting. She will not sit still at the piano. She shifts from side to side on the piano stool as she plays. He needs silence for his opening speech but he can hear her flicking through her sheet music. When he stops the rehearsal to work through some detail or other, he senses her moving around as though she is looking for a mislaid pencil, then fumbling for something on the floor. He can hear a strange clicking noise, whatever it is. This distraction continues until he stops, moves to the edge of the stage and looks directly at her. He catches a glimpse of something large and furry on her lap. What is it? Absent-mindedly, she lifts it up in the air with one hand while waiting for a moment to resume playing. Oliver can see it clearly now. It is a large ball of wool, and hanging from a thick needle is a half-knitted something. *What in God's name*, he thinks. *She's fucking knitting, she's fucking knitting while she's playing the piano.*

He asks the obvious. 'Are you knitting?'

She looks up at him, a pale diffusion of a face looming forward in the dark. He cannot grasp her exact expression but suspects an indignant one.

'Pardon,' she says lightly.

'Are you knitting? You're knitting.'

'Shee thish?' She holds her knitting up clear of the piano.

'A right Madame Defarge we have here,' he mutters, but loud enough for her to hear him.

'Shee thish?' She bellows at him this time. 'What do you think thish ish?'

Oliver is a little taken aback by her manner. 'It looks like a scarf or shawl of some kind.' He raises his eyebrows in disbelief that he is taking her question seriously and answering her.

'You may shink it's a shawl of shome kind, but this shawl represhents the washted moments of my life in regular and pearl.'

Oliver shakes his head, completely bemused by her.

Edith continues. 'All the time I am waiting for you to make up your mind, your dithering about, your "will I come on shtage right or shtage left, now which looks shtrongest?" and your "why am I giving her the bunch of flowersh at *thish* moment? Maybe I should wait for the music to peak and *then* – or maybe I should throw the flowersh into the audience" and "oh the light ish too bright in my eyes" and "who hash removed my markings on the shtage because now I don't know where to shtand"!'

The silence is so intense you can smell it.

Oliver speaks quietly and slowly. 'It all has to do with the timing, Madame Defarge.' He grits his teeth. '*Everything* has to do with the timing. Particularly after such a disastrous matinee.' He indulges for a moment in the idea of the Bastille, the guillotine poised above her neck. '*Ev-ery-thing.*'

She looks up at him. They lock eyes. 'It sheems everything has to do with the *washting* of time, if you want my honesht opinion.'

'I don't want your honest opinion.'

'It's not ash though you've dishcovered the Holy Grail – it'sh a trick, get on with it.'

'It's an *illusion.*' His voice is steady. He cannot believe her impertinence. She was a much nicer person when she was hungover, he thinks.

'Well, you'll need to cheat the rug a little further downshtage in your *illushion* or else they'll shee the trapdoor.'

Oliver does not move, or speak. How had he not seen that? The one detail that would blow the illusion. He gathers himself for a moment. Maclagan should have checked. *He* should have checked.

Edith throws her knitting on the floor of the orchestra pit and lights up a cigarette.

She is raising his game. He checks the position of the rug from the auditorium – *she was right, damn it* – and continues with the rehearsal.

She is on cue every time. All he has to do is ask her once. She understands exactly what is needed. The all essential timing, it becomes apparent, is in her bones.

Four

The first evening show at 6.45 sees Oliver at the top of his form, as it does Edith, who outshines the orchestra, hitting every nuance and beat. Oliver is heartened by her. He's glad that Sullivan did a runner and hopes Edith will now be booked for the rest of the run.

Word of mouth draws more than the usual number of patrons to the Empire Theatre for the 8.45 show. People are very keen to see this Mr Oliver Fleck, Mysterious Illusionist and Hypnotist, some are even standing in the aisles. Earlier, there had been a slight scuffle at the box office, a misunderstanding over tickets, then a swift resolve as the management apologised and offered both parties the best seats in the house. There were jealous looks from the other patrons waiting in the queue, smiles on the faces of those recompensed. Eventually the call came from front of house for the ladies and gentlemen to take their seats.

The running order is the same as the earlier shows, the double act Wilson & Welsh is followed by Mlle Sabine (this time with becalmed cockatoos), then a group of Eccentric Dancers, an Irish Impersonator, a Sword-Swallower and a Fire-Eater, however, Gordon

McGregor 'The Foot Controller' is laid up in his dressing room with a twisted ankle and has been replaced by Baritone Barry Bristow.

Now, Oliver walks out into the broth of smoke and sweat of a full house. He stops centre, stands solid and still, takes his time, lifts his head to the gods. A large, ominous shape haloed in a gold spill of light. Silence falls across the auditorium.

He gestures to the orchestra to play but holds his gaze on Edith. She nods and smiles at him. There is a clear ring of brass, a swift kiss of strings as the violins pitch in, then bass chords rumble and growl from the piano as Edith hits the keys. His choice – the opening strains of Beethoven's Symphony No. 7 in A Major, a lulling distant thunder like the sound of his blood. His heart is beating fast. Yet everything is contained. The orchestra struggles with the slower pace, not the serio-comic accompaniment they are used to, but Edith happily works her elbows up and down like a wingless bird trying to take flight. The audience senses the vibration, sees the attentive regard in which the conductor holds his head and shoulders, his right arm extended, the baton pulsing, and a hush falling over the house. The low thunder of music creeps closer, lightened by a fresh breeze of violins, and another burst of brass. The crystalline ring of a xylophone now vibrates through his bones, his pulse lifts, he breathes deeply, feels every pore in his body open to the music and to the heat of a full house.

He takes off his tailcoat – revealing his shirt and bow tie, starched and pristine white – and hands it to Maclagan (who in stark contrast to Oliver's generous frame is a wiry shackle of flesh and bone). He brushes back his hair, his handsomeness fuelled by the burning light which now rises in his eyes. He raises his arms, thrusts his chest forward, takes the weight off his tailbone, bounces a little on his feet, ready to present 'The Appearing Woman'. A loud cough from the second row, another from the back, then a chorus of coughs from the balcony, but he keeps his flow, he does not lose concentration.

Maclagan now offers him a folded cloth. Oliver cracks it like a whip and it opens as splendidly as a sail in a tailwind. Dust motes jiggle like a frenzy of sea flies in the footlights. The sail becomes a momentary parachute, then falls to cover a rosewood table which stands on a rug concealing the trapdoor, its secret opening hidden from view. With his right hand he slowly smoothes his hair back then extends his arm towards the table, banging his foot upon the wooden stage floor. He spreads his fingers wide. The xylophone intensifies. He grabs at the air with his outstretched hand and suddenly the cloth begins to rise. He can feel the audience's trepidation like a prickling on his skin. Something is taking shape beneath the cloth. They watch in amazement as the cloth continues to rise, up and up, each moment pirouetting blissfully into the next. Then with a flourish he pulls the cloth from the rising shape and reveals a woman – Millie Evans – standing on the table. There is a large gasp from the crowd. Millie smiles and is about to speak when Oliver raises his hand to her. He addresses her in a strange churring mixture of vowels and consonants, a demonic mumbo-jumbo. She closes her eyes and begins to sway to his deep and sonorous song. She leans into the air as though testing her weight against it, her arms floating upwards from her sides. He has hypnotised her. Suddenly he claps his hands. She falls from the table, her skirts billowing as she moves through the air, and he catches her in his arms.

The illusion is a huge success and in his bloody-mindedness he knows it. The audience are on their feet. He feels it fully, inhabits himself. A pinprick sparking in his brain and then a delicious, clear surge right through his body, bringing him out of his head, up into a pure and singular world. It's like a drug to him and he cannot get enough of the heat and charge. This pressing need to perfect, this hunger, which it seems he can never sate.

From the orchestra pit, Edith watches him, sees how his bulk of bone and muscle does not apologise for itself. On the contrary, she thinks, it inhabits more space in the world than is decent. But his brutish presence has nothing to do with the size of his body, he stands about five foot eleven, he's not a colossus. No, that physical charge he possesses is all to do with what his body displaces: the air, temperature, perception – as though he generates his own climate. There is an immediate handsomeness about him, she thinks, the eyes have it, their gaze is unflinching, intelligent; the way they fix on the darkness in front of them yet still blaze with blue fire. His features are blunt and strong – nose, forehead, chin – his lips soft, expectant. His shoulders are broad, his hands large and expressive, and his wrists although sturdy are slim, leaving plenty of room in his sleeves, fortunately enough considering he's an illusionist, she laughs to herself. When he smiles – when he smiles at her – there is a taut, elegant rise to his cheekbones. But there's another kind of smile which he turns on for the crowds, an appropriation of a smile, one that gives a sinister cast to his face, as though he is stubbornly challenging the 'bastards out there' to challenge *him*. That's the smile she sees on his face now as he stands centre stage.

Oliver places Millie on her feet and Maclagan leads her slowly to the side of the stage, where she stands like an automaton. The audience mumbles – is the woman all right? Will she be woken from her trance? – as they sit uneasily back into their seats.

Now Oliver steps forward to the front of the stage, his manner less flamboyant, his gaze fearless and direct, as though he has a much weightier matter on his mind, as though he is dismissing the audience after wooing them. As a result they appear to want him all the more. He carries the import of what is to come in his body. He does not have to move a muscle to communicate that what they are about to see will contradict all that their senses will tell them, they may even be afraid.

'Let me warn you,' he says, 'this has not been rehearsed. I do not know what will happen. Anything is possible. Those of a delicate disposition should leave now.' The other performers are drawn to the sides of the stage to watch. Oliver lifts his head to the back of the theatre. 'But to those of you who stay, come with me,' he adds. 'You know you want to.'

He looks at Edith once again, her fingers poised over the keys, her face a picture of concentration, before the stage falls dark behind him and the strains of Beethoven rise once again. Edith detects a devilish hue to his expression now, as though a manic clock is ticking inside him. She feels a shiver run down her spine as she plays. It is as though Oliver's real trick is to disarm the audience by allowing them to think a little less of him; by wanting them to assume he will not pull off the next task he has set himself.

With one hand Oliver lifts an object from the shadows and brings it into the light. It is a small square case. Moving close to the audience, he slowly opens the front panel of the case. Inside it is empty. The table from 'The Appearing Woman' now stands within a curtained recess, which has been erected behind him. He walks upstage, closes the case and places it in the centre of the table.

'Ladies and gentlemen.' He lifts his head as he speaks to catch the blaze of light. 'Is it not odd? This gathering? You and I? Here under this roof at this moment in time. Is it not very odd that we should tolerate each other? That you should sit and wait for me to demonstrate some truth or untruth? Have *paid* to sit and wait. And odd that I should demonstrate it – whatever *it* is. Do you not say to yourselves – what am I doing? How has my uncertainty propelled me here? To this theatre. Why do I accept so much?' He pauses, breathes deeply. 'But, dear audience, I ask nothing of you – I ask not for your respect, nor for your affection, and certainly not for your pity. For this is all your doing. This counterfeit, this masquerading of the truth. Look at your shabby lives, how you settle for so little. You know nothing, are certain of nothing. Just like me. So, let's agree on the sham. Let's at least be honest with ourselves. You come here because you want to witness all that is depraved and grotesque, do not lie. You want me to shock and appal you, to horrify you. So, ladies and gentlemen, allow me to give you what you want!'

He turns to the case and opens it again. Inside the case is a head with snake-like hair – a replica of a sleeping Medusa. The audience respond with a collective intake of breath, so lifelike is the head.

Slowly he lifts the case containing the head and holds it above shoulder height. It appears as though there is only dark empty space beneath it. Keeping his gaze firmly on the audience, he shouts, 'Wake up, Medusa!'

The eyes of the disembodied head open. They stare out at the audience like two huge black coals. Then suddenly they move from side to side. A woman in the audience screams. There is a momentary panic, low sounds of reassurance, then silence. The music stops.

'Speak, Medusa!' Oliver proclaims.

The grotesque black mouth of the head opens and a long green tongue protrudes.

'*I travelled through a Land of Men. A Land of Men and Women too. And heard and saw such dreadful things. As cold Earth wanderers never knew*,' the head wails.

Oliver turns to the head. 'What dreadful things? Tell us, Medusa!'

The lips of the black mouth part again. The eyes grow wider. '*The Babe begotten in dire woe – The Woman Old – The Beggar and the Poor, blind and age-bent – Terror strikes through the region wide – The Stars, Sun, Moon all shrink away – A desert vast without a bound*

- And nothing left to eat or drink - A dark desert all around!' The audience appears stunned, then there is murmuring as their sense of unease grows.

A woman shouts from the back of the stalls. 'It's the end of the world! That monstrous thing is predicting the end of the world! We're doomed!'

The audience looks around in disbelief. A family gets up to leave, their young daughter visibly upset. Another rumble of panic in the stalls.

Edith is completely enthralled by the spectacle, even though she has seen it all before, knows the mirrors attached to the legs of the table reflect the stage floor so as to make it appear continuous to the back of the set, knows that Maclagan - this scary Medusa - has his body draped in black cloth to prevent it from being seen.

Oliver raises his arm to settle the crowd, then turns to the head. 'Enough, Medusa!' he says, drops his arm slowly and places the case back on the table, closing the front panel. 'Do not be afraid,' he addresses the audience. 'Put your trust in me.' He turns to the case. 'Now, leave us, Medusa!' He opens the front panel of the case once more to reveal that the head has vanished and in its place is a heap of straw.

A man in the front row, amazed at what he has seen, slowly begins to applaud, others follow. Oliver walks slowly over to Millie, who still stands in a trance, and guides her centre stage. He claps loudly in front of her and she wakes up. She smiles broadly at him then turns to the audience to take her bow. Oliver bows too. Soon the whole audience is on its feet.

Oliver steps to the front of the stage. He takes another bow. He smiles at Edith who raises her hands to him in applause. No sooner has he left the stage than the audience calls him back. Eventually the curtain falls.

'You ran eight minutes over!' Fred Felix is furious with Oliver as he comes off stage.

'Apologies,' Oliver says, pushing past him in a hurry to get changed.

'What do you mean, apologies! They're going to drop my act at the top of the second half to make up time – I've just been told – and Minty's all primed to go on. You can't do that to a dog!'

'Fuck the dog!'

'Didn't you see his act?' Teddy Lewis, who is getting ready to perform his paper-tearing routine, corners Fred Felix. 'It were bloody marvellous! Who would want to watch a man with a singing mongrel after seeing the head of Medusa come to life – and a mongrel who can't even sing to boot!'

'You cheeky bugger,' Fred Felix snarls back and shoves his finger through the paper Eiffel Tower Teddy Lewis has been carefully holding in his hands.

Oliver meets Maclagan in the backstage corridor. Maclagan's face is painted black and gold. He wears a medusan wig. In his hand he holds a long green wax tongue.

'Great work, Maclagan! The "Medusa" illusion worked a treat. Who was the plant this evening?'

'Oh, Maud's a lady friend of mine—'

'Is she indeed?'

'Leaves an awful taste in your mouth, so it does,' Maclagan says, smacks his lips together.

Oliver loosens his bow tie. 'Be a bit quicker on the windlass next time for "The Appearing Woman", Maclagan. We can't give the audience any time to work out how it's done.'

'Well, maybe employ a lady who's not so fond of her meat pies. I was sweating like a pig under that stage turning that bloody windlass.

I thought Millie would never budge.' Maclagan heads up the stairs, his medusan tresses bouncing as he goes, then he stops and turns to Oliver. 'Oh, Fred Felix is having another party in his dressing room after the show tonight.'

Oliver grins. 'Don't think so, Maclagan – not after last night. Anyway, Felix wouldn't be too pleased to see me now that I've bumped him off the bill. He might set Minty on me.'

'You could always hypnotise the little bugger.'

'Who, Minty?'

'No, Felix,' Maclagan says with a deadpan expression. 'Get him to give me back that half-crown he owes me.'

Oliver watches as Maclagan disappears up the stairs then closes the door of his dressing room. He removes his make-up, changes out of his costume, then quickly makes his way towards the orchestra pit to find Edith and thank her. But Edith is nowhere to be seen.

Five

He spots her the following morning amongst the ferns. Having attended a lecture at Belfast's Elmwood Hall on 'Spiritual Communication and Mediumistic Phenomena', given by a Dr Henry Proteus, an expert in the field of science and the paranormal (he believed none of it), he now walks the Botanic Gardens. As he saunters, musing on the ludicrous suppositions of Proteus and on his ridiculous name, there is a shower of rain and he takes shelter in the Palm House.

It is the bright ring of her voice that he recognises immediately. He is overcome with the desire to call out to her but he holds his tongue. He follows her voice into the Fernery of the Tropical Ravine, where the heat thuds and the dank smell fills his head and throat.

Edith strolls with an elderly female companion and a dapper-looking gentleman. The gentleman has a neat moustache and beard and carries a walking stick. They move slowly under a frothy canopy of giant leaves. From the large cast-glass dome light drips slowly upon the ancient fronds. Her voice leads him on as it echoes throughout this luminescent Garden of Eden, circling the fat waxy bracts of the succulents, and the stiff leathery leaves of the Bromelias. He follows her past the slender bamboo and the broad-leafed taro, with its vibrant bloated stems of red and black. She and her companions climb the wrought iron steps to the balcony and gaze down into the steamy sunken glen, while Oliver stands below them. He takes in the acrid smell of spoiled earth, the burst of intense sweetness from a nearby breadfruit. He feels himself to be in some kind of phantasmagoria. Around him the roots of the plants are like twisted feet and claws, their fibrous sinews reaching into the soil, their camouflage thickening as they spread. Above him, her voice. Within him, the budding of some joy.

She leaves the unbridled prehistoric energy of the Fernery with her companions, all of them bending their heads against the rain as they make their way to the miniaturised exoticism of the Alpine House. Oliver follows them, feeling the shock of the reduction. He touches the plants that she touches and lets the alpine thistles prick his fingers. Saxifrage, crocus, gentian, earliest snowdrop.

He should say hello to her. But he doesn't. He has lost his tongue in the rarefied air of the Alpine House and wants to remain hidden from her. He watches her leave and stands rooted to the gravel, which lies spread underneath his feet.

Later the same day, Oliver enters the auditorium and takes a random seat to mentally rehearse his act. The work lights are on above him. In the silence he hears a belch from the seat in front. He leans forward and looks over the row of chairs to see who is there. It is Edith, curled up across the seats asleep, the shawl she has been knitting now finished and covering the top part of her body, the arm of one of the fauteuils lying across her waist, as though splicing her in half. Is she playing tonight? He hopes she is. Gamy for certain, he thinks as he looks at her and, yes, a little too cocksure of herself. One of her sleeves is rolled up exposing her forearm, her slender wrist, her smooth pale skin. She has taken off her boots. She wears black woollen stockings. He looks at her feet. A worn rim around the edge of the stocking reveals the shape of her toes underneath. They are like a cluster of stone fruits, their exquisite increments in a row of perfect rounds. He is taken by their tidiness. He wants to touch her. He'd love to see her bare flesh (is it possible at Felix's party he already has?), her legs, a shoulder.

Before the first show that evening, Edith appears at the door of his dressing room with shaving implements in one hand and a tin kettle in the other. A cotton apron and towel are draped over her arm. She does not seem surprised to see him.

'Hello, Oliver.'

He stammers it out as though he is choking. 'Hello – Edith.'

'I didn't know Harry was sharing with you.'

'Harry?' Oliver ponders for a moment, then realises she is re-ferring to Harry Gardner, 'Eccentric Comedian', whom Oliver has toured with before. Tonight he has been booked at the last minute to replace Fred Felix. Felix has apparently been laid low with the flu, although Oliver has his suspicions that Felix isn't ill at all but is having a new hairpiece fitted instead. 'Oh, yes.' Oliver tries to sound casual, but his mouth has gone dry and his heart is thumping. 'He's gone up to the roof to feed the pigeons.'

'Oh, I see. I can wait.'

'You know Harry, then?'

'Yes, I do. He's practically family,' she replies. 'He's a cousin of my Aunt Hilda – the woman you saw me with this morning at The Botanic Gardens – and he'll be staying with us while he's in Belfast.' She puts down the shaving items on the table. 'Did you enjoy the gardens?'

And he'd thought he couldn't be seen, *fucking eejit*, he wants the ground to swallow him. Out of embarrassment he stammers again, making his curiosity all the more heavy-handed. 'And the gentleman you were with?'

Edith looks at Oliver. 'Oh, that's Mr Willy Pilson,' she says coyly. 'Mr Pilson is very fond of my piano playing.' She holds her gaze on him.

Oliver coughs to clear his throat. He feels a fresh knob of heat gather in his chest at the mention of the dapper Mr Willy Pilson, then swiftly shakes it off. 'You're playing for the acts again tonight?'

'I am,' she says, and walks over to Harry's dressing table. 'Hope you're not too disappointed.'

'Of course not.' Oliver turns to look at himself in the mirror.

'I was told you got a great mention in the *Evening Telegraph*.'

'Indeed.'

'May I?' She points to the folded newspaper on the dressing table.

'Be my guest.'

Edith unfolds the newspaper and begins to read the notice aloud. '*Something of a thrill ran through the crowded theatre last night as Illusionist and Hypnotist Oliver Fleck performed at the Empire. This man of magic performs with utmost skill and innovation. His "Medusa" trick caused the audience to jump to their feet and there followed a great shout of general applause. This is not to be missed! I'd say!*' She looks over at Oliver. 'Though I bet you've never had a bad review.'

'It's not about the reviews.' Oliver busies himself applying his make-up.

Edith smiles then reaches into the pocket of her skirt. 'Oh, and this is yours, I think.' She hands him the Prussian blue cravat, then rests her haunches against the table and folds her arms.

Oliver takes the cravat and gingerly places it in the drawer of his dressing table. After a moment's silence he blurts out, 'I don't think it was appropriate what I did at the party that time—'

'Better than paying a fortune to a quack to pull my tooth out,' she says, smiling again. She presses her cheek with her finger, testing the new hollow in her gum underneath the skin.

'I mean – did I do anything else? – I mean did we—?'

Edith turns to him. 'You don't remember?' She looks perplexed, a crease between her brows. She is just about to continue when Harry Gardner arrives at the door. As soon as he sees Edith he opens his arms wide to embrace her.

'Ah, now everything is right with the world!' Harry wraps his arms around her.

'So lovely to see you again, Harry. How have things been?'

'Marvellous – bloody marvellous,' he says with a dour expression on his face.

'That good, eh? Here.' Edith laughs and pats the chair beside her. 'Sit down and let's get you beautiful, shall we?'

'Those pigeons would peck you alive.' Harry turns in a little circle before he sits down, brushing the dust of bird feed from his clothes. 'You know Oliver Fleck, don't you, Edith?'

'I do indeed.'

Harry sits in the chair, tilts his head back and closes his eyes. In a very businesslike manner, as though they have done this a million times before, Edith wraps the cotton apron around her waist then places the towel across Harry's chest and shoulders, fastening it around his neck. Into the small bucket she pours hot water from the tin kettle. She takes a clean cotton handkerchief from the drawer of his dressing table and soaks it in the water, wrings it out, then places it over his face, pressing it down gently with her palms. Harry lets out a great, long sigh. Edith removes the cloth and dips the brush into the water, working the soap into a lather. Oliver watches the slight wobble in her hips as she moves. Edith strokes the brush along

Harry's jaw, covering it with suds, then reaches for the razor. She catches Oliver looking at her. Oliver averts his eyes and goes back to his make-up.

'Where was the last stopover?' Edith asks Harry as she shaves him.

'Nottingham. What an ordeal. The crowd was savage, plain and simple. I'm just not understood in Nottingham.'

Edith wipes the razor on her apron, leaving a piping of lather across her hip.

'Just in Nottingham?' She tips Harry's head back with her fingertips, then bends her knees to get a better view of where she is to shave under his chin.

'Must be wonderful to be so perfect, Edith,' mumbles Harry.

Edith laughs.

Oliver watches her in the mirror. He should be rehearsing with that girl from the Dalby Dancers, his new assistant for tonight's performance, but he now feels compelled to stay.

'How is Harriet?' Edith asks Harry.

'Well, thank God.'

'And Bertie?'

'Fine. He's ten now, can you believe it? How did that happen? I'll have to put a brick on his head to stop him growing! He's a good lad is Bertie. I don't mind saying it but I love that boy to bits.'

'Ah, Harry, you're such a sop,' Edith says, wiping Harry's face slowly with the towel. She cleans his ears of suds, checks the smoothness of his skin with her fingers, rubs his temples and combs his hair.

Oliver catches his reflection in the mirror, a fret line is etched across his brow. He now feels a tension rising in him, like a spring being wound tighter and tighter, and with it a spread of loneliness that he can neither rationalise nor bear. He rises from his dressing table and leaves the room.

*

The following night there is a last-minute misunderstanding by the booking agents and Harry Gardner is switched to appear at the Gaiety instead. Oliver is alone in the dressing room. Edith arrives, holding the shaving equipment in her hands. Oliver is just about to explain but before he can say anything she asks, 'Fancy a shave?'

Oliver nods.

Edith arranges all the shaving accoutrements on Oliver's dressing table, together with the towels, the tin kettle from the kitchen and a small basin, which she has already half filled with hot water. Oliver pushes his chair back from the table to give Edith enough room to stand in front of him. He tips his head back while Edith drapes a towel around his shoulders. Then she leans over him and presses the towel against his face.

'Harry will not be a happy man,' Oliver says in a muffled voice.

When Edith removes the towel, Oliver's eyes are closed but his mouth is slightly open.

Edith bends down and ever so gently kisses him.

Feeling her mouth on his brings such a lightness to his heart that he feels like crying. He pulls his head back a little, looks up at her and holds her face in his hands as though, already, he cannot bear to let her go. Then he kisses her softly.

That night turns out to be the best performance he's ever given. He cannot see Edith from the stage, the glare of the footlights is as usual too intense, but this time she plays so well that he feels connected to the very strings and hammer of the piano, the wood from which the piano is made, the vibrations of its chamber. Tight and essential. She is filling his head with a clear purpose as she plays. There is no weight or drag. Everything flies. All details shine in full relief. Even the corolla of the artificial flowers he pulls out of his top hat are beautiful in their artificiality. Now, even the word corolla bounces in his head as he performs – *corolla, corollary, corona.* The audience applauds. They are on their feet. He looks down at Edith. A beautiful pale bloom in the darkness.

And just as beautiful a flower, he thinks, on their wedding day six months later in Huddersfield where she joins him on tour. She wears a broad-brimmed hat, which frames her face. Confetti peppers her shoulders, a snowdrift in early autumn. Her wedding bouquet is a huge carousel of long-stemmed yellow roses, speckled with sprigs of yellow conifer, which relax outwards as she holds them. A pattern of velvet flowers decorates her neckline. The pleats of her full-length cream silk dress fall in elegant straight folds, except across her abdomen, where they open and spread just a little too much.

Six

Huddersfield, 1907

The alarm is only in his mother's voice but that is enough. Bertie Gardner now runs as though his life depends on it. Outside the cold night air snaps and catches at his throat, but he sucks it in, his lungs a rasping bellows to keep his inner fire alight. He bows his head against the sudden ripples of fresh wind and spits of rain, which swirl up and around him. Not fully informed as to the *why* of the alarm – after all, the house seemed calm – he engineers his own excitement. Urgency comes from his body's swift motion, the speed of his gangly limbs, the feeling of his feet fast and flat against the cobbles through his flimsy shoes, his heart banging in his chest. He imagines a criminal ahead or, better still, he is the criminal, fleeing the scene of his crime, the police in hot pursuit. He darts between a cab and a horse cart, is nearly clipped by the horse's hooves, continues across Beast Market and down on to Kirkgate. At St Peter's Church he turns left down Cross Church Street, heading across the tram tracks and continues all the way down Queen Street. On the corner of Victoria Street a scrawny mongrel scoots right in front of him, nearly tripping him up. Bertie carries on without breaking pace. He must find Mr Oliver Fleck – the gentleman who rents the flat above him – and tell him to hurry home to his wife. Mr Fleck, it was made clear to him by his mother, is needed immediately. His mother, standing on the top landing holding a wad of towels in one hand and a basin of steaming water in the other, had yelled, 'Hurry,' at him louder than he'd ever heard her yell before. Mrs Fleck may be ailing or may have cooked a nice meat pie, doesn't matter to Bertie, it's secondary now to the rush.

Heavy purple clouds drift slowly across the night sky as though curious of Bertie's haste, and begin to spill their thin wintry showers over the town of Huddersfield. Needles of frozen rain sting his face as he runs. Each of his cheeks is now a robin's breast budding in the silvery light. His mouth is tight with purpose. He cannot let his labour slacken, he must get to Mr Fleck as quickly as possible.

Bertie whips on, turns the corner on Victoria Street leaping over a heap of manure piled on the cobbles, cuts down Bull and Mouth Street and finally reaches the Theatre Royal. He swings down the side of the building to the stage door and barges through it.

'What d'you want?' the stage doorman snorts like a cab-horse.

Bertie is breathless. 'I'm to tell Mr Oliver Fleck to come home immediately, if he's here.'

'Show's over. He'll be in the bar, Upper Circle.' The doorman nods towards the narrow door on his left.

Bertie opens the door and heads up the stairs. The smell of alcohol and tobacco hits his nose as hard as the darkness of the stairwell hits his eyes. He takes it all into his body like heat. He reaches the crush room first, empty of people now, and rushes through to the bar where, in a quiet dimly lit corner, he finds a group of about nine or ten people drinking and smoking. There is a serious tone to their conversation. Bertie hears the occasional phrase – 'short-term contract', 'fair wage', 'the syndicates' – lift from the blend of voices as he searches for Mr Fleck, his hands and his cheeks tingling as he stands.

'Mr Fleck?' he calls.

Out of the group a figure arises.

'I'm here. What is it, lad?'

Bertie's eyes contract as he tries to get a clearer picture of the man who responds to the name, a broad frame bleeding into the space, a voice as deep and resounding as a well. The man moves forward and the paltry light from the low-slung chandelier illuminates him a little more; handsome features, hair brushed back from his face, his gaze direct and grave. Yes, that's him, that's Mr Oliver Fleck all right, Bertie thinks, I recognise the stance of him, he's grizzly, like a bear.

'You've to hurry, that's all I know.' Bertie sniffs loudly but to no avail, the loose egg-white snot which has been hugging his nostrils now oozes down on to his top lip. He wipes it away with the back of his hand.

Oliver is suddenly in motion. He grabs his hat from one of the tables.

'Jesus – Edith!' he says, and lunges towards the door.

'No sooner out than in again.' Mrs Harriet Gardner rolls her left sleeve up to her elbow to prepare a length of arm and holds her body in a deep wide squat. She glares between Edith's open legs. A wet grey-pink fissure with the hard smooth segment of a head now pulsating within it, like a quarter segment of a musk melon or cantaloupe. The segment is pushing out then pulling back as though testing the adequacy of the aperture against which it presses.

'This little dear doesn't want to come out at all,' says Harriet. She makes a coaxing sucking sound with her mouth as though she is enticing a frightened kitten from under a bed.

Edith has been remarkably quiet throughout the whole labour. Harriet had commented on it, of course, had said that never in all her years had she assisted such a calm birth where the woman wasn't howling, screaming, cursing, or doing all of the aforementioned. The word aforementioned had floated in its peculiarity like a sliver of thin paper in and around Edith's head, a four-syllable distraction from the pain which was engulfing her and indeed threatened, she felt, to extinguish her from this world. Edith had clutched the word, saw the syllables break up and reassemble in her mind a thousand times.

Although Edith appears calm the internal experience of her labour is of seismic proportions. There isn't a screed of her left to complain, or howl or scream. If she does not hold complete focus she is certain she will die. The beast has woken and now there is no stopping it. She cannot allow herself to slip into her own terror. Her enormous belly pulses and undulates like a bubbling cauldron of newly forming flesh.

As the labour progresses, the merciless vice-like grip of the contractions stretches not only the neck of her womb but everything else until her whole body feels like a birth canal. Everything has loosened: her eyeballs from their sockets, her teeth from her gums, each and every bone – humerus, clavicle, fibula, tarsal – rattling slackly from its cavities, muscles and ligaments unravel, membranes snap. With the increasing pain of each contraction she sees Maclagan at his windlass, turning the handle, cracking her bony girdle. Maclagan, the gentlest of men, now hardened with purpose, the look of rank determination on his face, his eyes ferret-like and steely, the tension of the windlass mounting. Edith is a machine, she's wood and wire and metal and steam.

The kettle sings and Harriet runs briskly to the kitchen. She refills her basin with boiling water.

'The longest labour I ever attended,' she speaks as though she is talking of a Mass or a service as she comes back into the bedroom, 'and you'll never believe this, but it's true, the longest labour I ever attended lasted three days and three nights, and that's no word of a lie. God love the little thing, hardly more than a child herself, and I swear the baby that came out of her was twice the size she was, I mean to say . . .'

Harriet has a habit of not finishing her sentences. A trait which under normal circumstances is tolerated affectionately by everyone, but for Edith, in her heightened state, it becomes unbearable. She is left wondering – *you mean to say what? What do you mean to say, for the love of God? Don't leave me hanging. Please.*

Harriet places the kettle by the door and wipes her hands on the towel, which is tucked into the pocket of her apron. She squats once again to examine the baby's head, her face crinkling in consternation, a sheen of sweat across her forehead. The head has retreated and is hooded by Edith's flesh.

'I'll slip the hand up in a minute,' says Harriet. 'Growing up on a farm has its compensations.' She laughs lightly.

For Edith the thought of any intervention at this moment, from anything or anyone, is untenable. Not that she doesn't want her pain to ease – oh, she does – but the thought of even more flesh and bone inside her, while she is already bursting with both, is unthinkable. *There is no more room for you to intervene, Harriet, I am as full as I can be.*

How long she has been in labour she has no idea. Time has lost all contour and function. The mighty new clock is her cervix, an austere and cruel timekeeper. At first the contractions had crept up on her like a gnawing toothache that was becoming more and more insistent – although she was still able to go about her business, doing the laundry, sweeping the kitchen floor, making the bread. But just as she had kneaded the dough and covered it with a cloth to keep it warm, a contraction landed itself on her with such brute force that she collapsed like a house of cards, water spilling from her loins. She had mopped the floor with difficulty and crawled over to the bed, but lying on her back or her side was too painful. She had made her way out to the landing to call for Harriet. The contractions then came fast and furious, although seemingly making no advancement in the coming of the baby. Each time that Harriet checked Edith she would reassure her that she was doing fine and pat her forehead with a wet cloth. But Harriet still had time to go back and forth to her own flat several times to organise dinner for Bertie, put two sheets and a tablecloth through the mangle and rub the fire grate, the fender and the fender irons with a dry leather.

The contractions continued without any sign of the baby well into the night and into the early morning hours, and in her exhaustion Edith had no choice but to surrender – to let go of herself completely: her body, mind, identity. Too much valuable energy was being wasted remaining who she was. So, she reduced herself to only mouth, ear and eye, spoke politely when Harriet spoke to her and never even asked for water.

'Yes, I think I'll slip the hand up in . . .' Harriet stops talking as though distracted by a distant sound then continues, recounting how she had attended her sisters giving birth, all four of them, that's eleven births in all, and how they had attended hers, though she was not so lucky. She had lost so many she felt like a mere conduit for God Almighty, unable to hang on to either flesh or blood. But in the end He had blessed them with Bertie. Oh, how He had blessed them.

'I'd say Bertie has found Oliver by now,' Harriet nods and smiles, 'and I reckon he'll be coming up those stairs any moment.'

After their wedding in Huddersfield, Edith had been due to return to Belfast to live once again with her Aunt Hilda while Oliver continued on tour, his plan being to join her for a time once the baby was born. However, just before she was about to purchase her ticket for the boat, news reached them that her Aunt Hilda, a woman of considerable years, had died peacefully in her sleep. At the funeral Edith and Harry had never seen so many flowers. After their respects had been paid, Harry had insisted Edith return with him to Huddersfield and within the same month the flat above the Gardners had become vacant. With the selling of the family home after Hilda's death, Edith had received a modest sum, certainly enough to help pay for rent while Oliver was away. It had seemed the ideal solution as Oliver knew Edith would be well looked after having Harriet around, and as the rest of his tour was to venues in England and Scotland, he would be within easier reach once she went into labour. As luck would have it he couldn't have been closer, playing at Huddersfield's Theatre Royal.

The previous night Oliver had slept in the front room, tucking himself into the armchair and covering himself with his coat, while Harriet had pottered in and out to tend to Edith. Around seven o'clock in the morning Harriet had announced that Edith was still a long way away from her delivery.

'What can I do?' Oliver had felt helpless.

'Go about your daily business, Oliver. I'll stay with her. I can send for you if there's any change.'

'I have a matinee and an evening show – the last night of the run – of the season—'

'Whatever it is, go and do it. She'll be ages yet.'

'And there's talk of a meeting after that – about the strike.'

'Strike?'

'The Entertainers Union, Harriet – the Variety Artists' Federation – didn't Harry tell you? They're advising we strike.'

'He never said a—'

'It's only talk at the moment.'

'And I hope it stays that way.'

42

'But I can come back and forth.'

'No need. Just do what you have to do. I'll send Bertie when—'

'When?'

'—when the time comes.'

Bertie stands red-faced in the hallway looking up at Oliver as he scales the stairs to the second floor. Once inside, Oliver hears Harriet's gentle chatter from the bedroom and no noise from Edith and assumes the baby must be born. Confidently, he pushes the bedroom door open.

It's not a common feeling for him, to feel startled, but at this moment he does, very. He sees a mangled apparition – his wife sprawled out on the bed, partly covered in crumpled blankets, an unfamiliar purple hue to her half-naked body. He sees the ceramic bowl by the bed and the blood in the bowl, he sees the wet towels and spattered napkins. He sees the protrusion of new flesh between her legs, and at once thinks of the disembowelled lamb he had come across as a boy on Fathom Hill, attacked by foxes, its eyes gone, its blank sockets lifted to the cool grey sky, waxy clots of blood, too much softness.

'So sorry, Oliver,' Harriet is down on her knees at the end of the bed. She turns to look up at Oliver. 'Bit of a false alarm, I'm afraid. Still not quite there yet.'

Oliver nods his head meekly and leaves the room.

As soon as Oliver has gone Edith feels her body heaving. She moves like a sea monster rutting the seabed. She senses something now, something in the rush of her blood: there is more than one baby.

'No sooner out than back in again.' Harriet is shaking her head at the curd-covered skull which is once more bulging through the grinning slot between Edith's legs then disappearing.

'Right, let's go, shall we?' Harriet rolls her sleeve up over her elbow and extends her arm. But just as she is about to slip her hand inside Edith, the head of the baby suddenly emerges in full – a blossoming pale pink vole, blunt nose, short ears, eyes wide open. Harriet shrieks with delight.

Edith pushes with as much strength as she can muster.

'Hold, hold now, take it easy, girl, nice and easy now.' Harriet tempers Edith's efforts. 'Wait now, on the contraction, otherwise you're pushing water up a hill and all that good work'll come to nothing.'

Edith holds as steadily as she can but she cannot imagine anything harder, every fibre of her body is screaming push.

Harriet keeps a firm hand on Edith's belly. She feels the grip of muscle tighten.

'Now, lovey, now!'

Edith pushes.

A little body appears in its crusade from the dark maternal lagoon and into the airy world. Its skin immediately registers temperature, senses perhaps the smell of warm bread from downstairs, the smell of carbolic soap on Harriet's hands, the homely smell of its mother's blood. Harriet guides the baby out and immediately wraps it in a blanket. But before she can say 'Oh my Lord, a beautiful boy,' she is taken by the baby's gaze, its eyes full and alert, its head turning and looking back towards his mother. Harriet looks at Edith. Between Edith's legs, another pulsing head appears.

'Oh my God – who would have thought – you're having twins, my dear!'

At this exclamation, the second head retreats and disappears. Harriet secures the blanket around the newborn boy and places him in the straw basket which has been especially prepared – for one – and arranged on a squat table by the bed. She bends over Edith once more and looks between Edith's legs as though she's looking through a spyhole at a peepshow. She makes a tut-tut sound with her lips and tongue as though she is disappointed.

Edith has gone very still. She has no strength left to push. She is alive but feels as good as dead. This second child is on its own. Edith's eyes are closed. The baby boy in the basket mewls – a tiny, faraway sound as though coming from three or four streets away.

The second baby holds back, shows no sign of greeting the world. It's only when Edith falls into a stark, shocked sleep that the second baby slips out, and so quietly and gently it is as though it is afraid of waking her.

Seven

Frosted raindrops pepper the bedroom window, and the wind outside blows tirelessly. Inside, Oliver is transfixed by the sight in front of him. He stands in the bedroom staring at Edith and the two babies sleeping. He cannot quite believe what he is seeing. Two! Not one, but two! Not just his child, but suddenly his children. These tiny, squirming beings, pale as grubs. These little creatures are his son and his daughter – yes, the second baby is a beautiful girl – an alien part of him now realised and full of promise. This is where the world turns, he thinks.

The sleeping figures of Edith and the babies look like a painting. The late morning light coming in through the tall sash window infuses flesh and wood, cotton and nail, bone and hair, skin and feathers, tin and milk. Everything which had previously been separate and distinct is now connected. It seems to Oliver, as he looks at them in the bed, that there are three babies, not a mother and her two infants. They possess a pure tranquillity as they sleep, something, Oliver muses, that sleep has never offered him (no, never peace, rarely comfort – and that fear he has on waking up, ever since he was a child, the fear that he'll open his eyes to an altered world – no, never a tranquil sleep).

He does not let his eyes wander from them for a moment. The terrifying possibility of them ceasing to exist is already ripe. His protection of them now is paramount. His providing for them will direct everything in his waking hours. They are here and I must do all I can to make the world a good place for them, he says to himself. He feels a growing and genuine hope.

He had not shown a great deal of interest in Edith's pregnancy and had often become impatient with her when she complained of fatigue, or how difficult it was for her to find any position in the bed which was comfortable. But his impatience had been masking his fear of what was to come. He felt he had no control over any of it. And the birth had been difficult for Edith – for the babies too. He was glad it was all over now. And Edith has survived and the babies have survived and they are healthy, and now they are sleeping. All is well.

Soft flannel, golden hair, pink lips, the warm milky breath from their mouths. He is enthralled by it all – by the smell of them, the size of them, their perfectly formed miniature fingers and toes. And look at the size of these clothes, he says to himself, as he holds up the little cotton nightshirt which Edith has taken off the girl – his daughter, he reminds himself. Now his daughter has her head tucked down into her chest. The wool blanket in which she is wrapped covers her forehead and eyes, the back of her tiny curled hand rests on her chest and her little lips bunch and loosen as though she is searching for the breast. Oliver tiptoes towards the bed and reaches forward to pull the blanket back from her face. As he does so she opens her eyes wide to him. She gulps at the air around her and begins to cry, pumping her tiny arms up and down, kicking out under the blanket. She looks terrified. Oliver cannot deny the momentary pause he feels in his soul at his daughter's distress.

'Shhhhh. Shhhhh.' But she cannot be consoled.

Edith stirs and, still half-asleep, offers the crying infant the breast and soon all is calm again.

Harriet calls in to see how Edith and the babies are doing, bringing with her some bread and butter pudding. She puts the kettle to boil on the trivet of the small kitchen stove and busies herself tidying the flat, washing the dishes that have been left on the kitchen table. She sweeps the floor of the front room, pulling up the stiff sash window just a little to allow fresh air into the flat. Then immediately closes it when she feels the bitter coldness of January blowing in. She makes a huge pot of tea and brings a cup into the bedroom for Edith.

She finds Edith sitting up in the bed, a sleeping infant on either side, and Oliver curled up at the bottom of the bed fully clothed, in fact still in his overcoat, and asleep. Edith takes the tea and pudding gratefully. Harriet puts one baby in the bassinet and sits in the chair next to the bed holding the other. After eating and drinking, Edith is able to tend to herself for a moment, although just walking to the washstand is an ordeal, her body aches, her breasts are sore and her head, her shoulders and her back feel as though they have been stuffed with cotton then beaten with a hammer. Harriet informs Edith that another bassinet is on its way, offered by a friend of hers who has no use for it.

'Bertie will bring it up to you later,' she says with a smile.

After washing herself Edith climbs back into bed.

Harriet offers to take both babies down to her flat for an hour while Edith sleeps and shoves Oliver awake so that he can help her with the infants. Oliver is offered his daughter to carry. He takes her in his arms and, still in a groggy state, follows Harriet down the stairs. The baby girl opens her eyes and fixes her gaze firmly on Oliver. This time she does not cry but her bottom lip curls downwards and begins to tremble.

By the time he wanders back up to the flat Edith is fast asleep. He fixes fresh candles beside the bed in case she needs them. Then he lies back in the armchair in the front room.

He sees a future looming bright before him like a winter halo around a full moon. From the last tour he has accrued a decent amount of money, enough to keep them – his new family – in rent and food for a few weeks, possibly a month. That's a luxury in itself, he thinks, being able to take the time to live, to *be*, and not have to worry about money. How many could boast that? And at this time of all times, when he has become a father. Then there is the fee still due from his appearances on the Burton Tour in Bradford, Leeds, Chesterfield and Derby the previous autumn during which he had premiered 'The Magic Mirror'. Once that was paid it would certainly boost their funds. Yes, the sooner he can get them to pay up the better. 'The Magic Mirror' had worked beautifully. He remembers how he had swung on the moment of impact like a mental acrobat, how the atmosphere in the audience pulsed with expectation. Then the play of mirrors, the quick switch, the artful beauty of distraction, his assistant, Millie Evans, pulling the mirrors towards her so that she was hidden completely in the cabinet, the audience just didn't see it coming, or Millie going – Oliver smiles at his own quip – it had all happened so fast.

As the January afternoon gloom descends he gets up and lights a candle. His mind is teeming with ideas now, racing with bright colour and words and music and images. Energy is bubbling up inside him. He goes in search of a cigarette which he knows he has in a pocket somewhere, scoffs the piece of bread and butter pudding he sees on the kitchen table, finds the cigarette in the pocket of his black waistcoat hanging behind the door, lights it, inhales, feels the smoke peppery against the roof of his mouth, against his throat. Then feels it surging into his lungs like electricity. A point between his eyes expands and his head loosens. He lies back in the armchair, holding the cigarette lightly between his lips, his fingers shaking slightly from the cold. Stares at the framed tapestry hanging on the wall opposite him with its words 'Behold the fire and the wood, but where is the lamb?' embroidered in cardinal red. Contemplates it. Then he's up again, searches now for liquor. There's whiskey left, he knows, in the kitchen cupboard. He finds it, welcomes the healthy amount that's there – almost a full bottle – lies back in the armchair again with the bottle in his hand, blows out the candle, pulls on the cigarette, a whirl of pictures in his head, words, symbols now and fractions, sounds, and as he closes his eyes his eyelashes make the sound of thunder. His eyes feel as solid as bullets and as heavy. Then comes a strange pressure in his head. He drinks whiskey and inhales deeply through his mouth as though to release the pressure. He drinks more whiskey. A black expanse. And blacker. More whiskey. He feels thirsty now, but too groggy to get up. Feels cold. Senses light on his lids from somewhere but knows he has blown out the candle. Did he get up to blow the candle out? Feels his mouth dry, dry as sandpaper. Where is he exactly? Hears noises on the street. Someone shouting. A tramcar in the distance. Gets the sensation that his eyes are open when they're closed as though he's staring at the inside of his eyelids. Moving pictures. Shapes flickering like black flames. More blackness. Then his body floods with the smell of new skin, the taking and giving of milk, a mother's perspiration and sanguinity, this strangest phase of his life. Edith and the babies! The thought revives him like no other. He opens his eyes slowly. He gets up from the armchair and walks to the bedroom with his mind spiralling. He wants to wake Edith. He opens the bedroom door.

Harriet, by all accounts, has already brought the babies back and they and Edith are fast asleep in the bed. On the floor beside the bed are two bassinets now. Strange, thinks Oliver – he hadn't heard

Harriet coming back into the flat with the babies, or Bertie, who must have delivered the second bassinet from the neighbour. The bedroom is in much more of a disarray than he remembers – it looks as though a number of restless nights have passed not just an hour, a few hours. Edith is slumped width-wise across the bed, her head and upper body camouflaged with a quilt, her legs though covered mostly in her shift are sticking out over the side of the bed as though she is sliding down a laundry chute. Towels and nappies and baby clothes are strewn across the end of the bed and on the floor. There is a basket he has never seen before on the floor beside the window containing baby clothes and blankets. A large and rather rusty perambulator sits in the corner of the room. Good God, thinks Oliver, how did that get here? Oliver notices how the fresh candles he had fixed for Edith have now burned right down to their base. He looks at the window. The light coming through the curtains is not evening light, he realises, but the pearly limelight of morning. But which morning? he now wonders. Unsettled, Oliver turns to Edith. She is a curl of utter exhaustion in the bed.

'Edith,' he calls, 'Edith'.

One of the babies now stirs, its tiny cry sounding more like the fret of a kitten. The baby girl no doubt, he thinks. Then the other baby responds by crying too. Edith groans from underneath the quilt.

He goes into the front room, stands at the window and looks out. The wind and rain have stopped. The sky is an ink-blue pearl. Across the street, a shopkeeper is pulling up his awning while a younger man scuttles around him with a large basket of vegetables which he dumps on the pavement. Must be around seven thirty in the morning if they're opening up, thinks Oliver. A whole twelve hours has passed then? – that black expanse. Surely not. He picks up the whiskey bottle which lies underneath the armchair in which he slept, looks at it, empty, shoves it under the kitchen sink. Splashing water on his face from the tap and running his wet fingers through his hair, Oliver feels oddly refreshed and not tired or even groggy now. He throws on his overcoat, still warm from his sleep, pops his Borsalino on his head – a wedding present from Edith, bought before she left Belfast at Robb's department store on Castle Street – takes an empty hessian bag from the kitchen cupboard and makes his way down the stairs and out into the street. He'll make Edith breakfast. He'll get fresh bread at the market, some honey would be good for her. He'll make cocoa.

He walks the stretch of Beast Market towards St Peter's Church, cuts up Lord Street. The sky brightens. He waits for a buggy to pass, waving at the driver as though he knows him well, then crosses the street by the graveyard, continuing past the post office then turning left to the market on Brook Street. For some reason he cannot explain to himself, the streets feel brand new and full of brand new things. The people who are out walking and going about their morning business seem intriguing to him, full of purpose.

He reaches the market. Vendors shout out their wares. The flower sellers screech their winter catalogue of heather, thistle and hellebores. People barter over vegetables, meat, horse meal, fish. Oliver purchases fresh bread, dripping, honey, a bunch of leeks and two pieces of bacon. He decides to buy flowers for Edith. The flower seller outside the drab stationer's shop at the Byram Street end of the market offers him the best of a bad lot, a pinched seasonal bouquet of reeds and laurel, which nevertheless holds a certain charm as twisted amongst the green there is a bright speckle of yellow conifer, a favourite of Edith's.

Each item he buys fills him with a lightness. He shakes each hand that sells to him and comments on the cold morning that it is, and on the threat of approaching rain. The sellers nod in reply or throw out a witty remark. With the honey vendor Oliver refuses the change due to him. 'I'm sure it's worth it,' Oliver says, smiling broadly at the man and holding up the pot of honey. 'It's for my wife – she's given birth to twins.' The honey vendor, despite the bemused expression on his face, tips his cap at Oliver, jiggling the farthing in his hand as though it's a die he's about to throw. Oliver stands ready to embrace conversation. The honey vendor turns away and attends to his next customer.

He stops and takes in his surroundings and it feels like the first time he has done so. He had never realised before how handsome – if he could ascribe that word to inanimate things – the centre of Huddersfield is, with its none too high stately buildings and its neatly cobbled streets. Its architecture is charming to the eye, he thinks. Even the vegetables around him look regal as he walks through the market, the cabbage heads and cauliflowers, the carrots and potatoes – wondrous things. He takes in their hue and solidity, the ridges of soil which mottle them, their length and texture. He buys some kale, rolls an onion against his cheek before he buys half a dozen, feels the coolness and dryness of a turnip's skin on his. Smells a parsnip, its reek of burnt sweetness. Bites into an apple, as fresh and crisp as snow.

Oliver feels the weight of the hessian bag in his hand, the sway of providence as he walks. He is bringing home breakfast to his wife, who is sheltering their future, their son and daughter (he would soon get to know them apart). He gets an excited rush when he thinks about the names they will decide on. Edith's father was Archibald Henry Foster and her Scottish-born mother, Hettie Marie Lawlor. Good names to choose from – though Archibald might be a mouthful for the boy.

Then there were his own parents of course, Louisa Grace McKay his mother – a lump gathers in his throat as he thinks of her – both

Louisa and Grace are beautiful names for a girl. He imagines his daughter's companionship, her hand tenderly taking his, the skip to her gait beside him and he sees their life ahead as a continuum of wonderful possibilities. There is nothing they cannot do together. He will find work – a good stretch of work – he's bound to on the circuits, certainly after the reaction he's received here at the Theatre Royal, and the children and Edith can travel with him. But then why depend on the circuits? Isn't it about time he created his own one-man show? After all, Bill Garner had done it, had created his one-man show called *The Talking Trickster*, a mixture of tricks, comedy and music, and had brought it to America to great acclaim. And Garner was about as talented as a stuffed goose, thinks Oliver. So if Garner can do it, then, with the reputation he has built for himself, he certainly can too. His good friend and teacher The Great Bandini, long dead now, would be proud of him if he went out on his own. In Bandini's honour, then.

Oliver now feels his blood move like mercury in his veins, his body rising with its roll and flow, his mind filling with the swell of invention. He must put everything into this. He'll need more money – what with overheads and new materials to acquire – but he'll find it, he'll certainly find backers, he'll make a healthy return.

What name shall he give his daughter, then? – his life's breath – Grace? Louisa? A possible echo of his mother's gaze, or cheek-bones, or smile. Imagine. Would he know that if he saw it in his own daughter? The gift of his mother in his daughter's eyes.

And for the boy? His own father was Harold. Harold James Fleck. Oliver feels a tightening in his stomach. He inhales deeply to banish a rising unease and with that takes in the rich savoury smell of sausages from a nearby cookshop. It pulls him to the moment and banishes his melancholy. Sausages! – that's what I'll bring back for breakfast. Sausages! He turns on to North Gate towards the cook-shop passing a beggar crouching by a laneway. If only my hands were free, Oliver thinks as he picks up his pace, I would throw the bastard a coin.

When he arrives home Harriet has the kettle set to boil on the stove and is sweeping the landing outside his flat.

'Thought I'd make some tea for Edith,' she says to Oliver brightly, then her tone changes. 'Think you might try to give a hand?'

'Certainly,' Oliver replies. 'Will I get cups, milk?'

'I don't mean for the tea,' Harriet looks soberly at him. 'I mean all round. I mean it would be good for Edith if you could stay with it, Oliver.' She holds her gaze on him. 'Last night you were . . .'

Oliver waits for Harriet to finish, taking a moment to consider what Harriet might be implying. Then, 'But I've just been to the market. I bought breakfast!' he holds up his hessian bag for her approval.

'No, I don't mean—' Harriet drops her head. 'Stay alert, Oliver, she needs you.' She continues talking to Oliver as though she is talking to her shoes. 'By the way, Harry's home. He's called in with Bertie to see the infants. I hope you don't mind?' She lifts her head and looks everywhere except into Oliver's eyes.

'Not in the least, Harriet.' Oliver smiles. He's delighted Harry is home. 'Have some breakfast with us, why don't you.' He holds up the bag again.

Harriet raises her eyebrows in surprise at the amount of provisions Oliver has packed into the bag. 'Smells good,' she says cautiously.

'Well-seasoned German sausages – the best smell in the world. Let's eat them while they're hot. First I'll poke my head in.' He gestures to the flat. 'I want to hear how Harry got on.'

'Yes,' Harriet says simply, concern still colouring her voice. 'Why don't you do that, Oliver?'

Inside, he finds Harry Gardner chatting to Edith. Bertie stands behind his father.

Edith is up and dressed and sits in a chair at the table cradling one infant in her arms. She has made an attempt at freshness despite her obvious tiredness. She has put on her best skirt of green crinoline, which she would normally only wear on an evening out. With the skirt she wears a workaday white cotton blouse over which she has wrapped a shawl. She has gathered her hair into a loose bun at the back of her head. She wears a small straw hat. The combination is an odd mix, Oliver thinks as he looks at her tenderly, particularly the wearing of the hat indoors, as though she had just come in from the street to visit herself.

Harry holds the other infant in his arms, staring down at it as though he can't quite understand how it got there. Bertie stands with one of his hands on his father's shoulder, holding his cap in the other.

'Good to see you, Harry! Hello, Bertie,' Oliver says.

Bertie nods his head and smiles at Oliver.

'And you,' replies Harry. 'Congratulations, Oliver. Oh, they're beauties, the two of 'em.'

Harry offers the infant to Oliver. Oliver reaches out and takes it.

'Finally a father, eh,' he says as though talking to himself. 'Finally a father.' He looks up at Edith. 'Which one is this?' he asks, awkwardly adjusting the position of the baby in his arms.

'That's Agna,' says Edith softly, 'your daughter.'

'Agna?' Oliver stares down at the tiny wrinkled face.

'Agna, from Agnes, meaning pure. Agna Louisa.'

Oliver can feel Agna's little body tense as he holds her. She wriggles under the swaddling.

Edith rises slowly from her chair and offers the boy to Harry.

'And what do you think of Harold – after your father – for the boy?' she says.

Oliver looks at her. 'No, not Harold – begging your pardon, Harry,' he quickly turns to Harry beside him.

'Edwin then, after your brother?'

'And not Edwin either.'

'But wouldn't it be nice to keep it in the family?' Edith asks.

'You never said you had a brother,' Harry says.

Oliver ignores them both. 'What about Archibald? Archibald will do just fine – Archie. I think Archie's a great name.'

'Archie it is then,' Edith concedes.

The two men stand side by side gently swaying the infants.

'How shall we tell these twins apart,' Oliver laughs.

'But they're so different,' Edith says, 'they're not identical at all.'

Oliver looks from one baby to the other. Every crease and fold of them looks the same to him.

'I remember Bertie just this size,' Harry says, 'and now look at him, nearly as tall as his old man.' Harry beams at Bertie who does a little shuffle on his feet at the comment, as though embarrassed by his own growing.

'I expect Bertie'll have his own some day,' Edith remarks, nodding towards the young boy, 'and then you can enjoy it all over again.'

'God willing,' Harry says.

Oliver and Harry continue to sway from side to side, each man's gaze fixed firmly on the baby they are holding.

'How was the tour?' Oliver asks.

'Diabolical,' says Harry softly. 'Six matinees a week on top of the evening shows is a killer, Oliver, and then nothing to show for it. The wages are prehistoric. And I'm not getting any younger.' He makes a face at the infant in his arms.

'There's talk of a strike, you know that?' Oliver studies Agna's tiny nose.

'I do. But how can we live if we don't work, Oliver?' Harry rocks Archie.

'It's right to make a stand against the theatre owners. Do you think they would work for a pittance?'

'But they won't rebook me if I refuse to do that many shows or ask for more money.' Harry makes a cooing sound now, Archie gurgles. 'And there's been complaints before to no avail.'

'It'll all work out, Harry, you'll see.' Oliver takes Agna's little fist and kisses it.

'True enough,' Harry says.

The men are quiet. Bertie stands beside his father. Edith is content to sit and watch. A stillness descends on them all.

'Agna Louisa,' Oliver murmurs.

'Well, I've never seen the like.' Harriet arrives. She holds a tray with a plate of buttered bread and sausages and a pot of tea. 'Well, I've never seen the— Have you men gone soft in the head, give those babies here to me.'

She puts the tray down on the table. She takes Archie from Harry and puts him in one of the bassinets, which has been brought in from the bedroom. She reaches out to take Agna from Oliver. Before Oliver surrenders Agna to Harriet he savours the weight of the infant in his hands, a tiny weight, which now intensely occupies his life, and feels a contentment he has never felt before.

On the way to the market to buy fresh bread the following morning, Oliver picks up a copy of the *Huddersfield Daily Examiner*. Nestled amongst the ads for face creams and moneylenders there is a small article concerning the opening of one of the first purpose-built cinemas in Colne, Lancashire. He had heard talk of a cinema venue being built but had dismissed it out of hand, believing there wouldn't be enough of an audience for films alone. But there it was, due to open its doors to the public the following month. There's room for us all, he thinks.

At the baker's stall Oliver buys bread. He crosses over to the stall of an itinerant seller on the margins of the market to buy butter. The thin grey-haired woman is busily talking to a market porter and pays no attention to Oliver. Oliver waits for a moment, then as calmly as if he were picking a wild flower from a meadow abundant with wild flowers, lifts a pat of butter wrapped in wax paper from the stall and puts it in his bag. He walks on slowly through the market. No sleight of hand or distraction had been implemented in the taking of the butter, just plain stealing. Only right, he says to himself, this is small fry, the seller will not miss such an insignificant item or the money I would have given her – she would have been charging over the odds in any case – think instead what it will bring to my family. It's all in the balance of things – and how many items would I have lost over the years? How many things in the course of a tour would go missing? How many times might I have been swindled?

Oliver is becoming more and more comfortable with the justifications he is providing for his action. Still, they matter less to him now than the rising feeling of unexpected elation simply from knowing he has stolen. It is the simplicity of the idea which, he feels, has a beauty all of its own. It fits. The courage to steal does not enter the equation, daring doesn't come into it, nor the buzz of outwitting the merchants, and certainly not regret, or guilt or fear. It just feels right, as though the ownership of those items was his from the very beginning. There is parity in the whole process, because there is redistribution.

Oliver continues through the market, dodging those noisy sellers who now approach him with trays strapped around their necks offering seedcake, combs, pigs' feet. He passes a butcher's stall and, without hesitating, lifts some ox kidneys wrapped in butcher's paper from the edge of the stall, and slips them into his bag. One clean manoeuvre and he has them. On leaving the market he eases two green apples into the pocket of his greatcoat.

He wants to be intimate with Edith but, climbing into bed that night, Oliver feels he might get a fright at what he finds. He pulls the blankets up and over him and settles quietly, the bed warmer than he had expected, not having slept there for four days, or is it five now? Six perhaps? He is due to leave for Belfast the following morning on the start of another tour, a six-month stretch, although he plans to make the trip back for the children's christening in a few weeks' time.

Edith lies on her side facing away from him, her hair a cornet twist on the pillow. Agna and Archie are both asleep in their bassinets at the end of the bed. He is not sure whether or not Edith is asleep and he is wary of waking her if she is, but all he wants is to be held. Will her body recognise his after being occupied for so long by other skin and bone? Will the industry of her body, all the building and assembling of the past nine months, and now the controlling of temperature and letting down of milk, this intricate new agency of hers, will it reject his body as paltry and unproductive? A beautiful machine, thinks Oliver as he lies beside her in the dark, that's what she has become, a miracle maker.

Oliver stretches out his hand towards Edith under the blankets. Edith does not stir. He places his palm on her bare upper arm then slides it down to her waist. He feels her flesh underneath her cotton shift. A looseness in both cotton and flesh. He remembers how firm and large her abdomen had been close to the birth, a frightening, rippling expanse which seemed as though it would never stop spreading. He had been nervous to embrace her the way he loved to, to encircle her completely in his arms and squeeze her, and he had missed that. Now, the same abdomen displays the soft roundness of desertion.

He pushes his hand up under her shift, feels her cotton drawers, the shape of the towel she needs for the bleeding, moves cautiously across this once familiar body. He slides his hand up her back, feeling himself getting hard, and reaches around her stomach, which startles him in how it flops towards the mattress. He instantly thinks of old Mrs Doohan who used to visit his boyhood home in Eden's Cross. How creased and flabby her face was. As a boy he had believed the rumour that Mrs Doohan worked in a tripe factory where her job was to take the tripe – which had entered the factory as smooth as velvet – and push her face into it, and that's why the tripe was as wrinkly as it was. Oh dear, he feels his erection fading. He moves his hand up to Edith's breast, hoping to resurrect himself a little, and pushes his fingers through her night brassiere, then cups her breast with his hand. The breast feels vast, unchartered and weighty, her nipple much larger than he remembers. He feels himself aroused, wants to sink right into her, be swallowed by this new and doughy wife of his. He feels something small and prickly against her breast and picks it off with his fingers – a crush of yellow conifer from the bouquet of flowers he had brought her from the market. Edith turns her head towards Oliver.

'Just hold my hand, Oliver,' she says quietly, 'that part of me you'll recognise.'

He takes her hand and interlocks his fingers with hers, feeling the familiar coarseness of her palm against his. As he lies with her he thinks how much they have shared in the short time since they met at the Empire Theatre in Belfast. A swift and intense courtship, marriage, and now parenthood. The night of Fred Felix's party, Edith had subsequently informed him, had been the night the twins were conceived. She had described the whole event to him. He blushes at the thought of it now, how little he remembers of that night. In fact, if he is to be perfectly honest with himself he remembers nothing at all. Just the crucifying hangover the following morning and his Prussian blue cravat left like a chalk mark around her thigh.

But meeting Edith has breathed fresh air into his life. And when he goes off on tour again tomorrow he will miss her sorely. He will miss his children. As he lies in bed holding her hand his heart opens like a mollusc's shell and inside it he feels love as soft and as pure as oyster flesh.

Eight

Belfast

Oliver accepts the top hat that Maclagan offers him. Shows the inside of the top hat to the audience – clearly empty. Pushes his hand into the hat and pulls out a seemingly endless flurry of paper ribbons, which he revolves rapidly in the air. The audience applaud.

Next, he signals to Maclagan who moves to a wooden box at the edge of the stage and takes out two blank framed slates. Oliver places a piece of chalk between the slates and secures them with a rubber band. He asks a woman in the third row for her name. 'Tess!' she calls out. Oliver holds the slates high in the air. A mysterious loud scratching can be heard. When he separates the slates the name 'Tess' is chalked in large letters on each one. The audience stare in disbelief, applaud once again.

Maclagan swiftly brings him a broad-bellied decanter full of water and an orange silk bag.

'Ladies and gentleman,' Oliver says, 'everything will happen in the instant.' The hypnotic elegance which colours his voice seems to pique the audience's interest further – some women blush, feel he is speaking only to them. 'I have no need of moisture, earth or time to cause the seeds to root and the flowers to bloom.' He leans forward to a woman in the front row. 'Madam, what flower do you prefer – a mignonette, marigold, violet?' The woman is too shy to answer him, drops her head a little as she smiles, and fans her cheeks with the piece of cheap paper she is holding. 'For you, then, into this glass bottle I shall drop the seeds of each.'

He shakes the contents of the silk bag into the decanter and covers it with his top hat.

'Now, let each flower grow!'

Suddenly, he raises the top hat to reveal that the decanter has completely disappeared and in his hand, instead, he holds a magnificent bouquet.

'Madam,' he says to the woman in the front row and presents the flowers to her.

How on earth . . . ? he can hear from the audience. They applaud him again.

With a gracious sweep of his hand he takes another bouquet out of his hat, then another, and another, offering them to the ladies seated in the first few rows, who are now eagerly extending their arms out to him.

But he is merely warming the audience up, toying with them.

Now Maclagan binds Oliver's eyes with a cloth. Maclagan steps down into the auditorium and requests personal items from members of the audience, then holds each item in the air and asks Oliver to identify it. Blindfolded, Oliver describes each item accurately – a large copper coin from Tripoli, freshly minted, belonging to a gentleman at the front of the stalls; a breastpin dotted with five rubies which are obviously fake (a groan from the lady at the back of the stalls who owns the breastpin, and a guilty look from the man who sits beside her); a small bottle of 'David's General Mucilage' belonging to a portly American gentleman in an aisle seat, who confirms that he does indeed suffer from gastrointestinal problems; and there are more items from the audience selected by Maclagan which Oliver describes in detail – a cigar lighter, a handkerchief embroidered with three tiny lemons and the place name 'Sorrento'; an opera glass with a chip on the casing of one of the lenses. It is as though, by describing something so private and so personal about these people, Oliver is describing the people themselves, revealing something unique and precious about them to the rest of the audience. That's what they feel is happening. They feel indebted to him for choosing them. They are not being duped, they are being honoured.

The reaction from the audience fizzes like an electric current through his body. He takes the blindfold off. The audience give a rapturous applause. There is the obvious magic, the mechanics of the illusions deftly handled, but there is also the sense of the man filling the space. He stands centre stage.

A slick fizzle in the ink blue sky as a firework spreads. Then a crack of mandarin, lemon and green before the light dissolves. A small crowd has gathered to watch as each spear of light ascends then falls, illuminating Belfast's City Hall which, still weathering construction work, sits callipered by scaffolding like an enormous stone invalid. Hoarding fronts the quadrangle. Behind it rises the ghostly shape of the Queen Victoria statue, mummified by a wrap of white cloth. Above the heads of the crowd rosettes of drearily coloured rags, left over from the New Year celebrations, hang in a line from nearby lamp posts.

After the show at the Empire, Oliver walks along Royal Avenue and arrives at the Grand Central Hotel. Around the pillars which support the lavish white stucco ceiling in the lobby are twists of holly berry. A forlorn Christmas tree, past its time, its branches sagging, stands to one side of the reception desk.

He checks his reflection in the panelled mirror which greets him at the top of the staircase. Unable to find his Prussian blue cravat before he left the flat in Huddersfield – lost no doubt in the bundles of flannel pilches, nightgowns, baby caps and woollens – he now wears a burgundy one which is stippled with fine silver dots. Maclagan was sent out that afternoon to Robinson & Cleaver's Department store to buy it. Good choice, Maclagan, Oliver thinks now, stylish yet not overstated. He gives it a final twist and pull, then continues up the stairs to the second floor, adrenaline still coursing through his body from the reaction to his evening's performance.

He reaches The Heron Suite and opens the door to a room full of people. At the far end a woman sings by the piano. A waiter approaches Oliver and politely asks to take his hat and overcoat. Then a different waiter offers him a glass of wine. A huge blackcurrant jelly stands in the middle of the table just inside the door. The jelly is surrounded by an odd mix of sandwich and pastry plates, capons and a sausage terrine.

Oliver feels a hand on his back.

'Oliver, my good man! You decided to grace us with you presence after all. What in God's name are you wearing?' Sydney Brown stares at Oliver's cravat. Oliver is now in no mood for small talk. He wants to talk business with Sydney Brown. His run this week at the Empire drew a huge crowd and both 'The Appearing Woman' and 'Medusa' were resounding successes. What he needs now is for Sydney Brown to book him next season as the headline act.

Oliver adjusts his cravat. 'Surprised you don't like it, and you a man of such substance, Sydney?'

'Please don't tell me you're turning into an *artiste*!' Sydney says loudly. There are a few ripples of laughter from nearby guests. Sydney Brown lifts a glass of whiskey from the tray of a passing waiter and shoves it into Oliver's free hand, removing the barely drunk glass of wine from his other.

'What did you think of tonight's show?' Oliver asks. 'The audience loved it, said it was brilliant.'

'Wasn't there. Didn't see it,' Sydney Brown remarks casually. 'But this is why, Oliver,' he continues, pointing to the people around him. 'Patrons. Heard of them?' He tightens his lips and lowers his voice. 'You wouldn't have a theatre to be fucking brilliant in if it wasn't for them.' He pulls back, takes a moment to compose himself. 'I have great plans for the Empire Theatre,' he says, sticking his chest out. 'Great plans.'

From the crowd a young woman graces Sydney Brown's side.

'Hello, Sydney,' she says in a squeaky voice.

'Daisy! Another thing I have great plans for! Daisy, you've met Oliver Fleck before, haven't you?'

'No, but I've heard so much about you. It's a pleasure to meet you.' Her lips move stiffly. 'How exciting your life must be.'

Oliver doesn't quite know how to respond.

'I like your cravat,' she adds flatly.

'Thank you,' says Oliver.

Daisy gives a faint smile then moves off.

'Pretty little thing but unfortunately a bit like fucking that black-currant jelly. No resistance whatsoever.' Sydney turns to go. 'Oh, and before I forget,' he grins at Oliver a little too widely now. 'Sign the dedications book like a good man, will you? It's over on the piano. I don't want you to miss your chance to say what a wonderful theatre manager I am.' Then he backs off with his arm raised in the air as though Oliver is a long way off instead of only a few feet away from him. 'Let's have lunch, one o'clock tomorrow, downstairs,' he shouts and turns to a tall gentleman who has just arrived and is handing his coat and top hat to a waiter. Oliver watches as Sydney Brown shakes the tall man's hand and then walks with him to a door to the left of the suite. They disappear through it and are gone.

What had Sydney Brown meant by saying he had great plans for the Empire? Was he implying that Oliver should be an important part of these great plans of his? At lunch tomorrow he can make his case, although he knows he'll have to spend most of it listening to Sydney Brown talking about nothing other than Sydney Brown.

Oliver turns. Daisy is back. She is staring at him. She has a ring of icing sugar around her stiff lips, a pastry in her hand.

'I need to sign the ... book,' Oliver says to her. 'Nice to talk to you.'

Daisy says nothing, her slight frame dangling as though she is hanging on air.

Oliver is just about to move off when he feels a hand on his arm.

'How lovely to see you again.'

He turns to the voice. The woman who has just spoken to him has a large swirl of pepper grey hair arranged neatly on her head and a heavyset chest. Though she smiles broadly her eyes are dead.

Oliver stares at the woman. He has no idea who she is. He smiles back. 'Delighted to be here,' he says graciously.

The woman takes Oliver by the arm towards a small group of people standing near the piano.

'Let me introduce you,' she says to Oliver, her smile widening. The woman waves her hand casually in an attempt to catch their attention. 'Now, everyone. This is Oliver Flack.'

'Fleck,' he corrects her, politely.

'Oh, I do beg your pardon. Sorry – Oliver Fleck. The Flacks are a different breed altogether. Sheep rustlers, I believe – or petty criminals.' She laughs. 'Do forgive me.'

Oliver gently releases his arm from her hold.

'Please meet Mr and Mrs Orbach,' she continues. 'Mr Orbach was once one of our biggest linen producers.'

Oliver automatically extends his hand to Mr Orbach. 'Delighted to meet you, sir.'

Mr Orbach squints at Oliver and slowly raises his hand.

'It's Oliver Fleck,' the woman says again to Mr Orbach, leaning in to him and shouting into his ear. 'He does magic tricks.'

'I'm an illusionist.'

'Magic tricks?' Mr Orbach echoes the woman and wags his head disparagingly.

'No, not magic tricks,' Oliver insists. 'I create—'

Mrs Orbach now interjects. 'But what is your profession, Mr Fleck?'

Oliver turns to Mrs Orbach, notes how distinctly manly her features are, the angular jaw, the patrician nose. 'That *is* my profession,' he says.

The Orbachs stare at Oliver as though unable to comprehend what he has just said. Mrs Orbach's face runs the gamut from mild curiosity to disgust. She gawks then screws up her features in an attempt to understand what Oliver might mean. Oliver lets the silence between them hang.

Mrs Orbach leans in to Oliver, tapping his arm with her fan. 'I think you're having a little fun with us, aren't I right?' She grins. 'Tell us what it is you really do?'

Rather than indulge the Orbachs by explaining, he decides to have a little fun at their expense. 'I make boxes,' he says, picking the first idea which comes into his head.

Mr Orbach perks up. 'Oh, manufacturing! Yes, that's the business to be in.' Mr Orbach tweaks his moustache with eager fingers. 'Industrial or domestic?'

Oliver hesitates. 'Eh – coffins. I make coffins.'

Mr Orbach nods his head approvingly. 'Excellent stuff. Oh, there's a chap has just escaped from a coffin in Boston – that Houdini fellow. Read about it in the *Boston Herald*. Billed as the only conjuror in the world who strips stark naked!'

Oliver had heard of the stunt, of course, had thought the 'naked' pitch attention-grabbing and tiresome. 'And still nothing to look at!' Oliver pitches in.

Silence. Then Mrs Orbach releases a high-pitched laugh, like a cat being gutted alive. Oliver feels the pressure of it behind his eyes. He looks at her big teeth, her ruby lipstick spread like jam across her lips. When the laughter stops, her mouth remains open. Nothing is ever *that* funny, he thinks.

'The Flecks,' muses Mr Orbach. 'There's a barrister called Fleck I met recently in London. An Edwin Fleck. Know him? He's been making quite a name for himself tackling those ghastly restraints on trading liberties. That case a while back – Norris vs. McVeigh and Cooper Co. Ltd. – handled it superbly. Moved into Family Law now by all accounts, though God knows why, not as lucrative as Criminal. He originates from this side of the water too, Carrickfergus I think. Curious, never came across the name Fleck before and now, in the one week, I've met two of the bastards.' He turns to Oliver. 'You must know him.'

With the mention of Edwin's name Oliver feels a grip high in his chest. He clears his throat. 'Eh . . . no . . . I don't.'

'Never heard of him?'

'No,' Oliver replies abruptly.

'You must know him, he—'

'Excuse me,' Oliver says, feigning business to attend to elsewhere in the room, 'but I must have a word with . . .' and he waves his hand vaguely in the direction of the table of food unable to finish his sentence. Oliver takes his leave of the Orbachs. He jostles through the crowd, a thin seam of perspiration rising on his forehead as he senses a growing agitation within him.

The smell in the room is solid: body heat, perfume, alcohol, the sweet whiff of freshly baked pastries. Oliver hasn't eaten since breakfast: soda bread and potted herring left over from his dinner the evening before, hardly enough to sustain him through both the matinee and the evening performances. Now, he's starving.

He downs his whiskey then lifts another from the tray of a passing waiter. He takes a pink coconut meringue from the cake stand. He eats eagerly, takes another. Then another. He feels a sour heaviness in his gut for, despite crunching as hard as he can on the meringue, he cannot drown out the name of his brother – Edwin Fleck – which now echoes loudly in his head.

The following afternoon Oliver sits opposite Sydney Brown in the restaurant of the Central Hotel. His brain feels as tight as a dried pea. Sydney Brown is staring at him. Oliver attempts to stifle a yawn but can't manage it.

'Boring you, am I?' Sydney Brown says, feigning a childish pique.

They have finished their meal of braised kidney, onions and charlotte potatoes. Sydney Brown's chin is spotted with sauce.

'Excuse me.' Oliver yawns again. 'Sorry. I've been up since three this morning, working on plans for a new illusion—'

'The price of genius,' Sydney Brown interrupts Oliver and leans across the table. 'You've just got to learn to pace yourself.' In foreplay, Brown purses his thick lips then sticks his fat cigar into his mouth. Oliver tilts his body back against the chair, looks around to see if he can attract one of the waitresses' attention. He'd like a coffee.

Sydney Brown presses his face into a smile, which doesn't suit him. 'Talking of pacing yourself – that young one I've just hired. You know her, Betty Byrne? The blondie?' He runs his tongue against the inside of his bottom lip.

'Can't say that I do.'

'She kicks like a fucking mule. Never seen energy like it. Would give a man half my age a heart attack.' Sydney Brown sucks on his cigar again. He blows a small cloud of smoke into Oliver's face. 'Just as well I'm in the full of my health. Those thighs of hers could crack a man's neck if he wasn't careful. Eh?'

Oliver is still looking for a waitress.

'You hear me, Oliver?' Sydney Brown's voice has a metallic drag to it.

Oliver turns to look at him. 'Yes, sorry . . . I . . .'

'It's just that for a second I thought you weren't listening to me – or interested in what I had to say.' A pause, then Sydney Brown laughs loudly, throwing his head back. His tongue has a yellow-cream coating.

Oliver nods and smiles. He is reminded of Mrs Orbach and her gutted-cat shriek – no, nothing is ever *that* funny, he thinks. 'Oh, you know me, Sydney, I hang off every word you say.'

Sydney Brown has a bloated reptilian look about him. His eyes are pale, deep set and small, the skin around them slack and scaly. He has a weak jaw and a wide nose. His nasal cavities are full of wiry hair. His hair is always slicked back but Oliver once saw it without its usual oil and comb job, when he had unexpectedly called into Sydney's office at the theatre, and was shocked to discover it had a womanly wave. Sydney Brown wears only the best of clothes. He pays himself handsomely. He pays the acts he hires miserably, and worse than that he flaunts the fact. There will always be a part of this man, Oliver thinks as he looks across at Sydney Brown, a part of him that will always remain grubby and cheap – common even, small-time, mediocre certainly – no matter how expensive his clothes or how powerful he thinks he is. And there is a strange smell coming off Sydney Brown, despite his expensive clothes, which Oliver cannot place, a slight fruitiness mixed with sour milk.

'Next season, I want you to put me in as the finale.'

'You won't believe the acts I've already lined up for next season,' Sydney Brown steamrolls over Oliver's request, talking loudly so everyone in the restaurant can get a piece of him. 'Hotfoot from London, no less, Tom Barker – do you know him, of course you must – he's fabulous. Those monologues of his are magnificent!' Sydney Brown clenches his teeth around the end of his cigar. 'I'll be throwing eighty quid a week at that man. Well, I do my best to keep my people happy, you know that, Oliver – and an act like that, from London. London!' He says it like he can't believe his luck. 'They'll all be flocking to the Empire after that, all the best London has to offer.' Sydney Brown's lips are getting wetter by the moment. 'Only the best. Only the very best.' He grits his teeth. 'Do you know how much I paid myself last year, Oliver. Have you any idea?'

Oliver shakes his head. He's thinking of the twenty-five pounds Sydney Brown has offered him for a week's stint in the Empire. 'I wouldn't know, Sydney.' Oliver has gone off the notion of coffee and just wants to leave.

'Guess.'

For the moment Oliver is willing to play along, 'Oh, perhaps two—'

'Eleven thousand pounds, Oliver, that's the kind of money we're talking about. Eleven fucking thousand pounds! I mean, that's already the kind of money we're talking about.'

Sydney spreads himself wide in his chair, then snaps his fingers at a passing waitress. 'Apple tart, darling,' he says. 'Oliver?'

'No, thanks, I'm full.'

'Oh, go on, have some.' Sydney Brown scowls at the waitress. 'Two,' he says, 'with custard,' pouting as he speaks as though his mouth is full of it already.

'Sydney. I can do that. Better than Barker. I can bring the audiences in. You saw the last three shows, they were fighting over tickets. Book *me* as the finale, forget Barker.'

'And two whiskies!' Sydney Brown shouts after the waitress. 'Mackinlay's!' He turns back to Oliver and continues as though Oliver has said nothing. 'Look at her. An arse on her like a horsehair mattress. Listen – I've made great contacts along the way, you know, international contacts I'm talking here, and it's all about to come together. Take The Great Deneto, for example – now there's a performer of immense talent. New Yorker, born and bred, you know. And a good-looking man. And what a dancer. Can swallow three bayonets one after the other and still do the polka. Has something about him that man.' Sydney searches for the word. 'Flare. Command. Deneto stands on that stage as though he is about to have sex with every member of the audience.' Sydney Brown sits back, a broad self-satisfied grin on his face.

Oliver shifts in his chair.

'And I mean not just the women!' Sydney goes on. 'Well, the women love it – but I'm sure, secretly, the men do too. They feel they can't get enough of The Great Deneto. But do you know what I'm going to tell you—'

The apple tarts arrive. Sydney drops his voice to a curd of syllable and vowel. 'He's what I call a bed-wetter. Doesn't know he has it so good, pisses on everything because he thinks he's Mr Wonderful. A little too arrogant when he talks to me. Thinks he can dictate the terms without the hard work. I'm paying him two hundred pounds for the week – well he's an American after all, and a talented one, but he's still a lazy tender-balled little bastard.' Sydney Brown's eyes are focused mid-distance as though he is picturing Deneto right there in front of him. His face becomes a grimace. A bleb of custard sits like a pustule on the corner of his mouth. Suddenly, the end of his fat tongue finds it.

Oliver holds his gaze on Sydney, notes the shift.

Sydney Brown points his cigar at Oliver, belches. 'Now, as for you—'

'Well, if it isn't Sydney Brown!' A short chesty man approaches the table with both arms open, ready for an embrace. Sydney rises from his chair, a huge smile widening his face.

'Arthur Bonner! What has you here? Good to see you!'

'Life's been treating you well, Sydney.'

'Oh, can't complain.'

'And business?'

'Never better, Arthur. You're making a pretty penny, I'd say.'

'Who's counting at this stage?' Arthur Bonner laughs. He slaps Sydney Brown on the back. Sydney Brown slaps him back.

'Got to move on, Sydney.' Arthur Bonner points to a table in the far corner of the restaurant. 'Damn architects. I ask them to design me a country house and they want to build me the Taj Mahal! Oh dear, well, what can you do!' Arthur Bonner slaps Sydney Brown on the back again, ensuring he gets the last word. 'Good to see you, Sydney.'

Sydney Brown laughs a tight little laugh and sits down.

The whiskies arrive. Sydney Brown is quiet. He lifts his glass and drinks. It's a while before he speaks. 'What an ass,' he says eventually, wiping his mouth with the back of his hand. His mood has gone sour. He raises his eyes sharply to Oliver. 'Drink up,' he snaps.

Oliver takes a slow sip.

Arthur Bonner can be heard laughing from the far end of the restaurant.

'Old acquaintance?' Oliver doesn't want the opportunity to taunt Sydney Brown to pass.

'Can't abide the man,' Sydney Brown says with grim disgust. 'Thinks he's got class, educated at Campbell College. Fucking mummy's boy.' An awkward silence follows.

Oliver fills it. 'About next season—'

Sydney Brown looks at Oliver. 'What about it?' he growls, shovelling the rest of his apple tart into his mouth.

'I want to be the headline act. And after that I want you to be the first to book my one-man show at the Empire.' Oliver holds his gaze on Sydney Brown, sees the colourless centres of his eyes widen. 'Yes, Sydney – I want to do a one-man show.'

Sydney Brown swallows the last of his apple tart, licks his lips, takes a large swig of whiskey from his glass. 'You've the talent to be a headline act, the talent to have your own show – there's no doubt about that, Oliver. No doubt about that at all. But it's not a question of talent.' He throws his napkin on the table. 'Do you really want to know the reason why that'll never happen?' He sits back in his chair. 'The problem is, Oliver, you're homespun. You're too fucking Irish.'

Nine

Huddersfield

Edith lies in bed with Archie on one side of her and Agna on the other. She pulls the cotton sheet over herself and the babies, arranges the blankets over the sheet, then tucks the shawl – 'the washted moments of my life in regular and pearl' – around them all. It is early morning and the house is quiet. She settles back, takes the opportunity to savour the stillness, the lack of demand on her. The babies fed regularly, as usual, throughout the night, Archie gulping like his little life depended on it, Agna much more cautious, stopping every so often as though she was listening to the twist of a night breeze or a folding cloud. Harriet will bring breakfast up at eight o'clock and help wash and dress the babies. But for now, for now, she can lie calmly surrounded by the smell of sleep, allow her body to be infused by it and fooled into thinking that it sleeps too, as though just for a moment she has written herself out of her own present. The shock of motherhood has blurred all the boundaries that previously existed for her. The physical, the emotional, the psychological: if the babies are fed then she is fed, if her children are happy then she is happy. I am here, she muses as she turns to look at them, but also there. There is a sinking heaviness to her bones, which anchors her to the moment. And the moment spreads, elongates, has weight. She readjusts her head a little on the pillow or spreads her toes and that seems enough of a thing to do, has a satisfaction of its own, a value, is in itself a complete and done thing. Then on to the simple next. She knows that the duties of her life are still there, still waiting to be attended to, but the wet loaf of a brain she now has diminishes their importance. This makes her smile because it doesn't matter, none of it does. There is just this huge chunk of love which she carries around for her son and daughter. Carries around twenty-four hours a day, every second of every day, and everything else has taken on a different significance. Before, when she was in the middle of her life, things felt relevant. Now things feel relevant only in their relevance to them. All other concerns are trivial. Her son and daughter draw everything to them, affection, fussiness, altruism, a benevolent light.

She wonders about the day above her head, the deepening dawn. Clouds coming in from the east carrying the vapours of other worlds, dropping them on to her roof. Those big sky cows. Heavy and dense and groaning across the blue, offering their frothy milk to the earth as they glide. And she thinks of the first time she re-members seeing the sky, her earliest memory perhaps. She must have outgrown the blades of grass in which she sat and looked up. Maybe a swift or a sparrow caught her eye and she followed its flight, or maybe a bee, or perhaps her mother brought her slender arm up and out to the blue above, her floral printed sleeve falling back as she pointed, the pale reveal of her mother's arm guiding her gaze like she had painted the ceiling of the world just for her. These clouds are elemental: expanse, cold, warmth, sky, mother. And with this the smell of dock, its sap along her skin, a rank balm to ease the nettles' brush. She remembers the smell, yes, but not the sting, a curl of hair falling over this memory of sea green grass and mother blue sky. A memory of summer light beyond the deep ditch that wound its way through two fields and sometimes caused a cow to get stuck, once an old ewe. Inviting her away from the mountain shadow and the chill of granite. She sees herself clearly with her small feet upon the earth, and two huge fields laid flat before her, the nettles waiting. A feeling of calm accompanies the memory, of where, she is not sure, somewhere north, she thinks. Time with her mother amongst nature and no outside complications to bother them. A sense of time loosening, educating them. A wide tranquil world of seeing and looking and seeing more.

She remembers her parents – both dead now – with immense fondness. She was eleven when her mother, Hettie, died of pneumonia. She still misses the tenderness of her mother's touch, her gaze – yes, she had just turned eleven and had no brothers or sisters. And she remembers how she would watch her father – a girdle maker – work at the kitchen table after Hettie died as though he were merely occupying himself until she returned, not wanting to believe that she had gone for ever. During those nights, watching her father work, she became a witness to the contraptions of female imprisonment. It was more than a lesson in sewing, she thinks now, for her father, whether conscious of it or not, had instructed her in the ways of control and conformity, enabling her to recognise and be wary of such things in the world. But the very item which was designed to restrict her as a woman, to pinch her desire to an inch of her breath, was actually setting her free, for every girdle her father sold brought in more money and helped her gain an education. She had an interest in music and he had paid for piano lessons, though what he would have made of her playing the music halls she was not sure. He had often said, with a smile on his face and love in his eyes, that hers was an unconventional nature.

Archie stirs, his tiny fingers scratching the air, then he settles again. She sighs deeply, adjusts her head on the pillow. She wonders what the park looks like at this early hour – Greenhead Park, on the other side of the train lines, just beyond West Parade – covered now, no doubt, in winter's pearl. When the weather warms she will take the children in the big black pram and show them the trees and the fishponds and the growing grass – as her mother showed her the sky – and they will feed the ducks bread. And as autumn laps at summer's hem, and before the petals weaken on the evening primrose and the wind exposes the nub of the blossom's cup, she'll ask herself what is precious? And she'll tell herself her son, her daughter. That placid acceptance now vibrates in her mind as pure and as warm as an owl's song.

Ten

Belfast

That night in his usual Belfast digs, a modest room on Joy Street, Oliver lies back on his narrow iron bed and stares at the darkness above him. He is cold. He feels as though he could be buried alive, down deep in the cold earth. He rolls over on to his right side, pushing his hands between his legs in search of some hidden warmth. He draws his legs up to his chest.

His thoughts are racing. He thinks of the crowd's consistently enthusiastic response to 'Medusa' and he knows he can work the audiences harder, he knows he can headline the bill. Lunch with Sydney had drifted well into the early evening, followed by more drinks at the Garrick Bar, but a sense of belligerence had grown within him, fuelled by the irritation he was feeling after his conversation with the fatuous Orbachs, angered by Sydney Brown's easy dismissal of him, haunted most of all by the mention of his brother, Edwin – yes, of course it was his brother Mr Orbach had been referring to. Since then there has been a shadow hanging over him, a feeling of disquiet which he can't shake off.

He hears coughing coming from the room next door. He pulls

himself up out of bed and fumbles for the safety matches on the dresser. He lights a candle, which offers him a small globe of comfort, finds a cigarette stub, ignites it from the flame and breathes in deeply.

The window rattles as a crisp night breeze lifts outside. The wad of newspaper that he had used to fasten the window frame last night has dislodged itself but now he doesn't have the presence of mind to fix it. His head is still too tight with whiskey. He climbs into bed and settles on his right side facing out into the room, pulling the blankets up and over his arms and chest. He places his head deep in the pillow, cradles his balls to guard the kernel of body heat which is growing there. He clenches his toes, feels the soles of his feet tender and sore. He shapes himself into a whorl, neat for his size, tries not to move in the bed as the cold shock of the sheet is always fresh. A fucking stone bottle wouldn't go amiss, he thinks. His breathing is the only sound he is aware of now as the hollow in his chest widens.

No one comes to the door – no one is expected to come to the door, and yet he waits, as he lies there, waits for the knock, for an echo of his childhood.

The night is so long, he thinks, when you're waiting for it to pass. And there's still a lot of night ahead. He shifts in the bed. Looks at the length of burning candle that remains. He feels like a rock at the bottom of a dry well and he yearns for a pair of warm arms to hold him. Edith, he sighs, pushing his head into the blankets.

He hates it. He hates the night. He hates falling to sleep. He hates not falling to sleep. More than that, he hates the thought of how he might wake up. How the world might be utterly changed when he opens his eyes.

*

He is ten years old. He feels the hot rasp of his breath against his pillow. His hair is sticky with sweat and his heart is pounding. He has woken up on his left side and an overwhelming sense of dread now floods his body.

Had he woken up on his right side, facing out into the expanse of the room, his brother Edwin stretched out like a long, twisted rope in the bed across from him, he would have felt the sweet rush of relief loosen his head. But waking up facing into the rough plastered wall fills him with a sense of foreboding. On both the day the giant sycamore tree had died and the day the rusted clout nail had lodged itself in Edwin's cheek he had woken up on his left side.

He keeps his eyes half-closed so that he cannot see the wall in front of him in full relief, the canopy of his eyelashes his intimate guardian. There is no other sound. He can hear only the pounding in his ears. What if the worst has happened? What if he turns around to find the world has vanished? That nothing is left except a vast, grey desert. Or just as frightening – that the world has stayed exactly the same as he left it the night before: his clothes hanging on the peg on the side of the wardrobe, his shoes by the washstand near the door, his cotton flannel draped across the wooden towel-horse, his prayer book resting on the little stool at the foot of his bed with its ribbon bookmark drawn tightly to its spine – except that everyone in the world has disappeared? Everyone except for him.

He swallows the small reservoir of saliva which has gathered in his mouth, yet feels his gullet like a dry stick in his chest. He tells himself the world must still be there, that it is – as his mother had once said to him – only childhood superstition that makes him believe the worst. He opens his eyes a fraction more and squints into the solid murk of the wall.

He hears the stout melancholy call of a wood pigeon from outside his window, a familiar and welcome sound which puts the world back in its place. A moment later there is a short, sharp snort from Edwin. He exhales deeply, feels a melting in his gut and chest, a pulse of courage, and slowly turns on to his right side. So the world is still there, as it should be. Edwin in his bed on the other side of the room, his blanket half covering his face like a highwayman's disguise, one arm thrown back over and above his head, a silver line in the shadow, firing his pistol to the sky to beckon his fellow highwaymen to join him; or perhaps a cocky salute to his unfortunate victims, the fine jewelled ladies cowering in their carriage which he has ambushed on the edge of town. Edwin wears the clarity of a dreamer on his face – as though nothing is beyond the realm of the possible – and gives another sharp snort.

The curtains across the window are now fringed with the morning's spill and a jigsaw of light and shadow fills the room. He pulls back the edge of the curtain to look out. Close to six o'clock, he reckons, judging by the light, the sun yet to lift its head clear of Fathom Hill, which rises behind the house in a gracious rinse of purple. Sometimes he scales Fathom Hill alone and with an eager step. Occasionally with his father, who stabs the earth with his blackthorn stick and ploughs an arrow-straight path across its crest. But the best times by far are with Edwin. On their descent they both feel their bones jangle like rings of loose keys as they run, unable to prevent the weight of their bodies propelling them forward. Their feet thud upon the bracken-laced ground making their bellies feel full and empty at the same time. Laughing together all the way to the bottom of the hill, they fall on the grass verge by the cinder path, gasping for air. As brothers together they borrow from the mountain and the sky to build their boyish games of soldiers braving war, pirates in their quests for gold, adventurers conquering the highest peaks. At night they sometimes talk until morning breaks, at school they listen for each other's voices through the rickety wooden partition which divides the schoolhouse into classrooms, and last summer Edwin had rescued him from the girdled sycamore tree by the stackyard which they had both been forbidden to climb. The sycamore was diseased and had been girdled to quicken its demise and although it still looked strong it was brittle and sapless. Yet he had insisted on the climb and had then found himself stuck. Edwin had immediately gone to rescue him but the branch he had clambered upon had snapped and he had fallen, gouging his cheek on a rusted clout nail protruding from the stackyard gate – the crab-claw-shaped scar still marks Edwin's face. To save him from a beating, Edwin had taken full blame and had never told on him even though it had been his fault for climbing the tree in the first place. He turns around to Edwin. He is glad to have an older brother to look out for him.

Oliver glances up. Above Edwin's bed hangs a framed tapestry with the line 'My soul waiteth for the Lord more than they that watch for the morning' in peacock blue neatly embroidered by their mother. On his own side 'Behold the fire and the wood, but where is the lamb?' in cardinal red.

Normally Edwin is the first to wake and get washed, hogging all the clean water from the floral ewer for himself and, after splashing his face, chest and underarms with it, leaving it mixed with the mottled scum of his sleep. Edwin is fifteen, and since Easter – now it is the end of June – he has been shaving the thin black stubble which has been regularly appearing on his lower jaw and so the leftover water is now often spiked with hairs. Although Oliver is a little in awe of this new ritual, he doesn't like the feel of his brother's hairs against his skin.

But this morning Oliver is awake first and despite the initial sense of foreboding the ebb and flow of the day could still be teased in his favour.

He remembers it is Saturday. Today, he, Edwin and their mother and father are to take the train from Eden's Cross to Carrickfergus.

First, a visit to the Council Rooms at the Town Hall has been planned, where, as a member of Larne Rural Council, his father is to have a meeting with local councillors – an attempt to settle a dispute over the distribution of funds for the new library. Then his mother plans to pay a visit to the music shop in town. Afterwards there'll be a chance to glimpse the local regatta from the harbour. Perhaps he'll get ice cream or cake.

He slowly pulls back his blankets and places his bare feet on the wooden floor. There is an intake of breath from Edwin and Oliver turns to check him, but Edwin remains asleep, grinding his teeth under the blanket, no doubt testing the efficacy of his stolen pearls. Oliver quickly puts on his underwear and socks, then his trousers and shirt. He combs his hair and tidies his collar. A piss in the chamber pot, he decides, would definitely wake Edwin, so this morning he will use the outdoor lavatory instead.

He bends down to lift his shoes from under the washstand and his prayer book from the stool. The floor creaks loudly beneath him. Suddenly Edwin sits up in the bed, straight as a poker, and glares at Oliver as though he had just been given some shocking news – the realisation that his plunder is merely paste, his lady prisoners are policemen in disguise, aiming their dainty pistols at his head.

'What are you doing up?' asks Edwin, wide-eyed.

'Dunno,' stammers Oliver.

'You washed and all?'

'Yes.'

'How come?'

'I can't be late for prayers,' he says to Edwin and scrambles out through the door.

He enters the kitchen with a bounce in his step. His mother has already arranged the breakfast delph on the table – the settled promise of ordered things: cups, saucers, butter dish, spoons, milk jug. There is the smell of warm bread. He hears his mother in the scullery filling the kettle, but the tea will only be made after prayers are done. He stands beside his chair knowing that his mother will be surprised to see him up and dressed before Edwin.

She appears in the doorway of the scullery wearing her floral apron. Christened Louisa Grace – although he has never heard her called anything other than Grace or mother – he thinks that she has the kind of face where the space between her features seems right and regular (although perhaps – he has considered since – it is only the symmetry assigned by a child's love). Her hair reminds him of the colour of a hay ruck which has sucked up summer and she always wears it parted in the middle and pinned in a neat bun at the back of her head. Her skin is clear and pale, her eyes sea green and her lashes fair. She is not a tall woman but she is neat and evenly proportioned which gives her, by illusion, a sense of height. When she wears her frameless glasses she always looks puzzled. When she smiles it is an unending harvest.

Last night his father, Harold, had brought Edwin out with him to the Larne Poor Law Guardians meeting in Kilgiven and had said that they would not be back home until after ten o'clock. The house had become soft in their absence. A small fire crackled in the kitchen grate, and an unhurried tick sounded from the carriage clock on the mantelpiece. His eyes wandered from the tulips of flame to his mother's face, then to her hands as she worked her needlepoint.

'Your father and Edwin will be in the thick of it by now,' she had said gently, not lifting her head from her canvas, her frameless glasses perched on the end of her nose.

He nodded in reply.

'In the thick of it,' she repeated. 'That gives me a little time.'

She had placed her needlepoint – the stitching of yet another Biblical phrase – carefully on the small table beside her chair. Then standing and smoothing down her skirts she left the room. Moments later he heard the rich dark tones of Beethoven's 'Pathetique' coming from the front parlour.

His father had forbidden her to play Beethoven in the house. Only Schubert or Chopin were permitted. Beethoven was not fit for a Protestant household, his father had stated firmly, as it aroused only godless desires, although he had thought his father godless himself when he had said it, hammering the table with a tight fist, his face and neck an angry red.

He loved it when his mother played Beethoven. Always tame at first, her playing intensified quickly, pitching finally into a kind of abandoned frenzy, until he could feel the music shaking his very bones. He was a sycamore seed floating earthward, the dusk gently falling around his shoulders. Then he was spinning skywards, caught on a tailwind up to a great height, up over the sycamore from which he had fallen, his arms catching the night blue air, the pulse of his heart racing, and his two feet hanging like an anchor below him, as though his blood had filled his shoes.

When his mother had finished playing, the silence over the house felt as taut as a drawn bowstring and he had once again returned to earth. She came into the kitchen and sat in the chair opposite him, a breathlessness lifting her chest, a speckled blush dotting her cheeks as though she had, just the moment before, stepped out into the night and been star-burned. After playing Beethoven he seemed to see the words she was thinking but not saying, like a vapour escaping off her. Simple words: flutter – rush – float – rise. And not only the words, but the beautiful wide spaces which existed in between them. From her he learned to see the unseen. To look beyond the solid facts of the world as they presented themselves.

'A little while yet before they're home,' she had lowered her head and resumed her needlepoint, a rib of private joy guiding her hand. 'Tomorrow, when we go in to Carrickfergus, you and I will buy some sheet music while your father attends his meeting. Beethoven's "Moonlight" perhaps. No need to say a word.' She had spoken like a girl home late, happily damned.

Now she stands in the doorway of the scullery, smiling at him.

'You're early this morning,' she says, a lightness to her voice. 'Edwin up?'

'He's still in bed,' he replies, so pleased that his mother is pleased with him.

'Prayers shortly.' She puts the kettle on the stove.

On his way to the outside lavatory he checks the tin bucket in the yard inside which he has created an aquarium for the cloudy mass of frogspawn he collected in the spring. He is worried that his earlier sense of foreboding means that they may have come to some harm. He is relieved to see that they are fine, darting amongst the waterweed and flicking their liquorice-black legs as they move. Over the weeks he has watched the cloudy mass become tadpoles and the tadpoles become froglets. Their tails have shrunk. They have lost their gills. Soon he will be able to bring them back to the marshy ditch by the cinder path where he found them. He pulls the bucket away from the stone wall of the outhouse and into the middle of the yard so that it can catch the light as it falls. He tickles the surface of the water, feeling a swell of pride in the froglets' determined growth. He thinks he will name every one of them as he sets them free. As he straightens he can see the beginning of the cinder path, which runs all the way into Kilgiven town where he and Edwin go to school. He throws his head back, looks up at the sky, watches the clouds as they shift and change above him.

He uses the lavatory and washes his hands under the tap in the yard. He is already seated at the table with his mother and father by the time Edwin enters the kitchen. Harold checks his pocket watch.

'You're late for prayers.' Harold sits squarely in his chair, his large hands resting on the leather-bound Bible he uses for the morning readings. Grace has her head bent. Oliver moves his eyes quickly from Edwin's face to his breakfast plate and back again.

'I'm sorry,' says Edwin, looking chastened.

'He's growing, Harold, that's why he needs his sleep. Look, his trousers are creeping up his legs before our very eyes.' Grace gently shakes her head as though to remonstrate the perils of growing up so fast.

'If I want your opinion, I'll ask for it.' He turns to Edwin. 'Make sure it doesn't happen again.'

'Yes, sir,' Edwin says quietly and sits down at the table.

Harold slowly opens the Bible, finds his page. 'And the mountain burned with fire unto the midst of heaven, with darkness, clouds, and thick darkness.'

Oliver looks at his father. The hairs of his moustache are as straight as a horse's tail but his thick dark brown hair peaks at the front without coaxing.

'For the Lord thy God is a consuming fire, even a jealous God.'

His father's voice fills his head with a colour for which he has no name. One that he might find lining the insides of a steel pot or vacant tin.

'And the Lord shall scatter you among the nations, and ye shall be left few in number among the heathen . . .'

As soon as the reading is finished Oliver grabs the butter knife from the middle of the table but in the process knocks the jug of milk on to the floor. It smashes on the tiles. The milk sprays Harold's trousers and spreads out at his feet. Oliver immediately stutters an apology, staring with a terrified look in his eyes at his father and then down at the mess on the floor. Grace jumps up to fetch a tea towel to mop up the milk.

'Sit down. The boy will clean it. And then be duly punished.'

'Harold, no,' pleads Grace. 'It was an accident.'

'It's carelessness, that's what it is,' says Harold, leaning back in his chair.

Oliver fetches a cloth from the scullery and kneeling down wipes up the spilt milk on the floor. He doesn't dare attempt to wipe the milk spots he sees spattered on the lower half of his father's trousers. He places the broken pieces of the milk jug in the cloth and takes them out to the scullery. He feels sick to his stomach. There it was – the proof. Every time he woke up on his left side the day did not go well. Why did he imagine it would? Things never did. *Ye stupid eejit, Oliver Fleck*, he says to himself, *ye stupid, stupid eejit*. He returns to the kitchen.

'Now, get my blackthorn stick.'

'Harold, it'll only make us late if we fuss. Let's have breakfast and then, when we're back from our business in Carrickfergus, perhaps then consider a punishment.' She touches Oliver gently on the shoulder, an attempt to reassure him that she will intervene if and when the time for a punishment comes.

Harold pauses for a moment. 'Let him do without breakfast then,' he concedes.

Oliver can feel tears well up in his eyes but he makes a promise to himself that he will not cry.

As they make their way along the seafront at Carrickfergus the Flecks skirt the regatta. Despite both himself and Edwin asking if they can watch the boats set off, their father insists they continue on into the town. Harold's meeting with the local councillors is due to take place in twenty minutes and he does not want to be late. Grace suggests that most of the councillors, if they have any sense, will be attending the regatta themselves and perhaps the boys are right, perhaps they should stop awhile and watch, or perhaps she can wait with the boys while he goes to the meeting. But Harold will hear none of it. All the councillors called will be attending, he says, and regardless of that he believes that every councillor fares better in the eyes of the community when their families offer visible support. They will walk with him to the Council Rooms at the Town Hall and then wait in the atrium at the upper end of the main corridor until the meeting is over. Only if there is time after the meeting will they take in the festivities at the harbour.

Grace sighs. She turns to Oliver and makes a face to show that she is just as disappointed as he is. But somehow – and it has happened before – Oliver cannot feel an ease with his mother in the company of his father and brother. Some balance of power alters between them when they are all together and his mother becomes an isolated thing. The feminine affectations she displays towards something which pleases her, and which he would enjoy witnessing if they were alone together, are now an embarrassment to him. When his mother exclaims how pretty the ladies' hats are as they walk through the crowds on the seafront and presses her hands tightly into her chest in appreciation, he turns his head away from her. When she remarks how beautifully the sunlight flickers on the water in the harbour and gives that little shudder she always gives when something makes her happy, he clicks his tongue in disapproval. There is something in the stern look of his father and in the resigned expression of his brother which prevents him from appreciating her reactions, as though he is sensing that these are the weaknesses of women he must arm himself against. And in not acknowledging her he denies himself the same pleasure. He dips his head to the ground.

'I wish I'd worn a different hat now that I see how pretty the ladies are dressed with their summer fashion.' As she speaks Grace gingerly touches her neat brown felt hat. Harold, Edwin and Oliver do not respond. Oliver can feel his stomach tighten.

The meeting is longer than any of them had expected. When Harold eventually appears at the doors of the main hall, shaking the hands of his fellow councillors by way of a thank-you and goodbye, Grace and the boys ask if they might have an early lunch as all of them are hungry.

In Dobbins Inn Hotel they have fish pie. Harold orders whiskey. Over the course of the lunch a line of perspiration breaks out across his forehead and his eyes narrow as he talks about the discourteous behaviour of the fund managers at the meeting, pointing his finger at Grace as though she is one of them. He slaps a flat hand on the table making the cutlery ring, raises his voice, bites the air. He finishes his whiskey and orders another.

Grace wipes the corners of her mouth with her napkin. 'I was hoping, Harold,' she says politely, 'after we finish our meal that I could pay a visit to the music shop in the town. I can walk there myself, I know where it is, and I could meet you all by the entrance to the castle. I want to buy some sheet music – Chopin or Schubert. I have put money aside from the housekeeping allowance to cover the purchase.' She looks expectantly at Harold.

'That money is to go back into the housekeeping allowance. I will pay for the sheet music.'

Oliver clicks his tongue again. He knows that the true purpose of his mother's visit to the music shop is to buy Beethoven, after all, isn't that what she had said to him the night before ('Beethoven's "Moonlight" perhaps. No need to say a word'). He wishes now that he had not been privy to his mother's secret desires. He feels himself hardening against her.

Harold shakes his head. 'We will go together. I will not have you walking the town unaccompanied.'

'But I am perfectly able—'

'That's the end of it. I'll hear no more about it. Whether you think you are able is incidental. I'm sick of you constantly undermining my position in this family.'

Grace bows her head. Edwin and Oliver sit quietly.

Harold checks his pocket watch. He orders tea for Grace, and another whiskey for himself.

In the music shop Grace leafs through the sheet music, which is displayed on the stand by the door. The shop assistant, a small man with an impossibly tiny beak of a mouth, waits patiently behind the counter, tapping his fingers on the countertop as though to a constant rhythm in his head. Harold, Edwin and Oliver stand like three stone pillars behind Grace. Harold's impatience is growing by the moment.

Oliver watches as his mother becomes more and more flustered. He knows she will not now be able to buy the sheet music she wants with so many eyes upon her. The shopkeeper rolls out from behind the counter and over to Grace.

'Can I help you find something, madam?' Inside his mouth is a small clapper of a tongue ready to trill. 'Who or what might you be looking for, may I ask?'

'Oh ... Chopin's Etudes?' There is a shakiness to Grace's voice which makes her sound as though she is about to cry.

'That would be under "C", madam, not under "B".' He moves forward to assist.

'Oh yes, of course.' Grace steps back a little from the stand. 'I'm sorry.'

'Ah, here we have "Tristesse",' the shop assistant says with a smile and a flourish of his hand. 'A beautiful piece of music, if I may say so, earnest and controlled.' The pale bead of his tongue moves up and down as he speaks as though independently alive. 'Will you be purchasing it now, madam?' But as he asks the question of Grace he looks at Harold.

Harold nods. Grace takes a deep breath and looks at Oliver for moral support of some kind, a recognition of yet another disappointment, but he bows his head to the floor.

'May I just glance through it to make sure it's at the level I require?' Grace asks.

The shop assistant looks at her curiously. 'It's a fine arrangement, madam, I can assure you, but it's certainly for the more accomplished player.'

'Yes, I have no doubts it's a fine arrangement,' Grace continues, 'but if you could just give me a moment before I purchase it.'

'Of course.' The shop assistant gives a little bob of his head and walks behind the counter, drumming his fingers upon its surface again. Harold takes out his pocket watch, looks at it and gives an audible sigh. Turning his back on Grace for a moment, he looks out of the window. Just as he does so Oliver sees his mother lift another sheet of music from the stand and slip it into the Chopin she holds in her hands. Then she moves swiftly to the counter.

'That will do fine,' she says and turns to Harold. 'Thank you, Harold.'

Harold releases another long sigh. 'We'd better get going,' he says, placing money on the counter.

Oliver is shocked that his mother has stolen the sheet music. He watches the assistant roll Chopin's Etudes – with the Beethoven, he's sure, hidden inside – and tie it in a neat roll with a length of ribbon.

'I hope you enjoy it, madam,' the shop assistant's pink tongue rattles.

'I will,' Grace says smiling and follows Harold and the boys out of the shop.

They stand for a while watching the festivities at the harbour. The race is coming to a close and the last of the boats are lazily approaching the shore. Oliver finds a blue toy kite not much bigger than his hand tucked into a seaside shrub. He takes it with him. Then they make their way to the station to catch the two forty-five back to Eden's Cross.

Oliver glances up at his mother as they walk along the street. There is a soft and faraway look in her eye. When she turns to him he sets his face with a look of disapproval.

Had she fallen straight down she would have landed on the tracks. Then the full horror of the accident might have registered sooner and the reaction of the people in the station might have had an urgency to it.

But when the bearing plate buckles and the trestle snaps, the section of the footbridge on which Grace is standing swings down and back, the momentum of which flings her like an empty satchel on to the platform behind her. Then a bounce of her temple against the stone. An immediate lank flatness to her body. The people on both platforms, their attention drawn upwards to the collapsed segment of the bridge, take a while longer to notice the woman lying by the arched pillar. It's something by-the-way. Is that a woman who has fainted or has someone dropped their coat?

More than the usual number of people had been using the station's footbridge that day because of the regatta, though no one had been aware that the piton on the bearing plate was ready to pop: not the flagman who had stood under it adjusting his cap in the heat, not the porters who had crossed the footbridge time and time again that day with folding chairs and picnic baskets, not the stationmaster who, from early morning, had patrolled the busy platforms in an effort to ensure the safety of the public, who though warned were still insisting on standing too close to the platform's edge.

Just before the Fleck family had crossed the footbridge, a dozen burly businessmen had crossed, enough to finally undermine the wooden supports perhaps or shift the piton a deadly fraction. Harold and Edwin, who followed close behind the group of men, had already cleared the footbridge and descended the steps to await the train from Eden's Cross. A pace behind them, Oliver was pretend-flying his small kite, lifting it up at arm's length, and twisting its frame in the air. Lastly, Grace, walking with her head bent, her sheet music tucked neatly into her basket. On reaching the middle of the footbridge Oliver had stopped and out of boyish curiosity had levered himself up on to the railing of the footbridge, pushing his foot through the cast-iron lattice and shouldering himself over the top in order to get a view of the railway track below. As he climbed down from the railing the string of his kite snagged on a loose iron rivet and Grace, catching up with him, reached to untangle it.

He had looked at his mother as she unwound the string from the rivet – an instinct to check on her, a pull at his conscience that he had abandoned her for most of that day – when the cracking sound cleaved the air. But nothing moved. There seemed to be an endless stillness in fact, giving him more than enough time to witness the look of poised curiosity on his mother's face, as though she was wondering what on earth the sound could be – an echo of wood and metal in the station's chamber, so close and at the same time so far away. The judder and split came seconds later. The side on which Grace was standing jolted downward, separating it from the main segment of the bridge on which he stood by a few inches. A crude black brushstroke of a line, a thunderbolt in the wood. Grace instinctively reached for the handrail to steady herself. He held his gaze on his mother as she looked down at the fault line and saw no panic in her eyes as she lifted her head, only a kind of perspicuity before the drop. Grace's body followed the curve of the collapse directly, her arms outstretched, as though she was a trapeze artist just missing the bar on the peak of the swing. The space that had once held her let her go. He watched his mother as she fell, her eyes upon him, her lips parting in bewilderment. She hit the stone floor of the station. A blood song from her mouth.

Now there are screams from the passengers waiting on both platforms, some looking towards the fallen woman, others to the carnage of the broken bridge, still others at the frozen figure of the boy. He stands on the remaining segment, now a stark, jagged promontory jutting into nothingness, as though he were a tourist taking in the view. A tiny kite hanging from its undercarriage, swaying gently in the breeze.

A whistle pierces the air as a flagman raises the alarm. There is a ripple of panic in the station. Two porters jump down from the south-side platform and cross the tracks to Grace. The stationmaster shouts out a warning for people to stand well back from the footbridge and platform's edge. Another porter climbs carefully up the steps to the remaining segment of the bridge, to Oliver, only too aware that it too could collapse at any moment.

Oliver watches as a man on the far platform raises his arm and rushes to the small crowd now gathered around his mother: a doctor, who happened to be attending the regatta. He cannot see his father anywhere. As he turns he sees Edwin circling in confusion at the foot of the steps, amidst the burly gentlemen who are still straining to figure out exactly what has happened. Then a porter takes Oliver gently by the hand and guides him down the steps to the platform.

His blood fixes like rust in his veins. His body is cold. He starts to shake.

He sees his father being escorted past him by another porter, towards the station's exit, the porter insisting it is too dangerous for them to cross the tracks to reach Grace. His father argues with the porter, his arm raised in emphasis, his head is tilted back as though he is trying to see over the crowd. Oliver turns from the porter who has been holding his hand and follows quickly to catch up with his father, out under the archway of the station and into the bright sunshine, the street busy with people unaware of the accident that has just happened inside. Then he's back in the station on the other side. Cold stone feeling in his gut and a fresh approaching terror as he makes his way towards his mother. The crowd which has gathered around her parts a little. And then her small shape on the platform, curled on her side like a child asleep. He stands looking at her now. A green shawl with a weave of red ribbon, which someone has thrown over her, covers her face. A seep of blood the shape of an ear, and matching the ribbon's colour, grows huge and wet on the wool. His father kneels, touches the shawl, pulls it back, hide then seek, finds her, the cream of her skin, the blood ear growing and a stranger's hands upon his father's shoulders, helping him stand. His father now nodding his head in earnest conversation with three men in uniform. An ambulance is on its way, they say. No one is to move her, instructs the doctor. The crowd leans in closer to get a better view.

His mother lies on the station floor, one of her hands rests by her hip, her palm open to the station's dome, her fingers curled and relaxed, an artist's study. No one is to move her, repeats the doctor. He kneels at her side, slides his fingers under the green shawl to feel her pulse then lifts his head to Harold.

A pigeon flies right through the crowd, startling itself more than the people. Oliver looks up as the pigeon settles on the cracked steel girder of the footbridge above him. It shifts along the edge in an awkward sidestep, ruffling its feathers then stretching its neck. The pigeon's throat begins to vibrate, although there is no sound, like a baritone marking his score at rehearsal, saving his voice. It jerks its tiny head from side to side as though mocking him, as though suggesting that by waking up on the wrong side that morning he has caused this to happen. Did he not register the sense of foreboding when he woke? Could he not have made himself wake up on his right side? Made himself, had he really tried? Did he not fear that the world would change in an instant? The worst that could happen has happened when he hears the doctor pronounce his mother dead.

In the hospital corridor Edwin stands stiffly beside him as he cries. There is still light in the sky when they arrive home but he is sent to bed. He feels a strange relief in the midst of all that has happened that his father has forgotten to punish him for breaking the milk jug. But the following morning he finds his bucket aquarium lying on its side and empty. The froglets lie burned by the old stone trough in the yard.

*

As he lies now in his room in Joy Street he replays the fatal fall in his mind, like he has done nearly every day of his life. The simple aerodynamics of it. The kite and his mother. What was saved and what perished. In replaying it he sometimes allows himself to alter its course and so suffer the resulting shame of his alteration. In his own version of events he saves his mother. At the moment the bridge collapses he is on the platform looking up and sees her skirts billow and spread around her waist. She becomes as airborne and light as her sheet music, rocking gently from side to side, a smile on her face, an enjoyment even. The only shock, a length of leg revealed as her skirt blossoms further outwards, a secret receptacle full of stocking and petticoat for those below to gawk into as they tilt their heads upwards to watch her indecent arrival. He catches her in his arms before she falls on to the platform. He saves her and his blue toy kite falls on the tracks.

He wishes he hadn't been impatient with her that day, or felt embarrassed by her or had hardened himself against her. If she appeared to him now, right now in this dreary room, he would tell her how sorry he was.

He turns on to his right side. He can't dislodge these memories as he lies alone in his digs. Can't shift them. Where would he shift them to? They belong to the dark. And so does he.

Eleven

Huddersfield

Bertie Gardner slips his finger inside his shirt collar to loosen it, stiff as it is from his mother's starching. He twists his neck from side to side, gains only a little purchase. He pulls the ends of his worsted jacket down to neaten its line, fingers the buttons along the front that have been secured tightly by his mother with a needle and thread. Now the buttons don't wobble as they used to or threaten to fall off at any moment. His trousers have been lengthened as far as the hem will allow, a span of sock can still be seen, but at least the socks are darned. He has grown over the past few months, his mother isn't tired of telling him; 'We'll have to put a weight on your head to slow you down, Bertie!'

That morning he had buffed his walnut-brown leather shoes to a warm shine and had brushed his hair twice, because after he had shaped it neatly his father had ruffled it again as he passed him in the hallway. Now, he stands beside his father in the church. On the other side of the font stand his mother and Edith – his mother is holding Agna, Edith is holding Archie. Oliver is standing beside the vicar who reads from the tattered slab of his bible, his fingers twitching on the paper. The vicar's voice echoes around the cold vestibule. When the east door is opened by the parishioners, coming and going, a thin wind skips in, swivelling leftover confetti around the marble floor and blowing it into the corners of the church.

Oliver had travelled up from Grantham the previous day having organised a replacement for his slot at the Theatre Royal – Fred Felix and Minty the dog. He looks up at the stained glass windows above him. Panels of emerald green, sulphur yellow, sloe blue and crimson red, illuminated by the morning's January gloom, depict the trial of Abraham's faith. The light holds the story: God commands Abraham to offer up his only son; Abraham and Isaac clave wood for the burnt offering; Abraham is about to slay his son, Isaac, when the angel appears. What kind of perverse test is this? Oliver wonders. Why bring a father to that brink to prove a point? What kind of a God would do that? How could any father even consider such a request? He thinks of the tapestry his mother had embroidered, which hung above his bed in Eden's Cross, which he had taken with him when he left, 'Behold the fire and the wood, but where is the lamb?' It registers differently in his mind now he is a father. Oliver looks across at Harry and Bertie and smiles. A glimpse of future – a vision of himself and Archie together, side by side.

When the twins were born, Edith and Oliver had asked Harry if he would consider being godfather to Archie. Harry had responded by saying that he would be honoured to. But later that same day there was a knock on the door.

'A word, if I may.' Harry looked preoccupied.

'Yes, of course, come in,' Edith said.

Harry stood just inside the threshold beside Edith. Oliver joined them. 'It's about the christening and me being godfather to your little boy. I was thinking – and tell me now if it's not what you would like – but I have a favour to ask of you.' Harry rubbed his hands together as he spoke. 'Bertie is a young man now and I was wondering – if it was all right with you both – if *he* could be godfather instead of me. It would mean a lot to him, and let's face it, your children will see a lot more of Bertie than they will of me in the years ahead. And he'll be a good role model for them. He's a good lad is Bertie. It's just a thought' – and here he hesitated for a moment – 'and it would mean a lot to me too. They'll carry on after us, you know.'

Edith had been genuinely moved by the earnestness of Harry's request. She turned to Oliver who stood behind her nodding in agreement and then she held out her hand to shake Harry's. 'Consider it done,' she had said warmly. 'Consider it done, both myself and Oliver would be proud to have Bertie as Archie's godfather.'

Oliver now looks around at everyone else in their small party. Edith wears a paisley shawl around her long navy coat and wears her hair more loosely than usual under her felt hat. It makes her look younger and a little less tired. There is a dewiness to her skin, a lustre he hasn't seen in a while. Harriet has been moist-eyed from the moment they stepped into the church and, now that they are gathered around the christening font, tears are streaming down her face. Harry in his suit looks the consummate gentleman.

These are the people he most cares about. For the first time he feels a genuine and deep sense of family. He has never been so conscious of it before now. These people show nothing but warmth, kindness, love and loyalty. They are people he can depend on. And now to have children himself – now he understands family.

The vicar signals to Bertie to step forward for Archie's christening. Bertie takes Archie from Edith and holds him over the font while the vicar pours water over Archie's forehead. Bertie's face alters, his gaze widening as he feels the weight of the baby in his arms. He's taking it all to heart. The baby brings the man out of the boy.

A lump rises in Oliver's throat. He wants to believe that life can be good for them all. He must do the best for Agna and Archie.

Now Harriet steps forward.

'In the name of the Father, and of the Son, and of the Holy Spirit . . .' The vicar pours water on to Agna's forehead and her little body tenses. Her limbs go stiff and her eyes grow wide at the shock of the cold water, the echoing sounds around her, the sensation of her suspension over the font. She cries so loudly that, at the first opportunity, Edith rushes to take her out of the church.

After the ceremony Oliver finds Edith and Agna on the steps of the church. He takes Agna, now swathed in her blanket so that only her tiny nose and mouth can be seen, and when the others join them they walk back home.

Harry and Oliver sit in the Gardners' flat, each with a glass of ale. The table has been set. A cream linen tablecloth, its edges decorated with tiny white roses, has been spread out. On top of that is a pale pink table runner. The best of the silverware has been laid out, together with the best of the delph. A gravy boat and candlestick sit proudly in the middle of the table, and the salt and pepper have been decanted from their usual boxes into pretty glass canisters.

The two men are alone for the moment. Harriet is in the kitchen with Edith getting the last of the meal prepared. Bertie has been sent down to Filton's Grocers to get lemonade.

'We lost four before Bertie,' Harry says.

'Good Lord.' Oliver leans back in his chair.

'I know. A little careless, you might say.'

'No, I mean, hard on both of you.'

'Not all made it full term, mind you; two miscarriages, one boy stillborn and premature. The little girl lived longest, eighteen months. She died of diphtheria. Nellie was her name. A ringer for her mother.' Harry smiles. 'A real charmer if ever I saw one.'

'I'm sorry to hear that.'

Harry nods then shifts gear. 'I hope whatever is holding up this tour I'm supposed to be on is sorted out soon, I have a living to make.'

'Don't worry, Harry. The theatre owners are asking for too much and paying too little so that's why no one's moving yet. But they can't afford not to sort it out. You'll be back on the road by February, you'll see.'

'There you have it.' Harry takes a slug of ale. 'Yes, back on the road. Having said that, I don't like leaving her, Oliver.' Harry nods in the direction of the kitchen where Harriet is busy preparing the meal. 'She hasn't been herself lately. Won't tell me there's anything wrong, of course, she's never been one for complaining – that's my job!' Harry nods and manufactures a smile. 'But she works hard, too hard.'

'Bertie is here. He'll look after her.'

'Oh, he's devoted to her there's no doubt. And she fusses over him like you wouldn't believe. You've seen her, Oliver.' Harry shakes his head. 'But he's a lad! Has to be tough. It's not an easy world out there.'

'True enough.'

'I wish I could do something else, Oliver, anything else. I'm getting too old for this business. It isn't getting any easier – and for what?'

'We've both put in the time, worked hard over the years, but there's plenty of life in us yet, Harry.'

'Well I have to keep working, don't I – no choice. But the love has gone out of it, Oliver, long ago. And I'm not earning anything halfway decent.' Harry takes another slug of ale. 'And that cinema up in Colne – it's getting houses I hear. That's bound to affect us.'

'Yes.'

'There's a meeting over at the Albany Club tomorrow about a possible strike. You can make it?'

'Yes, then I'm off to Burnley.'

Harry takes a deep breath. 'I fancy starting up a bakery – everybody needs bread, Oliver. Bertie could work with me – after he does his schooling of course – and then he can take over. Open shops all over the county. I'll be able to retire and live the life of luxury I've been dreaming of.'

'Sounds good to me, Harry.'

The two men sit quietly. The sounds of pots and pans shifting on and off the stove drift in from the kitchen.

'That was a good day, Oliver, all told.' Harry nods at Oliver and smiles.

The door opens and Harriet and Edith bustle in with bowls of potatoes and carrots.

'Hope you men are hungry. I've made enough to feed an army.' Harriet heads back into the kitchen to get the meat and gravy. Edith tends to the twins.

'Don't forget the mushy peas,' Harry shouts after Harriet.

'Who said we had mushy peas?' Harriet calls back from the kitchen. 'Mushy peas is for any old day of the week! Asparagus! Something special for a special day!'

'Oh – I don't like the sound of asparagus,' mumbles Harry.

Bertie comes racing into the room and thumps himself down on the seat beside his father, plonking a bottle of lemonade on the table. Agna startles at the sound and begins to cry. Edith lifts her from the pram. Then Harriet and Edith take their places at the table. They say a scant grace, in honour of the day that's in it. Harriet lifts the lid of a small bowl to reveal a cluster of mushy peas.

'Ah, I knew it,' Harry beams at Harriet. 'You know how to make a man happy!' He lifts his glass. 'Now – a toast – to family.'

They all raise their glasses. 'To family!'

*

Once inside the Albany Club Bertie looks for his father and Oliver amongst the crowd which has gathered in the main hall. The meeting has been called to support the Variety Artists' Federation in London. There is talk of a strike regarding the recent contracts offered by theatre owners who are barring performers from appearing in any theatre within a five mile radius while performing at theirs, in some cases for up to twelve months, and the theatre owners are still demanding six matinees a week with no extra pay.

The atmosphere in the hall is charged. Tempers are fraying and the meeting has not officially started yet. After a few minutes, the chairman, a stout bald man with glasses and a thick moustache, steps on to the small raised platform. As he takes his seat someone shouts for, 'Action not discussion!' The heat is up. The chairman attempts to calm the rising disquiet. Another person hollers that the theatre owners should be taken out and shot.

A strident female voice comes from the back of the hall. 'We're the ones who bring in the crowds – we're the ones who make the money for the theatres – if it wasn't for us *they'd* be out of business. A decent and fair fee is not much to ask!' The crowd erupts.

The chairman thumps the table with his fist. The noise eases.

'Every single performer here today,' he begins, 'has to eat, has to pay for a bed at night, needs shoes and clothes to wear – I understand all this. But the truth of the matter is if we don't find a working solution the syndicates won't give us a second thought. None of you will be rebooked. The theatres will look elsewhere – anywhere – for cheaper, and they'll get it!'

'We need protection for a basic level of pay,' another voice pipes up, 'we need contracts guaranteed, a pro-rata payment for matinees.'

'Hear-hear!'

'We want a minimum wage agreement and none of this messin' around,' pitches in a tall man at the side of the hall. 'It's hard getting the work but much harder getting fucking paid for it.'

'We have to take this a step at a time.' The chairman gets to his feet.

'It's already been too long! It's time for an agreed code of practice, or else we strike – that's all there is to it!' a man shouts up from the front.

Another man from the crowd chips in. 'There's the maintenance of props alone – no one's taking that in to account. Who has to fork out for that? – us! And some of us have children to feed!'

'That's your problem for having them in the first place!' the woman behind him retorts. There is a scuffle.

'Calm down! Calm down!' shouts the chairman.

Oliver looks around him. What a godforsaken lot, he thinks. He feels a twist in his gut. He turns to Harry who looks exhausted and concerned.

Just in front of Oliver, a little man with a shock of black curly hair speaks with such a shrillness to his voice it attracts everyone's attention. Immediately the crowd hushes. 'We are performers!' he proclaims dramatically. The crowd murmurs. 'We must take what is offered to us in the true tradition of the business. We make magic out of the little we have. That is our art. That is what makes us true artists!' Someone laughs loudly.

Oliver can feel his blood beginning to boil. He surprises himself by shouting over the little man's head to the crowd. 'In the true tradition of business, and as professionals, the deal must benefit all concerned. So why allow the theatre owners and producers to renege on their end of the deal by not paying performers – that's not business!'

A cheer from everyone.

The little man rises on to the balls of his feet. 'But we must be grateful for the opportunity to create—'

Oliver looks down at the man. Is this what we've been reduced to, he thinks. Willing to accept so little? 'Amateur horseshit! What is it about performers that people just hate paying them? What in God's name is that about?'

Heads are nodding.

Harry puts his hand on Oliver's arm to calm him, but now Oliver is fired up. His pulse is racing, his fists are clenched.

The little man swivels right around on the balls of his feet until he is facing Oliver. His chin is tilted upward, his eyebrows arched. 'We are minstrels!' he says, his eyes widening in earnest, a sanctimonious smile spreading across his face. 'And minstrels take whatever they are given like the birds of the air take—'

'Minstrels! Minstrels!' he roars at the man. 'Where do you come from? Sherwood fucking forest?'

'Oliver, just leave it,' Harry interjects.

Oliver pushes his nose right into the little man's face. 'Where's your fucking lute 'til I shove it up your fucking arse!' He pulls back then with a tight fist punches the man in the face. He collapses in a heap.

Two men step forward to restrain Oliver. Harry backs off.

The meeting collapses into mayhem.

Twenty minutes later Harry finds Oliver sitting outside on a bench in the foyer of the club. Oliver is looking somewhat chastened. They watch as the little man is carried past them in a chair, his nose a bloody carnation in his face.

'That was so unnecessary, Oliver. You'll be lucky if you get off with a caution.'

'Jesus, I'm sorry, Harry, I don't know what came over me. I really don't. It was when he said – *minstrels*. Jesus, what hope is there if we think like that.' Oliver drops his head.

'Well, whatever it was came over you it didn't help.' Harry points as the man in the chair is manoeuvred out the door. 'Looks like the strike is on in London.' Harry gives a deep sigh. 'What happens if everywhere else follows suit?'

'Something will shift for the better.'

'I couldn't do it, Oliver, I just couldn't. I'm barely bringing in three pound a week at best and that's when there's work, but I couldn't afford to lose that.'

'I know, Harry, I know.'

'I couldn't go on strike, but I couldn't cross a picket line neither. What are we going to live on?' He sits beside Oliver.

Oliver remains silent.

Bertie arrives. 'There you are!' he says, beaming at the two of them. 'That was one good punch, Mr Fleck.'

Twelve

Belfast

He misses Edith and the children. He's done Hamilton, Norwich, Ipswich, Paisley and now he's back in Belfast. The same cold digs. Maclagan's in the next room, a comfort, though a small one.

That afternoon he had met with his theatrical agent Jimmy Hewitt in the Garrick Bar for champ and ale. Hewitt is an accountant who runs his agency as a sideline. Oliver had anticipated some bristling conversation about his career, ideas about where they should go with it, what decent work they should chase, move him on from these cul-de-sac jobs. But Hewitt offered nothing but limp platitudes – something amazing will turn up, you mark my words, Oliver, you never know what impresario might be in the audience of an evening and snap you up, talent always wins out in the end, you know, that little bit of exposure will do you no harm – as he sucked the soft potato off his spoon, his moist lips pulsing around the food before he swallowed, chuckling to himself between mouthfuls. What exactly he was chuckling about Oliver had no idea, but it had really begun to annoy him. Hewitt had an air of readiness about him, of efficiency, which ultimately came to nothing, like a weak cologne applied to cold skin.

Now he senses a loss. Can't pin it down. He takes a drink of whiskey from the glass on the small table beside his bed. Then another. Feels exhaustion overtake him. He sinks into some form of sleep where dreams exist as anchorless miniatures behind his eyelids. Not real dreams as such, merely disconnected pictures playing themselves out in the oval arenas inside his head, then disappearing again: a dog in a barrel; three men in a tree; snow falling among chestnuts; Edith's mouth, a soft-gummed cavity, empty of all her teeth; the frogs he had found burned by the old stone trough now alive and as big as geese; the girdled tree weeping blood in the backyard of Eden's Cross; his father and brother sitting with him at the kitchen table. His father and brother as clear in his mind now as though they were right there in the room with him.

*

Harold, Edwin, Oliver. Three men at the kitchen table – two of them hardly men – having treacle bread, milk and tea. The silence in the room is as solid as the walls.

There is a bubble in Oliver's chest ready to burst and he might just as easily dissolve into laughter as tears. He can see his mother sitting at the table opposite him even though she is not there. She is dead and her chair is empty. But he can see her nonetheless, her head held in that patient tilt, her gaze moving from plate to table to wall without investment, her hair pulled back from her face and pinned into its usual neat bun. He remembers once when she turned her back to him and had quietly asked him to check if her hair needed neatening. He had said that it was perfectly pinned and she had smiled at him and said that nothing was perfect, that only God's work was perfect, but she said the words with such glibness she diffused their power. And he had realised for the first time that God may not exist.

Now he is certain God does not.

Across the kitchen table his mother is looking at him, wondering why he was so cold with her the day she fell from the bridge. The pressure in his chest tightens. To stop himself crying, or laughing, he coughs loudly.

'Excuse yourself,' his father mumbles.

They finish their breakfast in silence. A thin spread of morning rain against the kitchen window. The wind at a distance. Damp leaves kissing the front steps of the house.

Oliver looks at his mother's chair again. He cannot see her now.

Harold finishes his tea, pushes his empty cup and plate away from him, then stands up from his chair and leaves the kitchen. Oliver will tidy up – a sudden and unspoken roster now alternating between himself and Edwin – while their father attends to other business.

Edwin sits for a moment longer at the table. 'Your frogs,' he says. 'Ever find out who burned your frogs?'

Oliver says nothing, dips his head, doesn't want to talk about it.

'It's a shame,' Edwin says flatly, then goes to get his coat.

Oliver takes the plates and cutlery from the table over to the sink. He dumps the remaining scraps of bread from Edwin's plate in the backyard for the foxes. He washes the dishes in cold water and dries them with a teacloth. He washes and dries the knives and cups. He wipes the table. A heavy black pot, in which dinner had been brought to them the evening before by their neighbour Mrs Doohan, sits unwashed on the draining board. When he looks inside it he can see a line of crusted grey potato. He leaves the pot where it is, pulls the plug from the white centre of the sink and lets the cold water drain away.

It is only half past seven in the morning but already he is dreading going to sleep that night. And it will not matter what side of the room he wakes up facing tomorrow morning or the next, or the one after that, because now he cannot change anything one way or the other. Now there is only this sinister, agitated present to exist in without his mother.

This morning, Harold brings Edwin with him to work at the council rooms. Edwin will learn the rudiments of land evaluation as Harold now expects Edwin to follow in his footsteps. Oliver leaves for school. It is his first day back since his mother died, a week since the funeral, and almost two weeks since the fatal accident, which now replays in his head without attachment. He does not know what to do about this.

He walks along the cinder path to school. He sits in his usual place at the back of the classroom. The other pupils turn and stare at him, their eyes shining hotly, then look away when he lifts his head from his desk. Miss Lavery asks the class to welcome him back, and in a crush of obedient voices, they chime, 'Welcome back, Oliver'. They answer Miss Lavery's questions about rock formations and tidal erosion. Miss Lavery explains how sedimentary rock is formed. She asks Oliver a question. He says nothing. He does not feel like answering. Miss Lavery smiles and turns to the blackboard. The sun spills in through the open window. A heady waft of dung lifts off the fields.

After school is over, the expectation that his mother will be at home when he arrives is so strong that he feels a lightness to his step. Even as he twists the handle of the back door her presence in the kitchen seems completely possible. She might be making jam or peeling potatoes, or sifting flour for pastry. The tedious events of his day, he knows, will become interesting as he relates them to her.

But as soon as he pushes open the back door into the empty kitchen, a seam of stilted air greets him and the world stops again.

He waits for their neighbour, Mrs Doohan, to bring dinner. He doesn't like Mrs Doohan. She is a stranger in his house and he doesn't want her there. Mrs Doohan pushes her face too close to his when she speaks to him and her breath reeks of bog and vegetable roots. Her skin, though plump, hangs loose and wrinkled around her jowls, her eyebrows are heavy and wiry, her lips wide and flat. She fusses over his appearance and the state of the household. He will not stay in the kitchen while she is there. He will make an excuse about schoolwork, will thank her for the food, will go to his room.

Mrs Doohan arrives with meatloaf and champ. She shakes her head at the way the cutlery has been arranged in the drawer; at the way the plates have been left in a heap on the draining board. She looks delighted to find the untidiness and disorder around her, evidence to suggest that of course she is right, that the male of the species cannot look after themselves, indeed *should* not look after themselves.

She leans in to him. 'You eatin' everything?' A whiff of onion, yesterday's buttermilk, some smell of decay.

'Yes, Mrs Doohan.'

'Who threw the bread out in the yard?'

'I did,' he says stiffly. 'I left it for the foxes.'

'Just what I thought.'

He is expecting her to scold him but instead she lowers her voice and tilts her head to one side. 'Always brings better luck when you nail broken bread to a tree.'

He has never heard of such a thing but he nods his head as though he has.

'Protects you from the unseen,' she says, her eyes wide as though she's looking right through him. She lifts Oliver's hands and inspects his nails. Her own fingers are filthy and feel sweaty against his skin. 'They need a better cleaning, so they do.'

He says nothing. Everything about Mrs Doohan needs a better cleaning.

'Let me see now, give me a big smile.' It is the same routine every time she calls. He smiles at Mrs Doohan although he feels like crying. This is not an attempt to lift his spirits but to inspect his teeth. Mrs Doohan squints, her jaw dropping in concentration. She nods her head as though to say 'now' and he opens his mouth. She looks inside, the tip of her tongue licking her lips as though in furtive pleasure. She closes his mouth with her hand. Next, she pulls down one of the lower lids of his eyes with her finger and shakes her head again.

'I've never seen such a bloodless child. Nettle soup, that's what you need. I'll make some for you tomorrow.'

'Thank you, Mrs Doohan,' he says, the taste of her finger still in his mouth.

'Have you washing for me to take, then?'

'Yes, Mrs Doohan.' He goes into the adjoining scullery and brings out a muslin bag filled with clothes. He hands the bag to Mrs Doohan. He hates that she washes his clothes, and Edwin's clothes and his father's, not so much their shirts and socks, but their underclothes.

'It's ready to eat,' she points to the meatloaf and champ. 'D'ye hear me?'

'Yes, Mrs Doohan.'

'I'm only doing the best I can for ye, ye poor mite. That's all I can do.'

'Yes, Mrs Doohan.'

'Bringing ye food is about all I can do. D'ye hear me? There's goodness in the bringing and goodness in the food.' As she speaks saliva dribbles out and down at the corners of her mouth. 'So whenever you eat, think of me, and of the goodness I'm bringing.' She smiles and shows her rotten teeth. 'Sit down now and eat it while I'm here to watch ye. It'll give me great satisfaction to see it going down ye.'

He feels sick to his stomach. He thinks of the previous meatloaf she brought to the house, how charred it was on the outside, how raw it was in the middle; and of the champ she delivered yesterday, bland lumpy potato, the scallions wasted and rotten. 'Sorry, Mrs Doohan, but I have schoolwork to do. I'll eat afterwards.'

Mrs Doohan appears dissatisfied but says, 'Off ye go then,' as if she doesn't care less.

He leaves the kitchen and goes upstairs.

He sits on the top landing listening for Mrs Doohan's departure. He hears cupboard doors being opened and closed, then water splashing around the sink, the sound of clattering delph, the dull clang of the oven door. Finally, after twenty minutes or so, he hears the back door bang shut.

As he sits on the stairs his thoughts break into flat singular pieces. He looks up at the ceiling above him. Lets the weight of his head fall back, feels his throat stretch. He stares at the knotted strings of dust webs which have gathered in the high corners of the stairwell. Wonders, are they spider-made or simply dust, and if it is just dust where has it come from and how does it appear to have gone upwards into the corners of the house if dust is supposed to fall down.

The house without her has now become a series of empty spaces, where the laws of housekeeping have been desecrated. Each empty space is connected by short empty corridors, punctuated by an empty stairwell. Everything has lost its colour, definition, contour. The walls, the windows, the ceilings, the floors are now held together by shadow, nothing is illumined by the light, falling either from candle or sky.

He sits on the landing until his father and Edwin return from Carrickfergus at eight o'clock that evening. They pick at Mrs Doohan's champ and meatloaf. It is cold and undercooked. He throws the leftovers in the yard for the foxes. They go to bed.

*

As the weeks pass his father begins to take the occasional day off work, something he would never have done before, and eventually stops going to work altogether. Edwin brings home the backlog of planning applications for his father to attend to. They are left unopened on his mother's chair in the kitchen while his father stays in the front parlour in his dressing gown. All day, every day now, he stays in his dressing gown and never leaves the house.

Each night Oliver brings his father in a portion of whatever Mrs Doohan has cooked – a curl of fatty mutton, some kale – collecting the dirty plates and cups from the previous meal. His trepidation is growing each time he enters the room, he cannot say why, something to do with how his father is changing since the death of his mother, the gaunt unshaven look of him now, the grey brown stubble souring his features, ageing him, reminding him of vagrants he has heard about in stories, who are dangerous and up to no good. His father sits staring into the empty fire-grate. He removes the chamber pot his father has started to use. Pours the beery broth down the outside toilet and rinses it out with hot water and soda.

Each night he hears his father moving about downstairs, the sound of a desk drawer being opened, what sounds like the heavy thud of a wooden lid, the clink and clatter of glass, and cannot figure out what small businesses his father is occupying himself with. He resists the temptation to go downstairs, afraid he may encounter an even more pitiable decline.

By the end of the summer Edwin is offered a position in Belfast by the prominent land valuers Hendrick & Ferguson, with rooms where he can stay and an increase in salary, a substantial portion of which he will be expected to send back home. Edwin accepts.

On the day of his departure Oliver watches as Edwin packs a canvas bag with clothes, books and shaving equipment. He also packs the tapestry his mother had embroidered in peacock blue and hung above his bed, 'My soul waiteth for the Lord more than they that watch for the morning'.

'You're the man of the house now,' Edwin says. Oliver feels his body tighten. A new reality is dawning on him. He doesn't want Edwin to leave. He doesn't want to be left alone with his father. He follows Edwin along the cinder path to the station at Eden's Cross. They wait for the train.

'Please, Edwin, don't go.'

Edwin turns to him, straightening his shoulders as though to add years to his young frame. 'I have to. I have to send money back to Father and you. Who else is going to do it now?'

'Please, Edwin, I'm afraid.'

'I have to go.'

'Take me with you, then.'

'I can't.'

'Why not?'

'Just can't.'

'Please.'

They hear the chug of the train approaching. Oliver grabs the sleeve of Edwin's coat. 'Please, Edwin, don't go.'

'You'd better scarper.' The train pulls in. An elderly porter walks slowly over to help the few passengers alight. As Edwin steps up into the carriage he turns to Oliver, his head bowed. 'It was me who burned your frogs,' he says. 'In case you're wondering.' His face is paler than usual, highlighting the scar on his cheek. A short dark crease rises between his brows. He turns and disappears into the train.

Oliver watches as the train pulls away from Eden's Cross then walks along the cinder path alone.

With Edwin gone the evenings seem interminable, a length of darkness that he has never known before. The same evenings he had known sitting watching his mother sew by the fire have nothing to fill them now except the blackness beyond the flicker of the candle's flame, and the dread of what his father is becoming. He sleeps in fits and starts, thinking that any moment his father will bang his fist on the door and enter his room with the scowl that draws darkness up and into his eyes, giving him a terrifying cast. Maybe he might beat him.

He cannot believe that Edwin burned his frogs. His father, yes, he would have expected that, but not Edwin. Why? When Edwin had known how much he had cared for them. He thinks of their shrivelled carcasses, their crisp, curled gills, their plaintive leathered heads. How they must have suffered. A surge of hate swells up in him, frightening him in its newness and clarity, but also affording him a sense of strength.

But how can he be the man of the house at ten years of age? His father is the man of the house. Out of the blue he gets an inkling of what it might be like with his father dead. A thought as thin and light as the steam from the black kettle when it finishes boiling for tea. Just wisps past and is gone. But it returns a moment later, bulks out in his mind. An image of his father lying dead in a coffin, people calling in to pay their respects. Edwin arriving home from Belfast to say a few words, the nodding of heads, hymns at church, a day when the rain falls mercilessly. The fantasy grows. The heavens opening, the coffin filling with water, a double death just to make sure. The claggy earth falling around their feet, weighing down the lid of the coffin. An eternal clay seal allowing nothing to escape. The coffin dissolving into the soggy mire, flesh and bones separating, a swim skin of clothes, limp rags, a third death. As many deaths as is needed. Bog man. Peat man. Troll. With his father dead, some days he might do nothing, only what he pleased. He would sleep easy in his bed and not lie awake frightened of the knock at his bedroom door or whatever it was lurking outside. Then he would know what it was to be the man of the house.

Summer is over. The night before he is due to go back to school he is woken by a loud sound like the complaint of an injured cow. As he lifts his head from the pillow he hears it again. He gets out of bed and stands at his bedroom door. It is his father howling. Is he hurt? Has he had an accident?

He opens his door and walks across the landing. He moves down the stairs, afraid, gingerly pushes open the door of the front parlour to see his father sitting at the table in his underclothes with the barrel of a pistol in his mouth, his shadow spreading and twisting with each flicker of the candle flame.

He cannot speak, can hardly breathe. His body starts to tremble. *Please do not look around and see me seeing you.* Shadows lick the hand that holds the gun. And now that he sees it he would not wish his father dead. He knows there is no redemption for suicide, no forgiveness, and his father will go to Hell. *Please don't see me seeing you.* His foot presses lightly against the wooden saddle of the threshold and it creaks. His father twists his head towards him, his eyes are ovals of black marble, the barrel of the gun pressed against the inside of his left cheek. He can feel a drag to his bowels, a spoon of urine now on his nightshirt. His father stares defiantly at him – there is something prehistoric about him, some shame so old – pushing the barrel of the gun up against the roof of his mouth.

He runs back upstairs to his bedroom. He never knew his father had a pistol. *What if he shoots me, then shoots himself?* He recalls the story Mrs Doohan told him of the two elderly brothers who shared a farmhouse out in Ballinbeg. The older brother had lost both house and land in a spurious bet and had shot his younger brother dead and then shot himself out of remorse it was said, but Mrs Doohan said it was nothing to do with anything other than drink. The brothers weren't found for days.

He pushes the door of his bedroom firmly closed behind him. His heart is beating fast. The darkness keeps its hold on the hours. Father turned bogeyman. All night he waits. Nothing. A spadeful of silence. Maybe his father has already killed himself? But surely he would have heard the pistol fire? Although there are other implements in the house which can kill. Why not the knife that guts the herring? Or the smooth heavy stones his mother used as weights to pin the washing on the hedge to dry? In the pockets of his father's long coat they would take him down to the silted bed of the Kilgiven River. Home was now a different terrain to navigate with the distrust of everyday things. The kitchen knife for slicing bread and spreading butter. The length of rope on the end of the broom handle which his mother looped over the latches of the windows too high for her to reach. The smoothing iron on the stove. Rat poison in the outhouse. Soda crystals in the scullery. Disinfectant in the outside lavatory. He needs to hide them all. He'll hide the large fish knife too, and the knives from the kitchen drawer, he'll hide the hammer and saw. He will stuff them in a sack and hide it under a hedge along the cinder path, and cover it with leaves and grass.

The following morning he comes downstairs in dread of what he might find and is bewildered to see his father dressed and shaved and making breakfast. Soda bread in the pan. Eggs in a bowl ready for scrambling. He looks for any sign from his father that he remembers the night before – the pistol inside his mouth. But nothing. Instead his father turns to him and asks casually if he would like some breakfast. He hears himself saying yes. His father turns back to the stove and pours the eggs into the pan, whistling as he cooks. Out of the corner of his eye he catches sight of the bread knife on the counter and feels reflux in his throat.

He sits with his father at the breakfast table eating small amounts of scrambled egg. His eyes keep wandering to the bread knife. His father tells him that today he will attend to the planning applications which await his approval. Next week he will bring them back personally to the council rooms at the Town Hall in Carrickfergus. 'Eat up, son.' Why is his father talking about going back to work when by now, having stayed away for so long, his position must surely have been filled?

'You're back at school today?' Harold stands up from the table and brings his plate to the sink.

He looks at his father. 'Do you think Edwin could come back home now?'

'Now?' Harold turns around, a severe look darkening his face.

'Now that . . . you seem . . .' He cannot finish. He is feeling more confused by the moment. After all these months during which his father withdrew from the world, now to behave so normally.

'Edwin has his own life to lead. He's making proper roads into what he's doing. Now, you make your way to school.'

Harold pats him on the shoulder, then lifts a pile of papers which sits on his mother's chair, leaves the kitchen and goes into the front parlour.

The howling begins again two nights later. He sits up in his bed listening. His father is shouting out his mother's name, then the familiar arc and slide of his one-sided argument, the pacing across the front parlour. A hard knot gathers in his head. It was a mistake not to hide the implements and stones and poison and the pistol – where is the pistol? He can hear noises in the hall now. Then his father's footsteps on the stairs. He jumps out of bed and scrambles into his breeches. He pulls his socks and shoes on as quickly as he can. The footsteps and shouting are getting closer. In his panic he dashes to the window and climbs out on to the ledge, scraping his leg badly against the latch as he does so. His legs are trembling. He holds his body flat against the wall of the house. He looks to his left towards the gable end of the house but there is nothing to give him purchase. He hears his father shout his name. Roar his name. He slides his body down keeping as close to the wall as he can. Though they are shaking violently he places his hands on to the sill and lowers himself off it. He hangs by his fingers. Another shout from his father and his grip loosens. A loud thumping on his bedroom door. He falls down into the yard, smacking his shoulder against the flagstones and twisting his ankle. Stunned, he scrambles his way to the outhouse. The door is stiff and creaks as he pushes it open. He closes it tight behind him.

The sooty darkness inside is choking him. He spreads his fingers out and touches the damp walls, sliding his hand along its cold surface until he reaches a corner. He tucks himself down on the outhouse floor, hugging his knees, trying to make himself invisible.

The night passes and he is woken by a crow scraping its talons along the tin roof of the outhouse. Claw against tin, the sound amplified as though it were a flock of crows. He moves with great difficulty. His shoulder hurts and his body is stiff and cold. He struggles to his feet, amazed that his father did not find him, amazed that he had fallen asleep. A thin wedge of grey light coming in around the outhouse door enables him to see its handle and he tugs at it. A sharp pain shoots up his leg as he places his right foot on the ground. He stands in the yard and looks up. The window from which he jumped last night gapes like an open mouth. A spattering of light rain surprises him for the sky above him is a clean blue. He moves to the back door of the house, opens it and cautiously hobbles inside. The kitchen is empty. He checks the rooms downstairs for his father. He slowly climbs the stairs. His parents' bedroom is empty, his father's clothes are missing from the wardrobe and all his personal items are gone.

He checks his own bedroom, he looks everywhere in the house, but his father is nowhere to be found.

His ankle is badly swollen. It does not, however, appear broken, able as it is to take his weight. He bathes his feet in a metal bucket in the scullery using carbolic soap to wash away the soot that streaks his skin. He dries his feet and tightly wraps a tea towel around his injured ankle. He improvises a crutch from a thick hazel branch he finds lying in the yard.

He searches drawers and boxes and cupboards in the house for any of the money Edwin sent, feeling a renewed pang at the thought of Edwin leaving him, burning his frogs. He also searches for the pistol he had seen his father with. What he would do with the pistol he does not know, but he feels that if he did find it, it might rule out the possibility of his father using it on either of them if he ever came back. He looks everywhere but he finds neither money nor pistol.

What he is shocked to find, however, are empty bottles of whiskey stashed inside the piano. Twenty, thirty, maybe more. His father might have had a whiskey on a special occasion – the day they went to Dobbin's Inn Hotel in Carrickfergus – but he had always been vehemently opposed to alcohol in the house, had lectured on it to both Edwin and Oliver and made them pray when they had heard about the two dead brothers in Ballinbeg. But then that would explain the beery piss in the chamber pot, the rancid smell in the room, the tangy metallic reek off his father's breath. Yet never once could he say that he saw his father drunk. Not the understanding he had in his head of what it was to be drunk: the lout unable to stand, slurring his words, talking stupid talk, falling over. No, he had never seen his father like that. He had never heard his father slur his words or seen him fall. Troll man. Bogeyman.

He stands alone in the house. Now the silence will only change at his behest. If he hollers, or sings or whistles or cries. Although he has promised himself he will not cry. Unless, of course, his father returns, and then he might.

A momentary jolt when he realises that Mrs Doohan will arrive at six o'clock with food – or something resembling food. He takes the twine he found earlier and wraps it around the handle of the back door and then again around the hook on the doorpost. He jams the back of one of the wooden kitchen chairs against the handle to keep it tightly shut. He locks the front door. He pulls all the curtains closed. All day he waits in the semi-darkness.

At six o'clock he hears Mrs Doohan's footsteps on the gravel. She muscles up the back steps and attempts to open the back door. She bangs her fist against it. Then she calls his name. Then his father's name. Finally, a crunch of gravel and then silence. When he feels certain she has gone, Oliver looks out of the kitchen window. On the back steps sits the black pot. He'll leave it there.

That night he keeps the front and back doors locked as a deterrent against his father's return. He organises three candles in their holders on the hearth. He sits in the armchair listening to the ticking of the clock and, in the distance, to the foxes calling to their young.

He hardly sleeps. In the morning he eats stale bread from the pantry, drinks buttermilk.

And the days pass.

Gradually his ankle mends. He cooks for himself with whatever food is left in the pantry, as Mrs Doohan has stopped calling with her black pot. Every evening he locks the front door and barricades the back door with a chair. One afternoon there is a knock on the front door. His heart skips a beat. He looks through the window to see Miss Lavery standing on the step. He is suddenly flustered. He makes it to the front door in time to catch Miss Lavery just before she is about to close the front gate behind her. When she hears the door open she turns.

'Oliver, you're here after all.' An expression of relief spreads over her face. 'Are you all right? Is everything . . . all right? I was in the town visiting a friend – and I thought I would call to see how you were doing.' She catches her breath and says pointedly, 'Is your father there?'

'No, he's gone to work.'

'To the council offices?' she seems perplexed. 'I thought—'

'No, to a meeting in Belfast.' His voice is a weight in his throat.

'Oh.' Miss Lavery looks into the hallway behind him. 'Can I come in?'

He hesitates. Then finally, 'Yes.'

Miss Lavery follows him into the back parlour. She looks around at the disarray in the house. 'Oh, and I brought you these.' She hands him a small basket of jam bakewells.

He takes out one of the bakewells and eats it, then immediately eats another one, then another. Whether or not it is the taste of Miss Lavery's baking or her kind round face or both, he starts to cry. He tells her the truth about his father, that he has disappeared and that he has no idea where he has gone. Miss Lavery admits that she suspected his father had been struggling with some manner of terrible demon since the loss of his wife. To reassure him she tells him that things will turn around and that they'll find his father and bring him home and that everything will be as it used to be. He keeps his head bowed as she talks.

'I wondered if you were still at school,' Miss Lavery says. 'I'm not teaching there any more. I'm married now and am to have a child.' She pauses for a moment, a pink dot rising on each cheek. 'You can't stay here on your own, Oliver, you know that.' She talks briskly now. 'I would gladly take you myself but I am leaving for England to start a new life. But my sister would have the means to take you and look after you. She lives in Belfast. And you could attend school there.'

He feels a sick churn in his stomach at the thought of Miss Lavery leaving Eden's Cross.

'I can take you to Carrickfergus station Friday coming and see you on to the Belfast train. My sister, Mrs Lytton, can meet you at the other end. I will write to her to let her know. She'll be delighted.' Miss Lavery smiles at him. 'Do you know Edwin's address?'

He nods. He goes to the sideboard in the hallway and opening a drawer pulls out a piece of headed notepaper. Miss Lavery copies Edwin's address into a small notebook, which she takes from her bag, and hands the paper back to him.

'Have you written to Edwin to tell him your father has . . . ?' Miss Lavery cannot think how to finish her sentence.

'No, Miss Lavery.'

'Well, I will write to Edwin and let him know where you'll be for the time being. Don't worry, I'm sure your father will come back.'

The train approaches Belfast and the city quickly makes itself felt, flinging out lines of stone and tile amongst the trees, grass and hedges. Then a solid slide into rows of brick, slate roofs, yard walls, terraced houses. Factory walls hem in the train on either side. The sound of the train hammers back at itself. Chimneys are smoking, the earthy sweet smell instantly inside his head as he breathes.

As he steps off the train and on to the platform he spots a woman standing alone by the archway, her eyes scanning the passengers as they alight. She is of a similar build to Miss Lavery, although not as tall. The woman turns her head. She moves cautiously towards him.

'Are you Oliver Fleck?' She raises her eyebrows and speaks loudly. He nods. 'In that case you'd better come with me.'

The Lytton family sits around the huge kitchen table. A taut and uncharacteristic silence has momentarily fallen over them with this stranger in their midst. Mrs Lytton is the first to break the silence.

'Now, Oliver, you're in the room at the very top of the house so I hope your legs is strong.' Mrs Lytton rubs the front flap of her apron as she speaks, then rubs the top of Margaret's head – her youngest girl who sits to the left of her – then rubs her hands together as though they need warming, then rubs Ned's face, who sits in a high wooden chair to the right of her. 'Well if your legs aren't strong now they soon will be,' she laughs loudly, then all the children laugh and everyone begins to speak at once. There are no singularly discernible words, merely noise. The unbridled energy of the Lytton family is something that is totally unfamiliar to him. Voices hitting him like flints of stone and setting fire to his head. He feels shy and bewildered in the midst of it, conscious of his own quiet reserve, and strangely misses the loneliness of Eden's Cross – of home – where the tangible absence of his mother could at least remind him he was once loved.

From his room at the top of the Lyttons' house he can see across the city of Belfast, the Cave Hill in the distance and beyond that, he knows, quite some way beyond, is Eden's Cross. He removes his few belongings from his bag and places them on the bed. The last item he takes out is the tapestry his mother embroidered for him, which he had slipped out of its frame (as Edwin had done) and taken with him. The thought of her words in his hands calms him. He pushes the tapestry under his pillow.

The following week he starts at the local boys school. He attempts to work hard although he finds that his concentration is poor. A worry overshadows him. There has still been no word of his father's whereabouts, but if his father does return to Eden's Cross (Miss Lavery will no doubt inform him where Oliver is), will he then have to go back and live with him? He doesn't want to do that. Alternatively, if his father does not return, how long will have to stay with the Lyttons?

There has also been no word from Edwin despite the fact that Miss Lavery said she would write to explain the change in Oliver's circumstances. He needs to find Edwin. Perhaps if he can overcome his animosity towards Edwin they can become close friends again, look out for each other as they once did, create new adventures together. He searches for the headed notepaper with Edwin's address on it and finds it. It is Mr Lytton who shows him the location of Edwin's place of work, pointing to it on the large map of Belfast which hangs on the back of the door of the newly installed WC.

As he makes his way to Hendrick & Ferguson Land Valuers on Gloucester Street, a stone's throw from the White Linen Hall, a new thought strikes him. What if Edwin tells him to scarper again? What will he do then? He will need to be able to persuade Edwin not to abandon him. He won't mention the burned frogs. Or perhaps he should mention them straightaway and say that it doesn't matter that they died.

He climbs the dusty stairs to the office where Edwin works, becoming increasingly nervous with each step yet yearning to see him again. But when he asks for him the young clerk tells him that Edwin Fleck is no longer working there and has accepted employment in London. He is so taken aback – he hadn't considered that option at all – that he doesn't even think of asking the clerk where in London and with whom or for how long, but instead walks slowly back down the stairs and out into the street, feeling a dark unpleasantness flood his body.

By the time he is thirteen he no longer goes to school. The Lyttons seem none the wiser. There is so much commotion in the household

that he can easily come and go unnoticed. Most mornings he walks
to the River Lagan. There he watches the men and boys work the
steam tugs. Smoke and soot from the city's chimneys mingle with
the noxious fumes from the gasworks beyond the embankment and
make his lungs feel brothy and thick. Unlike Eden's Cross, life here
feels very close to his skin.

He gets occasional work ferrying people in the rowboats across
the river. Sometimes, at low tide, he scours the exposed parts of the
riverbed hoping to find dropped coppers amongst the stones and
pieces of rusted tin, gathering silt on his shoes as though the Lagan
is tagging him and claiming him for its own. Once he found a half-
penny when he kicked over a rib of rotted wood, a glint in the river's
sludge, as the sulphurous reek of the Lagan burned his nostrils. He
avoids making contact with the other boys who ramble there, all
with the same intent as he – to find something of value among the
dirt. They eye each other with suspicion, aware they are each other's
trespasser, and they set their faces hard. Some wear boots, others are
barefoot. They walk heavily with their heads down as though the sky
has settled on their backs.

Other mornings, he heads towards the clothes market where he
gets a few hours' work helping the respectably dressed women search
for a bargain. The women take their time to inspect the quality of
the remnants and old clothes which he offers them. They ask him to
rummage through the bundles that are strewn across the backs of
wooden handcarts to see if he can find some silk or decent cambric.

One evening, while sitting in the WC, he spots a short article in
that day's *Belfast Newsletter*, which Mr Lytton has left folded and
lying on the floor. The article is headed 'Man Found'. As he continues to read he can feel a chill sweeping up his spine. 'A man found
in a flat in the city's York Street district has been announced dead.
The body has been conveyed to the Central Police Station to await

examination. Murder is not suspected.' There is no reason to think that this article in any way should relate to his father, except the detail, 'The man, in his late fifties, was found with a pistol and had wounds to the head'. He feels unsettled and, at the same time, filled with a light hope he finds hard to explain.

He tears out the article and is just about to leave the paper on the floor when he notices a 'wanted' advertisement in the amusements column for a call boy at the Alhambra Theatre. He has no idea what a call boy is but perhaps it might be more regular and reliable work than ferrying the rowboats or selling clothes at the market. He tears out the advertisement, stands to adjust his breeches and slips the two pieces of paper into his back pocket.

The following morning he makes his way to North Street and pushes open the side door of the Alhambra Theatre. Inside it is dark and it takes a few moments for his eyes to adjust. When he explains why he is there the man sitting behind the hatch tells him to take the stairs two floors up, then knock on the large black door on the left-hand side. As he makes his way along the narrow corridor, which skirts a large wooden screen at the back of the stage, he can hear music playing, a bar or two on piano, voices lifting, music again. He hears a woman laughing, hears the sound of hammering, someone shouting from above him, the boom of a drum, more laughter.

He stands for a few moments in the wings and looks out on to the stage. He feels his senses heighten. He thinks it looks like a picture book that has come to life, the warmth of the light is so intense. Onstage a woman looks as though her clothes are on fire as light spirals off her sequinned costume every time she moves. He stares at the woman's legs as she turns and it's as if she is turning just for him. Her legs are covered in a black transparent netted material, which follows the shape of them all the way from her ankles to up and over her knees. He has never seen this much of a woman's legs before. The muscles in his own legs feel hot and his heart presses against his chest.

Beside her a man in a golden turban waves his arms in the air to the music. He claps his hands and asks for the piano player to start from the beginning, 'IF YOU PLEASE!'. The music starts again. There is a clash on a cymbal.

'You looking for someone?' He turns around to see a small man in overalls.

'I'm here for the job of call boy.' Oliver takes the newspaper cutting out from his trouser pocket.

The small man points to a door at the back of the stage dock. 'You've two flights of stairs to go yet,' he says sharply.

He turns to look back at the stage. The woman sees him and smiles. He smiles back. The man in the golden turban raises a sword in the air, then points it at the woman and begins to talk to her in a kind of gibberish. She closes her eyes, sways from side to side. Then the man places his hand on her shoulder and guides her behind a small screen. He walks quickly back to the front of the screen and proceeds to push the sword through its centre. When the screen is pulled away Oliver expects the worst, he can hardly bear to look, but the woman has disappeared and the sword is revealed stuck fast into a cushioned bolster. The thrill is in its impossible speed. Oliver is amazed, transfixed. But the best part is when the man in the golden turban brings the woman back. Withdrawing the sword, he spins the screen and makes the woman reappear and Oliver feels a heightened rush right through his body as though the whole world has settled in beautiful regularity in his head and heart.

He knows which music hall act prefers which dressing room and who would never use dressing room six because it is, apparently, haunted. He knows not to immediately enter a dressing room after knocking, that decent seconds must be allowed to give the occupier time to attend to any indiscretion if needs be. He knows never to question what the performers ask him to purchase for them – whiskey, pasties, bread, ale, remedies for headaches, once ladies undergarments for comedian Larry Rowan who said, as his temples reddened furiously, they were a gift for his girlfriend. One other time a small dog, when the lady baritone Beryl Parson's Pekingese was found dead in the props room, poisoned, it seems, after eating a bag of pewter.

Two years now working as a call boy has sharpened his sense of discretion.

He works hard, timing the acts, giving the calls, changing the name cards on the dressing room doors as each week passes, cleaning up after the dog acts if and when they leave their mess on the stage, and he takes pride in his work.

He is particularly excited this evening for The Great Bandini – the illusionist and hypnotist in the golden turban he had seen that first time he had entered the theatre – is to perform once again at the Alhambra. Every time he watches Bandini's act he is mesmerised. Tonight he is sure will be no exception and he will position himself to get a clear view from the wings.

Now the Todd Brothers are performing their comedy sketch involving an endlessly rotating ladder which they climb while reciting 'Yesterday, upon the stair, I met a man who wasn't there. He wasn't there again today, I wish, I wish he'd go away'. During the sketch he gives the five-minute call to 'Lion Comique' Eddie Long. Then he brings a letter up to the top floor dressing room for Arabella whose act, 'Arabella and Her Dancing Chickens', is the last one on before the interval. Although Oliver thinks Arabella beautiful to look at with her long ebony curls and her plump round lips, he has always found her act a little artless. As usual when her turn comes Arabella will light the candles underneath the chickens' cage. The flames will heat the metal plate of its specially constructed floor. The music will start and Arabella will carry the chickens in their cage out before the noisy crowd. The chickens will dance on the metal plate. They will have no choice. They will hop to the scald of the music and the searing heat. The ridges of their feet will grow crimson red as Arabella twirls in her milkmaid's flounces and shows her thighs to the boozy men in the front row.

'Come in,' Arabella squeaks. He enters her room to find her lying back on a makeshift bed in her dressing gown, one of her legs raised aloft and a length of stocking showing. Above her hangs the emerald sequined dress belonging to the snake charmer Sally Streight, which Arabella is gently stroking with her toes. Gas lamps burn on either side of her mirror, two more lamps on either side of the doorway. The emerald dress sparkles and glints in the light as she toys with it.

On a chair beside the bed sits the feathered headdress of Lollie Keane, World's Crack Rifle and Pistol Shot. On the rack above it is a huge coiled rope, juggling batons of various sizes, hoops, a crate of rabbit food and a hessian bag stuffed full of coloured satin ribbons. Altogether the scene is a gilded treasure trove.

'My lovely,' she says to him, 'don't you think I'd look ravishing in that dress?'

He says nothing in reply. The side of Arabella's gown has fallen back revealing a porcelain crescent of breast. He hands her the letter.

'Oh, thank you,' she says, waving the letter like a fan in front of her face, a long black curl falling against her throat. 'Would you help me get into it, lovely?' She points at the green sequined dress and smiles at him, then stands up from the bed and removes her dressing gown. She wears only white satin knickers and stockings. It is clear that Arabella is very much a woman and not the child milkmaid she projects in her act, perhaps a woman as old as Miss

Lavery was when he was at school. As she walks towards him he can see the thickness of Arabella's make-up, the red lipstick applied well beyond the natural line of her lips, the curled webbing of the black wig against her temple.

He cannot look at her milky-moussed breasts and yet he can see nothing else. He has seen women's breasts before – when female performers use backstage as a quick change area or when the Poses Plastiques present themselves in a state of undress onstage as 'Chaste Venus Rising from the Sea' or 'Aphrodite with her Foot on a Tortoise' – but Arabella's breasts are without doubt the most splendid of them all. He helps Arabella into the green sequined dress, closing each of the small glassy buttons at the back with trembling fingers. Arabella shimmies from side to side in front of the mirror admiring herself in the dress, then lies back down on the bed and calls him to her.

'Why don't you give me a cuddle,' she says in a tiny voice and she pulls him down beside her. The sequins of the dress are sharp and dig into his face and neck.

Even though the lights are on he is completely in the dark. His heart beats like a drum as Arabella fumbles with his trouser buttons and he finds himself stiffening. When he pushes inside her he presses his open mouth hard against the sequins of the emerald sequined dress and feels he is eating the world.

There is a sharp knock at the door, then he hears Eddie Long shouting, 'Arabella, have you seen that call boy?' and Oliver is up on his feet. He quickly buttons his trousers then stumbles to the door, not looking back at Arabella on the bed. He races past Eddie Long, whose eyebrows arch in surprise, and makes his way down the stairs to the side of the stage.

Arabella is due to perform in ten minutes and The Great Bandini has yet to grace the stage. Oliver sits beside Arabella's chickens, five white Leghorns in a rectangular metal cage, and Bandini's golden turban awaits majestically on the props table beside him. He stares wide eyed at both. His heart is thumping madly in his chest, his body shaking, some new fuel rising in him. He cannot believe what has just happened. With sequin scars along his cheek and brow, the mark of his manhood, he is filled with a gentle glory. As he waits for the act to finish he leans over the cage. Inside, the chickens jab and worry the air. He instinctively brings his lips close to the metal bars and makes a small churring sound to settle them. The chickens dab and flick their tiny heads as though whatever they were in pursuit of has vanished and they are frantically searching for it. He continues making his sound, keeping it smooth and insistent. The chickens turn their heads to him and push their bodies against the metal bars of the cage, their feathers barbing. He caw-caws and draws them in. The clockwork motion of their heads winds down as he keeps his throat song going and soon the chickens press themselves still. An opaque film of skin slides across their eyes until they are milky and fixed, their eyes' rims stilled ovals of orange rind. He has sung them into dream. He has hypnotised them. He stops and straightens. He feels a sudden burst of heat in his gut and a thundering in his blood as he assesses his efforts. And now a simple flowering that might never have happened if it weren't for the chickens. Something in his head has dimmed, disengaged, as though it is all too much or too exciting or too true. A lightness floods his heart and all sense of his loneliness evaporates.

In gratitude the chickens do not move. He has freed them from their infernal frenzy and has released something marvellous within himself.

*

As he lies now in bed in his Belfast digs, the sound of Maclagan's snoring coming through the walls from the next room, he thinks about his life. How he moved from the bleak existence of Eden's

Cross, from the dark hold of his father, the abandonment he felt from his brother, to the world he now inhabits. And what would his mother have made of it all? Proud of him, he hopes. Never in his wildest dreams had he ever imagined the path his life would take. Never had he anticipated a career so far removed from the world into which he was born. A rich and varied world amongst such a coterie of disparate souls in which he had found a place, where the opportunity for redemption endlessly presented itself. Stepping out in front of an audience offered the possibility, each and every time, of a public transformation – the frightened, nervous boy becomes the man who is afraid of nothing.

Thirteen

Huddersfield, 1908

The Monday morning moon is as pale as goose skin. Edith rises. Dresses. Pours water from the ewer into the basin, scoops up a handful and splashes her face with it, feeling the complaint of cold against her skin. Then she presses her face into a flannel. She puts the kettle on to boil. She lights the fire in the main room, which she had set the night before, stockpiles some wood beside the range in the kitchen. She gathers laundry from the bedroom, collects other items from the kitchen and scullery. She sorts out the linen, separating the few items of white linen, collars and body linen into one heap, coloured cottons and woollens into another, coarser kitchen cloths and towels into another. She finds an ink stain on the cuff of her cream cotton blouse and places that to one side – she will attend to it later with some hot water and soap jelly – also one of Archie's shirts is badly stained with grease, to that she'll apply yellow soap. Once the kettle has boiled she pours the hot water into the small boiler on the range which she uses for scalding, dissolves some soda in the water and stirs it with a large wooden spoon. A tub sits on the floor containing a heavily soiled sheet, which has been soaking overnight. Agna had been sick. Edith is happy that the child is fine now and no longer suffering from a high temperature. She carries the tub down the stairs and into the yard, the fresh, crisp air biting at her cheeks, and draws the foul water off into the drain. Back in the kitchen she checks the sheet and seeing that it is still stained, places it back into the tub to be resoaked. She fills the kettle again. She hears the children stirring, then Archie appears in the doorway in his nightshirt. His feet and ankles are filthy after playing yesterday by the coalhouse in the yard – he had fallen asleep the instant Edith had brought him indoors. She bathes his feet now in a small metal bucket in the scullery using carbolic soap to wash away the soot which streaks his skin. Agna arrives by Edith's side, clings on to her skirts and apron while she washes Archie. Archie splashes the water with his toes as he sits on a stool singing a little song to himself, then once Edith dries his feet he drags them through both piles of dirty washing, spreading the coloured cottons and woollens across the floor. Edith collects them and sorts them out again, placing the white linen and collars in the boiler and pressing them down under the water's surface with the wooden spoon, Agna still clinging to her skirts. She makes tea with the remaining hot water from the kettle and while it's brewing she dresses Agna and Archie. She slices bread and butters it. Takes a jar of jam from the small pantry. Sits with the children at the table and has breakfast. Outside, an enfeebled sun grows stronger in the sky as the clouds lighten and fray, revealing here and there lozenges of blue. After breakfast Archie plays with Agna, corralling their wooden cows and sheep in a square of carpet. Edith washes the breakfast dishes, then dries them. She places the washboard in the sink, plugs the sink, and half fills it with lukewarm water. She sprinkles soda in the water. She washes the coloured cottons and woollens one by one. She hears Bertie from the flat below calling to his mother who has gone out to the yard. She dries her hands on her apron, opens the front door and calls down to Bertie. When he arrives at the top of the stairs she gives him some money to buy eggs, buttermilk, potatoes and candles. Back in the kitchen she rubs the coloured cottons with soap, using one layer of cotton against the other. She works the more stubbornly stained cottons along the washboard. She gives the clothes in the boiler a stir with the wooden spoon. She hears a loud knock on the downstairs front door. Hears Harriet going to answer it. She stirs the cottons. She remembers her mother had a saying, 'For the time being soon becomes the way it is'. Like when Mrs Noonan, their neighbour who sold tea and lard and flour from the hatch in her kitchen, found a baby outside her front door wrapped in a ladies' wool coat one winter morning. Mrs Noonan had said that she would take care of the baby 'for the time being', meaning until his real mother was found, and she still had him as a strapping lad of twenty-two. Or when her mother had mended a broken broom handle by inserting a metal pin in its centre and tying it with twine, saying that would do 'for the time being', meaning until she got a new one, and the broom was never replaced. Or when her father had offered their front parlour to the members of the local workers' union, of which he was a member, for meetings during a heavy snow and she had to sit at the kitchen table instead to work on her reading 'for the time being', meaning until the snow had cleared. And so comfortable did it feel going over her reading while only inches away her mother rolled pastry, spraying her book with flour and sugar, that when the meetings came to an end she continued to use the kitchen table to read from that day on. It was her mother's way of explaining that sometimes a temporary change in circumstances can become fixed and then feels normal. We adapt, she would say, to the strangest of circumstances much more quickly than we think. So, 'for the time being' she cooks and cleans and washes and tends to her children and life has a new order so different to her life playing piano in the music halls, so different to the unpredictable, transient and chaotic world that she had once revelled in, that at first it will feel strange but in time, she trusts, will feel normal. Archie comes to her with two of his fingers stuck in a thimble. Edith stops stirring the cotton and frees his fingers. She kisses the hurt away. She wrings each piece of coloured cotton with her hands, squeezing out the soap suds, then rinses them all in clean hot water. She wrings each piece of cotton again, her hands now red. She soaks the stained sheet in another tub with more hot water and soda then piles the clean linen into a basket and, tapping Archie on the behind to go play with Agna, she lifts the peg bag from under the sink and walks downstairs and out into the yard. The day will offer little to dry the clothes, so overcast and cold as it is, but she hangs the washing on the short line, giving the clothes another wringing when they're pegged. On her way back into the hall she meets a neighbour, Mrs Murtagh. Mrs Murtagh asks how Agna is. She's doing well, Edith replies, her appetite is up so that can only be a good thing. That's right, agrees Mrs Murtagh without missing a beat. That's right, Mrs Murtagh says again, nodding at the floor, then she heads out the door to the street. Edith walks upstairs and back into the kitchen. She mops the floor, which is wet from the washing. She thinks about getting out to the park later, she'll put the children in the pram and head off to Greenhead Park. She'll walk and feel the fresh air around her. They'll bring bread for the ducks. She remembers how as a child she used to go to Bog Meadow with her father, an urban haven for kestrels, reed warblers and herons, a traipse south east of Belfast city, not far from where they lived, where the wet earth smelt of copper. She loved to go there. It felt as though they were hiding out in the open. Under a bigger sky. She felt lost in something wiser. The slash of blue amongst the bricks released the pressure in her head and the bland drag to the marshy ground beneath her feet suited her mood. She sweeps the floor of the main room and stokes the fire. Bertie brings back the groceries and tells Edith that his mother wants her downstairs. He'll stay and play with Archie and Agna. Archie jumps with excitement in a little circle on the floor, Agna runs and buries her head in her mother's skirts. Edith places the groceries on the kitchen table, she'll make some pea soup later, some mashed potato. She lifts Agna up in her arms and kisses her cheek. She walks downstairs and goes into Harriet's flat. She finds Harriet in the kitchen smiling, the biggest smile she has ever seen on Harriet's face. Harriet is standing beside a brand new combined washing-wringing-mangling machine. Edith helps Harriet with her laundry to see how the machine works. Bertie, Archie and Agna stand and watch the spectacle. Edith and Harriet are giddy with gratitude as they drag the washed clothes and sheets through the mangle. They laugh and laugh. The laundry is done in half the time. Then they play rummy at the kitchen table, betting with buttons and smoking cigarettes.

Fourteen

Edinburgh

A funny old time of it I've had, it's true. You see, my wife said to me when I came home from work, she said, I'm very poorly. Oh yes? I said. Oh yes, she said. I've a pain in my eye you wouldn't believe. Of course I know how she got that, you know. So I said to her, do you take sugar in your tea, my dear, and she said, why, Harry, I do! I do take sugar in my tea! Do you think it's the sugar what's giving me this unmerciful pain in my eye? Well, I said to her, next time you have a cup of tea try taking the spoon out before you drink it. She wasn't happy, oh no. Well, she said, 'You've done it now'. She said to me, just you take me to the doctor first thing in the morning. First thing in the morning? I said. Yes, she said, first thing in the morning. Well, I set the clock so early we got up before we went to bed. Oh, she said, you've done it now . . .

Oliver waits in the wings of the Empire Edinburgh, as Harry Gardner performs his 'You've Done It Now!' routine to an eager crowd. He watches as Harry struts across the stage like a gamey rooster, with his too short trousers, his oversized shoes, his shabby black coat and his starched white shirt front which sticks out like a parched tongue. He holds a small japanned sheet-iron tray in one hand.

It's snowing outside dear, she said, it's very cold. Very cold? I said. Yes, she said, very cold. Well, I said, why don't we go on a holiday. A holiday? she said. Yes, I said, a holiday. But, she said, you're always sick on the first day you're at sea. Well, I said, why don't we start the voyage on the second day then? Oh, she wasn't happy, oh no. You've done it now, she said . . .

Each time Harry says 'You've done it now' he whacks his head with the small japanned sheet-iron tray and the audience howls with laughter.

Even though Oliver has seen this routine of Harry's time and time again he never tires of it.

And he is excited to perform tonight, to feel that delicious clarity in his head, feel every movement he makes become sharp and exact, feel the adrenaline course through his veins. He'll concentrate on one of his hypnotic routines where he takes a so-called volunteer from the audience – a young man he has hired as a plant – and places him in a trance, inviting other members of the audience to come up on stage to touch him before shielding him behind a curtain and making him disappear. It never ceases to cause a stir. Oliver will then perform his mental magic routine with the help of Maclagan, who will move through the auditorium selecting personal items from the audience, which Oliver, blindfolded, will correctly identify and only when he has finished will he make the young man reappear and awaken him from his trance.

He casts a glance behind him to check that Maclagan is ready, sees the trapeze artists who are on after him warming up. Sees Dolly Melford, Serio-Comic Vocalist and Dancer, poised to go on after Harry. Checks the large clock above the props table. Harry's right on target. If Dolly keeps it short he'll have the full twelve minutes.

From the dark of the wings he sees a figure move towards the side of the stage. The spill of stage light catches the figure. A woman. Oliver stares at her and feels instant confusion. He is totally and instantly beguiled by her, by her large eyes, her full mouth, her crescent-shaped cheekbones, her pale, smooth skin, her dark lustrous hair, her generous bust, her neat waist, her ample rump. Yet, at the same time he notes the firmness of her Adam's apple, its unmistakable maleness. Then those beautiful eyes again, deep and endlessly dark, looking now just at him.

'You must be Oliver Flack.' She is beside him now.

'Fleck,' he corrects her, but politely, and he smiles.

'That's what I said – Flack.' She drops the vowel and catches it again. Her voice is hard to place. Italian, he thinks. South American, perhaps? Perhaps not. It has an occasional growl to it. He stares at her Adam's apple.

'I'm Eurielle Hope,' she says. 'I'm closing the first half of the show.' Could someone help her with her hair, she asks quietly, tilting her head to one side, the stage light catching a line of hairy down along her jaw. Closing the first half? Doing what? Must be one of those female impersonators, Oliver thinks, look at you, you adorable creature, a marvellous singer to boot I'm sure – he stops himself midtrack, swallows hard, but he cannot take his eyes off her. She is one of the most sublime creatures he has ever seen. An angel. He takes a deep breath. Still it's not natural. Not natural at all. She's obviously not a woman. Or is she? He takes another deep breath. Anyway, there's work to be done, he reminds himself.

'The stagehand will help you,' Oliver says, and points to the young man at the props table.

'Thank you,' she says and walks back into the darkness. God, she's beautiful, he thinks. His eyes follow her until she's gone.

Harry finishes his act to rapturous applause. He passes Oliver as he comes off stage and Dolly runs on.

'That bloody tray,' he raises it in his hand. 'Why did I ever think—? It's not just the pain in my head, it's my bloody ears! Ringing like the bells of Old Bailey.' Harry sticks his finger in his ear and wiggles it furiously.

Oliver laughs.

'I'll be deaf by the end of this tour. Must change my act before it kills me.'

Oliver turns back towards the stage and waits for his act to be announced. He catches a glimpse of a man sitting in the front row of the auditorium and for one brief, sickening second he thinks he sees his father. It's the way the man hangs his head, stares coldly in front of him while everything else around him is alive and warm. The hairs of the man's moustache are as straight as a horse's tail and his thick dark brown hair peaks at the front, just like his father's. It can't be his father, he knows. His father was never found after he disappeared and is surely dead by now. He gets a flash of the newspaper clipping, 'Man found dead . . . with a pistol . . . wounds to the head'. Regardless, his father would be too old to be alive. But the intensity of the moment is enough to fill Oliver with dread. He starts shaking. It comes back to him as though it were yesterday. The creak of the wood on the stairs, the heavy pad of his father's footsteps, then the knocking on his bedroom door, the turning of the handle. His father standing in his room, a darkness in the dark. He calls Oliver's name. Oliver pretends to be asleep. His father moves over to Oliver's bed and sits on the edge. Shakes Oliver to wake him, calls his name again. Oliver fearfully turns to his father, looks at the dark shape sitting beside him on the bed, feels his heart racing. Even in the gloom Oliver can see how bloodshot his father's eyes are, how his lips are dry and badly cracked, how his hair is matted on the top of his head. There is a yeasty metallic smell to his breath.

'I've always tried to do the best for you . . .' His father opens his mouth to whatever conversation has been going on inside his head. 'But how could you possibly know how hard it was.'

Oliver keeps his attention on his father for fear of angering him. He cannot judge what his father might do. The image of the troll comes into his mind. The gun in his mouth.

'Are you a good boy?' his father continues, leaning into Oliver. 'Do you hear me!' he roars. 'Are you a good boy?'

'Yes, sir,' Oliver stammers nervously, hugging his bedclothes around him. His father crashes over Oliver's answer, hardly hearing it, 'And what kind of a son does that make you, then?'

Oliver remains silent, not quite understanding what his father is meaning. Is it a genuine question? His father squeezes his eyes tight like they are stinging from lack of sleep, then opens them again. He rubs a hand across his forehead. 'That makes you a son who doesn't know his own father. Wouldn't you say . . . wouldn't you say you don't know me at all, boy?'

'I don't know.' Oliver's voice is tight in his throat. He wants out of this. His wants his mother's embrace.

His father slaps his hand down on Oliver's shoulder, gripping it tightly. He begins to shake him as he searches the air for words. Oliver can feel his father's hand is warm and sweaty even though the weight of it is making him cold.

'What am I trying to say to you, son?' he shakes his head. 'Nothing – I'm saying nothing – I'm saying nothing to you.' He stares into the darkness and gives a sneering laugh. 'You,' he says again but louder. 'You' – he points his finger right into Oliver's face

– 'because that's what *you* are, *you* are nothing.' He stops talking. Then he roars at Oliver, 'Do you hear me!' Oliver can't help it, he wets the bed. His father raises his eyes to the ceiling. Suddenly he straightens himself. 'Time you got some sleep,' he says gravely and lifts the stunted candle from the nearby table. He hangs his head and stares into a kind of nothingness like he is talking to some version of Oliver that doesn't exist, then stands, drifts to the doorway and is gone. Oliver shrinks under his blankets. His heart is beating as fast as he has ever felt it beat. He looks over at Edwin's empty bed. If Edwin had been there with him he would not feel so scared and alone.

Onstage Dolly sings at the top of her voice and does a saucy little sidestep.

Well, I never saw such a palaver before
Can hardly believe it's true,
The blight of my life
Vanished straight out of sight
Left me to paddle me own canoe—'

The audience cheer and whistle as Dolly dances off, then suddenly, 'Ladies and gentlemen – I give you the great Illusionist and Hypnotist Oliver Fleck!'

Oliver feels a shiver across his soul. He shakes himself. Walks out on to the stage determined to give his best performance yet. But during his opening routine where he makes a bunch of flowers appear – a mere teaser before the main event – the spring mechanism fails. With a flurry he presents instead a stump of a tube to the audience, no radiant display, the flowers still stuck in their tiny packets along the shaft of the prop. Under such circumstances he would normally flourish, win the audience over, embrace the predicament, improvise and use the disaster to charm them (and it isn't even that much of a disaster, let's face it, he thinks as he stands on stage). But for some reason, which he can't quite figure out, he begins to tremble and his mind goes blank. He tries as best he can to avoid looking at the man in the front row, but his eyes keep searching him out. The audience senses his nervousness and begins to heckle. Maclagan stands upstage unsure of what to do, waiting for Oliver to show the audience he has fooled them, is merely playing with them – a double bluff. But Oliver doesn't move. He stands frozen on the stage like a picture of a man waiting for a tram, looking lamely at the flowerless tube in his hand, incredulous at his own incompetence, bemused at his shaking limbs. The band plays him off.

That night Eurielle sits with him in his dressing room and reassures him that these things happen to everyone, and that it will all pass, *Don't let it shake your confidence.* She pours whiskey, asks him about home. He opens up gladly, tells her about Agna, Archie, and Edith, about how much he loves them. He cries on her shoulder. She strokes his cheek.

He promises himself he will not lose it. 'I've been down that road before,' he says to her, 'where I felt everything slipping away from me. The first time I travelled to New York I arrived with two suitcases and ten dollars to my name. 1891, wasn't it? My first glimpse of the city, like nothing I had ever seen before, the sheer scale of the buildings cutting into the sky like a colossal forest, people weaving through the streets. The city pulsed, I could feel it instantly – you've been to America, Eurielle, you know what I'm talking about.'

He drinks more whiskey. 'Bandini's death had left me floundering. He had collapsed in the middle of "The Indian Basket Trick" at the Buffalo in Belfast. And in one moment I lost a mentor and a friend. I sat in my flat for days knowing I had to make a choice, either to give it all up or to carry on. Then the image rose in my mind, *I would take America by storm*. I worked the music hall circuits hard for the next two years. But the more I stayed faithful to Bandini's illusions, his coin tricks, portfolio tricks, ball tricks, the more lacklustre the whole thing felt. It was becoming too safe. And all the other illusionists I came across were merely crude fucking amateurs, excuse my language. What I needed was to challenge myself, develop new illusions, become bolder. Tap into the revival in extrasensory phenomena and the new fascination for electricity. Not always a popular choice with the managements though, they frequently asked me to, "Tone it down, Fleck". But I welcomed their rancour, felt charged by it. I began improvising with new and sometimes bizarre material which even Maclagan was ill-prepared for, my attempt at knife throwing being one of them, good God!'

He laughs, takes another mouthful of whiskey. 'Some managements here became too nervous to hire me. But America, yes, America would welcome me, I knew it would. Using mental magic and hypnotism I could perform at the drop of a hat at any venue. I took whatever came my way in the city's beer halls, concert saloons and dime museums. Living amongst a flotsam of comics, acrobats, blackface minstrels, sword-swallowers, tattooed ladies and manikin goats. Over the next three years I played New York, Baltimore, Cincinnati and Boston, earning a reputation for pushing things more than most. But I knew what I had to offer. I drank, I don't deny it, had my share of women, had my run-ins – I remember one night grabbing a heckler by the throat and nearly strangling him.'

He drinks more whiskey, breathes deeply. 'The first time I saw her was in a dingy saloon on Belona Street in Boston. Maryjo Shearer, the daughter of a schoolmaster from Burndale, Massachusetts. What age was I then, twenty-nine or so? And she was nineteen. That night

I remember I had introduced an act called "The Transparent Turk", a fellow with a great gaping hole in his chest from a blast of a Russian chassepot, claiming, *You can use him as a window!'*

He laughs, throws his head back. 'Well, I thought it was funny, don't you think it's funny? Anyway, afterwards I joined the "waiter girls" in the smoke-filled back room. Sat myself at the card table crammed with the empty whiskey glasses from my earlier bet with a freak merchant from Mexico. Next to the whiskey glasses, a revolver. I lifted the revolver and shoved it into my mouth, right up against my cheek, my lips closing over the shiny black barrel. There wasn't a sound in the room. As I raised my eyes I found her standing by the door, holding a pile of Anti-Saloon League pamphlets in her hands, her pale skin looking metallic in the light. I span the barrel. Then I fired the gun. She didn't even flinch. There were screams from the others, horrified gasps, everyone believing that the blood oozing from my left ear was real. But of course they were wrong, it was all a set-up. I lifted my head, pulled the gun back out of my mouth and smiled at the crowd.'

He drinks more whiskey. 'It was ... becalmed ... that's what it was ... becalmed ... her radiance ... her innocence ... all the more striking amidst the tawdriness, and for the first time in a long time I felt my heart warm ... so much so ... that when the evening was over I followed her all the way to Burndale. I rented a clapboard house and stopped drinking. I helped restore her father's outbuildings, learnt how to cut and shape wood, how to mend roofs, how to repair beams and supports. Every morning I was up before sunrise bathing my new-found resolutions of abstinence and piety in the pearly light, and it thrilled me.'

He sighs, shakes his head. 'But, you see ... you see ... what I eventually learnt about Maryjo was that everything about her was as straight as her mud-brown hair. She soon began to voice her dislikes . . . the way I ate my food . . . the way I swaggered too much when I walked down the town as though I had designs to own the place . . . the way I whistled too loudly in the park, and prayed too loudly in church. It began to irk me, you know, like an itch I couldn't scratch. She found fresh fault in me with every passing day until one evening after supper I rose from my chair in the kitchen of her parents' house, turned to her and said, "The fire is getting low, Maryjo," and left. On the train back to New York I drank for the first time in a year. Ended up being hauled unconscious out of the carriage at Washington. I went home, worked hard, God did I work hard, earned a consistent stream of good reviews, even performed for a season at the Olympia in Paris to great acclaim. I returned to America five years later, this time playing the larger houses as part of the Kelton and Albert cartel, and looked her up. We met at the Floral Arms Hotel in Burndale. It seemed to me that she had hardly aged at all. I wasn't surprised to see her accompanied by a husband and three children, I knew she had been keen to start a family. But I was taken aback by their obvious happiness. They had a pride about them, which made me envious.'

He sighs deeply, takes a slug of whiskey, then shakes himself. 'But that was years ago, all in the past, and what in God's name did I think I was doing with the gun? A bizarre imitation of my father? For Christ's sake! And what kind of a fucking name is Maryjo, anyway?'

He drains the bottle of whiskey. 'No, I've pulled myself up from nothing, time and again. And now, I *have* a family. I have Edith. I have Archie and Agna. I'll not let that slip away from me. I'll keep it together no matter what.'

He turns to Eurielle. She's gone. He starts to cry. He clambers over to the makeshift bed. A fresh flush of tears as he puts his head on the pillow. He falls asleep.

He wakes the following morning surprised to find himself still in full costume and in his dressing room. Then with a sting he remembers his bedtime reminiscences with Eurielle, and splashing cold water on his face, brushes them casually off to one side.

Fifteen

Huddersfield

22 Thomas Street
14th December 1908

D*ear Oliver,*
    I'm sending you this hoping that it will reach you at the Palace Theatre in Aberdeen in time for Christmas, but without a package because it may not. I'll keep the package for when you're home. I've taken up knitting again – you'll be pleased to hear – so you can guess what your present might be. How is life in Scotland? Is there snow? Here, it's snowing and very cold. The butter in the mornings is as hard as a brick and last night the milk in the table jug was frozen solid. The children are coming on great and getting bigger every day, and in Archie's case, bolder too. He's a rascal. Bertie has the patience of a saint with him because Archie's always wanting to play and follows him everywhere. Bertie's like his big brother. I cannot believe the children are nearly the full two years. Agna is only a little worrisome. She won't go with anyone but me and frets something terrible when I leave her to play outside, although not for the last while since it's gotten cold. Harriet says to leave her be but it upsets me when she cries and she has the most beautiful smile when she has a mind to use it, which I wouldn't have the heart to miss.

We are making preparations for Christmas, the second Christmas without you. Harriet and I have made jams and pickles and I have a few toys put away for the children. They will miss you. I have been receiving the money you have been sending but it would be lovely to hear your news. Say hello to Harry for us when you see him on the tour. I know Harriet has written to him too. I hope audiences are turning up and enjoying the new illusions you are presenting but that the piano players everywhere are terrible! I'll finish now because my pen is running done.

With fondest love,
Mdme Defarge

P.S. Your present is a scarf and mittens – and yes I have knitted them myself – so perhaps I should post them to you after all to keep you warm in the frozen north!

Despite the cold Edith gets an idea for some outdoor air. Harriet is constantly telling her how good it is for the children. Although they are too big for the double pram perhaps they can sit in it on the roof of the meat shed. She unscrews the body of the pram from its base, springs and wheels, opens the kitchen window as wide as it will allow and climbs up on the draining board, dragging the body of the pram with her. The pram is heavy and she has to shift and turn her body this way and that, but with determination she gets it through the window. Stretching outside is the wide flat roof of Crampton & Sons Meat Purveyors. It is a sheltered spot, free from snow and now bathed in winter sunlight, shards of which colour the tiny yard below. With some wood she has found left over from Oliver's prop constructions she makes a base – a little lop-sided – on which to rest the body of the pram. When she places the children in the pram she ties a soft cummerbund around Archie, over his little coat, to prevent him from climbing out. She gives him some wooden spools, a metal cup and his wooden animals to play with. Agna, she knows, will not attempt to climb out. She gives Agna her little knitted doll and clothes she has made especially for it. While the children take the benefit of the fresh air for half an hour, Edith busies herself cleaning the kitchen, pleased with her resourcefulness.

As she looks out at Agna and Archie, Edith muses on her new role, this unchartered guardianship she has been afforded and which she is expected to navigate, and wonders if she's good enough. She feels that over the last couple of years she has forgotten the woman she once was, as though she is unable to remember the taste of summer sun in her mouth now that it is winter. Some transformation in her since the birth has opened her to all the possibilities of life's frailty. At any moment her good fortune might shift, slip right out of her hands, and in place of a confident disregard for the world she feels an ever-growing caution. She tries to draw strength from remembering her own mother's quiet and elegant resilience. She thinks of her Aunt Hilda (whose passing is still keenly felt), of her wilder and more unorthodox approach to life – a great source of inspiration to Edith now. She sorely misses both those wonderful women, wishes they were still alive to see her children, to see life's inheritance blossom.

And her father – whom she adored and who adored her – she draws strength from his memory. He had never once expected Edith to step into her mother's shoes and take over the running of the home. On the contrary he had believed adamantly that his daughter should continue her education. Edith had learnt to play piano at her mother's knee but to study music at a proper academy would enable her to teach it, and so he invited his half-sister, Mrs Hilda Smith, who then lived in Scotland, to move in and take over the household duties. Having recently become a widow and having no children of her own, Hilda was happy to do so.

Edith had at first thought her aunt quite mad, and not in any way organised in her domestic affairs. Her aunt knew neither how to cook nor sew, knew nothing of how to buy a neck of mutton or how to work a wringer or a mangle or manage a fire. But, as a keen botanist, liberal thinker and firm believer that it was imagination which shaped the world, she was stimulating company.

When Edith's father died Hilda had become her rock. She helped support Edith's education with her modest widow's inheritance but also encouraged Edith to get out into the world. Hilda was the one to suggest that Edith apply to play piano at the music hall theatres in Belfast when a position had been advertised in the evening newspaper. She had also, sometime later, introduced Edith to Mr Willy Pilson, a young associate of her deceased husband, who had by then become a successful auctioneer and estate agent. She knew he would be able to provide a financially secure future for Edith, should Edith want that. And Willy Pilson had taken a great interest in Edith. He had travelled especially over from Edinburgh to listen to her play at the Empire and the Gaiety, had sent her flowers time and time again, and had on one particular occasion ordered a carriage to bring her to the Central Hotel after the show for evening supper and – as it transpired – to ask for her hand in marriage. But that evening Edith had refused the carriage. She had been suspicious of Willy Pilson's motives – why *her*, she had thought, when with his money he could have had any classy woman he wanted – though now, as she mulls it over in her mind, there was no concrete reason for her to think that his interest wasn't genuine. But instead, *that* night, she had gone to Fred Felix's party – she instinctively presses her cheek with her finger as she remembers her missing molar, the gap still a dark round surprise when she opens her mouth. When she saw

Oliver in Fred's dressing room she had felt an immediate attraction to him. She watched how he was able to hold the attention of the whole room. He had a command about him, an energy which drew things to him, an immense charm. He had made her laugh and she had never felt so entertained by someone, not only onstage – she had stood at the back of the auditorium earlier that evening to watch him – but offstage too. And he had intrigued her, for despite his largesse there was also something very private about him, as though he was a series of secret letters waiting to be opened.

He had drunk too much, had kissed her too heavily and held her too tightly (she'd had to remind him what happened that night) – although remarkably through it all he had managed to be never anything other than genteel – and under his heightened attention she had never felt more brimful of her own being.

A few weeks later Willy Pilson had returned with the intention of asking for Edith's hand in marriage. That day as they walked the Botanic Gardens together with Hilda, Edith had suspected she was pregnant by Oliver but had no reason to believe a life with him would be possible. Marriage to Willy seemed the obvious and only choice. Until that is she had spotted Oliver following them through the Fernery and had felt her body flood with a heat more intense than in any Tropical Ravine. From the night she had shaved and kissed him she had decided that she couldn't be without him and had joined him on tour. Much to Millie Evans's dismay she had even worked as his assistant at the venues where there was no need of a pianist.

She remembers in Portstewart, on a few days break after the run in Belfast, how they had talked about their future plans. They had arrived in the town as night fell and had walked from the station along the promenade towards their bed and breakfast. They had held hands and said how lucky they were to find each other. She had talked of buying a house in the countryside, somewhere in County Down perhaps, a house with a garden at the back and a view of the sea from the front. A place surrounded by nature where they could raise their child – their children hopefully. Oliver would have a workshop at the end of the garden, surrounded by apple trees, and she would bring him raspberry water and marmalade pudding in the afternoons while the sun warmed the wooden swing seat on which she would gently rock their infant to sleep.

As they walked the promenade they had stopped to look out over the sea, at the long white furrows running across it and the huge scoopfuls of water breaking against the sea wall and flooding the boardwalk. They had walked past the changing huts, which looked like a dark huddle of forlorn passengers who had missed their boat. They had watched the light change as the moon rose. It was the kind of forgiving light which made them feel as though they had all the chances in the world to live a life of happiness together. They had looked out over the dark bay and at how, as the moon climbed higher in the sky, it dropped a corridor of pale primrose on the sea.

Yes, there is a magic between them – funny, she thinks, that she should use that word.

When the sun's light begins to shift off the roof and on to the backs of the houses opposite, Edith decides it is time to bring the children back into the flat.

While Archie sits up in his nightclothes chatting happily to himself, Edith undresses Agna. Agna makes no sound but simply moves her tiny hands in front of her face as though to whisk the soft rays of candlelight into the dark. The candle on the table has burned down to a stump and the flame is shrinking. Edith reaches over to encourage it with her fingers, fanning it a little, but it fades to a tiny red glow then goes out. As she presses on the wick it crumbles, leaving a black spear on each of her fingertips.

'Night, Mama,' Archie says.

'Night, Archie,' Edith says.

She strokes Agna's cheek. 'Night, Agna.'

Agna looks out at her from the dark.

She tucks the children securely into bed and goes to the kitchen in search of another candle, seeming to remember an offcut left on the windowsill, but she cannot find it. The flat is now cold. In the darkness she stumbles back to the bedroom, pulls open the curtains a little to allow the moon's light to filter in, and climbs into bed beside Archie and Agna.

Archie's round face looks like a tiny moon which has fallen from the sky. He squeals as Edith kisses his cheek. Edith then kisses Agna, whose head is partially covered with her shawl. A scoop of moon-light blesses Agna's forehead.

As the children sleep beside her she hopes their lives will be bearable and that they will give little stock to the pull and drag of everyday. She hopes they will always have enough, and know what enough is. And not to be lonely, she wishes that for them. She hopes that they will always have each other, Agna and Archie. That their survival will be worth it, their lives happy – not lives of pain or misery or loneliness. And she wishes mostly that they do not die alone. It is *her* luck that they are here, *her* joy. So please let it also be theirs.

She wonders what lies ahead for them. She hopes they find much to rejoice about in the world, find a plainness in their lives which keeps them steady. She pulls the blanket away from Agna's face. They are so helpless, she thinks. Action or inaction could kill them. Some have done that, she knows, some mothers have, and to ones so small, when they already have too many mouths to feed. If she knew they had nothing but a life of suffering ahead of them, would she do that too? Edith turns to them, feels a crippling heaviness in her chest.

Perhaps, she thinks, there is nothing to fear and their lives will run a smooth enough course. They will be hardy. Archie will grow up to be a strong man. He'll pack a punch and stand his own ground. And Agna will possess the grace and fierceness of a lioness, and find the good in everything around her. Neither of them have the need to fear God, there is already enough to fear. And God could learn from them, she's sure of it, could learn from their appalling innocence, from their astonishing trust in the world, their uncomplicated joy.

But the moments now are the rise and fall of the ribcage, the smell of their skin, the swaddling warmth. And love.

In the morning Edith asks Bertie to fetch a small tree from the market so she can decorate it for Christmas. Outside it begins to snow. A letter arrives from Oliver.

The Palace Theatre
Aberdeen
19th December, 1908

Dearest Mdme Defarge,

Your mittens and your scarf would be most welcome here to keep me warm, but even more so your truly wondrous flesh! Could you please wrap yourself in a parcel and post yourself to me. I think of you every moment of the day and night and wish we were together again. If only I could make love to you in a letter – to hear your voice, to touch you, to kiss you, to hold you. Sometimes when I think of you, you seem only like a wonderful dream. Those times frighten me. I need to have you with me. It is all so frustrating, so for the moment let us talk of ordinary things.

I am moving on to Glasgow after this, then Paisley. There may be a break when I can get home but I can't promise. The audiences have been mostly good, though Harry was bumped off the bill last night by Nellie Byrne 'The Cripple Girl with the Angel Voice'. She was called back three times until every member of the audience was in floods of tears –seemed like they couldn't get enough of poor crippled Nellie. Turns out she was seen after the show dancing like a ballerina down at The Bull Inn after a good few ports.

It's good to hear all your news. It's snowing here too. Sorry to hear that Agna is fretful but as long as she – and Archie, of course – is healthy that's all that matters.

I cannot wait to see you again. I cannot wait to see the children again. Kiss them for me.

I've enclosed money as usual. I will keep in touch and write again soon.

Enjoy Christmas without me, but don't stop loving me.

Yours forever,

Oliver.

Sixteen

On tour, 1909

Before leaving Troon to return home in April, Oliver is offered an unexpected booking replacing Dickie Mitchell 'The Whistling Genius' on a six-month tour on the Mosswood Circuit. He decides to take it despite the fact that he knows he won't get home to see Edith and the children as soon as he expected, but it's work. He also knows he needs to push through the stage fright he experienced when the spring mechanism on the flowers failed to open in Edinburgh, which after all this time is still managing to rattle him. If he stops now it might only allow the fear to grow.

He doesn't have Maclagan with him this time, nor Millie his assistant. It's all simple conjuring stuff, card tricks, coin illusions. He does Plymouth, Bath, Barnstable, Bristol. In Ramsgate he performs twice nightly. He has one week now in London before heading on to Bedford. On the London leg of the tour his evening schedule runs Queen's Theatre Poplar 7.10; London Shoreditch 7.40; Holborn Empire 8.10; the Oxford 9.00; Wilton's Music Hall 9.20; Holborn Empire 9.50; London Shoreditch 10.20; Queen's Theatre Poplar 10.50. Each evening on the walk back to his boarding house he picks a pub to stop off at, a few whiskeys to close the night, to still his head.

During this run he has been feeling some kind of reckless energy welling up within him, totally at odds with the meticulous preparation and strictness Bandini had insisted on, but it is this very energy which he feels is becoming essential for his survival on stage. It is fuelling the unquenchable thirst he has now developed to connect with the audience at all costs, all the more rewarding if the moment is spontaneous and unscripted (at the Empire in Holborn he had jumped off the stage into the auditorium). And it is helping to allay the creeping sense of boredom he is experiencing offstage, something he is finding increasingly more difficult to bear.

The night before he leaves for Bedford he throws up on the pavement outside the pub, leaving a steamy marigold of carrots and boiled ham melting the snow. Wiping his mouth with his handkerchief, he moves on, thinks he needs to shift things up a notch, can't go on like this. Tomorrow before he leaves he'll call on someone who just might be able to help him succeed.

The following morning a letter arrives from Edith.

22 Thomas Street,
Huddersfield.
13th September 1909

Dear Oliver,

I hope this reaches you before you leave London. How is the tour going? We are getting by well enough. The weather has been reasonable and we have spent days sitting out on the street, which has been good for Agna. We sit together on the front step and she is content just to be there with me and we watch Archie play horses and football with Bertie and laugh at their carry-on. The odd time we wander over to Greenhead Park where she loves to feed the ducks.

Agna isn't speaking yet, which is of some concern. Harriet said the doctors can test for deafness and such things so I'm of a mind to bring her to be seen, although it worries me what they might tell me, and if it turns out she has a hearing affliction it will be a hard thing for her to bear in life. She cries whenever she has a pain so I think that means her voice is in working order but I'm left wondering why she will not speak. Harriet says that all children are different and she'll come round in her own time.

I have decided to take some work on and Harriet said she is happy to keep an eye on Archie and Agna while I'm gone. I am pleased about that as it means a little more stretch in the money. It's ironing shirts at a laundry, which I think I'll be good at, considering the practice I have had.

Harry has been home a while now and we wish you were too. He said the circuit this time was tough, more matinees put in without warning. A friend of Harry's said there might be more work around the London theatres but I don't think Harry is in a mind to go. He said he doesn't have it in him any more. I wish he wouldn't talk like that as it makes me sad.

The money you're sending is still arriving.

Always yours,

Edith.

Folding the letter and slipping it into his pocket, he heads out, reaching Piccadilly within minutes, the wind lifting around him as he moves. His heart breaks at the thought that there may be something wrong with Agna's hearing. What kind of start in life is that for her? How hard for her if it indeed turns out to be an affliction. Though hopefully the doctor will find nothing to be concerned about. Is that a slight disappointment he's feeling? A niggle somewhere, not just the fear for her but some other unspoken expectation? Some need for her to be perfect? In one still so small he sees the mannerisms of his mother, a similarity around her eyes and mouth, the way she bows her head, her smile, the summer's glint off her girlish hair. She is a curious presence to him, some flicker of his life when love was whole, and it's as though he cannot bear the thought that anything might impair that.

He tries to keep focused. He quickens his stride. He has an idea he wants to follow through. He shakes off his thoughts about the letter. He crosses on to Regent Street. He checks his pocket watch, feels a shiver down the back of his neck. He needs to be alert. He arrives at St George's Hall.

'I do not permit vulgarity in my theatre.' Max Stapleton wears a neat black frock coat, a crisp white shirt with a lemon silk cravat, impeccably folded at his throat. Classical music plays from the large gramophone that sits beside his desk. Despite lying in the shadow of the adjacent All Soul's Church, the winter sunlight fills his office, which is sparsely but tastefully decorated.

Stapleton is on the telephone. As he waits for him to turn around, Oliver cannot help but feel a little disconcerted by the large portrait of Stapleton that hangs behind his desk. Replacing the telephone in its receiver, Stapleton signals to Oliver to take a seat. As he sits, Oliver feels two pairs of humourless eyes upon him.

Stapleton is one of the most successful magicians, if not *the* most successful magician, of the day, and everything around him rings of that success. 'You're not a vulgar man, are you, Mr Fleck?' He brushes his seat before he sits down.

'That's a matter of opinion,' replies Oliver, happy that Stapleton appears to know who he is.

Stapleton keeps a straight face. 'You're Irish,' he says as a statement of fact, not a question.

'Yes.'

'Interesting.'

'Is it?' Oliver can feel that shiver down the back of his neck again.

Stapleton leans back in his chair. 'I know your work. Saw you take the Vaudeville by storm. Why are you here?'

'I'm looking for venues for my own one-man show. St George's Hall being one of them.'

Stapleton slides his hand across the shiny wood surface of his desk. 'They shouldn't have let you in to see me. You must have sweet-talked them downstairs. Sensational, is it?'

'Sensational?'

'This one-man show of yours.'

'Well, yes . . . it will be. You have all the stage mechanisms I need here, a deep stage and full basement underneath—'

'Do I indeed? I have my own show here, Mr Fleck, which my touring companies take to the provinces. I'm hiring for the companies today, I'm not leasing the theatre to a loose cannon.'

Oliver balks at Stapleton's comment. 'There's always room to expand,' he says, regaining his composure. 'Develop a programme of a variety of illusionists and magicians here and you'd have something no one else has.'

'I already have something no one else has – my own theatre for my own show.'

'I still think collaboration makes for good business. I have fresh and exciting material to offer and—'

'Henry Lockley is the man I want to collaborate with, he's quite remarkable. I'm planning to present some of his illusions right here in St George's Hall, if he'll agree to it. You've heard of him, I'm sure.'

Oliver knows of Lockley's rising reputation. 'He doesn't have the experience I have.'

'What age are you, Mr Fleck?'

'Forty-three.'

'You see.' Stapleton nods his head.

'See what, exactly?'

'There it is. Lockley's a mere twenty-eight, already brilliant *and* he has time on his side.' Stapleton holds his gaze on Oliver, leans back in his chair. 'Today, Mr Fleck, I'm auditioning for two magicians for the touring show, a ten-minute slot each for an illusion I've created called "The Bottomless Teapot". Interested? If not, go, as you're wasting my time.'

Oliver does not reply. He sits trying to hold on to the fire in his belly, his sense of self-esteem, his worth. Stapleton squares himself in his chair. 'As you heard me say on the telephone, Mr Fleck, I do not permit vulgarity in my theatre so I think you should leave now.'

Taken aback by Stapleton's abrupt dismissal, Oliver rises slowly and reluctantly extends his hand. Stapleton does not reciprocate the gesture. Instead Stapleton's eyes tighten and a ridiculously small smile graces his lips. Oliver turns and leaves the room.

As he walks down the stairs he feels humiliated. What is wrong? Does he have delusions about his own talent? Is he fooling himself? Or is Stapleton right, is the whole business changing? Is it really all to do with age?

He collects his bag from his digs and heads to the station, just missing his train to Bedford. As he sits in the cold waiting area, a hard lump gathers in his throat. Yes, Stapleton's manner had irked him: the way the man had assumed superiority over him, had talked down to him, had lauded Lockley's talents over his. Bottomless Teapot! How dare he! Fucking ponce. Worse is the way he now feels he had somehow ingratiated himself by asking Stapleton for the use of his theatre, by needing something from him. Stapleton knows his reputation is solid, had acknowledged that much at least, but it had felt as though he had willingly handed his worth to Stapleton only for him to destroy it.

There is a familiar flood of unpleasantness in his body. A sickening hot swell spreading right through him. What is he to do? Surrender his thirst for achievement? His desire to make real his imagined future? No, his commitment won't be thwarted by the likes of Stapleton. And had Stapleton given him what he'd wanted, would he not now be crippled by a feeling of being indebted to the man? No, that would never do. The needing of something from someone then the crushing shame for needing it in the first place when it isn't granted.

Like when he had needed Edwin, and Edwin had left, and left again.

Not once while he was in London did he think of looking for Edwin or asking Edwin for help. But then Edwin, as far as he knew, had never attempted to look for him. He wonders if Edwin has ever seen him onstage, or read his reviews, or seen his act advertised in the newspapers. It would have been easy to find each other in London, if they had really wanted to. No, he would never put himself in that position with Edwin, to feel beholden to him. He couldn't bear that.

As he arrives back in Huddersfield at the end of the tour he finds a girl of about six or seven years of age standing on the front steps. She has ruddy red cheeks that seem too big for her face and a mop of twisted black curls.

'Hello,' she says brightly as Oliver approaches the open doorway. She holds the handrail of a large black pram and jostles it vigorously. 'Are you the magician that lives here?'

Further down the street a young woman empties a bucket of water on to the cobbles. A horse cab passes by.

'I am,' Oliver replies, bending to look into the pram. Where he expected to see a baby he sees a large black and white tabby cat, covered in a blanket, a grey tattered woollen bonnet tied around its head. The cat has a sour, resigned look on its face. Its one eye – the other by the look of it lost long ago – a pale peridot, holds on Oliver. Oliver suddenly wonders where the baby is, if there is one, and as he turns he sees a half-naked baby lying on the step beside him. Good lord, he thinks.

'Your Agna's daddy and she can't speak.' The girl is talking to Oliver but looking behind him, her cheeks reddening further.

Oliver is puzzled by the girl's remark. Just as he is about to ask her about the baby on the step she grabs it, shoos the cat out of the pram, and plonks the baby back in.

'What do you think you're up to, Dillie Lester?' The young woman with the bucket is now marching at a pace across the street towards the child.

'If you were any good,' the girl shouts back to Oliver, 'you'd magic her to speak!' She runs off, bouncing the pram across the cobbles.

Oliver makes his way up to the top of the stairs. The door of the flat opens.

'I thought I heard you coming.' Edith throws her arms around him, planting a kiss on his cheek. 'Your father's home. Say hello to your father!' she calls to the children, leading Oliver into the flat. Archie runs over to Edith, wrapping his arms around her leg and looks up at his father. Oliver rubs the boy's head.

'Good to see you, son.' He pulls a small bag of fudge from his suitcase and offers it to Archie.

'What do you say?' Edith leans down to Archie.

'Thank you,' Archie says, beaming broadly.

Oliver offers another bag of fudge to Agna. Agna stays sitting on the floor playing with her doll, Edith's shawl draped around her shoulders.

'Hello, Agna,' Oliver says gently. 'There's some for you too.' Agna looks at him briefly then dips her head again, pulling the shawl up and over her head.

Archie takes the second bag of fudge out of Oliver's hand and brings it over to Agna.

'Does she hear me?' Oliver turns to Edith.

'Oh, yes, she hears you – Doctor Campion tested her only last week for deafness and said that she responded to every sound he made, so her hearing is fine. It's just that she doesn't seem to want to speak, but I'm sure that there's nothing to worry over. You look tired.'

'It's good to be home.' He kisses her. 'Yes, it's good to be home.'

'Agna says she doesn't like fudge, so can I have hers?' Archie smiles at his father.

'Cheeky monkey!' Oliver laughs and dashes across the room to catch Archie, chasing him out of the flat and down the stairs.

Later that afternoon Edith leaves to go to work at the laundry on Seed Hill Road. Harriet checks in to see that all is well and brings up some stewed celery and buttered potatoes for Oliver and the children.

'Tell me what you think, but that new gas cooker we've hired from the Corporation works a treat. Every single thing I cook on that new contraption tastes wonderful!'

'I will, Harriet.'

'Harry had an awful job cleaning up after they . . .' She picks up a few of the children's garments that need washing.

Oliver looks at her.

'Oh . . . after they installed it – the last time he was home.'

'How is he?'

'He's in Barnstaple. Says there's nothing but half-naked poseurs and mechanical dolls on the bill.'

'Sounds great.' Oliver smiles.

'I can take the children if you want.'

'No, thank you, Harriet, they're fine with me.'

'You seem tired. Have you been sleeping all right?'

'Not really.'

'Drinking too much, I dare say.'

Oliver looks at her. Shakes his head dismissively at her, but there is a serious cast to his face. Harriet blushes.

'Well, if you need anything, you know where I am.' Harriet bustles out the door and is gone.

Oliver opens his suitcase, lifts out his props and arranges them on the table. Some of them are in need of repair. He sits at the table to inspect them. Archie climbs up on the chair beside him and watches as Oliver works to reattach part of the wooden frame of one of the blank slates and adjust the spring mechanism on the flowers. He is aware of Archie's concentration. He slips his hand into the orange silk bag which he normally uses to hold the 'invisible' seeds in 'Madam, what flower do you prefer – a mignonette, marigold, violet?' and instead pulls out a small mouse made of blackened cork. Oliver places the mouse on the back of his hand. Fixing the length of thread which is attached to the mouse's head to his shirt buttonhole, then interposing one hand over the other in a contin-uous smooth movement, Oliver makes the mouse run as though by magic.

Archie laughs and points. 'Look! Look at the mouse! Look, Agna.'

From the corner of the room Agna lifts her head to watch.

Oliver keeps the mouse running, delighted with Archie's reaction.

The more the boy laughs at the running mouse the more Oliver keeps his hands moving and the more his heart lifts. He feels another presence beside him. It is Agna. She stands back from him a little, amazed at the running mouse. Then she steps forward and gently rests her hand upon his arm.

Seventeen

Huddersfield, 1910

In the *Huddersfield Chronicle* he reads a rave review of The Great Deneto's new illusion 'A Woman Appears', at the Empire in Croydon. It rounds off: '*A Giant Success. Deneto thrills with his Magical skills! Magnificent!*' He had always suspected that this American illusionist – the bed-wetter, as Sydney Brown had called him – had stolen some of the finer details of his 'Appearing Woman' illusion. It happens, he knows, happens all the time, ideas are taken, reworked, he's done it himself, but it riles him when it's done to him. Bastard, mutters Oliver to himself. The review mentions another illusion of Deneto's where he shoots eggs into a tub of water and ducks emerge from the tub. Though Archie would love that one, he thinks.

Below that there is a notice advertising Henry Lockley's appearance at St George's Hall: '*Celebrated illusionist and hypnotist Henry Lockley in a series of new and original magical problems. You'll be amazed.*' Folding the paper under his arm, he walks towards the Cloth Hall Exchange off Half Moon Street and waits in line for a call box. When one becomes free he calls his agent, Jimmy Hewitt, in Belfast.

Normally, he would never make a call to Hewitt, it is just too expensive, but bitterly disappointed at his reception from Stapleton he needs a lifeline. What Oliver could do with now are names, one or two producers, get Hewitt to set up a few meetings, do the introductions, sell him, earn his fucking crust. Oliver has played London before many times, knows he has made his mark on the entertainment fraternity, all Hewitt has to do is ratchet up the game, get them eager to meet him, take on his idea of a one-man show – he has plenty of material and lots of ideas for new illusions. Yes, Hewitt needs to sell him! He dials the number and is put through to Hewitt's office.

Hewitt stutters a 'Hello' when Oliver announces himself on the telephone, surprised as he is to hear from him. 'Someone dead, Oliver?'

'Jesus, no, Jimmy. This is business. Ever heard of that?'

'This must be costing you a small fortune, Oliver, ringing from Huddersfield.'

'Never mind that. Listen to me. I'm planning to build a one-man show—'

'Who for, Oliver?'

Jesus, Oliver thinks, *is the man clued into anything*? 'For me!' Oliver clenches his jaw.

'Oh right.'

Oliver takes a deep breath. Calms himself. 'Hear me out, Jimmy. I need you to contact some producers in London, good ones, mind you. I need to meet them, get someone to take me on. I know I can create something sensational. You need to prime them, get them keen.'

'Oliver, you can't be doing that.'

'What do you mean, I can't be doing that?'

'You're thinking too big, Oliver. No one's going to take the chance to back something they don't know anything about.'

'God damn it! You know I have a good reputation. It's your job now to support that!'

'Now, Oliver, my good man – heh-heh-heh – let's not allow ourselves to be carried away here.' Hewitt begins to laugh through his words, lacing his whiny Northern Irish accent with the kind of smug pomposity which drives Oliver mad. 'It's all very well for you to have your grand ideas but – heh-heh-heh – we've got to be practical about this. These producers you're suggesting I contact, well – heh-heh-heh – are, frankly, very – heh-heh-heh – busy – heh-heh – people.'

Oh, you little pile of mediocrity. 'Well, in that case let them be busy with *me*.'

'We've got to get you on a good tour Oliver, eh?'

'I've just done two in a row, Jimmy!'

'The Benson Circuit or the Donaldson. Keep an eye out for a wee fill-in.'

'Another fill-in! You must be joking. Never again. And not at this stage of my career.'

'Oliver – heh-heh-heh – we should never say – heh-heh – never. Plenty on my books would be very – heh-heh – happy with a fill-in.'

'Well I'm not.'

'There's "The Whistling Genius" Dickie Mitchell, I hear he's off for a week – bit of a long shot mind you as he's very popular, Oliver, and everybody wants him – spent some time in America, you see. Now he's having something taken out, his adenoids or appendix, can't remember which. Could suggest you for that, Oliver. But of course, as I said, it's a long shot. Can you sing? Dance? Whistle? What would you say? Can't promise anything of course, you know there's plenty – heh-heh – ready and waiting to step in and do the job for half the fee if it means working.'

'I've spent time in America too, Jimmy! And I've just spent six months filling in for Dickie Mitchell while he was having his fucking wrinkles injected with paraffin! What in God's name is wrong with you? Do you hear yourself? I have something great here, and all you can do is suck the good out of it.'

'I think it was that saddle nose of his they were injecting with paraffin, Oliver, not his wrinkles—'

'Jimmy!'

'Look, it's all about money, Oliver.'

'Yes, and I'd like to make some, you fucking twat—'

'Now now, Oliver – heh-heh – there's no need to use that kind of – heh-heh – language with me—'

'You can sit in your own pile of petty provincial shite if you want to, Jimmy, but I won't. God Almighty – I can't bear it any longer! You take every ounce of enthusiasm, every spark of potential, every flicker of creativity and you destroy every fucking piece of it. You just can't let it breathe. What in God's name does it take to rise above this infernal disaffected bog of small-minded fucking pigmies to have something grow – flourish even, God forbid, yes, flourish!' Oliver's bile is rising in his stomach, his blood is racing. 'You can't think beyond your own limp fucking dick, and all you want to do is to squeeze the life out of every single good idea until it's just as fucked!'

Oliver hears a click on the other end of the telephone.

Oliver and Edith lie back on their cast-iron bed sharing a cigarette. Through the window they watch the sky's changing blue, first the rinsed cobalt of a winter morning then the seep of afternoon purple – the world reduced to a simple square of sky. They listen to the wind, which at first brushes flimsily against the eaves of the house, like the rustling of a woman's skirts, but grows in intensity, snapping and whistling above their heads and drowning out the sounds rising from the street.

'The clouds are being torn to shreds,' Edith says, exhaling through pursed lips.

They watch as scattered pieces of cloud rush by. They begin to count them, anticipating when the next cloud will appear. Oliver's chest rises and falls in steady rhythm. Edith's head is nestled in the bend of his arm.

'Look, there's another one,' Oliver says, 'and another.' They watch as the clouds fold and shift their shape under the frivolous wind. Edith reaches over to the bedside table and stubs out the cigarette on a saucer.

'What time are Harry and Harriet due to bring Agna and Archie back from the cinema?' she says.

'Three o'clock.'

'That's been a nice day for them – visiting Harriet's nieces and nephews and then the cinema.'

'Yes, lovely.'

'Did you see that?' marvels Edith, another whisk of white against the blue. She turns to Oliver. 'Or are you dreaming with your eyes open?'

'I can't tell.'

'If only we had that energy, that endless momentum. Then we could always be awake.'

'I want to sleep right now.'

They lie and watch the clouds change. A galloping horse becomes a sleeping child becomes a giant fish.

'Don't you think it's possible we crawled out of the sea?' Edith asks.

'What about the world and everything in it?'

'What about it?'

'Nature – the animals, the fish in the sea, the birds of the air, the clouds above our heads.' Oliver lazily extends an arm up in the air.

'Who created all that? And if we created God, who created us?'

'Well, that's probably where my argument falls.'

'So, what do you believe, then?'

'Sometimes I believe and disbelieve the same thing. Sometimes I believe there is a God and at the same time believe that we are completely alone.'

'But it has to be one or the other,' Oliver arches his back to stretch it. Edith's body rises with the movement. 'It always has to be one thing or the other.'

'Does it though?'

'Yes, there can be only one truth.'

'Because we cannot prove anything,' Edith continues undeterred, 'then any number of truths are possible, any combination, a mixed state that we could exist in – there's our lives and then there's the version of our lives we tell ourselves and others.'

Oliver pushes himself up in the bed. 'I'm starving,' he says. 'Let's eat.'

'Where are we – breakfast, lunch?'

'What does it matter?'

'So what are you going to do?'

'Do?'

'About work.'

'I'm trying my best to get things moving. It'll be fine. Don't worry.'

'There's been nothing for a while now, Oliver.'

'Something will turn up.'

'Did Hewitt have anything to offer?'

'I don't want to talk about it.'

Edith releases her hand from Oliver's. They lie quietly for a moment.

'It would be lovely to have a garden. I'd love to plant shrubs and flowers with Agna. I used to garden with my Aunt Hilda.'

Oliver turns to her. 'The botanist?'

'Yes. But the tiny yard at the back of the house here gets little light.'

'I'll make a garden.'

'How?'

'I'll make a portable garden that Agna can carry to wherever the light falls.'

Edith straightens her back, suddenly interested. 'She would love that, Oliver.'

After eating some beef shirt and onion pie, Oliver makes his way to Greenhead Park, half a mile away, where out of view of the park keeper he digs up some geraniums, miniature ferns, and some tiny narcissi, making sure to preserve a good amount of soil around their roots. Back at home he gathers a few offcuts of wood left over from repairing his props. He builds a rectangular wooden box, not unlike one a hawker might use to sell chestnuts or cigars or whelks. He attaches a length of twine from one side of the box to the other so Agna can place it around her neck or sling it dispatch-style across her shoulder and rest it on her hip. He makes a lid for when she wants to transport it. He lines the base with a double layer of hessian and across it spreads a few handfuls of sand and gravel. Then he inserts the plants and soil. He waters them lightly. He tests the weight of the little box garden, light as a bag of apples. He sets it on the stone plinth in the yard beside the coalhouse. The sun slips off the flat roof of the meat shed and feeds it with light.

At three o'clock Harry and Harriet return with the children, Bertie holding Archie's hand, Harriet and Harry walking behind with Agna. Oliver tells Agna he wants to show her something and brings her out to the yard. Edith follows with Archie. As they stand together he lifts the lid off the box garden. Agna looks into it. She studies the tiny yellow-green protrusions, pushing up through the grainy soil, their papery tunics peeling around their rims as though

they are just waking up. She touches the frayed edges of the miniature ferns. She turns the wooden box on the stone plinth to let the
light do its work. Oliver leans forward to help her. Archie, curious
to examine the little plants, steps in. They stand together gently
sculling the sandy earth with their fingers, setting things right for
the alpines.

Agna bends her head to look closer at the garden when snowflakes
begin to fall on her neck. March. Nature's most indecisive month.
Only a moment ago the sun's rays were bathing the corner of the
yard. Now winter is falling around her head. She resists turning to
the sky, keeps looking down as the snowflakes pass her by and feels
she is falling with them from a great height, falling into the little
garden below her while Archie holds his hand out to catch them.
With her fingertip Agna wipes away the water shadows that the
snowflakes leave behind as they melt, off the tops of the alpine geraniums, off the miniature fern, and leaves a wet finger line through
the garden.

'Look up,' Oliver says, and she bends her head back. Snow falls
like petals, as though the sky is a windswept garden. The snow
clouds move their story along. A giant ship appears, lengthens and
becomes a dragon, the dragon's head becomes a bird and takes flight,
the bird's wing curls into a baby's face, engulfed by giant hands and
then fragments of blue begin to appear once again.

She turns to look at her father, his frame darkened by the light
behind him, and smiles.

For months Oliver has been working every day developing ideas for
his one-man show. He has turned down the few bookings which
have dribbled in, nothing of any worth, but he now needs something
halfway decent to materialise as their debts are mounting. After
such an intensive few years touring had he fallen out of favour with

the theatre owners and the circuit managers? It feels as though he is being tossed from one extreme to the other, and at the mercy of it all. Oliver walks to the call office in the Cloth Hall Exchange.

'Get me something decent, Jimmy, anything.'

'Oliver, my good man – haven't heard from you in so long – heh-heh – where have you been? How are you? You in Belfast?' Jimmy Hewitt's voice trickles down the line.

'I'm still in Huddersfield. I'm going mad to work, Jimmy, it's been months now. Y'know! But I've scaled down my idea for the solo show and if I can just get some bookings to try it out . . .' Oliver can feel himself getting hot under his collar. 'I know you won't get me the big houses, but . . . a good regional venue, a matinee somewhere.'

'Oh, still dreaming about that wee one-man show of yours – heh-heh – good man.'

Don't fucking 'good man' me.

Silence.

'I need this, Jimmy. I need to be performing, I need—'

'Oh, these days if you want to be a star you've got to get yourself up on the screen. That cinema over there in Great Yarmouth, the Gem, I hear is doing great business—'

'I'm not talking about wanting to be a star, Jimmy Hewitt! I'm talking about the craft, the work.'

'Yes, yes.' Jimmy adopts a serious tone, which sounds vaguely ridiculous. 'Well, any theatre of any decent size, Oliver, is out of the question. And I would add that the medium-sized venues can also be ruled out – most of them have been booked up already by the syndicates. You're asking for a lot, Oliver.'

'And this time I want my family to travel with me.'

There is an audible sigh from the other end of the line. 'I'll see what I can do.'

He replaces the telephone receiver and is just about to leave the

Cloth Hall Exchange when he sees Eurielle standing by the north door. She turns to look at him. He makes his way quickly through the hall, now busy with people, towards her, delighted that she has appeared just at a time when he feels disheartened with everything. There is something so familiar about her, he had sensed it the very first time they had met, some familiarity, which he still cannot articulate. She understands him. Eurielle. Eurielle Hope. So aptly named. Beautiful creature. As he approaches the north door two gentlemen walk in front of him obscuring his view for a moment, and when they pass she is gone. Oliver steps out on to the street but she is nowhere to be seen. He walks home wondering if he really saw her at all.

Eighteen

On tour

It's October before Hewitt is able to set up a string of regional venues in which Oliver can test out his one-man show, insisting it must only be the small-scale stuff or the venues won't take him.

This time the touring feels particularly exhausting. It is becoming apparent to Oliver that fewer people now want the kind of entertainment he is offering, drawn as they are to the cinemas, and the revue-style shows. This in turn has affected the confidence of the producers who, try as he might to convince them to back his one-man show, are reluctant to capitalise on his reputation. Despite his past successes, despite the brilliant reviews he has received, despite the fact he has proved himself time and time again, it all seems to come to nothing – he has to fight for even Jimmy Hewitt to believe in him – his own agent, for God's sake! And when this is over, what is there to go home to? he thinks. Days, weeks, months perhaps, of waiting for another booking. The grind of trying to start all over again. He knows he must continue to believe that he has something to offer, something exceptional, but the more time passes the more difficult it is becoming.

Their digs in Whitby are at the top of a dark narrow staircase.

They have been there a week now. It is cold and damp. The gas fire doesn't work. The bed linen is not fresh. Something is leaking somewhere. There is the constant sting of urine in the room. The toilet sits in the corner, a cold, bald stinking homage to modernity. Cracked no doubt, thinks Oliver, its contents seeping on to the linoleum floor. How posh to have an indoor toilet, he laughs dryly to himself. A wooden partition surrounds it at waist height to offer some privacy, but the base of the partition is rotten with the burn of acid, the floor swollen on either side, the floorboards at the back buckled. Streaks of mould mottle the wall and clusters of black spots speckle the pipes. In the opposite corner sits the iron stove, its hob plates ringed with rust. Loud voices can be heard coming from the room next door.

Edith lies on the bed and stares up, stony-faced, at the ceiling. Uprooting the children to such dreary surroundings has made her anxious, but instead of rallying with her usual resourcefulness she feels weighed down. Archie lies beside her, tired after trailing around the town.

Agna sits on the end of the bed. Her portable box garden lies on the floor beside her. She has added yellow sedum, spoon-leaved stonecrop, cobweb houseleek. She keeps the garden tidy, the little plants watered, deadheads them, imitates a light breeze for their leaves with her breath. She wraps her shawl around her head, creating a small peephole through which she can see into the room. She watches her father as he empties his bag of props.

Oliver lays his props out on the table that flanks the end of the bed, a way of preparing for tomorrow's performance. He has a forty-minute slot at some place called the Four Corners. He lines up a small cardboard box full of seeds, a transparent goblet and a selection of artificial bouquets folded into tiny packets for 'The Birth of Flowers'; a porcelain vessel and a metal cylinder, a pouch of flour, a candle – tomorrow he'll buy the eggs and cake – for 'The Cake Baked in a Hat' (a trick he despises for its pure laziness and lack of imagination – but the audiences love it); a decanter and a disc of glass the size of a penny for 'The Dissolving Coin'; a small wooden tray and coins for 'The Multiplication of Coins'; miscellaneous items – he's not relying on the venue for anything he might need – ink, matches, handkerchiefs; boxes for his 'Magic Boxes' trick. He looks at the arrangement of props and gets a fast, tart sourness at the back of his throat, a nub of fury rising in his chest – there's not one illusion or any grander display of his skills. He's been reduced to tricks. Pathetic. He looks at Edith curled up with Archie, not unlike a child herself, he thinks. Although he hasn't asked her, he hopes she will play the piano for him tomorrow, in fact he's counting on it. He looks at the huddle that is Agna under her shawl, wondering what in God's name is wrong that the child will not speak to him.

'You all right?' he barks at her. She doesn't move.

The noise from the next room gets louder. People are shouting. The wall between the rooms – a mere wooden partition – shakes as something heavy falls against it, a drunken body perhaps. Oliver thumps the wall and yells, 'Shut up!' Agna starts and begins to cry. Edith stirs and calms her. There is more shouting from the other room, laughter, the wall shakes again. Oliver stares at Edith, his colour high, his brow taut, his eyes pinched in anger.

'At least we're together,' he says coldly. He reaches into the bottom of the props bag and takes out a bottle of whiskey.

The Four Corners is a dingy, stinking pub packed with a raucous crowd. There is an improvised stage of two upturned wooden crates. Oliver goes through his tricks one after the other. The crowd pay little attention. Regardless, Oliver keeps his focus. When he gets to 'The Birth of Flowers' he raises his voice in an attempt to grab them.

'I have no need of moisture, earth or time to cause the seed to root and the flower to bloom. Everything will happen in the instant. Madam, he says, leaning forward to the woman seated at the table nearest him. 'What flower do you prefer – a mignonette, marigold, violet?'

'Bugger off.'

When Oliver asks if any gentleman in the audience would care to offer his hat for 'The Cake Baked in a Hat', he is met only with derisive laughter. He pours eggs and flour into his own collapsible top hat, the one he normally uses to produce an endless flurry of paper ribbons, and struggles with the sickening knot growing in his stomach.

Throughout, Agna and Archie sit with Edith as she plays the piano. It doesn't matter in the least that she is rusty because nobody appears to be listening.

Oliver is booked for six performances at the Four Corners and each evening it is the same. The crowd shows no interest whatsoever in his act. Each night after the show Oliver, Edith and the children make their way back to the miserable theatrical digs. Each night noise can be heard coming from the next room, a threatening sense to it. They do not sleep well.

At the end of the second week they move on to Middlesbrough where Oliver is hopeful that the venue will be bigger, a proper theatre. Jimmy Hewitt has secured him bookings with The Magic Palanquin. Off the train, and with Edith and the children in tow, Oliver goes in search of the venue first before looking for digs and finds it down a narrow side street off the main square. It's not a theatre at all, it's a magic shop, the owner of which takes bookings for children's parties and outdoor entertainment. Oliver can hardly bear to step over the threshold.

At the first children's party the eggs for 'The Cake Baked in a Hat' are grabbed and broken before Oliver can use them. At the second he is upstaged by an arthritic donkey who carries each child in an ever decreasing circle around a garden. At the third he is asked to leave after he holds a child upside down and shakes him vigorously in his attempt to find the missing coins for his 'Multiplication of Coins' trick.

In Harrogate he is booked into an actual theatre, the Crimson. It is small but adequate, has running water backstage and a clean dressing room. However, no one at the theatre has bothered to advertise Oliver's show. On the first two nights the auditorium remains empty. On the third night an elderly couple and a mother with her blind son sit in front of Agna and Archie, expecting a musical recital. During the short interval the elderly couple leave but the mother and her blind son stay. To a prickle of applause Oliver presents the bouquet of flowers, which he has pulled out of his hat, to the blind boy and his mother and wishes he was dead.

In Skipton, he does five shows at the County Council rooms. There is no piano, so instead Edith sits having tea in an anteroom watching the men play bridge. Agna and Archie play games on the steps in the echoing hallway. Each night the audience seems bemused when Oliver performs his tricks in relative silence as now he's not even inclined to do his usual patter. On the last night the council representative responsible for taking the booking fails to turn up with Oliver's fee. As payment Oliver lifts a bottle of sherry from the cupboard in the small grubby kitchen which serves as his dressing room, puts it into his props bag and leaves.

In Burnley, his show has actually been advertised and he sees that a decent-sized crowd has turned up, in what could be described as an equally decent-sized theatre. But the crowd hasn't turned up to see Oliver, he knows that, for after he performs his forty-minute slot in front of the red curtains, the same curtains will open for the star act of the evening – the picture double bill 'Rescued by Rover' and 'The

Dog Outwits the Kidnappers'. As Edith plays the opening chords of Beethoven's Symphony No. 7 in A Major – which now sounds just too grand – he walks out on to the stage with a shaking hand. When his show is over he throws his overcoat over his costume and sits beside Archie and Agna in the auditorium, watching them marvel at the screen, his world dissolving before his eyes.

At the bed and breakfast in Hartlepool the landlord's wife stands with Oliver and Edith in the dismal hall, rubbing the birthmark on her neck, a long purple teardrop of which she seems ashamed, and nods at the two children. Even though she isn't supposed to, she says she will take them for an extra three shillings.

Later that evening a knock comes to the door.

'Can't have that – smuggling children in!' The landlord's voice rattles like a spanner against a pipe. 'Didn't you see the sign? No dogs. No children.'

Edith pleads with him. 'But your wife—'

'She shouldn't have allowed it. No children, do you hear?'

'We paid three shillings extra for—'

'Get out – now! You can have your money.' The landlord stands with a red face at the door. Then he jams the door open with a door-stop as though to hasten their departure and barrels downstairs.

'That's what we'll do!' Oliver says.

'What?' Edith is close to tears.

'We'll smuggle the children in our suitcases into the next digs.'

'Don't be ridiculous, Oliver. There's no need. We'll just find another place that'll have them.'

'It's brilliant. I don't know why I didn't think of it before.'

'No, Oliver.'

Oliver works methodically as Edith watches him. He gathers their belongings and stuffs them into the large carpetbag and also into his props bag. The two suitcases are now empty.

Oliver lifts Archie into one of the suitcases. Edith rushes over to stop him.

'What do you think you're doing, Oliver? You can't!'

'All right, you do it then.'

'No!'

'We need to test this out in case it happens again. It'll be simpler all round. Tell Archie to lie down and close the lid over him.'

Archie stretches his arms up to Edith. 'No, I don't want to.'

'Please, Oliver, no.'

'Do it.'

Edith becomes increasingly agitated. She knows they need a place to stay, but thinks Oliver is being unreasonable. She looks from Oliver to Archie. Then furiously rubbing her brow, she tells Archie to lie down in the suitcase. Archie lies down.

'Push his head in.'

'I can't, Oliver.'

'I said push it in. We'll keep them hidden at the next place we try.'

'We won't need to. He doesn't want to go in.'

'For God's sake, woman, close the suitcase. The child will be fine.'

Edith places her two hands on Archie's head and gently twists it until it clears the edge of the suitcase. Then she presses an open palm against his cheek as though trying to flatten him.

'It'll be all right, darling.' She turns to Oliver. 'I can't do this.'

'He'll be fine.' Oliver is impatient to go. 'Quickly, they want us out of here.'

As soon as Edith lifts her hand away from Archie's face the boy's natural instinct is to follow it. He turns his head, two large eyes staring into hers.

'Mama!'

'Oliver, I'm going to lift him out. There'll be plenty of places which will take children.'

'Just do it!'

'But what if there aren't enough air holes for him to breathe?'

'There are.'

'But what if there aren't. We don't know how long it'll take us to find the next lodgings, or how long we might be kept waiting.'

'Either we hide them or we don't have a bed for the night.'

'Of course we'll find a room, Oliver, I don't know why you're behaving like this.'

'Mama!'

'Just stay where you are, Archie, that's my boy. Don't call out or make a sound. This won't take long, I'm so sorry, my love.' Edith closes the lid of the suitcase, exerting some pressure to secure the latch. A strand of Archie's hair gets caught on one of the fasteners, a turn of wheaten blond, and he cries out. Edith frees the strand and pushes it back in. Oliver grabs the suitcase and walks towards the door. Edith stands frozen.

'Sort out Agna. Pick up your things. Hurry, let's just get out of here.' Edith feels her stomach churn. She turns to Agna and lifts her into the other open suitcase. Agna points to her portable box garden.

'Yes, love, I won't forget it.' She pushes the child down, then presses the lid of the suitcase closed.

'Agna? Are you all right?'

A tiny finger pokes out of a hole in the corner and wiggles as way of a reply. Edith frets.

But Edith needn't worry.

Agna feels absorbed by the huge warmth around her. She is aware of the smell of her father from inside the suitcase, like the smell of pennies in her palm, of copper used, the smell of blood and sawdust on the butcher's floor, not unpleasant, but inhabited and solid, mixed with the smell of the macassar oil he uses in his hair. The lid of the suitcase lies across her shoulder and she feels a certain pressure around her body, which feels pleasant. Her eyes are wide open in the dark. The corner of the suitcase she is facing has a hole and when she looks through its frayed webbing she can see into the room beyond. Archie is nowhere to be seen. Shafts of weak lemon light leak in through the open door. Her father stands in its spill. She looks through the webbing that now divides the picture of her world into smaller bits. The segments of this new world feel just the right size for her and don't frighten her. She senses the warm air in her nostrils – her intimate breath – and she is soothed. She looks at her mother through a segment of the webbing. Then she looks through another segment and sees Archie's head poking up and out from the other suitcase, which her father has put on the floor. Then she looks back at her mother who appears concerned. She looks back at Archie who is now standing in the middle of the room. Then back to her mother who is crying, the portable box garden slung over one shoulder. She is able to choose the order of the story through the strands of the webbing, frame by frame.

Then she is carried, like a night traveller, out into the street. But she is safe. Unseen.

She hears her father demand his three shillings back from the proprietor, then say sarcastically, 'Yeah – we've stolen everything from the room and left the children behind!' She assumes Archie is back in the suitcase. She hears footsteps on the pavement. The sound of a passing cab. She senses the cobbles on the street as she is carried along it. Then the smoothness of the pavements. At the first two boarding houses they come across she hears the words 'full'. As the walk continues, this time along the seafront, she can hear the sea and the calls of night gulls overhead. 'Look, "Rooms Available"', she hears her mother say. A knock on a door. She hears voices. The rapid, confident patter of her father. The voice of someone she does not recognise. 'That's heavy luggage. What've you got in them – rocks?'

'Costumes and props,' she hears her father say confidently. 'You're actors?' 'No, I'm an illusionist.' 'Same thing.' 'No, it's not.' 'Don't want actor types in here.' She hears the small muffled sound which comes from the other suitcase. It is Archie. Then a distinct 'Mama'. 'But we're not actors.' 'And no children neither.' 'But we've no chil—' Then the sound of a door slamming. More walking, and through the frayed webbing she can see the stone pavements below her lighting up with small white petals. 'I don't care, Oliver,' she hears her mother shout. 'It's snowing, for God's sake.' Snowing? she thinks. 'Oliver, let's spend some money on a decent hotel.' 'What money?' her father laughs sourly. Through the webbing she sees stone steps. Hears a muffled conversation this time. Keys jangling. She sees carpet, stairs, a glimpse of her mother's coat, a wooden floor, she feels her weight being lifted up and up. She feels safe and warm in this sudden darkness. She feels invisible. And she can choose where to look and at what, and no longer is everything coming at her at once. Her mind has put on its winter clothes.

Nineteen

Huddersfield, 1914

A funny old time of it I've had, it's true. You see I've just been to the doctor and the doctor said to me that I'd only six months to live. So, I went home and I told my wife and my wife said to me, she said, 'Oh dear, Harry, you've done it now!' But it's not all bad news, I said. Oh no? she said. Oh no, I said. When the doctor heard that I couldn't pay the bill he gave me another six months.

Harry Gardner makes his way along Queen Street after the Wednesday matinee at the Theatre Royal in Huddersfield. He counts his blessings that this week he can head home between shows, change his socks, rest his feet, have a decent bite to eat. But there's more than clean socks and food waiting for him when he arrives home. Oliver, Edith, Archie and Agna have called in to see Bertie in his soldier's uniform.

They all stand now in a loose circle around Bertie who – a little self-conscious but more than a little proud – shifts from side to side in his puttees and boots, his woollen khaki tunic and trousers and his stiffened peak cap. Harriet fusses over the line of his collar. 'Well,

I don't think it's right.' She shakes her head. 'Lying about your age in order to get drafted.'

'Stop worrying, Mother.' Bertie smiles, mock rolls his eyes at her, then gives her a big hug. 'I'll be fine. Before long I'll be back and me and Dad will open that bakery he's been dreaming of, eh, Dad!'

Harry smiles and nods.

'Well, that's the thing, isn't it, Bertie being so tall, he'd easily pass for nineteen,' Edith says, standing with Agna beside her as Archie squares himself up beside Bertie, comparing his height. 'You've a bit of catching up to do, right enough, Archie.'

'I bet I'm still taller now than Bertie was when *he* was eight,' Archie says. He turns and pretends to fistfight with Bertie.

'You look great, son, we're proud of you. When do you think you'll be sent on?'

'Once drawing my identity discs is done, now that the inoculations are all sorted. In the next few days, I'd say.' Bertie holds Archie at arm's length. 'C'mon, Archie, you can do better than that!'

'Right, let's eat something.' Harriet wipes her eyes with the back of her hand as she heads out to the kitchen.

Harry turns to Oliver. 'She's not one bit happy about her boy volunteering – but what can you do? They keep telling the young men how much they're needed.' Harry sighs. The rims of his eyes are spotted with remnants of black liner.

Agna moves over to pretend fistfight Bertie now, ducking her head just like Archie did and throwing out her small fists. Bertie grabs her, lifts her in the air and spins her. She lets out a sudden, huge, joyous and unbridled laugh. A sound which fills the room, swings, echoes, blossoms as she moves. Her hair following in the slipstream of her spin, trailing out in horizontal ropes behind her, her mouth wide, her eyes tightly shut and creased in excitement and with the thrill of the movement. She laughs and laughs. And when Bertie, who is laughing now too, laughing with her, unable to resist the infectiousness of her laughter, stops turning, her head settles bumpty-bump on his shoulder, and her eyes are still closed shut, as the room is spinning in her head, and her mouth widens even more as she sighs in an arc of complete joy through the wake of sound, and Bertie holds her tightly, his arms wrapped around her and his head now pressed against hers, and he squeezes her and says what fun. And she opens her eyes and looks straight at Bertie and smiles at him and plants her two hands either side of his face, she leans forward and whispers in his ear. Yes, what fun, Bertie says again.

Edith, Harry and Archie stand enthralled at the sight, but Oliver drops his head, scowls at the floor.

'What a carry-on,' says Harry, his voice bright. He turns to Oliver, sees the surly expression on Oliver's face. 'Everything all right?'

'Fine,' says Oliver, his eyes lifting momentarily to take in the picture of Agna and Bertie – Agna's deep affection for Bertie as plain as day, an affection rarely if ever freely offered to him – then drops his eyes to the floor again.

'How's the flat on Prospect Street working out for you all?' asks Harry.

'It's fine. We only have the flat on a short lease. We'll be off again soon.' Oliver coughs, clears his throat.

'Off again? Me and Harriet were hoping you'd be around for a while. The place is not the same without you all, and what with Bertie enlisting—'

'We'd better get going,' Oliver says abruptly. He nods his head and approximates a smile at Harry, at Bertie. Then takes his leave, a chill of shadow remaining as he goes.

*

The large trunk that contains the apparatus of 'The Appearing Woman' is sent ahead by freight train to the first venue in Portsmouth. Oliver, Edith and the children follow on the later passenger train. But at Wolverhampton their train is delayed. Oliver becomes increasingly restless, stepping off and on the train several times in an attempt to determine what the hold-up might be. Then he sees them. Scores of soldiers trekking up the wide steps of the station and swarming on to the platform. Their uniforms are spotless, an air of keen excitement surrounds them. He watches as the stationmaster beckons two porters towards him, then blows sharply on his whistle. The porters enter the carriages at the front of the train and within minutes passengers begin to disembark, looking around in puzzlement as they step on to the platform. A porter approaches Oliver and asks him to gather any personal belongings and to leave the train as it has been requisitioned to transport troops to Folkestone.

Oliver, aware of the news that war has been declared, stands with his suitcase on the platform with Edith, while Agna and Archie wave at the soldiers who lean out of the windows of the train as it pulls out of the station. The Flecks wait for another train but the same thing happens. As time goes on the station becomes more and more chaotic with passengers being asked to disembark and soldiers arriving to board. Oliver's agitation grows by the minute. At this rate, he figures, it'll be nightfall before they reach Portsmouth. At the ticket office, after he pushes through the crowd, he asks the young woman behind the counter what other means of transport he can use with the tickets he has paid for, but she shakes her head and tells him that all concessions have been suspended. The Flecks have to find somewhere to stay the night in Wolverhampton.

The following morning involves another twelve-hour wait before they finally get a train and by then Oliver has missed his first engagement at the Portsmouth Theatre. The management are not happy when he arrives. Not only that, but the trunks containing the props and set have gone missing and no one appears to know what has happened to them. Without them Oliver can't perform on the second night at Portsmouth and the management decides to replace him with a clog dancer from Barnstable. That night at their digs Oliver's humiliation at the replacement act turns to anger.

The theatre management at Portsmouth refuses to allow Oliver to perform for the rest of the week – not even during matinees – and with no redress on his part. The clog dancer, Oliver is informed, has been a big hit with the audience, something – and he repeats their words to Edith with contempt – 'that they could have a good old laugh at'.

By the end of the week, with the trunks still missing and with an engagement in Reading looming, Oliver decides to modify his act once again, using his mental magic routine – the same kind that Maclagan used to perform with him – that needs few if any props.

At the first matinee performance both he and Edith are laughed off the stage. Edith had been ill-prepared for the mental magic act. Oliver had introduced her as a woman who possessed extraordinary clairvoyant powers as she sat blindfolded on the stage. He had walked among the audience selecting a gentleman's pocket watch for Edith to describe. As usual all the clues for the identification and description of the pocket watch were contained in how he phrased his question. Each word emphasised in his question related to a system of tables of articles, materials, colours, numbers and more which she had at one stage memorised. But Edith found herself unable to remember even the most basic elements of the system. Out of five items selected she did not guess one correctly. Oliver didn't have the heart to attempt to redeem himself with 'The Cake in the Hat'.

Between the matinee and the evening performance, Edith prac-
tises as though her life depends on it. Agna watches her from the
corner of the room in which they are staying, pushing seeds she has
found amongst her father's props into the grainy soil of her portable
box garden. Again Edith's memory of the clues fails her once the
lights go up. Before the act is even finished Oliver lumbers through
the auditorium, his hands clasped over his head, and disappears out
of the nearest exit.

There is no sign of Oliver that night nor the next and neither
Edith nor the children know where he has gone. The last two performances in Reading have to be cancelled. The theatre manager roars
at Edith that he will sue her for every penny she has. Edith, Agna
and Archie go back to their digs but they cannot sleep, worried that
Oliver has come to harm.

The three of them head for the next venue in Watford the following morning, hoping that Oliver will be there. Archie had, the
night before, made sure to pack his father's papers and his personal
items – his brush and shaving equipment, a packet of his cigarettes,
his shirt and waistcoat and his soap – neatly into his bag.

Edith and Archie have the few articles ready for the conjuring and
card tricks but they stand panic stricken in the wings of the theatre
in Watford at the thought that Oliver may not turn up. He appears
twenty minutes before curtain looking cold, tired and unshaven.

'What in God's name do you think you're doing?' Edith is furious. Archie stands beside her. Agna joins them, her shawl wrapped
around her head and shoulders.

'A little risqué for Watford.' Oliver nods calmly towards the netted
stockings and basque that Edith is wearing.

'Where have you been?'

'Doesn't matter.'

'Oliver!'

'Nowhere in particular. Walking.'

'You can't just disappear like that!'

'I'm here now. Let's do this.'

Edith throws her arms up in frustration. 'What's the point! We'll still have nothing to show for it.'

'Well, what do you suggest?' Oliver thrusts his face towards Edith, his eyes glaring.

Edith stands square and glares back. 'Ask Edwin for money.'

Oliver pulls away from her. 'What did you say?'

'Ask Edwin, your brother, for money. Write to him – ask him to help you out. We can settle our debts, find somewhere stable for the children – it will buy us some time if nothing else.'

Oliver is lost for words.

'He's your brother, for God's sake!'

Oliver shakes his head in disbelief. 'When was Edwin ever part of the conversation?'

'Please, Oliver.'

'No!' Oliver walks away.

'We read about him in the newspaper, Daddy.' Archie calls after his father. 'He's been made a judge. He's living in Belfast now.'

'And?' Oliver turns back to Archie.

'I'd like to meet him.'

'Would you now?' Oliver nods his head slowly.

'Yes.' Archie appears unfazed by Oliver's rising temper. 'He sounds important.'

Oliver glares at Archie. 'He – sounds – important?'

Edith steps in between them. 'It would be easy to make contact with Edwin and I'm sure he would be happy to help. He's family after all. And Belfast would be a good place for us to look for steady work, a regular job. There's work at the shipyards, in the linen factories. It would be a fresh start. And a good place for the children too—'

Oliver turns to her. 'Seems like you two have been making plans in my absence. You've probably written to him already, haven't you, telling him all about your miserable existence with his little brother.'

'No, Oliver, it's not like that.'

He turns towards Agna. 'And what about you, Ag-na?' He says her name as though he is taking a bite out of it. 'Would *you* like to see me grovelling to this brother of mine, eh? Would *you* like to see me go cap in hand to this very important man?'

Agna lifts her head to Oliver, her eyes brim with tears.

Oliver leans in to her. 'And what in God's name is wrong with you, child, that you can't open your mouth—'

'Oliver, leave her alone.'

'Does she even know how to speak?' Oliver throws this out to the air then sweeps back around to Edith. 'Why does she not talk to me? What does she say to you about me?'

'She doesn't, Oliver. She doesn't say anything to me, about you or anything else.'

'I should have marked her "Deaf and Dumb" on the census form that time—'

'Stop it, Oliver!'

'Or perhaps "Imbecile"!'

'Oliver!'

'It's never going to happen, Edith, I'll never ask Edwin for anything. Never. And that's the end of it.' Oliver stands and takes the three of them in. 'We'd better get ready,' he adds coldly. 'We're on in five.'

Not much improves in the response in Watford. The audience heckle and jeer at Oliver and Edith. Oliver fulfils every engagement but at the end of the week his wages are cut by a third. The theatre manager, a stocky man with cold grey eyes, simply shakes his head when Oliver approaches him. 'We all have to compromise, Mr

Fleck,' he says. 'It's a time of national crisis. Audiences can no longer be guaranteed but the theatres still have to survive.'

'But the theatre's been packed every night this week. Why cut my wages?' Oliver is livid.

'Now, don't tell me, Mr Fleck, you're so naive that you actually believe nothing has changed. Not a good idea to be seen putting your own livelihood before the war effort. News like that doesn't travel well. Sounds like you're stepping out of line in the hour of need. It's not make-believe we require now, Mr Fleck – there's a war on. We need morale boosting, we need an enthusiastic patriotism, we need rousing songs, not card tricks. Can you sing, dance or tell a joke?'

Oliver breathes deeply, but his gut feels as heavy as a lead balloon.

Before they leave Watford, Oliver gets word from the theatre that the prop trunks have been found. They are waiting at the Liverpool docks until papers are signed for their release. He tells Edith and the children that he is going to make his way back to Liverpool to organise the transport of the trunks up to their next engagement in Wolverhampton and that they are to travel on. On his arrival in Wolverhampton Oliver opens the trunks only to find that the windlass and the specially adapted rosewood table for 'The Appearing Woman' have been broken. He works through the night and into the next day in order to have everything ready for the first performance at the Empire Palace of Varieties. But by the time he utters the words 'Ladies and gentlemen . . .' he is physically and mentally exhausted.

Just as he is about to present the first illusion of the evening an army officer appears on the stage and announces that Oliver's show has to be cancelled as the venue is needed immediately to facilitate army recruitment. Army officers start setting up tables on the stage ready to take any volunteers from the audience.

Agna, standing in the wings, watches the glamorous songstress Ada Hill walk up and down the aisles of the auditorium inviting the young men to follow her on to stage to sign up for the war. Agna senses the rising tension in Oliver's body and sees his hands clenched white at his sides. She wonders what her father will be like that night when they go back to their digs. She covers her head with her shawl.

Twenty

On tour, 1918

Archie helps Oliver load and unload the sets, assists him in assembling the materials and hands the necessary props from the wings to Oliver and Edith, or runs to the under stage area to turn the windlass for 'The Appearing Woman'.

Meanwhile Agna, rather than helping out, seeks solitude, hiding under costumes and drapes in the dressing room, or muscling into some dark backstage corner where she feels she can watch the world around her and not be seen. The labyrinth of the theatre provides her with countless options to hide and remain silent and no one thinks her odd, for oddness is a normal thing in this domain. Sometimes from behind the stage curtains she finds some small delight in watching her mother perform, as her mother struts across the stage with her hand on her hip and her head held high before she pulls a big bunch of flowers out of Oliver's top hat, or thrusts her arm in the air in that decisive way she does when she 'appears' as though by magic from under a rising cloth. There is a predictability about it which pleases Agna.

She tends to her box garden – Archie builds a new wooden casing for the garden as and when it's needed – brushing the cushioned necks of the succulents which she has added to the ferns, geraniums and spray of marigold and teasing out the faded flowers with makeshift tweezers fashioned from a piece of wire, or lifting the crumbling detritus out with her pale fingernails, which are now delicate and beautiful and long.

For Archie, Agna and Edith a sense of family is keenly felt amongst the other performers on tour and they feel so much more at home than they did touring alone with Oliver's one-man show. Fred Felix has joined them, not only wigless but indeed flaunting his almost bald pate as part of his new act. Minty is long gone. Now Gladys the Yorkshire Terrier dances on her hind legs as Fred delivers Mel. B. Spurr's much-loved monologue 'The Man With The Single Hair'. The Ted Lennard Five are now The Ted Lennard Four, after a trampoline fiasco at the beginning of the season, where Ted Lennard himself misjudged a double front somersault and ended up in the orchestra pit with four broken ribs and a bloody nose. Elsie Smart the barrel jumper – who Edith is convinced was the one who wrote 'Go to Hell' in lipstick on Fred Felix's head at the party that night long ago – has changed her act a little over time. The barrels are lower and wider – considerably lower and wider – and while she still jumps into the barrel, or more correctly clambers in, she no longer jumps out but instead rolls herself slowly off the stage where two burly stagehands are at the ready to assist her out. Also touring with them is Dickie Mitchell whose whistling abilities have gone dramatically downhill since the reconstruction of his 'saddle nose'. Once rousing audiences to their feet with his stirring rendition of Tchaikovsky's '1812 Overture', he's now barely able to snort his way through 'Greensleeves'.

And on some of the tours Harry joins them. Stretched out on makeshift beds in Harry's dressing room between shows, Edith, Agna and Archie are entertained as Harry tells them stories about the everyday and the exotic, and they are transported by the softness and earnestness of his voice. It never matters that the stories Harry tells them are not true, not for a moment – they know that. What matters is his intent and his generosity in giving them. Stories of the Galapagos, he tells them. Oh yes, he was quite an adventurer in his early days before he took to the stage. The time he was shipwrecked, no less, on his way to dance for the King of Peru. He tells them of the creatures he saw there, lizards the size of people, birds with two beaks, snakes twenty feet in length or more and in Madagascar, the howl of the lemurs at night, the bulging trunks of the baobab trees, long-necked beetles who wrap their eggs in soft leaves, white fish with no eyes who swim upside down in underground lakes. As Harry talks, Edith and Archie lie quietly, and Agna takes his words captive under her shawl.

Oliver's search for his best illusion yet continues. He spreads his hands across the sheets of butcher's paper laid out on the table of his dressing room. He needs to bring his mind to what he wants to achieve. He could resurrect 'The Magic Mirror' routine, but he wants something even more spectacular. He works to scale, builds four basic cabinet frames this time. The illusion, as always, will rely on the exact and particular arrangement of mirrors and light. He constructs an arc of candles around the frames, orchestrating the shadows and illuminations to bring focus to its centre. He arranges the six small mirrors, which he had stolen earlier that day from a small ware shop, at various angles around the candles. Then he keeps shifting the candles to illuminate the mirrors so that it looks as though he can see right through to the back of the room. It is as disciplined as any scientific experiment. But to what end? What is he trying to make vanish this time? What if it was something grandiose, totally unexpected, a large animal, an elephant, perhaps? Or a pyramid of people, not just one person. Perhaps the illusion could be a version of 'Medusa' where the head doesn't just disappear to be replaced with straw but reappears in another cabinet in a completely different area of the stage. The cabinets themselves could be made of shimmering glass so that it looks as though nothing could possibly be concealed in them. With 'The Amazing Crystal Cabinets' added to his repertoire he could amaze audiences once again. But he knows that if he wants to raise the stakes, to realise something truly ambitious, he needs investment, money – there is no other way around it.

The idea, savagely resisted in the past, now fleshes out in his mind: yes, if he really wants to realise his dream he will write to Edwin and ask him for money. He sucks in the air, leans forward, sees his reflection in the mirrors, dictates a plea to the multiples of himself. *Dear Edwin* – he says calmly – *I am hoping that this finds you in good health. It has been a long time since we have been in contact with one another.* He pulls back from the table, takes a deep breath, leans forward into the mirrors again, continues. *It is a curious thing that our paths have not crossed over these many years. Having said that, estrangement between siblings can often become part of a family's history, particularly when the circumstances of that family suddenly alter, as ours indeed did. I am interested to know how life has been for you* – a slight shudder runs through his body – *As you may be aware, Edwin, I have been touring Britain over the course of the last number of years as an illusionist. My illusions and my experiments in hypnotism have been received to great acclaim. I now plan to create a splendid one-man show called 'The Amazing Illusions and Conundrums of Oliver Fleck'* – he winces at this lame invention of a name, then laughs it off, draws back again, cracks his knuckles, stretches his fingers, carries on – *On the strength of an already well-established reputation I have secured a certain amount of money which will go some way in helping me produce the excellent standards to which I believe this show should aspire. However, as the show will require high-quality apparatus and craftsmanship it is essential that I raise more money* – the multiple reflections grimace all at once – *In the light of this I am writing to ask if you would invest in this venture of mine* – come on, man! Get right to the point – *a loan of three hundred pounds would cover the necessary materials and labour. I will pay every pound of it back within a period of six months together with a nominated bonus, interest, call it what you will, of your naming and for your generosity. I would very much appreciate it if you would consider this proposition* – he blows air out through his lips, the mirrors mist a little, then clear – *My wife Edith and the children are well and I hope, if you have family, they are well too. I eagerly await your response. God bless* – God bless? God bless! When has he ever said that before! – *Your brother* – your brother – *Oliver.*

He shifts his position slightly and all his reflections disappear at once as though the light has swallowed them.

That night he writes the letter, finds Edwin's address in Belfast, puts the letter into the envelope and seals it. He hears the faint strike of the clock on the mantelpiece behind him. Midnight. He stands up from the table. He stretches his arms above his head. His back is stiff and his shoulders are aching.

The following morning he posts the letter, watches the creamy envelope slide out of his hand and down into the mouth of the red pillar box. Gone.

Arriving back at Prospect Street in Huddersfield four weeks later, the first thing he sees is an envelope waiting for him in the hallway. When he opens it he finds thirty crisp ten pound notes inside, exactly the amount he had asked Edwin for. No letter accompanies the money, merely a printed standard compliment slip from 'Fleck, Hamilton & Laird, Barristers, Devereux Chambers, Belfast'. The speed and coldness of the arrival of the money shocks him, and yet he's now enabled. He puts the money in his coat pocket, a tension rising in his chest, unsure of how it's making him feel.

Regardless, he says to himself, he needs to lose no time gathering what he requires. That afternoon, while Edith and Agna visit the market for provisions and Archie cleans the grate and lights a fire in the flat, Oliver heads off to the Theatre Royal. He seeks the help of one of the scene painters to hand paint the new chambers that he needs for his reworking of 'The Amazing Crystal Cabinets'. He describes what he wants – dramatic and colourful, doves, nymphs, angels – gets a price for the work which is more expensive than he had expected, but it'll be worth it, he's sure.

At the theatre he enquires into Maclagan's whereabouts, a long shot, he knows. However, one of the stagehands informs Oliver that, as his luck would have it, Maclagan since the beginning of the war has been working in the bar of the Tivoli in Leeds. Oliver contacts him and once Maclagan realises he'll be decently paid, he is happy to oblige Oliver on this new venture.

Next Oliver buys a second-hand Morris Oxford delivery van off a furniture dealer on Buxton Road which Maclagan will drive. Oliver has his name painted on the sides of the van – by the same scene painter who is at work on the Crystal Cabinets – along with some flimsily dressed exotic dancers. It's another unexpectedly expensive commission – or perhaps the little bastard is overcharging, thinks Oliver. He sticks with the title he had suggested in his letter to Edwin, which at the time he had shuddered at, 'The Amazing Illusions and Conundrums of Oliver Fleck', for the side of the van. Now he thinks the title intriguing, if a little old-fashioned.

The painted cabinets arrive and the finished product is exquisite. The wooden panels of the chambers are framed in panels of grisaille and decorated with paintings of exotic birds, half-naked women draped in silks, details of nature, Egyptian hieroglyphs, blazing stars and the phases of the moon.

He advertises for a female assistant and, after interviewing the four women who reply, decides on Peggy Taggart who has a jaunty gait and can also play the trumpet. As Edith won't be joining him on tour this time – she plans to look for regular work at the dyeworks as she's tired of moving the children around and concerned by their lack of schooling – he needs alternative musical accompaniment. He fires Jimmy Hewitt as his agent and hires the young and up-and-coming Dubliner Eric Blake. Why in God's name did he not think of firing Hewitt long ago? Blake will organise the bookings, publicise the events, get the whole thing rolling again. On the first leg of the tour, Oliver will travel across the northern counties of Ireland, testing the material, building up the routines, then bring the show to Scotland, before he finally takes it to London.

On the telephone Hewitt tells Oliver that he just can't fire him at the drop of a hat. But Oliver gives a deep laugh. 'You can't tell me what I can and cannot do, Hewitt, if you learn nothing else in this world learn that much at least.'

That night he brings home a large bouquet of flowers for Edith and tells her he has booked a table for dinner that evening at the White Horse Hotel.

The venues booked by Eric Blake turn out to be small, some barely more than a local church hall or meeting house. They are ill-equipped, with no running water backstage and an unpredictable electricity supply, hardly legitimate venues of entertainment. In many there are no trapdoors on the stage floor with no room underneath the stage for Maclagan to work the windlass.

As is expected he and Maclagan do everything from loading and unloading the stage set and props, to setting up, to doing the get-out, but now they have to advertise the performance as well, as Blake, he soon discovers, has publicised nothing. They play Donegal town, Strabane, Enniskillen, Coleraine, Magherafelt, Portadown, Newcastle, Bangor. Each time they arrive at a new venue they stick up the posters they have printed – another costly expense – and leave flyers in various establishments around the town. But despite their efforts few people turn up for the evening performances. At such times and in such settings, Oliver and his illusions appear incongruous – ostentatious even – and the Crystal Cabinets stand on the stage like flamboyant misplaced sarcophagi.

The Scottish leg of the tour brings an initial flush of enthusiasm but within two weeks of being on the road Oliver has to cancel four performances because of the lack of attendance. In Troon Oliver is double booked with a Christian temperance group, and there is a row over compensation with the management. Oliver loses his bookings for the whole week. The cost of transporting everything by ferry has eaten into the money Oliver had held over in reserve and he desperately needs to recoup his losses. By the fourth week Oliver is unable to cover the price of lodgings for himself and Maclagan – although as a matter of decorum he continues to pay for Peggy Taggart's bed and breakfast – so the two of them end up sleeping in the van. In Kirkcaldy the small crowd who turn up are expecting a faith healer and ask for their money back when Oliver yells that he cannot cure their ailments. And after twelve weeks on the road Oliver lets Peggy Taggart go as he cannot now afford to keep her on.

The most exhausting thing of all, however, is the loneliness.

He has never felt it this intensely before. He buys a catapult and a toy soldier for Archie and a small tapestry set for Agna in a shop in Kirkcaldy, remembering how when he had brought her liquorice on a previous visit home she had pressed her tiny hands against her chest and given a little shudder of pleasure that had reminded him so much of his mother that it had almost crushed him.

With the tour over, he and Maclagan spend their last night in digs. The following morning before going home to Huddersfield a letter arrives having been redirected first from Portadown then on to Eric Blake in Belfast and then on to Kirkcaldy.

He opens it and reads it as he walks back up to his room.

14 Prospect Street
Huddersfield
6th April 1918

Dear Oliver,

It is with great sadness that I am writing to tell you that we have received the news that Bertie has been killed in action. Harry called to us last night and told us so I thought to write to you straight away. I will relate everything he said. I have nothing more to say myself only that I feel such a heavy sadness in my heart and it is so hard to believe. Agna and Archie have taken it badly too.

Bertie had joined the offensive at the Somme and by all accounts the fighting has been vicious and a lot of men have been killed, all told, Bertie now being one of them.

Harry said that he and Harriet had written to Bertie often over the time he was serving but in the last letter they got from him, a few days before he died as it has turned out, he apologised for not having written to them in a long time, which he hadn't. He said that he had suffered owing them a letter and he was sorry but that he was becoming less and less able to talk about what was happening. Only that the trenches were full of mud and water and corpses and that you didn't know when you might be attacked with the shelling and shrapnel flying around and that only the day before he was lighting up a fella's cigarette and the fella was hit and just dropped out of existence.

Harry says it is a greater burden to have lost him than he could have imagined, and just as hard to think of the boy suffering and not knowing how much or for how long or in what way he died exactly. Harriet has taken it very badly and I am not sure if she will recover at all.

Keep us in your thoughts as we keep you in ours. Hoping you are in good health.

Sorry to bring you bad news.

Yours always,

Edith.

He climbs back into bed holding the letter. He breathes deeply and looks out at the morning. Rain falls in long grey streaks. As the clouds darken and roll slowly past his window it feels as though the light itself – or the lack of it – unearths the saddest part of him. He drops the letter on the floor then lies down on his right side facing out into the room and pulls the blankets over his head to close off the day.

Later that evening on the way home through Kilmarnock, while Maclagan downs a pint in the local hotel, Oliver drives to a visiting fairground attraction and throws the last of his money away on the side stalls.

Disembarking from the ferry from Scotland, he follows the route inland on the way back to Belfast. He can see the flanks of the Antrim Hills falling away behind him. Fathom Hill and beyond that Eden's Cross. How he feels it pull at him. His mother. There. The speckled flowers on her roof of grass. Why can't he bring himself to visit her grave? Why can't he bring himself still, now he's so close to it? To tend to the spear thistle or the restharrow or the cuckoo flower which may be crowding her. To eke out the moss from the stone grooves of her name. He thinks of the house in Eden's Cross, now cold without her, water bleeding up through the earth to claim it. What has happened to the house? he wonders. Is it still standing? Is it empty? Is there someone else who lives there now? It would surely have gone to Edwin as the older brother for him to do with as he wished. If Edwin had sold it, why would it follow that he would even contact him about it, or give him his share of the profit. A sudden thought strikes Oliver – the money Edwin sent him, was that what *that* was? If so, now it's all gone to waste.

It is late evening of the following day by the time he parks the van outside the house on Prospect Street. When Agna opens the door she is taken aback by the dark energy which encircles him. She is inclined to smile at him but instead she pulls back, drops her head as he walks past her into the room.

She turns to look at him standing by the window, a desolate shard. Not a word from him, no acknowledgement even of her existence, so lost is he within himself. Without himself. If she could say something to soften him she would, but she can't. So she imagines a white world around him where he stands. Allows winter to fall around his head. Allows the snowflakes to fall and then falls with them. Falls from a great height among the snowflakes, which are every word she never speaks. As soon as the snowflakes touch the earth they melt, but she continues falling. She is not melting. She watches the intricate snowflakes dissolve around her. She imagines her father rising up out of her words of snow. She takes his cold hand. She leads him across the cold earth. Away from his pain. She guides him to freedom, to grass, to hot bread and soup.

II

cold Earth wanderer

One

Belfast, 1920

Agna and Archie take it in turns to bring their father a hot lunch to the cabinetmakers in York Lane where he works on a casual basis, and on their way home to collect the regular dispatches of cotton from Mundell Bros. & Co. on North Hill Street, which Edith and Agna, as outworkers, will fashion into handkerchiefs and bring back for them to sell. Today Agna stands on the threshold of the door that leads from the small showroom at the front of the premises into the workshop at the back. In her hands she holds some bread and sausage wrapped in brown paper, soup in a small flask, a bottle of ale.

Oliver stops for a moment to take her in. At thirteen years old the round childish contours of her face have lengthened, her demeanour has taken on a deeper reserve. She hands him his lunch.

'Thank you,' he says.

She nods her head.

'Your mother at home?' He knows Edith is but asks Agna only to keep her here with him a moment longer.

Agna nods again.

'Archie hawking sticks?'

She nods again.

'Tell him I'll get him work here, I promise.'

Agna dips her head. Then, very quietly, she leaves.

She has never spoken to him.

He puts his lunch on a nearby chair and turns back to his work. He feels the sawdust cover every inch of him. It coats his eyelashes, fills his ears, his gullet itches with it. He feels as though he wants to shake out his lungs in the fresh air like a picnic blanket. The damn sawdust is probably floating in his blood by now, he thinks – a stream of claggy corpuscles clogging up his veins. The more elegant woods – the birch or oak – produce a sawdust as fine as ladies' face powder, which hangs merely a moment in the air before it is sucked into his lungs. But these cheaper woods – the pine, the fir – release a spongy dust which swells on the moisture from his breath and sticks to every part of him like a bloated second skin. His mouth feels swollen. There is the constant tang of eucalyptus on his tongue.

Oliver once again puts the saw to the wood. He checks the pencil line, which he has marked along the grain, and follows it with the saw. He has one more panel to finish cutting before the coffin can be assembled. He moves his arm evenly and slowly, despite the ache in his back and shoulder. He keeps to the line. A few minutes later an offcut of wood falls with a hollow clank to the floor.

At least his apprenticeship in carpentry with Mr Shearer, Maryjo's father, all those years ago in Burndale – cutting and shaping the wood, mending roofs, repairing beams and supports – hasn't gone to waste, he thinks wryly. And ironic meeting the Orbachs at Sydney Brown's party, the time he had told them he made coffins, and here he is making them. Perhaps he should consider the construction industry instead. Or the shipyard. Archie could work with him. There'd be more going on in the shipyard than in this damn place.

He straightens his body and looks over at Thomas Manger who is waiting to assemble the panels he is cutting. Manger leans against the wall on the far side of the workshop like a forgotten rake, his eyes bloodshot and wide with dread. What in God's name is the matter with that man? Dejection personified. Look at him. Not a move out of him. Oliver knows Manger doesn't mean any harm by his long silences and sad exhalations and hangdog look, but they drive him mad. It angers him catching even a half glimpse of that martyred face. At first he used to fill in the gaps in their conversations, found himself rambling on just for the sake of making some noise, but it soon became exhausting. Was he ever any different? thinks Oliver, looking at Manger. Probably not, as a baby, wouldn't put it past Manger to have stared at his mother's tit in abject fear. Oliver coughs loudly to see if this will change the arrangement. Manger shifts on his feet then groans quietly to himself. Ah – the bastard's still alive.

He first met Manger at the Empire Theatre. Manger had been frequently called upon to assist with the construction of sets in the days when Oliver had begun to make a name for himself. Oliver remembers the backdrop Manger had built for 'The Appearing Woman': with those beautiful horseshoe arches, those crested birds in their golden cages, that array of half-naked dancers wearing emerald green babouches. He was sorry that he had to sell the backdrop to cover mounting debts, for it had epitomised everything exotic in the world of illusion. Surprising for a man so curtailed as Manger. But building coffins was Manger's forte, a reputation he had earned since constructing a bespoke coffin for the renowned Belfast businessman William Sidden, twenty-five years ago now. The coffin had been described in the national newspaper as a work of 'world-class craftsmanship' and an influx of commissions had followed. Subsequently, Manger had been asked to build a coffin for the famous actress Dorothy Grant, and after that, for the philanthropist Henry Gordon. From that Manger had opened a funeral parlour on York Street, which he ran with his wife Flora and above which they both lived. Their slogan, 'From Manger to Grave', painted across the frontispiece of the funeral parlour made Oliver groan every time he passed it.

Manger, however, was not a man to respond to opportunity with any spark and had subsequently disappointed clients by defaulting on commissions, even during the war when many similar businesses had flourished. 'It's because he's on tablets for his nerves and needs to take things slow', was how his wife explained the resulting slump in business, both in the making of coffins and in the handling of burials, to anyone who cared to ask. Take things slow? Any slower he'd be dead, mulls Oliver now as he looks at Manger. Here is a man who has adopted the ways of the dead while still living, has let everything slip through his bony little fingers, let all his talent go to waste.

Oliver puts his saw down. He hears the drag of palettes outside from the shed across the yard. That'll be Divitt. It's Divitt's job to source the wood for Manger, to order supplies, to deliver the deal or pine or oak and have it ready for the construction of sideboards, tables, chairs, dressers, storage chests and coffins – whatever the customers have ordered.

Manger groans again, then slowly moves from the wall and begins to brush the floor. 'There's been a lot of trouble in the city', he says very quietly as he brushes; nevertheless Oliver is slightly startled by Manger's attempt at communication. It catches him off guard. Oliver says nothing. 'I see Carson wants to take things into his own hands', Manger says. 'But Westminster isn't happy. The Unionists aren't happy—'

Divitt appears at the door, sliding it open a little further and drawing a thin whisk of fresh air into the workshop. Manger stops speaking, keeps his head down.

Divitt is a small man, but wiry and strong, with grey, vacant eyes. He wears a large flat wool cap, which flops over his forehead. He stands silently, looking from Oliver to Manger and back to Oliver again, then he closes the door. Jesus, another luminary, thinks Oliver, that's all I fucking need.

'Leave it open,' mutters Manger, possibly to Divitt, but Oliver can't be sure. It could be to the floor or to the sawdust or to whatever the hell is going on inside the man's head. The door remains closed. 'Bastard – I know he can hear me. We'll choke in here.'

'Well – let's open the fucking door then, shall we?' says Oliver.

Oliver walks over to the door and slides it open. The air outside is heavy but at least it feels clean. Oliver stands and takes a deep breath. Just behind the low wall at the end of the yard he can see the Morris Oxford van which, although falling apart, he still owns and can least afford to run. It's madness to have brought it over from Huddersfield and to have kept it, but where else is he to store the apparatus for 'The Appearing Woman' and 'The Amazing Crystal Cabinets'? Maybe he should get rid of the whole fucking lot.

He feels as though he is starting all over again. That dream of a one-man show, where did that go? He had taken opportunities whenever they had come, made opportunities when there were none, had fought each step of the way to keep his head above water, to claim his place. And all for what? In the end – absolutely nothing. And coming back to Belfast had reduced everything to shit. There was no performance work for him to speak of. The place was too small to sustain him. The only things on offer were twenty-minute slots playing the backwater circuits at the mercy of the syndicates. The same fucking treadmill. Lumped in with second-rate crude novelty acts. Nothing had changed. Because nothing would. Everything going nowhere. But he won't go down that route again. No matter what. Helping out in Manger's workshop, however dull, means that, at least for the moment, he can make some money to keep them going. Yes, he's here now, making coffins. Fuck it.

He shouldn't allow this intense boredom to get to him, this excruciating mundanity – it's work, after all. But there's no crack out of Manger, nor out of Divitt. There's no spin, no lightness. He's drowning in a humourless dry rot.

Christ – what he wouldn't do to shake Manger out of it. Have some spark set the fucking place alight. Release himself from this purgatory, this halfway house. First he'd tell Manger to go fuck himself – then he'd get the juices going again, create something great, he'd show them, he'd show them all – get back on the boards with his best illusions yet – didn't they see it in him? Didn't they see it? All of them, they – them – all of them, what he is capable of? Weren't they remotely aware? Morons, all of them, every single one – every—

A large gap suddenly opens in his thoughts and for a second there is nothing. The rage is failing to push him up and out of this flat, bleak trough,

—fucking last one of them.

He stops. He looks at the sky above, at the roof of the shed opposite, at the palettes in the yard in front of him. Nothing rings, nothing has texture, or vibration or sheen. Everything is monotone. He can suddenly feel that same sense of foreboding he used to experience as a boy now flooding his body – that feeling he would get whenever he woke up on his left side facing the wall of his bedroom: that something was bound to go horribly wrong. He can feel that nauseous grip in his stomach at the thought that the world could, at any moment, become one massive and undifferentiated bleak, monolithic state, can feel himself flattening under the weight of it. He grips the doorjamb to steady himself. He looks down at his sawdust-covered boots, at the gaping hole in one boot's leather toecap. Then a hole in his sock just under the hole in the boot and under that, staring back at him, an almond of sawdust-frosted toe. The framing of his flesh in such a precise way makes him feel oddly pathetic: a tiny portal of leather and wool offering a final pasty reveal, which is so disappointedly predictable.

A fucking hole in his boots. At this time of his life.

In the distance he hears the weaving trill of a pipe band then the long boom of a drum, like the roll of a giant iron ball.

'Are they still marching? The twelfth of July's over,' he calls back to Manger.

Manger stops brushing the floor, shrugs his shoulders. 'That's why they call it the marching *season*,' he says then continues brushing.

Just then Archie arrives in the yard to tell his father he's got work in the Paint Hall at the shipyard for a few weeks.

Oliver smiles. 'Good lad,' he says. 'Well done, you.'

Archie looks soberly at his father. 'They kicked out the Catholic workers, pelted them with rivets, some of them had to swim the Musgrave to save their lives – that's the only reason I got the job.' Archie stands dispirited, troubled.

'I know, son, I know,' is all he can say. He looks across at Divitt who is working on the far side of the yard sorting lengths of timber. 'It'll all sort itself out, don't worry.'

Archie nods at his father as he leaves. 'See you later,' he says. He dips his head as he passes Divitt.

'Yes, see ye. And stay away from any trouble,' Oliver calls after Archie.

'I will.'

Oliver sighs. He's tired. Very tired. Hasn't slept in days. But the boredom is worse than the tiredness. And as he stands in the doorway, some smell now is putting him in mind of a stale steak and kidney pie – his overalls in the clammy air perhaps, the foulness rising off him, his body's sweat on the turn, the smell of baked kidneys gone off. That's all he amounts to. A fucking stale steak and kidney pie. His life crumbling like yellowed rancid pastry revealing only a shrunken filling. He gets a sudden blast of Mrs Doohan from his childhood in Eden's Cross – 'So whenever you eat, think of me, and of the goodness I'm bringing,' saliva dribbling from the corners of her mouth. He shakes the image off. No, not even the pie itself, fuck it, not *even* the pie – merely, the smell of one. He's a disaster. He's vapour. An utter failure.

Two

At six o'clock on the dot he leaves the workshop. He stops off at McShannons for a drink, buys a half bottle of Dunville's whiskey and heads for home. He opens the front door of the house in which he, Edith, Archie and Agna occupy the top floor flat and immediately gets a tart stable-yard smell in the hallway. Mrs Earwaker, the lodger who lives on the ground floor, is standing by the end of the staircase wearing a grubby apron and holding a chamber pot in one hand and a parcel in the other.

'This arrived for you, Mr Fleck,' she says, turning to Oliver and proffering the parcel. 'I was just about to go upstairs with it.'

'Thank you, Mrs Earwaker,' Oliver says, hesitating to take the parcel from her and thinking – *haven't you something more pressing to attend to?* He looks into the stinking chamber pot. *And is there no end to this decay!*

'Would you like me to open it for you too!' Mrs Earwaker says sharply, staring at him.

'No, that won't be necessary, Mrs Earwaker,' Oliver replies dryly over the rank copper-yellow swill, mustering as much dignity as he can under the circumstances. 'You're very kind.'

'And there's a letter for you on the sideboard – haven't you seen it? It's been there for days.'

'Yes, I saw it. I'll pick it up later.'

'Likely from the landlord,' Mrs Earwaker announces with a grandness which doesn't suit her. 'Or the bailiffs!' She turns on her heels making the contents of the chamber pot swirl rapidly around in the bowl. As luck would have it – or indeed not – a splat of urine lands on Oliver's boot, seeping through the hole in the toecap, then the hole in his sock so that he can feel the warm liquid against his skin. He gets a shiver up his spine. The sawdust should soak that up, he thinks, then banishes the thought. He quickly makes his way up the stairs before there is a chance Mrs Earwaker might follow him with whatever further bad news or bad odours she has to distribute.

He opens the door and finds Edith at the table in the sitting room writing in her accounts book, anxious as she has become to make every penny stretch, a pile of newly fashioned handkerchiefs in front of her, another pile of cotton waiting to be worked, a mound of knitting by her side. Agna sits in the armchair by the window. Edith is chatting to Agna but stops as soon as Oliver enters the room and lowers her head. Oliver feels a hard lump rise in his throat. He puts the parcel on the table, then takes off his boots and his socks. He removes his coat and hangs it on the back of the door.

Their flat in Belfast is shabby but moderately comfortable, although nowhere near as large as the one in Huddersfield. A threadbare rug covers half of the wooden floor and an odd-looking rose chandelier hangs from the ceiling. Out of his first few weeks' wages Oliver put money down to buy some furniture – the table at which Edith now sits, its four matching chairs, the armchair which hugs the window, a divan, a sewing table for Edith and a worktable for himself, also the blankets, curtains and linen they needed. But some of the furniture which came with renting the flat is badly in need of repair. In Oliver and Edith's bedroom – off to the left of the sitting room – the wardrobe doors are hanging off their hinges, and in Agna's box bedroom – off to the right – one of the legs on the bed is an improvised length of hose. Archie sleeps on the divan. The kitchen houses a range with a bottle jack and a meat screen, two chairs, another small table, a dish rack and a lead-lined wood sink. The place is littered with the paraphernalia Oliver has insisted he still needs to work on plans for new illusions – books, periodicals, note-books, papers, wooden boxes, rolls of fabric, offcuts of wood – and as a result it feels desperately cramped. For the price they are paying for the flat – eleven shillings a week – Edith had at least assumed it would be of some standing. It is disappointing most of all to Oliver, who is renting the flat from its original tenant ventriloquist Dessie Hobbs. Oliver had helped Hobbs only two years previously get his first booking at the Palace Theatre in Huddersfield. Now Hobbs is touring America to great acclaim while Oliver feels he's living in the squalor Hobbs has left behind.

Oliver walks restlessly around the flat in his bare feet. The framed tapestry embroidered with the words 'Behold the fire and the wood, but where is the lamb?' – the one that hung above his bed in Eden's Cross and now hangs on the wall of their flat in Belfast – is tilted to one side. He stops, straightens it. He looks at Agna. 'You all right?' he barks at her. Agna stays silent. 'Is there room for a piano?' he says suddenly to Edith.

'Sorry?' Edith looks up from her accounts book.

'Why don't we get you a piano?'

'Where did this notion come from? There's no room, I haven't played the piano in years, and anyway we couldn't afford one. I've over fifty handkerchiefs to do up in order to get a measly two shil-lings, what are you talking about a piano for?'

'Of course we can afford a piano. If that's what you want—'

'I never said I wanted one.'

Oliver lifts his hands in the air, points around the room. 'It would fit.'

'I don't want a piano.'

'I know it's a small room, but it would fit.'

'Where?' Edith is amazed at the suggestion. 'Just look how much stuff is in this room already.'

'We can move the stuff.' He catches Agna looking at him. He glares at her. She drops her head.

'Where?' Edith says.

'Get rid of it.'

Edith is puzzled at Oliver's sudden change of heart. All this 'stuff' as he calls it now was only yesterday 'the precious building materials of their future'.

'We could put the piano in the bedroom where the bed is, but we'd have to move the bed?' she says, calling his bluff, curious to pursue his reasoning.

'We can't move the bed,' he says with a strange and sudden firmness.

Edith looks at him. 'Why not? Why can't we move the bed? It's facing the door. If we turned it the other way—'

'I want the bed facing the door,' Oliver says, turning his head away from her.

'You do? Why?'

'I want to know when there is someone at the door.' He sits on the divan opposite Agna.

'But you'd know when there was someone at the door because you'd hear them knocking.'

'I want to know when there is someone at the door before they knock.'

Edith gives a broad smile taking this as a joke, but then her smile weakens as she sees that Oliver is serious. 'Well,' she continues cautiously, 'what about along by this window?' She points to the far side of the sitting room. 'I could use the ledge to sit on—'

'No, we couldn't afford a piano,' Oliver says quickly. He lifts a notebook and pencil that is on a nearby table and begins to write.

'That's all right. I never said I wanted one.'

'Should I light a fire? It's gone cold.'

'No. Save the logs. Put your coat back on.'

Oliver does not move.

'Or your socks.' Edith bites her words. She holds her gaze on Oliver who is scribbling furiously. As she is about to turn her attention back to her accounts book she sees the parcel on the table. She lifts it to inspect it.

'Oh,' she says. 'It's from the Gardners – it must be, the postmark says Huddersfield.' She opens the parcel. Inside she finds a pair of brown leather shoes, size nine. Her breath catches in her throat as she reads the accompanying note.

22 Thomas Street
Huddersfield
16th July, 1920

Dear Oliver, Edith, Agna and Archie,

I hope you don't think it odd but I've decided to send you the pair of Bertie's good shoes, which he bought when he was last home on leave. He had been sweet on a girl who lives over on Union Street and wanted to make an impression on her. They look good as new as he only wore them the one time and he wouldn't have wanted them to be wasted, and Harriet feels it's too strange a thing to see them still in the

*house. I would like Archie to have them. I know they won't fit him yet,
but one day they will.*

We are getting by.

All best to you.

Harry.

A weak complaint of wind whistles through the window frame. Oliver, in silence, gets up from his chair and sets about arranging some logs in the small grate as though to get a fire going but doesn't light them. Agna covers her head with her shawl. Edith gets up to go to the kitchen to fill the kettle with water and set it on the stove, tears streaming down her face.

That evening Oliver cannot sleep. He sits in the armchair in the front room staring through the window into the night, engulfed by the blackness it brings. Archie lies asleep on the divan, Bertie's shoes lying on the floor underneath it. Oliver is glad that tiredness has overtaken the boy, he'll have an early start at the Paint Hall in the morning. As Archie turns in his sleep his blanket slips down off his shoulders. Oliver gets up and adjusts it to keep Archie warm.

He moves to the table, which is littered with paper and materials, wood, nails, a roll of wire, a saw, a box of iron rivets he picked up at St George's market. He sits down, clears some space in front of him, drops his head in his hands. His mind begins to race with fragments that seem to come out of nowhere: Fred Felix in the blue chiffon dress all those years ago with 'Go to Hell' written in scarlet lipstick on his bald head; Maclagan in his medusan wig; Arabella and her five beautiful white Leghorns; Arabella and her two beautiful white breasts; an endless series of hinged mirrors lining an endless corridor; something huge which disappears – not just a person or part of a person this time but a tramcar, a building, Belfast's City Hall.

Bertie, dear lovely Bertie, lost to the cold earth. And Eurielle Hope. Where is Eurielle? Eurielle.

The door leading from Agna's box room opens. Agna stands at the doorway, her eyes soft and hooded but not completely closed. Is she awake? Oliver hesitates, then says a gentle goodnight to her. She smiles but doesn't reply. She looks into the far distance and Oliver realises she's sleepwalking. He moves towards her and reaches out to take her hand. Agna turns her upper body slowly towards him as though she is immersed in water and automatically extends her hand to his. With their palms enclosed, Oliver gently twists Agna around and begins to walk her back into the box room. He guides her into her bed and tucks the blankets around her, then gently, as gently as he can, he strokes her forehead with his fingers.

Her breath releases itself in an audible sound, which takes Oliver aback. He stands stock still, holding his own breath, waiting for the sound again. Was that her voice?

'Agna?' he asks cautiously.

Nothing.

'Agna?'

She is fast asleep.

'Talk to me.'

Nothing.

'Why won't you talk to me?'

Nothing.

'Please, Agna, say something to me ... anything ...'

His eyes fill up.

'Everything's all right, Agna, everything's all right. Sleep well.'

He turns, his heart as heavy as a stone. He catches sight of the portable box garden he made her when she was younger, sitting on the floor beside her bed, amazed that the little construction has survived all this time, that she has tended to with such care. He sighs, leaves the room and closes the door behind him.

The bottle of whiskey that he keeps in the kitchen cupboard is empty. He leaves the bottle on the table, searches for something else to drink, another bottle of gin, which he may perhaps have forgotten about (a ridiculous notion, he knows, always too keenly aware of exactly how much alcohol is in the house), a bottle of beer even, but no such luck. He makes his way into his bedroom and climbs into bed.

He lies in the dark. Without the whiskey the dark feels as though it is expanding by the second. He tries to fill his head with trivia, with anything, to keep the dark from swallowing him. He begins to recite the 'second-sight' system of questions he used in his mental magic routines, the familiarity of it might help, he thinks. 'What article is this?' he mutters, picturing himself on stage somewhere, the audience not yet where he wants them to be, a little restless, distracted, perhaps. He wants to pull them into the moment, to rivet their attention like a bolt to a girder.

Edith wakes up. 'Sorry?' she groans, lifting her head from the pillow, her hair rubbed to a frizz on the back of her head.

'What *article* is this?' Oliver says.

'What do you mean?' Edith turns to look at Oliver. He continues reciting.

'Each set has an arrangement of ten different articles. For every set there is a question, similarly worded, so as to give the impression to the audience that it is in fact the same question being asked . . . inflection . . . that's the trick . . . and rhythm . . .'

'What are you talking about, Oliver?'

Oliver continues at a rapid pace. 'The first question to be asked at the head of the set will provide the clue to which particular set contains the article which is to be described – there is a number assigned to every set and each particular article is conveyed by a word – the questions give the clue to the set. What is here? – fourth set. What may this be? – third set. What is this? – second set. What article is this? – Yes! Couldn't be smoother—'

'Oliver, you're babbling.'

'I'm not.'

'You are.'

'We have money.'

'No, we don't, Oliver. Jesus, no, we don't.'

'We have some.'

'But that's not going to last for ever – we need to live off that.'

'I'll find a way. I'll get the money somehow, from somewhere.'

'Oliver?'

'I can't keep working in that workshop.'

'Why don't you check the paper? Someone may be looking for a new act.'

'I'm not a *new* act.'

'You know what I mean.'

'I can do this, Edith. I know my worth.'

She turns to him. 'I just think that we—'

'You've got to believe in me, Edith.'

Edith sighs. 'But I do. I do.'

Oliver stares at the ceiling. They both lie quietly for a while. Then out of the silence Oliver asks, 'Has Agna ever spoken to you?'

Edith hesitates. 'Yes.'

Oliver nods his head gently, taking it in. Almost afraid, he asks, 'What did she say?'

'She told me about the first time she saw snow – the time you made the portable box garden for her and showed it to her in the yard.'

'Snow?'

'Yes. She said her head is a cold prison of words and the first time she saw snow the words trapped in her head began to melt just like the snowflakes falling around her. And she felt free and not afraid.'

'She said what?'

'And that when it's dark, or when she hides herself and makes it dark, she imagines snow.'

'Snow?'

'And sometimes she imagines all manner of weather at once, not just snow, but rain and wind and sun all together at the same time, and then her feelings fall, and all the wrong things fall out of her and are carried or twist or drift away, and she feels light as a cloud.'

Oliver is silent.

Then. 'And has she spoken to Archie?'

Edith turns on to her back and looks up at the ceiling. 'She always speaks to Archie.'

'She does?'

'Yes.'

'What does she say to him?'

'Normal everyday things, but quietly, so no one else can hear.'

Oliver sighs heavily. Why did Agna only talk to Edith and Archie and not to him? He wants to ask Edith if Agna has ever said anything about him. That would please him if she had. If she had acknowledged him in some way. But he doesn't ask. He is afraid to ask. He simply repeats the word slowly as though it's a word that he has never heard before but which might describe something deeper than love.

'Snow.'

Three

O ver the following months nearly all the things he steals are small and consumable. Most recently, a sweet mince pie, the remains of which have stuck to the inside of his coat pocket – the flakes of pastry, granules of sugar and parings of dried fruit still managing to find their way under his fingernails days later.

Now larger stolen foods crowd the cupboard in their kitchen, and the rate of stealing has surpassed the rate of consumption. At first Edith had simply been grateful that Oliver had thought to go by the market on his way home from the workshop. But as the days progress she becomes more and more concerned about the amount of food he brings back with him. How much does that mean he is spending? And how does he possibly think they can eat it all? There are now bags of potatoes and onions, boxes of apples, three loaves of bread at the last count, carrots, bacon. Some of the food goes off before they even eat it – unheard of.

At both the hardware shop and the jewellers the items he steals at first are small: a coat hook, a plain silver band, a silver comb. Then he brings home larger items which are not obvious necessities: spectacle cases when neither he nor Edith wear spectacles; a wrist brace when neither he nor Edith have a sprained wrist; a stuffed ferret, which upsets Agna, though Archie finds it curious; a percussion cap, a whip, an Indian headdress, a pair of crocodile belly cowboy boots. Edith is increasingly surprised – why on earth do we need rosary beads? Or a compass? Or an umbrella cover? Or a tuning fork? 'Are these items to be used for your illusions?' she asks him harshly. 'The illusions that you haven't been working on for years?'

Oliver registers the comment, feels its sting, says nothing, keeps his head bowed.

Edith adds up the cost of the food Oliver has left in a bag on the kitchen table – three shillings, ten and a half pence. Then she calculates the cost of the sundry items.

'Oliver, we can't afford to spend that much on food – or anything else that's not essential for that matter – we just can't. We're already behind in rent. That money could be used on other things. I'm putting a shilling a week into the clothes and boot club for Archie and Agna but I could have used the money which you spent on all this. Why are you making it more difficult than it already is!' Edith's tone hardens as she waves her hands at the items on the table.

In a voice which seems to drag behind him as he walks out of the flat he says, 'Stop worrying, Edith.' As he leaves he realises that he has never once thought of stealing whiskey, until now.

On the way to Manger's he calls into McShannons. A couple of weary labourers from the shipyard sit at the bar with pints, having finished their night shift. The rest of the place is empty. Oliver slips behind the counter and takes a bottle of Dunville's whiskey. Slides it into the deep pocket of his overcoat.

He heads for the workshop and works solidly all morning without a break. Then at midday he stands out in the yard. Blows the sawdust out of his nose. Breathes in the city air. He opens his lunch parcel, eats the warm bread, drinks the ale. He takes a slug of the stolen whiskey, then hides it.

Just before he is about to return to work, Divitt walks towards him and offers him a cigarette. Oliver accepts, takes a light off Divitt, pulls on the cigarette, blows out the smoke. Feels something open in his head. A light breeze shifts a scattering of sawdust around the door of the workshop.

Divitt takes off his cap. When Oliver turns to Divitt he is taken by surprise at the shape of Divitt's bald skull. He doesn't want to stare, but Divitt's head looks odd, misshapen, there is a strange dark hollow on one side of it. That's a serious dent all right, thinks Oliver.

Divitt says nothing. Oliver knows he'll have to be the one to start a conversation, if, that is, he can be bothered to. Divitt takes another drag from his cigarette. Rests into another silence.

'Where's Manger?' Oliver says.

'Gone to a funeral, I think,' Divitt says without irony.

'Do you think he'd want to buy this fucking hearse of mine, the Morris Oxford?' Oliver points at the van parked behind the wall. Mud covers the exotically and flimsily dressed dancers making them look as though they now wear scapulars and cowls.

'You selling?'

'I need the money, blast it.'

'You do?'

Oliver sighs deeply. Shakes his head.

'Thought you'd hit the big time, Fleck, the way you've been talkin' and all?'

'Well things have moved on a little differently than expected.' Oliver coughs to clear his throat, shifts from foot to foot. 'You always worked with wood?' Oliver says, changing the subject. He turns away from Divitt and looks down at the ground.

'Yeah.'

'Thought of doing something else?'

'I'm always doing something else.'

'Yeah?'

'Yeah.'

'Like what?'

'Have all sorts of – schemes running.'

'You have?'

'Yeah, I need to. I'm paid a pittance for this job. Wouldn't get a job anywhere else. Sure they've driven the Catholics out of Mackie's, the Sirocco Works, Musgrave's . . . where would I go?'

Oliver says nothing.

'But I'm making a fortune.' Divitt takes a long drag on his cigarette.

Oliver perks up. This is the most he has heard from Divitt. Thinks he should jolly Divitt along now, find out exactly what he means. 'Any to share around?'

Divitt turns and nods his misshapen head. 'You interested?'

Oliver sees Divitt is serious. He takes a moment before he answers. 'I'd never say never.'

Divitt chews on his lower lip. 'It's just I have a job needs doing.'

'Oh yeah?'

'That requires transporting something.'

'But you have a van?'

'Don't want to go using it for personal stuff, if you know what I mean. Prefer to use yours.'

'All right. Go on.'

'It's only a couple of dogs that I need taken off my hands, just for a while. Just until I say. You'll get paid. They're no trouble.'

Although it all sounds wrong to Oliver he's too glad of the offer to ask any further questions. 'I'll take them off your hands. I'll drive there now. When do I get the money?'

'Soon enough.'

Oliver lets a silence hang, sighs, might as well be doing something on the side, he thinks, no harm. Then keeping his eyes on the roof of the Morris Oxford, he says quietly, 'Did you hear about the man who drank a bottle of varnish?'

'No.'

Oliver tilts his head back and looks up at the sky. 'He had a terrible end, but a beautiful finish.'

Divitt nods his misshapen head. He stamps on the stub of his cigarette. Puts his cap on and walks back into the workshop.

That evening as Oliver arrives home after visiting Divitt's mill, Agna opens the door of the flat. She stands back as he brushes past her, his mood sullen, dour, three miserable-looking greyhounds tagging slowly behind him.

Four

He puts on his white shirt and his black frockcoat and trousers. He puts enough props in a small suitcase to give him a twenty-minute solo act. Small stuff: card tricks, coin tricks, a handkerchief illusion, and to round off, the trick that turns his stomach for being so pathetically crowd-pleasing – 'The Cake Baked in a Hat'. That has to be the worst. The only comfort being that if he gets nothing out of the competition he'll at least get something to eat. How fucking pathetic is that, he thinks, *the practical cake*.

He has been included in Class No. 3: Comedians, Acrobats, Ventriloquists, Musical Acts, Dancers, Magicians, etc. It's the 'etcetera' which worries him – God only knows what that's going to throw up, he's thinks, and in the literal sense of the word. He had heard about the Dentalist from Hungary at Burnley's 'Go-As-You-Please Competition' last season, who had spun from a rope by his teeth until he had thrown up all over the stage. Then there was 'etcetera' Daisy Daniels and her mind-reading duck at that competition in Colne, which Harry had described as one of the most excruciating acts he had ever had the misfortune to witness. But the crowds had loved it, for by the time Daisy's duck had quacked and waddled from one side of the stage to the other Daisy had removed every item of her clothing. This is what it had all come to. Novelty over skill. Flesh – for Daisy apparently had plenty of that all right – over good material. The crowd demanding pap and titillation. Fuck talent.

No, this would be different, he hoped. At this season's 'Go-As-You-Please Competition' finals at the Gaiety in Belfast he would win something, he was sure of it.

The first prize for each of the three classes is £7 10s, the second £2 10s and the third £1 10s, with a week's engagement offered to all three winners. Anything at this stage would help get him out of this hole. All he has to do is to simply get through it, not lose the rag or walk off no matter how much he wants to. The finals are to be held on Saturday night at the second house. He'll use the winnings to cover rent arrears and then the earnings from the week's engagement to offset some of his debts. He clips his suitcase shut, tidies his cravat and walks out of the flat to get the tram into town. He wants a drink. He keeps walking.

Backstage at the theatre it is mayhem. Oliver sits at the end of a corridor that is thronged with every kind of act imaginable, yodellers and whistlers and comic dancers, sword-swallowers, bell-ringers, jugglers, snake charmers, knife-throwers and other acts he hasn't the will to try to figure out. He sits clutching his small suitcase until someone calls his name, then slowly walks to the wings to await his turn after 'Morris McLeod – The Midget with the Musical Buttocks'.

As he waits in the wings he notices a rectangular metal cage sitting on a table. From where he stands he can see a spray of white feathers sticking out through the metal bars. He walks closer to inspect it. There are five white Leghorns huddled together in the cage. They peck and worry the air with their small yellow beaks. They stare at Oliver with orange-rimmed eyes. *Arabella!* he thinks. *Arabella!* She must be performing at the theatre. She must be here.

He instinctively looks around him, sees if he can spot her. After all these years how curious it would be to meet her again. She'd be quite an age now, he thinks. He tries to calculate – in her late sixties, early seventies at least – my God! he thinks, and still performing. There's tenacity for you. Inspiring! But she's hardly been reduced to doing competitions at this stage of her life – in the instant the irony of his conjecture stings him. He shakes it off.

He bends to look closer at the chickens, bringing his face up to the bars of the cage. And surely she wouldn't be let away any more with torturing these poor birds to make them dance, he thinks. He makes a churring sound, feels an awakening, a connection once again to some worth, to the belief he had in himself. He smiles. He keeps his throat song going. The chickens bob their heads, ruffle their feathers, jitter across the floor of the cage as though it is already hot. He 'caw-caws' to hypnotise them, moving his face even closer to the cage.

Suddenly and viciously the largest of the chickens strikes out and pecks a gash in Oliver's cheek just below his eye. He quickly pulls back from the cage. He touches his cheek, it is bleeding. He takes out one of the handkerchiefs which Agna has embroidered, and which he had planned to use in his act, and dabs his face. A moment later an assistant to the adjudicators calls him to the stage.

He performs his conjuring tricks but the injury has thrown him. With the pain of it he is only half concentrating. He drops the coins by mistake on the floor, picks the wrong card out of the pack, can't use the bloodied handkerchief in his new 'The Goblet of Ink' trick, and startled by a loud bang from somewhere in the theatre he messes up 'The Cake in the Hat' routine. Before the adjudicators have a chance to turn him down he walks off the stage.

Heading down the backstage corridor towards the exit, he passes a half open doorway. From the corner of his eye he sees someone sitting in the room, then catches the name 'Arabella' on the door.

He stops. He breathes deeply. Remembers that first time with her, *his* first time, a young man of fifteen. He had felt so alive it was as though God's angels had taken his arms and, while his feet were firmly on the ground, had stretched him to the sky. He instantly craves the innocence of that time, the hope he was filled with when everything seemed possible. Where had it gone? He turns his head slowly, leans forward to look through the crack in the door just to get a glimpse of her. Would she remember him if he prompted her?

Through the crack he sees her sitting in front of the dressing room mirror. She is wearing her costume, a child's smock for her 'little girl lost' routine, her bonnet rests on her lap. Her Bo Peep wig with its blonde curls is cocked to one side on her head revealing a tuft of ashen hair. She applies a rouge stick to the leathery flaccid skin on her cheeks.

Everything tumbles down in his brain.

'You,' she says, spotting him in the mirror.

Oliver sheepishly steps forward. 'Hello.'

She turns slowly round to him. 'What theatre is this?' she looks exhausted, pitiable.

'The Gaiety,' he says, hardly believing her state.

She holds her look on him. 'Where?' she says, her voice frail.

'Belfast.'

She turns back to the mirror. Stares at her reflection. 'How did I get here?'

At first thinking she is asking for a reminder of how she had travelled to the theatre, he is about to suggest by tramcar perhaps, but the look of utter desolation in her eyes shifts the meaning for him. He waits, takes a breath. 'I don't know.'

'And you.' She turns back to him. 'How did *you* get here?'

He drops his head. 'I don't know.' He stands on the threshold, doesn't move. 'I don't know how I got here.'

Arabella lifts a bony hand and points to herself in the mirror. 'You see that,' she says, stabbing the air with her finger. 'That, my friend, is what a casualty looks like. Just so you know one when you see one.' She bares her teeth at him in a strange tired grimace.

A sharp voice travels towards him down the corridor, pulls his attention away from her. 'Flack! Magician man! Is that you there?' It is the adjudicator's assistant.

He doesn't turn to the voice. 'Fleck,' he says quietly to himself.

'Sorry, magician man, you're out.'

He steps back from the doorway. Does not offer any goodbye to Arabella.

'No, don't be sorry,' he whispers to himself. 'Don't be sorry. That's fine. That's fine.'

He leaves the theatre. Walks along North Street. Takes Agna's handkerchief out of his pocket to dab his cheek, which, in the fresh air, has once again begun to bleed. He looks at the handkerchief. Agna's embroidery has created what looks like a face, a stitch of blue thread forming the shape of a crab's claw, just like the scar that the clout nail left on Edwin's cheek. Oliver's head floods.

He'll find Edwin, he'll pay him a visit after all.

Five

He stands in the study of Edwin's house. As he looks at the artefacts on the console table by the door he feels as though he is standing in a museum. There is a small cast of the Venus de Milo and a generously proportioned bronze Hercules. Above the table there is a large seascape on the wall, two Japanese prints either side of the expansive chimney breast and the fire screen in the grate is decorated with a mandarin's fan. He takes in the richly patterned wallpaper, the leather-bound books in the bookcase behind him and, in front of the bookcase, the large mahogany desk upon which a paperweight, an inkwell, pens and blotting paper are arranged in an orderly row. Everything has a refinement about it. A crystal decanter, half full of brandy – he lifts the stopper, breathes deeply, yes, brandy of some considerable quality, he thinks – and two glasses sit on the table to the right of the bay window.

Oliver approaches a display case, which sits on a walnut trunk to the left of the window. The display case is a beautiful object in itself – enamelled ends, polished oak cornices, the glass front of which is angled to allow a greater visibility of the objects inside. Oliver bends forward and looks into it. Inside are four elegant flintlock pistols, their wooden handles inlaid with emerald- and ruby-coloured stones and intricately decorated in silver wire. Mounted on the wall above the display case is a wooden and glass cabinet in which – symmetrically arranged and pinned according to their size – is a line of metallic black beetles. Underneath the beetles there is a line of exotically marked butterflies and, running along the bottom of the case, are six small frogs, each a deepening shade of green. Below each specimen a handwritten label in Latin. They are trophies of travel perhaps, or of a select acquisition, or perhaps the possessions of an amateur naturalist. He looks at the frogs – ironic, he thinks, considering it was Edwin who burned his frogs on the cinder path in Eden's Cross.

Oliver wishes Edwin would arrive, get this thing over with; he feels nervous. He cannot believe he has found himself in this position, arriving cap in hand at Edwin's house.

Suddenly he hears someone at the door and turns around. It is Edwin.

Edwin is the first to offer his hand. 'Good to see you again, Oliver,' he says quietly.

It has been more than forty years since he last saw Edwin but there is still a youthfulness about his older brother despite his grey hair. He wears the clothes of an ageing and respectable bachelor. The scar of the clout nail – that odd crab-claw shape – is now a faint silvery pink comma. Oliver is overtaken by a yearning for what they had together as boys. It takes him by surprise. He takes a deep breath, composes himself.

'Good to see you too, Edwin.' Oliver feels distinctly shabby in his brother's presence. The two men stand silently for a moment.

'Can I offer you some tea, Oliver? A drink, perhaps? Brandy.'

'Brandy sounds good.'

Edwin moves to the decanter. He pours the brandy into two glasses, turns and offers one to Oliver.

'Thank you.'

'Touring at the moment?'

Oliver takes a drink, perked up a little by the idea that Edwin has at least paid some attention to what he has been doing. 'Eh . . . between tours.'

'Your wife—'

'Edith.'

'Yes, you mentioned again in your recent letter – Edith. Is she well?'

'Yes, indeed.'

'And your children? How old are they now?'

'The twins. Thirteen.'

'Any family resemblance?' Edwin surprises Oliver by asking the question.

Oliver dips his head. 'They take after Edith mostly – although Agna has the look of Mother about her – just in the way – in her expressions. Yes,' he falters, 'Agna is very like Mother.'

'Agna, what a lovely name. And the boy?'

'Archie.'

'Very good.' Edwin drinks his brandy. He does not offer Oliver a seat, simply waits for him to continue, and appears to be in no hurry to make Oliver feel at his ease. Of course Oliver knows that it is up to him to broach the subject of money once again. He knows Edwin will not ask him why he has come to visit because Edwin has already guessed why, and will simply continue the pleasantries of the conversation, finish his brandy and then excuse himself to attend to some business. No, he will not help Oliver along in the conversation. Oliver will have to start the crawl. He will have to humble himself as much as is required, until he is not himself but the self Edwin wants him to be. It was always conditional, now that he thinks of it. The unspoken rule was that everything Edwin did was more important than anything Oliver did, or would ever do. Why else would Edwin have walked away from him in the first place, other than out of a sense of his own importance?

'And you're a judge now?'

'I was appointed six years ago.'

'Yes, of course, I knew that.' Oliver shifts uneasily from foot to foot.

A strained silence.

'And are you worried for your safety?' Oliver asks, desperate to keep the conversation going now that it has started.

'Sorry?'

'As a judge in Belfast … you might, well … attract the wrong kind of attention.'

'I keep vigilant.'

'It seems the threat of civil war is ever with us.' Why is he even bothering to engage Edwin in a political discussion? Why is he lapsing into platitude?

'It seems that the part of Ulster that fought hardest against Home Rule might be the only part of Ireland in fact to get it,' Edwin offers.

Another silence.

Oliver breathes deeply again, then jumps in. 'I'm sure you're wondering why I'm here.'

Edwin stands erect, waiting.

Oliver continues, growing more nervous as he speaks. 'Well, the money which I – which you – invested in my work, the materials for the illusions, the touring, for my one-man show, has of course been used wisely – eh – but …'

Edwin remains silent.

'But that was a while ago now—'

'Five years to be exact,' Edwin says.

'No, not five years.' Oliver is genuinely dismayed at the flight of time.

'You promised to pay the money back.'

'I did.'

'And?'

'Well ... times are – have been – difficult ... as I'm sure you can appreciate ... and eh ...' Oliver feels another slump in his confidence. 'You see, for a man in my position, for someone who takes risks – such risks – in their profession ...' Oliver is beginning to hate himself. Why does he feel he has to explain himself to Edwin to such an extent? 'Sometimes – sometimes –' he feigns a professional nonchalance, 'these risks don't always pay off.' He looks at Edwin. Edwin's expression remains cold. Oliver fills with shame.

'How much more do you want?' Edwin's voice is matter-of-fact.

Oliver's voice stalls in his throat. 'Eh – I'll definitely pay you back, of course, on both loans—'

'How much?'

'I hadn't thought of an exact figure ...'

'Last time I gave you three hundred pounds.'

'Yes – and believe you me, it really made such a difference – it – and—'

'Do you want the same amount again?'

Oliver hesitates. He has reached the point – how does he say yes and retain his dignity? He knows he doesn't have that luxury. He swallows his pride.

'Yes, please, that would be great.'

'Edith is able bodied?'

Oliver is confused by the sudden change of direction in the conversation. 'Sorry?'

'I'm asking if your wife, Edith, is able bodied.'

'Yes,' replies Oliver, confused.

'I need a housekeeper. I'll pay her for her services. Cooking, cleaning, sewing. The young woman who showed you in, Sadie, the new housemaid, has no experience. And I'm afraid my cook, Lily, is too elderly to do the work that's needed in the kitchen, although I will keep her on for some of the lighter tasks. But I need someone who knows how to look after a home.'

Oliver is speechless.

'And there would be work for your son and daughter as well. Archie and—?'

'Agna,' Oliver mumbles.

'That's how you'll get your money. If you need the full sum up front I'm sure we could come to some arrangement.' Edwin finishes the brandy in his glass, offers Oliver a half smile. 'Seems like a workable and fair transaction to me. Keeps it strictly business where we both contribute and gain. Don't want you to feel owing, Oliver, now, do we? At least not any more than you do already. Agreed?'

Oliver scrambles in his mind for words. He cannot catch one.

'Think about it. Let me know by the end of the week. I'll advertise the position then if Edith doesn't want it.'

Oliver stands rooted to the spot. It is Edwin who moves. He holds the door of the study open for Oliver. Oliver walks as though in a daze, stands facing Edwin at the door.

'What happened to your face?' Edwin says.

Oliver touches the scar from where Arabella's chicken had pecked the gash in his cheek.

'Eh . . . it was an accident . . . it's nothing . . .' Oliver says.

'See. We're more alike than you think.'

Oliver looks at the scar on Edwin's cheek, a mirror reflection of his own. He sees the brother who once watched out for him, who rescued him from the girdled sycamore, who he looked up to, now relishing his position of power to undermine him. The trust had gone. But maybe it had always been so, Oliver thinks. Maybe the protectiveness Edwin had afforded him when they were young was simply a means to control him, to make him feel beholden, the whip and sting of which would last a lifetime. He's sorry he's come now. He's sorry he's come cap in hand, to feel only his own dissolution. Should have known it would turn out like this. Offering himself only to be belittled by the brother he had once relied on.

'I eventually found out what happened to him. What happened to Father, if you're interested.'

Oliver lifts his head to Edwin.

'He died in London over ten years ago, in Clerkenwell, a stone's throw from where I worked, in fact. He was homeless, penniless. A drunk by all accounts. '

Oliver does not know how to respond.

'I never made any attempt to sort him out, help him in any way. I left him to his own devices.'

Oliver looks at the cold composure on Edwin's face. Sees, despite it, the young face of the brother who once slept opposite him in Eden's Cross, that impassioned dreamer who became so quickly restrained by the mantle of responsibility life had handed him. But life had handed it to them both, surely? How does the love within a family become so broken and then so redundant, as though it never had the right to exist in the first place? And yes, there was love between them at one time, he thinks, there was companionship. And there was love enough at one time for his father too. A boy's love for his father, for him to not want his father to harm himself with the bread knife or the length of rope on the broom handle or the smoothing iron or the rat poison, or to die alone and penniless in Clerkenwell. Did their mother take all the love with her when she died? Is that where all the love went?

'I'll see myself out,' Oliver says. He turns from Edwin and leaves the house.

'I'll take the work,' Edith says.

'You'll do no such thing,' Oliver shouts.

'I can cook, clean, look after his house,' Edith shouts back.

'Never. He wants to destroy me. Take everything I have away from me.'

'Oliver, that's not true, don't be ridiculous, it's a job he's offering, a well-paid job. I can't turn that down. There's little enough work to be had in the city now. It will mean we can pay everything back. We'll be indebted to no one. For once we'll have a decent life.'

'For once?' Oliver's outrage peaks. 'What do you mean *for once!* What in God's name have I been trying to do all these years!' The blood has drained from his face, his jaw is clenched, his eyes wide.

'I'm sorry – I didn't mean . . .'

'Oh, you *did* – you fucking *did!*'

'Oliver! Please!'

'No! Next thing you know he'll have you living in the house. Then Archie, then Agna. And *we'll* no longer be a family!' He throws the glass from which he has been drinking whiskey against the wall. It smashes into pieces. He turns and catches Agna pulling her shawl over her head. Archie sits solemnly in the armchair looking at the floor.

'Are we even a family now!' Edith screams at him.

Oliver walks out of the room.

Six

I t is six o'clock in the evening. Above him is a still, cold sky. Streaks of blue struggle to appear amidst the wash of grey and the threat of snow creases the horizon. There have been days now of heavy rain and hail.

Oliver stands in the yard of Divitt's mill. There is not a sound. He thinks that a dog is missing from the picture, an angry mongrel on a long rusted chain, thrashing the air and snarling at him – snarling at this stranger who has arrived unannounced in greatcoat, urban shoes, a smear of caution across his face. But there is no dog, though nailed to a tree on the other side of a large iron gate is a sign with the words 'Beware of the Bull' painted in fat white streaks.

He has parked his van in the lane of the farmhouse next to the mill where Divitt lives. Agna waits for him in the van.

It was Edith who had suggested Agna go with Oliver – a highly unusual thing for her to have done, but she had planned to take Archie to the pawnshops around town that afternoon in an attempt to pledge some of the articles which littered the flat. The rent man had called and had once again left with nothing and, fearing that the bailiffs may then be on their way, Edith did not want to leave Agna on her own. Oliver had promised Edith he'd sort out the situation with the greyhounds, had promised her he'd finally secure a deal on the van, had promised her he'd set everything to rights – *she was to stop worrying, for God's sake!* On the way to Divitt's he had stopped to place a bet, backing the favourite, a whippet called Trick of the Light at the 3.30 up at Celtic Park. Placed five shillings, lost, left with only a shilling and sixpence in his pocket.

When they had arrived at Divitt's mill he had said to Agna that he only had a bit of business to attend to in the next set of buildings beyond and that she was to wait near the farmhouse until he got back, that he wouldn't be long. He told her she could look around but not to make too much of herself about the place. There was still someone living in the house itself, despite how dilapidated and empty it looked.

Now Divitt comes out of a nearby shed, his sleeves rolled up, his trouser braces hanging down around his flanks, as though he has just been for a piss. He holds his cap in his hand. He stops and stares at Oliver, says nothing. In the dusk the dent in Divitt's skull appears more pronounced than usual as though darkness has pooled in its hollow. Oliver's stomach takes a minor lurch.

'What you here for?' Divitt says sharply, his breath like smoke.

'I'm here to get my money, Divitt. I've had those dogs of yours for ages now – months! How much longer do you expect me to hold on to them?'

'Until I say so.'

'I want paid now or else I'll get rid of them.'

'I'm afraid you'll have to hang on to them for a while longer, until I work out what to do with them. Last thing I need is to draw attention to this place, and that's exactly what they'll do. And you now for coming here. Don't worry, you'll get your money.'

'Give me my money now then and I'll go.'

Divitt throws his head back, looks up at the sky, then back again at Oliver.

'Want to double it?'

Walking into the yard only a few minutes earlier, Oliver had promised himself he'd keep this transaction clean. He would make it clear that he was in no mood for Divitt to be acting the lig or wasting his time. He had Agna to get back to, he had home. But he is derailed by the offer.

Divitt says nothing, just stands gaping at Oliver. Oliver stuffs his hands in his pockets, bends his head. 'Well—'

'You want more money or not?'

'Yes, I do.' Oliver blows out an exasperated sigh. 'Look, I don't give a damn if it's tobacco or meat or alcohol – *or dogs* – I'll pass on whatever. Yes, I'll do it. It's short-term. To get me out of a hole. I'll breathe a word to nobody. But only if there's some money up front.'

Divitt still says nothing. He picks at his crotch then smells his fingers. Oliver winces at the action, thinks – how was Manger ever afraid of this dozer?

Then Divitt walks towards Oliver, stops just a few feet away, a stench coming off him. Divitt smells his fingers again and now, this close, Oliver can see blood on Divitt's fingers and under his nails, still wet. Oliver looks down, there's fresh blood on Divitt's boots.

'Climb up,' Divitt says, indicating the thatched roof of the building to his right.

'What?'

'Your ticket to a few extra bob.'

Oliver looks incredulously at Divitt. 'You having me on?'

Divitt shrugs. 'You said you wanted in.'

Oliver looks up at the roof of the building. Reluctantly he mounts a pile of wooden crates stacked against the wall. The building is low enough. He is soon level with the thatch.

'Now,' Divitt says, 'slide your hand into the thatch.'

Oliver clears his throat. 'What?'

'Just slide your hand right in there.'

Oliver, increasingly unsettled, does what he's told and pushes his hand into the thick of the coarse thatch. It doesn't take long before his hand touches metal, lots of it. He moves his hand to the right and to the left. The thatch is crammed with rifles. Oliver quickly removes his hand, turns from the roof and climbs down into the yard. He shakes his head and raises a hand to Divitt. 'Not that, Divitt. Stolen beef, cigarettes, I'm in – but not that, not arms. I may be many things but I'm not a warmonger.'

'You're in anyway.'

'What d'ye mean?'

'You've seen them. You know I have them. No way out now.'

Just then Oliver hears what sounds like a woman sobbing. It's light and broken. He turns his head quickly. Is it Agna? No, it's coming from inside the thatched building. He turns his ear towards the sound for a brief moment in an effort to get a clearer hold on it.

'You're in now.' Divitt grins at Oliver.

Oliver turns back to Divitt. He feels the sick confusion of the moment, a watery churn in his gut. Manger had warned Oliver about Divitt and it seems Manger *is* right. There's something dark and primeval about Divitt, something sinister. Oliver's throat tightens.

'Having nothing to do with it,' Oliver says. He tries to hold his nerve as he walks away from Divitt. Gives himself just a casual sway, not a swagger, as though he has seen nothing unusual, heard nothing. How he wishes he had not come. He prays he doesn't get a bullet in the back, or a knife, or a pair of hands around his throat.

'Do you want your money or don't you?' Divitt spits.

'Having nothing to do with it.'

'No choice now, Fleck. You'll be back, or else—'

'Let's just pretend this never happened,' Oliver shouts back at Divitt.

'Oh, but it did – and you know it did. And I know where you live.'

Oliver gingerly steps through the muddy yard for fear of slipping. Skids on a crescent of cow dung. Not the dignified exit he was hoping for.

Oliver now skirts the fence along the upper field. He walks as though he is looking for something he dropped earlier or left there, a shovel or scarf. He moves keenly, lifting his feet in and out of the muck as though it is singeing the soles of his shoes, occasionally sliding sideways. He wears his town shoes, not even his boots from the workshop, so he has little grip. As he walks, the ends of his coat flap like the ears of a large dog.

There is a great agitation wheeling around him. He is thinking about Divitt, about the rifles. What's the blood on Divitt's hands from? And the woman crying – what's that about? Oliver keeps his head down, keeps moving. Perhaps it's innocent enough, he thinks. Perhaps he caught Divitt in the middle of killing a chicken. There's always chickens on a farm. Makes sense if he was killing a chicken. *He's a fucking madman!*

He feels a fury rising in him. In trying to make things better he's just made the whole situation worse, *fuck – fuck – fuck!* Everything's gone to shit. How did he not see the troublemaker in Divitt? *He's a right fucking madman!*

Meanwhile Agna has been looking around the farmyard and touching, cautiously, the old rusted machinery with its vicious spikes and chains, which sit at the back of the byre. The barns stand empty except for a couple of roller barrels in the corner and one or two miserable bales of hay and only a few irritable ducks in the yard. Everywhere a heavy rank smell of manure and meal and dirty thick green streams running under her feet.

Now she hangs off the large iron gate to test her weight against it, her arms dangling over the top bar, her knees bent and her rump low. From the gate she sees her father walking back towards her across the upper edge of the top field. She watches him slip and slide across the cold wet earth. Imagines him cursing under his breath, spraying his misty spittle into the dusk.

An evening bruise of clouds draws in overhead releasing loose spats of cold rain, which fall on the sodden earth and come to nothing.

Oliver stops by the upper fence, lifts his head to the adjoining field. There it is. The bull, a bullock to be more precise, a young Aberdeen Angus, hardly fully grown, as still as a cenotaph in the sludge. Slowly the young bull juts its muzzle upwards and sniffs the air then drops its head, locking its eyes on Oliver.

Without warning Oliver mounts the fence and jumps down into the field in which the young bull is standing. He strides towards the animal, an energy pushing visibly right up through his body. Nearing the middle of the field he stops and widens his stance as though in preparation for something. He looks down at the wet, cold earth at his feet. The young bull holds his position then shifts towards Oliver with a heavy waddle, its nostrils dripping strings of mucus. Then, as though uncertain of this intruder, it stops again. Oliver remains motionless, the stocky hold of his body a fine match for the young bull's.

Agna watches from the lower field. She can hardly believe what she sees. She feels a sickening crush in her stomach. Oliver had strictly forbidden her to go anywhere near the upper field, pointing to the sign nailed to the tree. What is her father doing? What is he thinking? She drops down from the iron gate and runs up the field towards her father as fast as she can, the heavy soil sucking at her feet. She wants to call out to him to come away, come away from the bull, Daddy, climb back over the fence, but the running uses up the breath for any words she might have had.

She sees her father tilt his head back to the sky and bend his knees. Then he begins to swing his right arm in a wide circle, moving it like the vane of a strange windmill as though it is dislocated from his shoulder, a great momentum gathering with the rotation – sky, earth and sky again. For a moment, as though confused by the movement, the young bull simply shifts where it stands. Then, as it becomes increasingly agitated, it blunders a few steps towards Oliver, snorts at him. Although it does not charge, anyone else would surely have turned and jumped over the gate, but Oliver stands where he is.

Agna reaches the fence and sees the young bull's head close and thrusting forward, its hair matted like an old teddy bear's with whorls of dried mud.

And then it seems to Agna to happen all of a sudden. The young bull is only a few feet away when her father clips his fist into the side of the bull's head. The contact is brief but its effect is immediate. The forelegs of the animal buckle and it collapses forward as though it has been shot, spreading its dung-encrusted rear to the sky and emitting a leaden bellow. Where before there had been solid muscle and bulk, now there is a softness and yielding. Under its long lashes the bull's chocolate-coloured eyes are wide and glazed. In a final slump the animal's back legs give way, its belly and jaw slap into the mud.

There was either great finesse to the manoeuvre or no finesse at all, simply brute force, or luck – a knuckle impacting on the exact point of an occipital nerve perhaps. Whichever it is, the bull is down. Oliver turns.

Agna stares at him in disbelief and shock.

Her eyes dart to the bull and back to her father.

'What's wrong with you?' Oliver growls.

Agna's mouth opens, but no sound comes out.

'What's wrong with you?' he hollers at her now.

Agna stares at her father. Why did you do that? she wants to say.

In her eyes Oliver sees the effect of his action reflected right back at him as clear as day. He sees the animal in himself. There is no denying it. She tells it all with her eyes.

In the instant, in the heat of his violence, a distilled contempt for himself now pours out all over Agna. He can't stop it. He yells at her now. 'What's wrong with you! What are you looking at! You feel sorry for that fucking animal? Eh? Eh! Do ye! Do ye! Well why not start feeling sorry for me! Eh! All the shit *I* have to wade through! You're just like your mother and the whole fucking shower of selfish bastards that I've had the misfortune to waste my life on – the whole fucking lot of you – and your brother's not much better, thinking the worst of me I bet, putting me down! I'm sick of you! Sick of the whole fucking lot of you! And look at you! You can't even open your fucking mouth to speak – what the hell is wrong with you, child! Well?' he screams into her face. 'Well?'

These words are lifelines he is throwing out – the more scathing the better, the more pointed the better, the more they would cut the rock and stick and pull him up out of his descent. He keeps throwing them at her, he cannot stop his rage at her. And inside he is listening to it all, to himself, but there is nothing he can do to stop it, he has to let it run its course. And when he has emptied himself of his words, he sneers and walks away from her, although that's not what he wants to do, he wants to fall like the bull, he wants to be slain. Troll man. Bogeyman.

Oliver rubs his hand across his mouth, adjusts his coat, straightens his collar, begins to casually scrape the mud off his shoes on the bottom rung of the iron gate. Behind him the young bull lies wheezing in the field.

Back in the van Oliver sits behind the steering wheel and drinks himself to sleep while Agna sits beside him and listens to the rain hammering on the roof.

Seven

Belfast, 1921

Every day a new humiliation. And each humiliation more searing than the last. The degree no longer matters. All action and reaction, the big and the small of it, is moving Oliver in the same direction: towards the final straw. And he knows it. And knows there is nothing he can do about it.

He is now having nightmares so frequently that they fill his waking hours. Nightmares terrifying in their bleakness where little happens but where he finds himself lost and alone on a plain of unending black ice. An unnameable threat always hovering close by.

What a fucking ride this is, he thinks. Even the weight of his own sadness cannot slow it down. He welcomes the sadness, at least it has a certain intelligence about it, it has an object, something to be sad over or about. At least the idea of reclamation comes with what is lost. But this damn thing, this wet mawkish rag wrapping itself around his soul, is suffocating him. He is slowly, oh so slowly, in this almost dead state, dying.

Oliver sits on the edge of the bowl. The smell of urine, both fresh and stale, gathers at the back of his throat. He lifts his head, looks at the tiles in front of him spread out like the pages of a dirty book. He looks at the mould between the tiles, a demon slime. Even the mould has a purpose, he thinks. Even it is doing what it is meant to be doing, leaving its mark on the toilet wall. He says the word 'mould' out loud. Hears it hang in the air. Says it again, and again, stripping it of its meaning so that it ceases to relate to what he is looking at. It is not a word any more but a slur he is making with his mouth. He utters his name, *Oliver Fleck*. Utters it again and again. He becomes another slur. Everything feels flat and black. There is nothing he can do. He is useless. He is a failure in every aspect of his life, in his work, in the eyes of his wife, his children. He feels hideous to himself. At least without a mirror in this squalid sordid hole he is not able to see himself. He could not bear that. The lump he is.

He sits on the bog, wearing his hat and overcoat, his bare arse poised over the cold, white bowl, an enormous ceramic gullet waiting to swallow him. 'Goddammit, it's fucking freezing,' he mutters quietly between gritted teeth. He folds his arms across his stomach and bends his upper body forward to trap in a portion of heat. The wooden seat, which rings the bowl and on which his thighs now rest, is at least gathering a little warmth, but the wind screeching over the top of the door and underneath it, spiralling up and down in wild miniature tornadoes around his feet and his shoulders, is petrifying. As for the wind that is coming up from the bog underneath him – God Almighty, it's arctic. He imagines what lies below the toilet, down into which he could slip or be sucked, and never be seen or heard of again. What a way to go. Down this gaping endless funnel of shite into the true dark yeasty bowels of the earth.

Suddenly he hears Edith's voice from the other side of the door. It startles some part of him, which part he is not sure. She sounds so close and yet so far away. Is the voice inside his head?

'Oliver, you're wanted.'

'Wanted,' he repeats meekly. Then, *Wanted?* Could that be true?

'Oliver.'

'Yes.'

'Are you there?'

'Yes.'

'Can you hear me?'

'Yes.'

'Will you be long?'

Silence, except for the wind of course.

'Oliver.'

'I'll be out in a minute.'

'It's OK. Just tell me.'

'Tell you what?'

'The money for the rent – where did you put it?'

There's a very distant scream he can hear. *I said I'll be out in a minute! Can you not give a man some peace, for crying out loud!*

'Oliver.'

Silence, except for the wind.

'The rent man is here.'

'Well.' Oliver struggles to maintain composure, he doesn't want to lose the readiness in his bowels. 'Tell him to come back another time.'

'I looked on the mantelpiece but I couldn't see it.'

Another scream in the distance. *That's because it isn't on the mantelpiece – Jesus – Jesus – Jesus!*

'Oliver.'

'Yes.'

'Where is it?'

'I – can you – it's – just give me a minute—'

'It's already ages overdue, Oliver. The rent man said months.'

A whoosh and whistle up from the bog, a cold snap across Oliver's arse.

Will you please let me finish!

'Oliver.'

Silence.

'Oliver.'

Then nothing.

Has she gone? He needs solitude without the thought of her hovering on the other side of the door. There's no dignity in the finish being heard.

'Oliver.'

Christ! She's still there.

'Yes.'

'I'm still here.'

'Leave me alone.'

'I'm only waiting.'

'Please wait somewhere else.'

'Just tell me where the money is.'

'It's complicated.'

'What could be complicated about it?'

'Believe me – it is.'

'Hurry up.'

'I can't – I'm trying but I can't go with you standing there.'

'I mean hurry up and tell me where the money is.'

'I can't when you're standing there listening.'

'I'm not listening. Not specifically listening. Not listening for that in particular.'

Oliver grunts, then releases a short involuntary moan.

'He says this time he's not moving.' Edith's voice sounds as though it's coming through the keyhole.

Silence.

'Oliver. The rent man is not going to leave this time without the rent. Oliver.'

'Yes.'

'He says he'll wait for you.'

'He knows I'm here? '

'I told him you were here.'

'On the bog?' Another short moan. 'What did you tell him that for?'

'He asked.'

'He asked if I was on the bog?'

'He asked what you were doing.'

A scream in the distance again. *Why didn't you say I was – out – somewhere – woman!*

Edith sighs. 'He's not taking no for an answer.'

Oliver squirms on the wooden seat. He hears Edith's footsteps fading and the back door of the house slam shut and with that his bowels slam shut too. He closes his eyes. He has missed the moment.

Nothing now except the cold and his freezing arse and not even the satisfaction of a half-baked crap. He stands. His bowels still feel heavy. He pulls up his underpants and his trousers. Pulls on the long chain of the cistern and gives another small moan as he looks down the bowl for there is no need to flush.

He soberly heads back into the house.

Only Agna is there.

'Where's your mother?' Oliver speaks so quietly he hardly speaks at all.

Agna lowers her head.

He walks slowly over to her. 'Agna,' he beseeches her.

Agna keeps her head down. The greyhounds whimper beside her.

270

He lifts the brown envelope that has been left on the kitchen table. 'Summons' is written on the front of it. He puts it in the pocket of his overcoat. Had he still been sitting on the bog he would have gladly flushed himself away.

Eight

E dith is in high spirits. She has struck another soft skull. The long-handled broom which she wields has hit its target with a hard whack on the sitting room floor. Edith looks at the head of the broom. A tiny pouch of flesh and bone has burst its seams underneath the clove-black bristles. Another mouse runs along by the skirting board. Edith lifts her broom. Archie angles his spade in the air. Agna raises her hoe then swings it in a loose balletic arc, chipping the ceramic shade of the gas lamp on Oliver's worktable.

'Careful, Agna!' shouts Edith. Agna moves to the divan and climbs up on it to watch the crusade. The three scrawny greyhounds cower in the corner by the door. Then another mouse appears, and another. Six, now seven mice, scuttling furiously across the wooden floor.

'Little buggers.' Edith releases her fury and brings the broom down in a series of unmerciful thumps.

The mice disappear into a gap in the skirting board.

'Now block the hole!' she yells at Archie. Archie drops his spade and dashes into the kitchen to the sink. He ducks underneath its ceramic front and grabs a rag from a small basket. Then he runs back into the sitting room and stuffs the rag into the gap where the skirting board has come away from the wall.

Archie swings back up and stands at the ready.

'And the one by the door. The hole by the door!' Edith shouts.

'That's now their only means of escape. It's blocked on the other side,' says Archie.

'Then thump the wall!'

Archie lifts his spade, whacks the wall. A crescent-shaped dent is left by the spade in the plaster.

'Sorry, Mother.'

A mouse darts furiously out of the hole, scutters across the floor towards the divan. Edith releases a deep, low groan at the sight of it. The quick movements of the animal always surprise her even though she prepares herself every time. Agna pulls her shawl over her head. The greyhounds fret and whistle in the corner, patting the floor nervously with tender paws. Edith slams the long-handled broom upon the floor several times before she hits her target. Another small skull caves in.

'Got it!' Edith says, amazed at herself.

'Poor mouse,' Archie says.

Edith lifts her broom, leans it against the stove, rolls up the sleeves of her blouse, clips back the strands of her hair that have come loose across her forehead, lifts the broom again and holds it mid-air. She's ready again. She nods at Archie. Archie slams his spade against the wall again, this time making Agna jump, and another mouse runs out of the hole, races across the floor to the window, disappears under the curtain which hangs to cover the pipes, reappears within seconds, confused, has nowhere to go, suddenly changing direction and running towards Agna who has jumped back down off the divan onto the floor and is moving in small circles with the hoe still in her hand.

'Agna!' Edith yells at her.

'Why do we have to kill them?' Archie says. 'Just let them be.'

Edith leans in and catches the mouse with the sharp edge of her spade. So accurate is her aim in fact that the head of the mouse snaps cleanly off. She and Archie grimace in amazement at the sight. A sparkle of blood splatters on the floor, framing a shiny slug of innards. The body of the mouse is a still furry purse, its head has rolled a yard away, firm and complete, as though it has never before been attached to anything, and now sits on the kitchen floor like a dropped walnut.

'Well, there you are,' Edith says, her mouth tugging down in disgust. She fixes her hair again, still holding the broom. 'While you!' – she shakes her broom at the greyhounds – 'You're just useless mutts, d'ye hear me!' The greyhounds shiver and apologise to her with doleful eyes.

Within no time at all, it seems, she has shovelled seven dead mice on to a length of brown paper and has left them on the doorstep for the foxes to feast on, though she knows the cats will get to play with them first.

Her efforts have revived her. She boils onions and potatoes for dinner – the last of the food that Oliver, daily, had brought home with him. Now it has swung the other way with Edith having to ration what is left.

Agna shifts her box garden along the floor from one side of the window to the other in order to catch the last of the evening light. The soil looks bare but nonetheless she strokes its surface, feels life from the few sleeping bulbs underneath her fingertips, blows her breath across their grainy roof to let them know she has not forgotten them. Then she hops up and drags her finger across the windowpane making pictures in the condensation which has formed from the steam off the bubbling water. A face with crossed eyes and straggly spiky hair squeaks into existence.

'Who's that?' Archie asks.

Agna smiles.

'That looks like you, Archie,' Edith offers, 'with a face on ye.'

Agna shakes her head for a 'no'.

'Who is it then?' asks Archie.

Agna leans over to Archie and whispers into his ear.

Archie laughs. 'Mrs Earwaker!'

'I'd say it's because Agna thinks you have a wee fancy for Mrs Earwaker,' Edith says.

Agna nods again and smiles.

'Awh, horrible!' Archie laughs. He crosses his eyes to match the face Agna has drawn on the windowpane and cups his hands on his chest. 'My darlin' Mrs Earwaker and your lovely bosom.' Agna laughs at Archie and affectionately ruffles his hair. She leans into Archie and whispers to him again.

Archie turns to her. 'You too, Agna,' he says affectionately.

Edith carries the pot of onions and potatoes over to the table. The greyhounds whine as they smell the food. Edith dismisses their begging with a brisk wave of her hand. The greyhounds are driving Edith mad. She has to try to find enough to feed them. They do nothing for their keep. They smell. They foul up the room with their waste. They follow her with imploring eyes that look as though they cannot believe the horrors they have been subjected to. Oliver had reassured her that he would only be minding the dogs for Divitt for a short time. The idea was to train them and race them like whippets, official racing, that was the latest in the racing world, the wins from which he'd get a cut, and that was a promise, not a bad thing to have a finger in a pie like that. But Edith is not convinced and could do without any thoughts of gambling being part of Oliver's plan. *Bloody dogs*, she thinks, *Oliver needs to get rid of these goddamn, bloody dogs*.

She sits with Archie and Agna at the table. As she eats the mash of potatoes and onions she decides that it's not too late. She will go to Edwin and she'll accept the position of housekeeper.

Nine

Edith begins working for Edwin within the week. She is nervous at first and feels peculiar that she should now be hired as her brother-in-law's housekeeper, but she is determined to get their lives back on track. Her schedule is manageable, considering the size of the house. She arrives at six o'clock to draw the blinds and curtains and open the shutters. She checks the boiler in the kitchen for water and puts the kettle on to boil. In the breakfast room she covers the carpet with a coarse cloth, lays out the black lead box for the cinders, the cinder-shifter and the fire irons, and after cleaning the grate she lights the fire. She strews damp, used tealeaves, rinsed the day before, over the carpet to collect the dust, then sweeps them up again. After that she serves breakfast.

Edwin is nothing more than courteous to her. He talks politely to her and addresses her as Mrs Fleck although she has no idea how to address him – what should it be? Your Honour? Judge Fleck? Edwin? So she mumbles 'sir', at first laughing a little through the word out of embarrassment.

When Edwin leaves for the Chambers in town she cleans the front hall, whitens the front steps, shakes out the mats and rugs then makes the beds and brushes and washes the floors. Lily and Sadie wash the breakfast dishes and sort out the laundry while Edith dusts the furniture and ornaments in the drawing room and polishes the silverware while listening out for any calls from tradesmen. Archie arrives to take the post and to run errands. Edith then attends to any ironing, prepares and leaves a light supper for Edwin on his return from work, empties and refills the bottles of drinking water in his bedroom and is then free to go home. It is Lily and Sadie's job to clear up the supper dishes later and rake out the kitchen fire to have it ready for the following day.

One morning during her first week working at Edwin's she overhears him talking to Lily about needing to hire a 'sleeper' – someone to sleep in his bed overnight for the purposes of detecting the presence of bedbugs – after having been informed that Sadie had found bites on her arms and legs. Edith, keen to keep her family in work, suggests Agna. Edith herself has done this kind of work in the past. The pest controller at the Gaiety Theatre in Belfast, a Mr Nummy, once got her a lucrative few nights' work testing the beds of the theatre's wealthy patrons, and Edith had taken the work gratefully. It was common enough for bedbugs to be a problem in the summer, but winter usually killed them off. Now, in those households that could afford cast-iron radiators and hot water heating, the rooms remained warm even during the coldest months. As a result bedbugs seemed to be thriving all year round. The 'sleeper' has to be bug-free and fresh to the house as the regular staff might already be carriers, so it stands to reason that Agna would be perfect for the job.

The following evening Edith walks Agna to Edwin's house. Agna is to make her own way back home in the morning. Edith is anxious for Agna and worries over the child's inability to communicate

– what will she do if she needs anything? How will she ask? – but she tries to reassure herself by thinking that at least Agna will have a night of comfort and warmth in the plush surroundings of Edwin's house.

If Agna rises in the morning with red welts on her skin after sleeping in whatever bed needs testing, Lily will be particularly satisfied. It will confirm her suspicions that these 'night riders' as she called them had been brought into the house through Sadie's carelessness. Edith knows that Sadie might well lose her job if Agna's skin shows evidence of bites, but what can she do about that. Perhaps Agna could take her place, she thinks on a practical level, and Sadie would surely find employment elsewhere. Regardless, Agna will earn three shillings for the betrayal.

As they walk together they feel the bitter cold of the night air slice through them. Agna wraps her shawl tighter around her head to shield her from the sleet, tucks her stiff, cold hands in under the folds, clenches her jaw against the January chill.

It is Lily who meets Agna at the side entrance of the house and tells her to go without delay to the small cloakroom opposite the kitchen. Edith says to Lily that she will wait for a while to make sure Agna is settled. In the cloakroom a bathrobe has been left out for Agna to wear. She hangs her own clothes on the hooks provided on the back of the cloakroom door and puts on the bathrobe. As a precaution her own clothes will not be brought into the main house. Lily then hands Agna a newly bought nightshirt and tells her to go upstairs to the bathroom and bathe before she puts it on. Towels have been left out for her and there is soap for her to wash with and, to Agna's delight, when she turns the tap lots of hot water spurts out.

'Rub that on you,' shouts Lily through the bathroom door. Agna looks around and sees a glass jar sitting beside the washstand containing a thick honey-coloured lotion. 'It attracts them – if they're there,' shouts Lily and leaves. With Lily gone Agna slips off the bathrobe and washes herself. Despite the fact that she has sweet smelling soaps, a plentiful supply of hot water and soft towels and flannels to indulge in, she is beginning to feel a little too exposed to enjoy the luxuries at her disposal. She stands stiffly in the bathroom of this strange house. It feels odd to be almost naked and not to be feeling cold. She takes in the warm comforting smell of the towel as she dries herself and then lifts the lid off the glass jar of lotion. It reeks of overripe apples. She applies the sickly sweet lotion to her skin and feels as sticky as goosegrass, then pulls the nightshirt over her head and down her body with some difficulty as the cotton now drags against her skin. She washes her hands and ties her hair back and up off her shoulders with a ribbon she has found in the pocket of the bathrobe. She opens the bathroom door only to discover Lily on the landing. Lily points to a door on the other side of the landing and disappears again.

Once inside the bedroom Agna looks around her. It is a large and oddly shaped room, tapering to a set of narrow French windows which, when she looks out through them, lead on to a small hexagonal balcony. A length of evergreen waves at her in the moonlight from the nearby tree. The curtains either side of the windows are made of heavy gold brocade and a giant tassel hanging from a tie rope encircles each one. She closes the curtains. A strong bounce of light from the electric lamp on the bedside table hits the patch of ceiling directly above it and spills eerily into the rest of the room. A large rug covers the floor. A dressing table and stool sit in a recess in the wall opposite the door. She stands in the middle of the room in the brand new nightshirt, feeling the soft rug underneath her bare feet. The air in the room smells of chrysanthemums and heat. A flinty, dusty smell, which catches in her throat, prickles her nostrils and makes her chest tighten as she breathes it in. As she looks around the room she senses the possibility that a number of personal items have been removed, as though Lily might suspect a thief in her. It has the feeling of a room in which someone has recently died rather than one in which someone has very recently slept. Having said this, everything about the room is so refined, she thinks. The wallpaper has a velvety embossed pattern on it and the fabric which is twisted in generous folds over the canopy of the four-poster bed has a lush, intricate design of peacocks, exotic fruits, crimson and orange flowers, fantastic curls of emerald green.

She walks over to the door and turns the key to lock it. She would like a life like this, living in a house that was comfortable and spacious and warm like this, with maids to clean and cook for her, with time on her hands to entertain and beautiful things to use.

She feels conscious of her diminutive frame in the large room. She moves to the bed. Immediately she notices a tapestry hanging on the wall to the right of the bed with the words 'My soul waiteth for the Lord more than they that watch for the morning' embroidered in peacock blue. It is just like the one that is hanging in their own flat, she thinks, the one embroidered in cardinal red and with the same neat stitching. A framed photograph of a woman rests on the table. Agna studies the photograph. The woman's features seem right and regular, not unlike her own. Her hair is parted in the middle as Agna's is and pinned back in a neat bun at the back of her head. Her skin is clear and pale, like Agna's. Who is she? Agna wonders.

She turns off the electric lamp, pulls back the eiderdown and slips in between the sheets. The softness of the mattress and the cool feel of the sheets are a shock to her. If she is to detect any evidence of bedbugs she knows the sheets will not have been changed. She detects a faint waft of tobacco coming off the sheets now that she is in their midst. Is this Edwin's bed? she wonders. She wriggles her body, tries to relax.

The night wind rattles the window frames, and an icy patter ripples against the panes. She lies in the bed in a state of intimate agitation. No matter how cold it is outside, she thinks, she will still be warm. She could walk around the room in her nightshirt through to the early hours of the morning and still not feel the chill of winter. A flush of guilt comes over her as she thinks of Archie and her mother back in the cold, damp flat. Where her father is she does not know. She thinks of the greyhounds huddled in some desperate weave, not wanting to move from their tableau lest they feel the piercing cold. She lies in luxury while they freeze. She feels tiny in the big bed. But, she reassures herself, she'll get paid in the morning and that's all that matters.

But she cannot sleep. She cannot even close her eyes. She turns on to her right side, shifts quickly on to her left. She wishes she had brought her shawl with her, not for warmth but for comfort, but even if she had she wouldn't have been allowed to bring it into the bedroom with her. Her body is now getting hot under the blankets. She throws back the eiderdown to cool herself a little. She feels another sudden rush of guilt with all this wasted heat. She turns on to her right side again and closes her eyes. The sleet and wind have eased outside and the room becomes heavy with silence.

She draws her knees up to her chest for comfort. Thinks she feels a bite on her thigh. Slaps it hard. Then pinches the skin. Smells the rise of sweet ripe apple, sighs, then turns again on to her left side, might only have imagined that she was bitten, pulls the eiderdown back over her.

She hears voices coming from downstairs. Both male. Hears footsteps on the stairs. A few moments later she hears a sound outside her door. She twists her body around, hears a click. Then, in the gloom, notices the handle of the door turning slowly. She sits upright in the bed, her breath catching in her chest. She remembers she had turned the key in the door so knows it is locked. The handle turns again. She climbs out of bed. Flat lines of flickering light spill under the door from the corridor. The sound of a heavy sigh on the other side. *Is that a sob she hears?* Agna's heart thuds in her chest. After a moment the lines of light break and dissolve. Then, a creak on the landing, and all is quiet. She tells herself not to be frightened. She breathes deeply. She imagines snow and summer rain, a midnight breeze teasing the alpines and the geraniums and the ferns of her portable garden.

From downstairs she can once again detect voices. She goes to the door, unlocks it, opens it, looks out, there is no one on the landing. But when she looks over the banister she sees Edwin and her father talking in the front hall. Her father wears the button fly collared shirt and bow tie he normally reserves for the stage. The shirt is grubby, the bow tie loose and shapeless. Over the shirt he wears his coat, shabby now and torn at the pockets. He holds his Borsalino in his hand. Why is her father here? Has he come to collect her? Was that him at her door just now?

Edwin stands opposite her father, dressed neatly in his housecoat. Her father is angry. She hears him asking Edwin why she, Agna, had been hired as a sleeper in the first place and what is she doing upstairs without his permission and the door locked. Edwin defends his position, saying that it was Edith who had given permission, in fact it had been Edith who had suggested it. Her father shakes his head.

'If you're not happy with the arrangement then in that case I'll get Lily to unlock the door and organise for a cab to take you both home,' Edwin says.

A silence between them.

Oliver moves in a half circle. He looks around him. He struggles to make a decision. He is half afraid that if he tells Agna to come home with him that she might shake her head firmly, find cause to reject him and worst of all in front of Edwin. 'Let her sleep,' he says finally. 'You've always done what you wanted to do, no matter how bad it made me feel, so why should you stop now.'

She watches as Edwin steps towards her father.

'Don't you think there's more to the story than your version of events?' Edwin breathes deeply.

Oliver's face creases in puzzlement.

'He didn't care about me either, Oliver, contrary to what you believe. He expected things of me, a kind of obedience which was suffocating, and I was as frightened of him as you were, terrified of him, hated him – he was a drunk – but even so I clung to him, did what he asked me to do, because mother had you, because mother always had you.'

Oliver looks at Edwin, his eyes wide. 'I know what you're doing. You're blaming me. That's what you're doing, what you've always done. But I couldn't do anything to save her, Edwin – for God's sake, what did you expect me to do?' Her father's energy rises, he shifts on his feet, his voice begins to shake. 'I would have done anything to save her.'

'You called her back.'

Her father stops moving, stands rooted to the spot. 'What?'

'You called her back.'

'What do you mean?' her father says, his face stark, questioning. 'I didn't call her back, she was already behind me on the bridge.

She was the last one to cross, in the wrong place at the wrong time. What! Would you have preferred that it had been me!'

'No, Oliver, that's not how it happened.'

Suddenly voices can be heard coming in from the side entrance of the house. It is Lily and Sadie, then the voice of a third party. Her mother? Lily opens the door of the kitchen and as loud as a fanfare shouts back behind her for Sadie to put the kettle on for God's sake and to see what bread there is for supper.

Agna looks back at her father and Edwin. They are face to face now, so close she can no longer hear them, Edwin talking heatedly in a low voice, her father's eyes incredulous, his face growing paler by the second. What has Edwin said to him?

Lily stops stock still in the hallway, surprised as she is by the two brothers, and apologises for disturbing them.

With that her father puts on his Borsalino and leaves the house.

That night she dreams she finds a boy hanged from the girder of a bridge by his mother's knotted stockings. In the dream the boy is already dead by the time she finds him but his eyes are open and he speaks to her in a gentle, relaxed manner. He had been watching the eels in the river below him as he was dying, he tells her, some of the biggest eels he had ever seen in his life, gathering in a swirling seething wreath below, creating a vortex for him to fall into and disappear, and he was waiting to drop, waiting for his mother's stockings to snap but they would not snap, they would not let him go. So Agna climbs up on to the steel girder of the bridge and gnaws at the stockings with her teeth until the stockings begin to fray, lowering the boy into the river. And the boy drowns after he's been hanged. When she wakes, Agna knows to pay attention to the dream, for that's what dreams are for, they tell us things we don't know we know, she says to herself, things which are right in front of our eyes that we don't even see.

Ten

He has arranged them in order of size. Every item is nailed to the wall. Firstly a row of buttons, then washers, then thimbles and razors. At the far corner near the window there are hinges, then spoons, forks, knives, then spectacles, spectacle cases, gavels, doorstops, serving spoons, umbrellas, hairbrushes, empty picture frames, candlesticks, lanterns, letter openers, candle snuffers, the stuffed ferret. Some have been badly broken in the hammering – a violin bow is in pieces – other items are dented.

The flat has taken on the dark and subterranean feeling of a dungeon, an industrial banquet of metal, wood and tin. There is a horrible strength in their numbers as though the pockmarked walls might collapse with this new weight upon it. Crumbled plaster lies on the floor, rims the edges of the room and covers the furniture, the rug, the bread and butter on the table.

Bizarrely the flat is now tidy – there is not one object lying on the floor, or spread across the armchairs or across any other surface. The only thing that sits on the floor is Agna's portable box garden, catching the fall of light by the window, the leaves of the succulents sprinkled in dust. But everything Oliver has stolen is now nailed to the wall like the leftover bread he had nailed to the tree as a boy in Eden's Cross. He stands back to take in the full view of the odd bazaar. Protect me, he sings it to himself, protect me from the unseen. Yes, there must be a song running in his head for he skips a little, then stops and delivers a timid bar or two to the air. His face has an increasing fall to it. He tries again, this time with more volume. His fist a faint punch in the air as he tries harder. A song about fruit and vegetables, his favourite and oh so sweet little carrot top, like her hair, like Agna's hair, his sweet pet, his daughter, so like his mother it makes him smile, brightens up his face, his favourite and oh so sweet little carrot top, talk to me. Please talk to me. A catch in his throat and his confidence falters. A strange plip-plip in his brain. No, perhaps not, perhaps that's not the song. He starts again but this time it starts with a sob, and he skips on the spot. Plip-plip in his brain again. He composes himself so that he can give what he can, what it takes. His new act will begin with a song and dance just like they all said it should, that's what the audience want, it's all they want, none of yer hoity-toity arty stuff now. Just give us an aul song and dance like a good man. But the sob won't go away, it's growing in his throat and it's getting louder, getting louder than the song itself, and that strange plip-plip in his brain again, coming out through the words and his skin and the music in his head. The words of his song getting louder, I didn't call her back, she was behind me on the bridge.

White rain falls in sheets through the unnatural dark. The city is etched in sleet. Brick and slate harden the northern wind as it howls. The iced air blows in bitter gusts and freezes the last wan ripples of winter light, and the earth has turned its shoulder to the sun. January, a month too bleak for most.

He walks through the streets of the city. He does not know where he is going, yet he keeps moving. He shoves his frozen hands into the pockets of his overcoat. He bends his head against the fitful wind, tugging down the rim of his Borsalino to shield his face. His ears are burning with the cold. His breath splinters through stiffened lips. He carries on walking, along the main street, turns left at the crossroads by the Post Office on Royal Avenue. All that is left is for him to yield to the weave of narrow streets, wherever they lead. Belfast, this city that had opened up the possibilities in him as a boy, through which he now walks, exhausted, will witness his closure.

Oliver digs his hands deeper into his pockets. He can sense a thin curl of warmth begin to circle his palms (or does he just imagine this?) but his fingertips are frozen. He moves his fingers painfully, eking out a corner of heat, tipping vaguely off the summons still in his left pocket, Agna's cotton handkerchief and the stub of a cigarette in his right. He remembers the change he had received from the racing bet he placed the day before and lost, one shilling and sixpence, the last of whatever money he has, and fumbles for it. He finds the shilling in his right pocket but there is no sign of the sixpence. He checks the inside pocket of his overcoat. Empty. Flicks a cold hand into the front pocket of his trousers. A tongue of icy wind licks at his thigh. Then frisks the lower outer panel of the overcoat to see if he can sense it. There it is. Feels neither relief that he has found it nor panic that he may not be able to retrieve it, he just corners it: he needs to eat.

Oliver does not know where he is going because he has nowhere to go.

He did at one time in his life. Call it purpose, a sense of direction, belief in himself. But not any more. His efforts have brought him to nothing, bar a threshold. But this time the threshold he finds himself on is as sharp and as clear as the crystal winter rain that falls around him, and like no other he has stood upon before. It is both ominous and oddly full of charm. For unlike other thresholds in his life, which bridged two possibilities, this one offers only one: he knows he can't go back.

He closes his eyes and stands in the bitter cold. He is so tired. He sways a little on his feet. Hugs his shivering frame. Tries to curl his numbed toes in his shoes, but he can't. He is a glacier a thousand feet thick and his bones are cracking under the weight of his frozen soul. The pictures of his life are now locked deep within him. The faces of those he loves most, lost in the cool lank light of an ancient ice.

No. Can't go back to Edith. Can't go back to his children. Now they are all distant frosted spirits, abandoned by him. Edith and the children disappointed in him, at home in their squalid flat a mile away from where he stands. Could just as easily be a thousand arctic miles away.

And he can no longer think of his mother the way he used to. Edwin had put him straight on that. Had told him the true version of events. Told him what had really happened that day on the bridge. His mother was not behind him as he seemed to remember, she had already cleared the bridge, was already on her way down the steps on the other side to Edwin and his father when his kite got caught and he called her back. She went back to him to free the kite and just before the bridge collapsed she pushed him out of harm's way. She saved him and then she fell. He called her back, otherwise she would not have died.

The sleet hardens to hail, pits the street, needles his skin. The night sky balks at what it has let fall. Time freezes and holds him where he stands.

The sudden inertia is torture but he cannot move. He stands, sensing that his stillness will kill him. Welcoming it. Then a small thought cracks. *So this is where it ends.* He'll be found, not in a heroic rescue on an ice-capped mountain, but here on a drab city street. An oddity in the winter squall. Discovered by a body of stern pathologists who'll carry him away and lay his stiff corpse on the mortuary slab and begin to hack and chisel at it to find out the whys and wherefores of his life and death. Hammering at his bones and organs, which are all as solid as rock, they'll nonetheless see how easily he falls apart, a pliable obeisance in the end which is unbecoming to a man, any man. They'll chip away, find cavity after cavity where, he had thought, there had been substance, efficacy, meaning. But the pathologists will prove, with the dissection of him piece by piece, that he has amounted to nothing. It will be plain for all to see. They'll say this man was built of nothing and came to nothing: look at his marrow, his sinews, his blood's film; all form-less. How fitting that he's disappearing before our very eyes. They'll mock his life's efforts to stay afloat, his desires to provide for his family, to love and care for them, yes to love them. Oh so sweet, little carrot top. But they'll overlook his acts of tenderness and kindness, his generosity, his willingness to laugh at himself – *those aspects of himself were there too, weren't they?* They'll overlook how sad he has become. You see, those attributes are not showmanship material.

And when his life is scattered on the slab they'll see no point in reconstruction. They'll let him melt into a piss-coloured pool of water and drip over the edge of the slab where he'll be caught by the shallow metal canister resting on the grubby tiles of the mor-tuary floor. A burden to himself and to his family, that's all he is. A defeated, self-deluded quack whose only function in life was to feed untruth. A freak. A fool. Thirty years as an illusionist working the music hall circuits. Finally exhausting himself by mediocrity and by the anxious churnings of his life because the pursuit of greatness was too delicious to relinquish. Strange, they'll say, that someone who tried so hard should find himself, at what should have been the height of his career, past trying.

Suddenly his Borsalino is whisked off his head as though lifted by a rifle shot, and it's gone. He barely feels the cold rain on his skull. He slowly opens his eyes. Feels his lashes tug with the drops of pearled rain that have frozen on them. How long has he been standing here? he wonders. Or was he not still walking? He was sure he was still walking. Now it hurts to breathe. He turns his head stiffly to look around him, a stabbing pain slices across his forehead. Where exactly is he now? How far from the main street? He looks up at the building in front of him, at its large arched doorway, its tight red bricks. On the façade above the doorway, he reads with difficulty the words HAMMAM TURKISH BATHS painted in large white letters. The lights are on inside. A warm glow through the mottled glass. The seduction of heat. Hot towels, steam, the sense of perspiration on his skin, unthinkable now. He unfurls his stiff, aching fingers to find the shilling and sixpence in his hand. He could get something to eat. A glass of ale perhaps. Could make his way to The Crown Bar from here. But instead he swallows the ice-cold breath in his throat, scores a frozen knuckle against the hardened stubble on his chin, slowly climbs the steps of the Turkish Baths and goes inside.

The heat hits him like a tram.

The cost of a bath and the use of the rooms for a first class patron is one shilling and sixpence and is stipulated on the sign hanging at the reception desk. Unless he wants to step outside and come back in through the second class entrance on Donegall Lane that's what he will have to pay. Fitting, is it not, the exact amount he has in his hand, leaving no change with which to buy food or drink. But even in his sorry state, Oliver experiences just a ripple enough of pride to prevent him leaving the baths. In any case, now that he feels the heat it has become the drug he needs.

But with the heat comes shame. Inside the cubicle Oliver peels his clothes off weakly, aware of their shabbiness, a feeble tang rising from his flesh as he undresses, his fingers so numb from the cold they are barely able to function. As he places his shoes in the metal basket given to him by the attendant, he notes how scuffed they are, the laces knotted in several places, each heel worn to a slant. Next his socks, threadbare and loose. Unbuttoning his trousers he feels the copper buttons, wrong-sized and stiff. He slips his trousers off and folds them loosely, placing them on top of his shoes. Next he removes his waistcoat, Edith's mending stitches like tiny green stalks bent by the wind over its flint grey lining. Next his shirt and collar – he can feel the line of grime on the collar with his fingertips – and lastly his vest and underpants, old friends. Oliver tucks the offending collar in underneath his underpants to hide it. He misses his Borsalino. The hat is probably by now trampled under hoof, foot or wheel. He could have placed it on top of his miserable pile of clothes, given the pile some dignity, could have hidden his collar and his pants underneath it, could have hidden them *in* it. Stepping out of the cubicle, the warm towel which the attendant has also given him tightly wrapped around his middle, Oliver walks to the attendant's desk and hands over his clothes as though they are the soiled exhibits of a forensic investigation. As the attendant reaches to take the metal basket from Oliver the underpants shift and the collar pops out from underneath them. He doesn't want the attendant to see the dirty pebble-grey tidemark along the inside of his shirt collar but he catches the attendant registering it. The two men stand silently. Then, the slight whiff of manure. Both Oliver and the attendant look at the metal basket, following the smell. One shoe is turned sideways against the mesh, a small thatch of horseshit muscled in at the heel of the shoe. A hiatus, and then the attendant carries on about his duties as though nothing has been seen or smelt. He hangs the basket at the end of the rail furthest from his desk, and then hands Oliver a token on which the number of the basket is engraved. Oliver takes the token in his hand and looks at the hole that has been pierced just north of its centre, through which a lace is threaded. Then as though he has won a medal for depravity, he hangs the token around his neck.

'Thank you,' Oliver says to the attendant, and feels an uncomfortable heat rise up to his neck where it swells at his throat and he coughs. Amazing, Oliver thinks, that, depressed as he is, he still feels shame.

Now flushed full in the hot room of the hammam, Oliver feels his body expand. It hurts in a delicious kind of way. He wants it, he needs it, but the tug and judder of the heat at his tense cold muscles is almost more than he can bear. He sighs as he burns. His thighs stick to the marble top of the bench. His arms and legs feel heavy. The heat is returning him to himself, but as he warms, Oliver senses that something is missing. Something that was part of him before the temperature of his body soared is now gone. He sits motionless, staring intently into the steam that surrounds him wondering what it is, as though if he looks hard enough he'll see it in the twisting vapours. What could it be? A memory of some kind, childhood or adolescent? A preoccupation, ancient or recent? Then he realises what it is: he can no longer see what his despair looks like. That constant companion of his. Despite how full of heat his body feels, his mind remains, in that regard, an empty cave. There is nothing in there except a damp rust lining his skull, a peppery saffron decay.

But there had always been a picture. There had always been some image of his despair to cling to. Every time Oliver had sunk into the depths his imagination had conjured some representation. Even outside in the freezing cold his despair had been visible to him. The old reliables: the obvious sinking ship, the ancient ruin, the abandoned house unhinged and haunted, the flooded forest or the rabid black dog, the syphilitic whore, mad, with rank flesh that withers and falls from her bones, the derailed train, its upended carriages filling slowly with the freezing green waters of the tarn, the dying soldier disappearing into the greedy earth, a swallow of winter fruits in the sucking mud. Once even the crumbling crust of a steak and kidney pie. Remember that. He has been all of these things. Always something tangible. Something he could see clearly in his mind's eye. Could watch, describe, could name. Now, for the first time in his life, Oliver's despair is faceless.

Why can he not imagine his despair as he was once able to? If only it would take some form inside his head, if only his despair would settle into an idea, be any one of those previous incarnations. Oliver thinks about this absence without emotion. The realisation sinks slowly within him like a rock falling through the sea to the ocean bed but never landing. At least there is the rock, he thinks. At least he can see that. Can watch it swivel in the blue currents as it falls, moss-green-hued, a ridge of tiny molluscs across its back, a seaside rock, nothing huge, a small rock. He looks down at his bare feet. His toenails need clipping, the big toe on his right foot displaying an especially twisted horny plate.

Sounds of the slap and pummel of naked flesh can be heard echoing from the high ceilinged rooms beyond. The functions of men: clay, steam, sweat. From the douche, the sulphur and the pine baths, the business of men: deals, propositions, lies. Voices rolling out in low serious rumbles despite the sign hanging by the attendant's desk asking patrons to be quiet when using the facilities, and to refrain from any earnest conversation.

Tucked into a small alcove in the 260 degree heat, which he is feeling so deeply in his body he might cry, Oliver thinks of the attendant. Oliver senses a punisher in the attendant. Yet the attendant had been nothing but courteous to Oliver. Focused when he spoke to him and with a gentle delivery. A feminine curve to his cheekbones, but a manly jaw. And skin sleek and shaven. And not unlike Eurielle, his angel. Where has she gone? Oliver had felt the attendant's scrutiny but at the same time had been impressed by his practical deference. This man is not a fraud, thinks Oliver. This man knows his place, can fulfil the promises he makes to himself, understands the mathematics of his life, his strengths, his limitations. He is not a disappointment to himself. Oliver breathes in the smell of juniper and peppermint as he sits, his flesh ruddy as though whipped by an impatient wind. That man could follow you around a room and you'd never know it, thinks Oliver, he has footfalls of vapour. That man could be an assassin with his measured manners, his imposing frame, his pristine beauty. Should have emptied my pockets, thinks Oliver, he'll go through my pockets. And find nothing of any interest. Damn.

Oliver sits alone in the hot room. Now that he has thawed he is a bundle of low-grade tics. The cold had kept them dormant. They reappear with alarming swiftness. Twitches and jerks. The cough, of course, but also the spasm in his gut, the splinter of chest pain which forces him to twist his torso to relieve it, the ache in his lower back, the ache in his upper back, the leg cramps, the need to stretch his jaw, the yawn. He tries to ignore them.

And now the drip inside his head. Plip-plip-plip. He tries to ignore that too.

For whatever reason, he remembers the last time he saw Sydney

Brown. Sydney had appeared nervous, had tightened his fat wormy lips, rubbed his large hand over his chest, looked at the papers scattered on his desk as though they needed urgent attention, couldn't even look Oliver in the eye. Then he'd lifted his head and said, 'We all fall out of favour some time or other, Oliver, yours has been a long time coming.' No, wait, has he just imagined this? The last time he saw Sydney Brown, is that what he said to him? Surely not.

His thoughts twist in fast bouts. He feels a grunting emptiness in his stomach.

Plip-plip. Yes, can't deny that he can hear that drip in his head. The constant drip which accompanies him now, a liquid metronome. Plip-plip-plip. The debt they are in. Plip-plip-plip. The rent arrears. Plip-plip. The filthy flat. Plip. The lack of food. Plip. His failing career. Plip. His failed career.

His limbs are growing heavier by the moment. A thin line tightens across his eye sockets, pinching them. He thinks of Edith, how he loves her, how he feels she despises him. He thinks of Agna, how his heart is broken; both his children lost to him. Trusted friends, or so he thought, deserting him. He feels as though he is staring at the back of his life. The excavation of his losses, the futility of his efforts, the constant self-mockery (he doesn't need the pathologists). The steam around him has more substance than he does, thinks Oliver. Oliver folds his arms limply across his chest. Even now with him in it the room feels empty. He could be living or dead, it wouldn't matter. And that can only mean one thing, that *he* is now the image of his own despair. *He* is what his despair looks like.

The ventilation flue, housed within the marble-topped wooden bench on which Oliver sits, complains with a rattle behind his calves, then hisses. The overhead light flickers for a moment then settles back to its steady satin glow. Oliver gazes into the air in front of him.

The door of the hot room opens and two men enter, moving to the opposite end of the room. They shuffle through the steam and sprawl across the benches like sated buffalo at a waterhole. Towels casual around their midriffs, tokens hanging around their necks. One of the men, broad shouldered yet lean, releases a salacious grunt as he rubs his genitals. Pops his breath through loose lips. The sound a little too intimate. The other man, stouter than the first, belches: a brief watery pocket and, eventually, the smell of soup. Oliver rests his back against the glazed brickwork of the alcove, able to catch the outline of the two men when he turns his head towards them yet out of their view. He feels invisible anyway, nothing but his ruminations leaking through his pores and evaporating. Blending with the silent deprecations of these men into one thick blanket of steamy testosterone and regret. The heat is getting more intense. Now too hot for Oliver. But he stays. He does not move. The weight of his bones anchoring him to the bench. A slimy glisten of condensation covering the walls. Oliver tips his head back and looks at the ceiling. A mosaic sky of Byzantine blue and citron. Droplets of water fall from the ceiling and plop on to the tiled floor like pebbles at Oliver's feet. An echo of the drip inside his head.

The two men, ignorant of Oliver's presence in the room, strike up a conversation, or continue an earlier one, the heat ferrying their syllables across to Oliver. Not that he wants to hear them. He wants them to be silent. He has no interest in their innocuous ramblings. He wants to hide in his own quiet shadow.

One of the men has an accent, which Oliver finds difficult to place: an American nasal sound definitely and yet there is a flat almost Germanic delivery to his speech. The other man has a London accent.

They talk in a slow rambling way at first, a few words here and there, as though their language has been cauterised by the choking heat. But Oliver can make out enough to know that what they are saying does not interest him – the fire at Hoddard's Emporium the night before, a dip in trade at the Mercury, the scuffle between the police and suffragettes outside the Town Hall. Oliver finds himself drifting in and out of attention.

Edith, he thinks, will be past caring where he is or if indeed he'll return. Before he left the flat her face had tightened into that familiar cold mask, the one he saw so often now, a hardness across her brow, her lips pressed thin, her eyes sharply focused on everything but him. She listens to his promises now with faint interest, as though she is trying to catch the low vibration of a distant train, not even wondering where it is headed, knowing that another promise would trundle along the same line, follow the same old trajectory, any time soon. But he had meant what he said, and every time he had promised her he had meant it: that things would be different. He misses the feel of her palm against his cheek, given willingly, her tender cupping of his jaw, cradling his indecisions, his doubts and his woes, her ability to banish those in one swift caress. He misses the feel of her body, the skittish amorous strokes along her skin, her arms wrapped firmly around his head and neck, smothering him in the milky scent of her affection. *Oh, Madame Defarge!* He misses her belief in him.

Archie too, he's lost the knack with Archie, can't talk to him as he used to, or laugh, and the boy has become quiet around him. And as for Agna, well that is a sorrow too deep to contemplate.

What went wrong with it all?

Suddenly the name Henry Lockley pierces the hot air of the room, moves like an arrow towards Oliver, is as sharp and as clear as a morning lark. And pricks him, wakes him from his steamy sleep.

Henry Lockley – yes, the name again, the two men are talking about Lockley, Oliver had heard correctly. Oliver's heart misses a beat. The Lockley who Max Stapleton had talked about so favourably when Oliver had met him in London. The Lockley who Stapleton wanted to collaborate with instead of Oliver. Now hailed as one of the greatest illusionists of the day.

The two gentlemen in the hot room have dropped their voices. Oliver strains to hear. The man with the London accent says that he attended the preview of Lockley's new illusion just the other evening. Not a public event, no press attending, really only a rehearsal, but well-staged at St George's Hall, the details of which are not to be disclosed at any price, you understand, sworn to secrecy, of course. Oliver holds his breath. It had been phenomenal, the man continues, like nothing he had ever encountered in the business, gruesome, horrifying and spectacular, and Lockley himself had announced at the end of the evening that the illusion 'will make the whole world spin'.

The American-sounding man coaxes his partner to divulge more of what he knows, tells him he can be trusted, that of course he will not tell a soul before it is shown officially to the public, and at any rate the papers will know about it soon enough. That's true, the Londoner replies, he pops his breath again, and indeed Lockley will be performing the illusion to the public shortly and people will be talking about it anyway. Without hesitation the Londoner continues, he cannot figure out exactly how Lockley did it but visualise this: a body in a box, two secret panels I'm reckoning, the body contorts to pull the legs up to the chest in the top half of the box, false boots at the other end – that's what I figured anyhow – then cutting through the box with a huge double-handed cross-cut saw, cutting the body in two, simple and beautiful, showing the audience the two halves of a body still alive, the boots wiggling, it's grotesque, the audience are aghast. Could there have been a second person in the box, hidden there already? the American offered. Now, I never thought of that, replied the Londoner, of course that could well be the case, never thought of that.

Tucked in behind the arched alcove of the hot room, and hardly daring to breathe lest he miss a detail, Oliver listens and relishes the sound of his resurrection.

Amazing, sighs the American. Lockley, you must admit, is a cut above the rest, if you'll pardon the pun, the Londoner quips. The illusion will be shown to the world at Finsbury Park in four days. It will be an absolute sensation and Lockley will be celebrated throughout the world. The two men settle. Muse on their exchange. Feel their vowels and consonants protected by the cloistered air. But Oliver has breathed them all in. Has felt them resonate within his skull and dissolve its rusted lining like acid. The straight plumb line of the idea, as smooth and as fine as a glass thread, falls from Oliver's head down into his gut. And when it pierces he knows just how brilliant the idea is. It is the exactitude of its landing point. A solid single clear arrival. He latches on to it, and knows he won't be letting go. Now *he*, Oliver, owns the epiphany, feels the thin needle at his exact centre.

How much time do I have? Oliver asks himself. How much time to devise his own version of the illusion and gather the materials he needs? Lockley is to reveal all in four days so if that's the case Oliver must perform tomorrow, the night after at the very latest, to make sure that he is the first to make the world spin.

What he needs to do is cool himself down, then quickly collect his clothes from the attendant. Now the attendant will recognise the maverick in him and instantly cast away all previous judgement. And Oliver will hand him the token, no longer a symbol of his paucity but a simple transaction among men who stand solidly in the world. Oliver will get dressed in the cubicle, slipping back into the smell of himself. Too late for any image of despair to come to him now, too late. What did he care for that now? Now everything is different.

He will leave the Turkish baths, head to the salvage yard in Smithfield, secure the materials he needs to build the apparatus, some sort of bargain with the tradesmen to be worked out. Or use what he already has. His mind lifts in a series of shifting sections like an expanding giant telescope, and everything around him begins to take on clarity. His mood becomes light, he feels unhampered by all the things that had been pulling him down. Genius, he says to himself, fucking genius. He will work it through, every detail, and get it right, get everything shipshape. The more beautiful the assistant the better. Yes, the more beautiful the woman he cuts in half the more heat in the act. They'll all be jumping to book him. Then he'll secure a solid solo circuit of Britain and, before long, America. They would finally see him as the brilliant illusionist he really is.

The two men sit quietly for a moment. Then, a long, low grunt from one as he stands. The other man stretches and, rearranging the towel around his midriff, stands too. They say nothing. The waiting is tortuous for Oliver. Eventually, they pad slowly across the hot tiles, as though the heat has aged them, and leave. Oliver counts to ten, then follows.

He walks naked to the plunge pool, his shoulders soft, his head erect. He climbs down the thin metal ladder harnessed on one side of the pool, immerses himself slowly in the water until he is completely submerged. There is not a jot of visible reaction to the iciness in his body. He opens his eyes under the water, a slice of intense pain from temple to temple, and he looks through the wet glacial fog, a freezing subterranean world which thrills him and makes him feel very much alive.

After so much deadness. After so much despair. Now this! The grace notes of a great plan. A happiness even. In the eyes of his wife – *Edith* – in the eyes of his children – *Archie, Agna, oh Agna!* – he will be somebody again.

Eleven

Sitting in the back snug of the Crown Bar, Oliver finds it difficult to hold his pencil steady. His hands, though warmer, feel twice their size. Oliver tries to draw a straight line across the sheet of brown paper that the barman has given him. Then another. He messes it up. The angles are wrong, the dimensions out of proportion with one another. He scrawls over it and starts again. He's trying to work in all the variables of the design, trying to recall everything he overheard from the two men in the Turkish baths. He wants to get it all down on paper as fast as the carnival of detail is happening inside his head. He takes another swig of whiskey. Starts again. The length of the box about so. Now, where exactly do the panels drop in? Where best to attach the hinges so that the box opens back smoothly into two halves? Or maybe he should plan it so that the box can be wrenched apart into two completely separate sections; a ghastly space in the middle for the audience to stare into and be amazed. Next, a concealed handle to make the boots move as though there are feet in them. What about the idea of a trick blade? No, it has to be real. Oliver takes another drink. A groove for the blade to slide into, narrow enough to enhance the sound of sawing, the rasp and tear of it. No, the blade has to be real. *Did I think of that already?* Another sup of whiskey. He can scatter sawdust discreetly from his pocket to make it look authentic. Or his assistant (who on earth will he get as his assistant this time?) could scatter some from inside the box. No, the assistant's hands need to be tied. This illusion needs to defy belief in every way. Oliver is fired up. This is simple, so beautifully simple. He'll have to look the part, exotic even. He'll reinvent himself. Not a turban, Christ no. Not a cape, too old school for him. Something new, something dynamic, something sharp, something modern. He drains his glass, spilling a drop of whiskey on to the page, wets the dimensions of the box's width, blurs them. Oliver rubs the spot, tears the paper. Bugger. Doesn't matter. He snatches the sheet of brown paper, folds it and pushes it into his pocket. Breathes hard. He wants another whiskey. Knows McCauley won't rise to adding a fourth whiskey to the tab, the bastard. Oliver runs his palm across the top of his head. As he stands, the whiskey hits him: an empty stomach, the rekindling of his desires, salvation just within his reach; a heady mix which underscores nicely the obsession racing at speed inside his head. His dirty secret. His furious design. His glorious reawakening.

Within twenty minutes Oliver is at the stage door of the Empire Theatre. He announces himself to the doorman who sits on the other side of a hatch. The doorman takes down a list of names pinned to the wall above his head and scans it. The man is shaking his head.

'I'm not on any bloody list!' Oliver is infuriated. 'I'm here to speak to Sydney Brown.'

The doorman looks blankly at Oliver. Oliver leans in a little unsteadily to the hatch, juts his chin forward, glares at the man. 'Sydney Brown. He's in his office?' Oliver takes the piece of brown paper on which he has drawn his plans out of his coat pocket and holds it in his hands, ready to deliver his great plan.

'And who are you?' The man talks slowly, looks at Oliver with suspicion.

The question creates an unpleasant swell in Oliver's stomach. The swell spreads up into his chest and down through his arms and legs, then a cramp in his bowel, a tightness at the back of his head. Oliver's response bottlenecks in his throat. He coughs, twists his torso to relieve the spasm which clinches, draws his lips back. He has always been known in this theatre. Who does this little bugger think he is, seethes Oliver. But before he speaks, Eurielle arrives by his side.

'What are you doing here?' Eurielle is about to put on her gloves. Her false eyelashes are like black butterfly wings drying on an evening breeze, dew at their tips. Then they float up majestically to reveal almond-shaped eyes of a pale woad blue, the slight hint of a turn in one eye. A faint down of hair graces her upper lip.

Oliver cannot believe she is right there in front of him again, as though she has miraculously appeared out of nowhere. He feels his tightened chest relax.

'I need to talk to Sydney.'

'He's gone, Oliver. Had a meeting with some American memory man at The Grand Central. You off somewhere? You look terrible.'

Shouts and applause can be heard from the auditorium. In response to the sound Oliver shifts from one foot to the other, is instantly restless, but says nothing. Eurielle notices his agitation.

'I need a drink,' says Oliver.

'Yes,' says Eurielle casually.

'Are you all right, sir?' the doorman asks Oliver.

'A drink of water.'

'Excuse me, sir?'

'You'll catch Sydney in the morning. He'll be in his office first thing. Come on . . .' Eurielle says softly, and smiles. 'Come on back up with me. I'll sort you out.'

'How was tonight?' asks Oliver.

'Oh, don't talk to me. Couldn't even remotely warm them up. So unlike me.'

Oliver's thoughts derail for a second – he has never seen Eurielle perform her act in all the years he has known her, never once. How bizarre, he thinks.

'I said, sir, are you all right? Can I get you a glass of water perhaps?' The doorman comes out from behind the hatch towards Oliver but is distracted by the delivery of a huge bouquet of flowers. He takes the flowers and when he turns around Oliver is gone.

Upstairs in dressing room number four – a dressing room which Oliver himself has used many times – Oliver finds gin and drinks it, a present to Eurielle from an admirer, apparently. Oliver sprawls on a small divan, on which has been thrown Eurielle's fur coat – yet another present. Eurielle lies in the makeshift bed. She is smoking. The dressing room looks like the inside of a wardrobe, with dresses on hangers clipped to hooks on the walls, scarves and wraps draped over every surface, shoes and belts strewn on the floor, hats cupping the edges of the dressing table and the corner stands of the bed, and underwear bunched on the chairs.

Oliver has taken his shoes and socks off and is examining his feet. 'Do you have scissors?' The gin has given Oliver a keen twist to his agitation now, on top of the whiskey. He wants to attend to incidentals: cut his blasted toenails, pull out the nasal hairs that have been bothering him – he can see one right now if he closes his left eye and looks at the edge of his nose with the right, it catches the light when he turns towards the beaded fringed lamp on Eurielle's dressing table, driving him mad, look at the length of it, he thinks, and each time he tries to pinch it between his fingertips and tag at it, the hair escapes him, his fingers slide right off it; now he can't find it, then he sees it again, rudely straight as though it has still a long way to grow – and his lips are irking him, constant tiny shaves of dry skin at the corners of his mouth, he has to get rid of those too.

'Oh, somewhere.' Eurielle stubs out her cigarette and reaches for another. Oliver jumps up from the chair, makes a feeble effort to direct his energies into looking for the scissors, waves a hand at the dressing table, jerks his body where he stands to hastily track the room with his eyes. Shakes his head, raises his eyebrows, frowns, bares his teeth.

'Jesus, Oliver, what kind of conversation is going on inside your head?'

'What time did Sydney meet up with that ... meet up at the Central?'

'Sydney won't be calling here, if that's what you're thinking. He knows what a bore I think he is. Anyway, he's more pressing things on his mind. Sit down, Oliver, there's time.'

Oliver dips his hand in his pocket. The brown paper plan rustles at his touch.

'Why not try to get some sleep,' says Eurielle, bringing a lighted match to her cigarette.

'Can you contort?' Oliver swings around to her.

Eurielle relaxes back on the pillows propped up against the wall. 'Yes,' she replies slowly.

'No, I mean contort inside a box, make yourself half the size—'

'I'm tired, Oliver, I've had two nightmare performances in a row,' Eurielle says flatly, blowing smoke out through her nose, then a thin rill of it wafts from her mouth. 'And no, I couldn't make myself half the size inside a box.'

He stops suddenly and stares at her. 'What size boots do you wear?' Without waiting for Eurielle to answer him, Oliver grabs at the various clothes on the floor, finds a pair of her boots – he supposes they're Eurielle's boots – holds them up to judge their size.

'I'll need two pairs exactly the same.'

'Well, you're out of luck.' Eurielle stubs out her cigarette carefully. 'Sleep, Oliver, why don't you sleep,' she mumbles. Then after a pause, 'Why don't you sleep with me?'

'Two pairs exactly the same,' he repeats. 'With the same markings on the soles.' Oliver stares at the boots in his hands, the light from the lamp on Eurielle's dressing table illuminating his face. Oliver stops, something catches his attention, the hair in his nose.

'And scissors – I need scissors.'

Eurielle lies back on the makeshift bed and is soon a heap of quilts. She snores lightly. Oliver watches her from where he sits on the divan. He has not slept. Perhaps a doze here and there, nothing longer than a few minutes, he suspects. He stretches his jaw. Twists his upper torso in the chair in order to ease out the tightening in his chest. Thinks he hears a distant sound inside his head, a soft plip-plip. He pulls Eurielle's fur coat and her dressing gown, which has been resting on his knees, up across his middle. The dressing gown smells of cloves and cigarette smoke. He cannot still his mind.

After the war, he thinks, everything changed. Audiences became so hostile, so eager for sensationalism, a bloodthirsty new generation. Well let them have it, if they want it. Let them have it.

His eyes dart quickly back to Eurielle. He coughs. Feels his leg begin to cramp. Stretches it. Coughs again. He licks his dry lips. A stab of pain across his forehead corrals Oliver's thoughts momentarily then, as it fades, they loosen again. He drinks more gin. It smooths the edges of his agitation and allows him a reprieve.

Edith had stayed at Edwin's that evening, long enough for her to feel that Agna had fallen asleep upstairs. Both Lily and Sadie had been out visiting friends but when they returned at ten o'clock Edith said goodnight to them and headed for home. While waiting in the scullery she had heard Oliver arrive, his tone agitated, and had become aware of an intense conversation between himself and Edwin in the front hall. She had attempted to eavesdrop through the scullery door but had been unable to make out what they were saying. After hearing the front door close she had left by the side entrance but had not found Oliver.

She now opens the door of their flat hoping to find Oliver there. A slant of light spills from the outside landing into the room. She looks confused at the pockmarked walls, the crumbled plaster on the floor. Archie is asleep on the divan, a claw hammer beside him. There are boxes on the floor full to the brim with objects. She can't even begin to work out what has happened. Two of the greyhounds are lying with Archie. One dog's head rests on Archie's hip, the other dog has tucked his head in under Archie's chin. Oliver is not there. Exhausted as she is she can't bring herself to waken Archie – whatever has happened, she'll find out in the morning.

She stands and looks around the dismal room. Working in the refined surroundings of Edwin's house makes the shabbiness of their own flat almost more than she can bear. Their home. A sinking ship when all is said and done. It's not just the pockmarked walls – from whatever has happened this evening – the metal latch on the stove door no longer works, the broom head is broken from the slaughter of mice, there are fresh mice droppings on the kitchen table, the windowpane is patched with a wooden slat, there's little food in the pantry and the flat is full of droopy hunched greyhounds.

Everything about them is falling apart.

She looks at the one greyhound who distrusts the unguarded nature of sleep and crouches shivering and petrified in the corner of the kitchen, a nervous wretch of a thing. Edith looks at the dog's eyes and is instantly irritated by their absolute neediness, but then she extends her hand to touch the animal's head. The dog does not shrink back but suffers her touch gladly, presses his skull against her palm to greet it. Poor mutt, thinks Edith. She lets the dog lick her fingers then quietly bids it to lie down. The dog obeys, settles forlornly, shakes from the cold, looks up at her. She takes the old sheet, which is rolled up to stop the draught coming in from under the door, shakes it and places it over the dog.

'Good boy,' she says gently.

She is tired, so very tired.

There'll be another three shillings tomorrow from Agna, and her own wages by the end of the week, and Archie is earning a little from the shipyard, on and off, as well as running the occasional errand for Edwin. But they won't be able to pay for the damage done to the walls. She can't bear to think about it.

She leaves both Archie and the dogs and goes into her bedroom. She unlaces her boots and slips them off but climbs into the bed in her clothes. The bed is as hard as it is cold. She buries her face under the blankets to catch a little of her own warmth. She rolls on to her back and stares at the expanse of dark ceiling. Her thoughts begin to gather pace. Is Oliver on his way home? If not then where is he? That morning as she left he had muttered about some business he had to attend to but she had not been able to make out what he had said and had been too tired, too dispirited, to ask him to repeat himself. But the look in his eyes as she glanced at him was distant and sad, resigned to some loss of self. He had turned his head away from her as though she was something he had been doomed to accept. There was no trace of wanting, of desire, of fellowship even. What had them so changed? She had once adored him and had felt adored by him. And now their only intimate moments were governed by pettiness and slight.

She so desperately wants to sleep but it seems this very desire to sleep is what is keeping her awake. Each moment passes with a heaviness, and even though she is tired and her body yearns for sleep her thoughts continue to race. What will become of them all?

She muses on a different life, the one she might have had if she had taken certain opportunities that had come her way. With Willy Pilson perhaps. Willy Pilson in the bed beside her now in his gentleman's pyjamas, a solid secure presence, his reading glasses folded neatly on the bedside table, the predictable rhythms of his breathing lulling her into a peaceful sleep, the calm measure of his pulse, her plainsong, her psalm. Good old reliable Willy Pilson. She feels the tightness in her chest loosen and a tiredness envelops her as a night cloud might swaddle the moon.

There is now a nervousness in the back of Oliver's mind, a newly awakened and persistent pulse of energy in his body, a readiness, a growing impatience. He looks over at the makeshift bed but there is no sign of Eurielle. She's gone. He is alone in the dressing room. Whatever dressing room it is, for now he does not seem to recognise it.

He does remember that he had not wanted to go home last night. He had not wanted to risk the chance of Edith derailing him, distracting him from his purpose just when he was fixed on it. Some quibble or criticism about his absence, or his having to explain himself to her about the money he spent at the Turkish baths, or her needing him to attend to some domestic triviality. It all dilutes, he thinks, it all dilutes the only hope we have to survive, we have to rise above all this, we have to pull ourselves out of the slurry. He suddenly remembers the greyhounds. Christ! The bloody greyhounds still have to be dealt with. Oliver checks his shoe. The manure still tucked into its sole. A lighter hue, drier, less of a smell coming off it. Edith'll be hopping mad by this stage, he thinks, no, he couldn't be doing with *that*! Dealing with *that*! He gets up from the divan. Now too agitated to stay in one place. Anyway the sooner he gets all the things he needs for the illusion, he thinks, the better.

He takes the remains of a cigarette from the ashtray, blowing the ash off the length of it, slipping it into his pocket, draining a glass of gin that sits on the dressing room table. Pours himself another straight gin and downs it in one.

He slips out of the theatre unnoticed. The dawn is a mere pink edge on the horizon when Oliver steps out on to the street. It holds the buildings around him in flimsy silhouette. The sleet from the night before has left the city chastened. Harsh, crisp lines fringe the kerbs and gutters. The tracks of carts, the imprints of hooves, mark the frosted surface of the road. Too early for the sun to have teased this ice-wrapped world out of its frozen sleep.

He misses his Borsalino, he rubs his head with his palm, and the cold punishes him as he walks. Nevertheless he smiles. He has his plan, he knows what he's about. The streets are slowly filling as people make their way to work. Oliver barrels towards Smithfield Market. Hasps, rope – *Jesus*, boots! He forgot to bring Eurielle's boots – perhaps he could find two identical pairs of boots at the market, there were bound to be boots there. Did he need a large mirror for the illusion? He'd get that at the theatre too. Building the box, that was the first thing. He'd have to patent that design – would he have to patent that? – no – in fact maybe he should go back to the theatre first – no – he'd go to Smithfield first and get all the smaller bits and pieces – and blood of course, a supply of fake blood. Sydney Brown will be amazed, amazed and yet not surprised, a little apologetic that he'd ever doubted Oliver – no, he needs to go and get the saw first, that's the first thing he needs to do.

Oliver crosses Lombard Street, on to Donegall Street.

He'll need to work all day and through the night – perform

tomorrow, or the night after – he'll need Sydney to give him the set dock, a couple of stagehands – who'll be sworn to secrecy, of course – get Eurielle's skinny arse out of her bed, well get her into that box and start sawing – no! he needs a new assistant, she said she'd never fit – and where did she disappear to anyway? – and, *Jesus*, the cross-cut saw!

He moves on to York Street. Walks with a determination that just about keeps the gin from fogging his mind. Always good to be a step ahead, he thinks. Got to keep a step ahead.

When he reaches Manger's Funeral Parlour he bangs his fist against the front door. After a few minutes he hears a jangle of chains. Even before the door is fully open Oliver is hollering at Manger. 'I need a cross-cut saw – thirty-six inches thereabouts.' He looks up. Sees 'From Manger to Grave' – awh, for fuck's sake, he thinks.

The door opens to a crack and a slice of Manger's scrawny face can be seen through it.

'You'll have to make it out to Divitt's mill, I've nothing here that size,' Manger says to Oliver, scratching his face with his grimy hands, the nails bitten down, a crescent of inflamed red at each tip. Manger's eyes are like dried salt lakes, huge, empty, yearning for colour. He stands at the front door of the funeral parlour, nervous of the real world, anxious to return to the dead.

'You must have something, Manger. In the workshop.'

'Have you ever seen a saw that size in the workshop? We only use small handheld saws, you know that, nothing the size you're looking for.'

'God damn it!' Oliver now wears the gin he has drunk like a second skin. It insulates his body and his mind, sharpens his attention, acts like a flint to his responses. Manger is irritating him with his timidity. Oliver wants to squeeze Manger's face, crush the flaky nasal bones, knead the paltry ripples of flesh around his jowls, get rid of that martyred expression once and for all.

'Divitt's mill, Oliver. But don't tell him I sent you. If he asks say you never even saw me. I think he's running some scams, something's not right. I've let him go from the workshop. There's still lots of trouble around here, Oliver, and I don't want any trouble from *him.*'

Oliver shakes his head. What is Manger blabbering on about? Doesn't matter, he's got to push on. 'I need something to eat, Manger.'

'Got fruit bread, no butter.'

'That'll do.'

'Wait here.' Thomas Manger closes the front door on Oliver, slides the chain back into its slot.

'For God's sake,' says Oliver, stamping his feet on the step. A face appears at the window above, a woman, then disappears. The front door opens again. Thomas Manger hands Oliver a small package wrapped in greaseproof paper.

'You'll have to pay this time, Oliver.'

'For the fruit bread?' Oliver says in disbelief.

'For the saw, Oliver. For whatever you take.'

'Yes, yes, yes,' says Oliver sharply. 'Fine.'

'You said that before.'

'You'll be paid, ye stupid blurt!' Oliver shouts at Manger. The woman reappears at the window.

'Not so loud,' says Thomas Manger meekly and looks up at the window.

'Afraid I'll waken the dead?' Oliver laughs.

'He'll be open late morning but I never sent you, right?' The door closes. Oliver unwraps the parcel in his hand and stuffs the whole piece of fruit bread into his mouth, throwing the greaseproof paper on the ground. He stands, tilting his head up, and quickly gobbles down the bread, like a snake swallowing awkwardly shaped prey. Then smacks his lips. He'd love a drink. He thumps the front door of Manger's house.

'Manger,' he shouts. 'I need something to drink, the bread's dry – y'know!' He waits. No answer. 'Y'know!' Still nothing from Manger. 'Bastard coward,' he mutters, turns quickly on the step and heads back towards the city centre.

A strange melancholy threatens to descend on Oliver as he walks, but he shakes it off. He has a job to do.

Twelve

When she wakes Agna can feel the bites from the bedbugs itch her skin. She scratches the bites through her night-clothes, feels their pinpricks of fire. She shows the welts to Lily – a red peppered trail along her arms and back, a few here and there on her left thigh. Then Lily tells her to get dressed. Just as she is about to get her coat from the back kitchen she lifts her head. In the mirror, just to the right of the washtub, she sees a man standing in the doorway. He wears a smart morning jacket and carries a folded newspaper in his hand. He has grey hair. He does not look unlike her father, only his frame is less robust than his, and his features are slightly more refined. Like the woman in the photograph. Like herself. It is Edwin, she is sure. Who else could it be?

Edwin hovers in the hallway for a moment then slowly moves towards her. Agna watches him in the mirror. He stares at her as though soaking up every detail of her face, her hair. She turns to him as he moves over the threshold of the scullery.

Lily arrives. 'Judge Fleck—'

Edwin gently raises his hand to her. 'Thank you, Lily, you can go now.'

'I'm sorry to say, sir, that we found—' Lily begins her report on the bedbug situation.

'Yes, that's fine, Lily, that's fine. A job well done. Why don't you tell Sadie to remove the bedclothes first and we'll take it from there.'

'But Mrs Fleck should be here to do that – it's her job—'

'Just get Sadie to do it for now.'

'Yes, sir. Anything else, sir?'

Edwin holds his gaze on Agna for the whole time. His eyes are alight and his face has widened into a childish beam as bright and clear as a summer's day.

'No, thank you, Lily,' he says eventually.

Lily turns to go.

'Oh, perhaps you might fix some breakfast for Agna before she leaves. By that stage Mrs Fleck will be here.'

'I will, indeed,' Lily says and waddles off.

'After all if the bedbugs get a feast why shouldn't you?' He gives Agna a big grin, which makes her laugh.

'I hope you were able to sleep, Agna,' Edwin continues, smiling.

Agna nods her head.

'I'll ask Lily to leave out some calamine lotion for you and your payment will be on the table in the hall, is that all right?'

Agna nods her head again.

'You know you're welcome here anytime, Agna.'

He stands before her as though unable to pull himself away. Then dropping his gaze he turns and leaves the scullery. Agna watches him. She hears Lily calling for her from the kitchen and turns to the sound. When she turns back she sees Edwin slumped against the wall as though the narrow channel of morning light has pinned him to it. His body begins to shake. She hears him sobbing.

Lily calls her again. She hesitates. Should she go to Edwin? Another shout from Lily and she runs to the kitchen.

By the time she leaves the house the bed she slept in the previous night has already been dismantled and Sadie is dousing the slats and crevices and springs with boiling water in the small yard outside. The blankets, sheets and pillowcases wait in huge piles to be washed. She walks along the main road which runs at the front of Edwin's house wondering why her mother hasn't yet turned up for work.

She thinks how gentle a man Edwin is, how considerate he seems, nothing like the kind of man she had heard about growing up, nothing like the man her father had many times shouted about. She had felt very easy in his company and he had reminded her of Archie. The same noble arc to the brow, the same smile, the proud forehead and the neat jaw. And it had never bothered him that she did not speak, he treated her kindly nonetheless, perhaps didn't even notice. She thinks about him slumped against the wall in the hallway as though everything about him had turned to shadow.

As she nears her flat she sees a horse and cart on the street. The back of the cart is piled high with boxes. Out of one box sticks the Indian headdress that her father brought home from one of his stealing sprees together with the stuffed ferret which had frightened her. The four sitting-room chairs are stacked beside the boxes. She enters the hallway of the house to find Mrs Earwaker talking animatedly to a tall man who holds a sheet of paper in his hands. Two men carry the kitchen table down the stairs, behind them another man carries Edith's sewing table. She hears her mother's voice coming from upstairs and pushes past the men to get to her. Reaching the top landing she sees her mother, white faced, pleading with the men who are carrying the divan out of the flat. Archie stands behind her, the look of fresh sleep still on his face, a blanket wrapped around his shoulders.

'Mrs Fleck,' the tall man in the hallway shouts up the stairwell, his voice as thick as curd. 'You were warned. I want you out by this afternoon or else you'll pay for this behind bars.'

The men continue clearing the flat, even taking Agna's bed with its piece of hose for a leg, and the wardrobe with the broken hinges. Agna rushes into the room to find her box garden. She sees it sitting by the window, grabs it, then looks around the room in disbelief. She sees the walls destroyed by holes, the wallpaper torn, the plaster cracked. She sees that the framed tapestry with the words 'Behold, the fire and the wood, but where is the lamb?' is the only thing hanging on the wall. The glass of the frame is broken.

'It's your father's handiwork.' Edith is on the verge of tears. 'Archie came home to find everything nailed to the walls last night.'

Agna looks at Archie, his face is etched with worry.

The three of them stand quietly together on the landing, a faint whiff of dog waste coming out from the flat. They hear Mrs Earwaker's voice rising in sharp pulses from below as she talks to the bailiff.

One of the men carries Bertie's shoes in his hands.

'They're mine,' Archie calls to him. The man stops, looks at Archie with disdain and drops the shoes on the landing. Archie slips them on. 'Will they take the dogs?' he asks, looking at the three greyhounds huddled in the corner of the empty room.

'I doubt it,' Edith says solemnly. 'Though I wish they would.'

'I think Daddy must have stolen them,' Archie says.

'What do you mean?' Edith says.

'Yesterday when I was buying whitening for Edwin at Herevetz's shop, I heard Mr Herevetz talking about it.'

'Heard him say what?'

'Saying there was three greyhounds gone missing from the track owners up at Celtic Park who're wanting to do greyhound racing as well as the whippets.'

'But isn't your father minding them for Mr Divitt? Was that not the "official" plan?'

Archie lifts his head to look at his mother. Takes her in. 'Mr Her-evetz said whoever stole them was in deep trouble. The police and all are on to it. And whatever way, if Daddy's minding stolen dogs – even if Divitt stole them first – Daddy's still part of the crime.'

'Why didn't you tell me?'

'I'm telling you now.'

Edith and Archie look over at the greyhounds in the corner of the room.

'Those wretches win a race?' Edith says. 'They can hardly stand.'

Two of the greyhounds are huddled together, heads entwined like the arms of lovers. The third greyhound stands shivering, limp-limbed, dripping misery and diarrhoea. The idea that the dogs Oliver had agreed to mind for Divitt were stolen was not beyond the realms of possibility.

'I'll bring them back to Divitt. The bailiff is bound to say some-thing to somebody, then they'll be on to us,' Archie says.

'I think it'll be fine, Archie. I think we should just leave the dogs where they are.'

'I'll bring them back and everything will be all right again.'

'No, Archie, I really don't think—'

Archie takes a deep breath. He stands tall in Bertie's shoes as he speaks as though he's found a new confidence in wearing them. 'I think Daddy is worried that he might be thought part of the crime of stealing them. That's why he hasn't said anything. I think he needs help.'

'There's a lot going on, Archie, I don't think it's just about the dogs.'

Archie looks over at Agna whose eyes are wide with intent.

'Do you think I should bring them back, Agna?' Archie asks her.

Agna nods her head.

Archie moves towards the dogs. 'All right, Agna agrees. That's it. I'm going to bring them back to Divitt then, leave them back at the mill. I know where it is. Daddy won't have to worry any more, once they're off our hands. He won't have to worry that the police might call.'

'Archie—'

'I don't even have to say anything to Daddy. When he comes home from Mr Manger's it will be like a good surprise.'

Edith drops her head. 'What home?'

'What about the bailiffs?' asks Archie.

'Don't worry, I'll think of something.'

'Where is Daddy anyway?'

'I don't know, Archie,' replies Edith. 'I don't know.'

Archie sets pots of water out for the dogs while he searches for rope. The dogs move their heads nervously from side to side, passing their muzzles across the pots before they drink as though sensing some shift. They lap at the water. They circle around each other. Archie improvises a collar and lead for each of them, but they are reluctant to leave the flat and pull on the rope. Archie encourages them to move with him, attempts to reassure them like a shepherd guiding a nervous flock. There is a sense of righteousness about him now that he has made the decision to return the greyhounds to Divitt and to take affairs into his own hands. He wants to set right the wrong his father has committed by stealing the dogs, or by being partly involved in their stealing. Put an end to it. All of it. Get everything back on the straight and narrow. The dogs are not their property.

As they walk down the street everything appears to spook the dogs, a change in the breeze, the movements of people passing them on the street. They weave around Archie's feet in short desperate trots, bending their heads back and up every so often towards Archie, their eyes darkly suspicious. But Archie is lighter in his step. He's doing the right thing.

A half-hour walk out of the city and Archie reaches the mill. He walks across the muddied yard with the dogs to the back of the building and pushes open the slatted wooden door, which leads into the storeroom. The storeroom is empty. Once inside the dogs become increasingly agitated, ducking their heads low to the ground, dragging their haunches, their thin tails now tucked deep in under their rumps.

Then Divitt appears. It is the first time Archie has seen him without his cap and it gives him a hard feeling in his stomach. The skin on Divitt's bald head is smooth on one side, an almost baby shine to it. On the other side the skin pulsates over the huge dent. It looks impossible that any person could be alive with this catastrophe etched out on their skull. A palm sized fontanelle, the brain merely a porous membrane away, easy to poke with curious fingers, open to the elements. Without a hat this indentation would fill with rain, thinks Archie as he stares at the disfigurement. The dogs cower and fret at Archie's feet. Archie searches for the courage he had on leaving the flat just a short while earlier. He reminds himself he is here to do a job. He swallows the sour water build-up in his throat.

'I'm bringing the greyhounds back to you,' Archie says, trying to keep his gaze on Divitt's face and not his skull, a tear in his vowels. Divitt says nothing. The fontanelle pulsates. 'With all due respect, Mr Divitt,' Archie has to swallow more sour water before continuing, 'my father doesn't want to be a part of your schemes any more. Now that the dogs are returned we can just forget all about it, because it's quits now.'

Divitt does not move. He stares at Archie. One of the greyhounds wets the floor, a stream of yellow piss snaking towards Divitt's feet. A warm rank smell.

'I'm sorry, Mr Divitt, sorry for your trouble.' Archie can feel any courage he had evaporate, he watches the piss pass Divitt. He looks up at the ceiling of the storeroom. He looks down at Bertie's shoes on his feet. This'll put things to rights, he says to himself, pretending to be brave.

Divitt remains silent. Archie doesn't know what to do now. He drops the ropes attached to the greyhounds as a final gesture in a settlement which so far has been only one-sided. The greyhounds scamper into a huddle trying to hide behind Archie.

Looking down at the dogs, at their eyes wide with terror, Archie suspects now that he shouldn't have come. It was a mistake to return the dogs. He should have stayed well away.

'Do you know what your daddy's been doing?' Divitt says, the words crackling through the yellowed spittle that cobwebs his mouth. The voice is thin, grating.

Archie's body stiffens. He wants to check that the door is still open behind him but he cannot bring himself to turn. 'No, sir,' he says, his voice shaking.

'The greyhounds is only small fry. Just something to rile an as-so-ci-ate of mine who I don't particularly care for.' Divitt pokes his tongue out a little through his dry lips, says the word 'associate' as though he is spelling it out in his head as he says it. He possesses the glee of a child ratting on a friend. He moves towards Archie. 'Your daddy's took advantage of those poor families. None of them thought of checking. Furthest thing from their minds what with them crying and all. When the bodies come in he was always the first there to measure them. Said he wanted to get the coffin to fit them best. It was all a yarn. Took what he found. Rings, pins, neck-laces, watches. Finest gold and silver. Replaces them with tat, if he replaces them at all.' As Divitt speaks he thrusts his face closer to Archie, then bends his head as though on purpose to weaken the boy. The pulsating skull only inches now from Archie's face. Archie feels a wateriness at the back of his knees. When Divitt lifts his head, he grins at Archie, showing a jumble of teeth. 'Then there was the fraud. Charging for mahogany' – the word rattles first at the back of his throat before it comes out – 'but ordering deal. More besides. For handles and wheels and nameplates. Overcharging then slipping it all into his pocket.'

Archie cannot believe what he is hearing. He wants to run. Divitt moves closer. Divitt steps on one of the greyhound's paws and leans all his weight on it. The poor animal yelps.

'Not saying that I would tell, but your daddy could go to prison for a very long time if I did.' The same kind of yellow discharge webs the inside corners of Divitt's eyes. 'Sometimes I goes with him to measure the bodies. Once I saw him take the wooden leg off a dead man, inside the leg was a stash of notes. Said nothing to the family. Kept it all. Did he buy you shoes with it?' smirks Divitt, tapping Archie's foot with his own. 'Doesn't look like it. Them's you're wearing seem too big for ye. Probably drank it up then pished it down. He likes to drink, eh?' Divitt pauses, looks straight into Archie's eyes. 'Another time I saw him kissing a dead girl on the mouth. But I wouldn't tell on him for that. That's hurting nobody. That's the kind of thing I like to do myself – and more besides.' Divitt exhales deeply as though finishing something in his head, his breath is foul. He tips his head back and looks at the ceiling of the storeroom, black hair grows in long matted streaks up his neck, a peppering of sawdust in the hair. 'But the stealing, the fraud – them's a crime.'

Archie says nothing. He is afraid of Divitt. Senses that the man could clearly harm him like he has the dogs and the dead girl. Is sickened by the smell of him, by the damaged skull, by the thick wiry hair on his neck. But he cannot believe what Divitt says about his father. His father would never behave like that, never. Then Archie thinks of the greyhounds, how they came to be in the flat. He thinks of how his father can go missing for days and come back with a strange, discomfiting energy. He thinks of all the materials his father brings home for new illusions when money is so tight.

Divitt smiles at the ceiling. 'Your mother.'

Archie's head is suddenly hot at the mention of his mother. He doesn't want Divitt to talk about her. He doesn't want the man to know or say her name. The room feels airless, suffocating.

Divitt looks at Archie and repeats, 'Your mother.'

'Yes, sir?'

'She works up at the judge's house, doesn't she?'

'She does, sir,' Archie says, his throat aching. Then in an effort to deflect from his mother, he adds, 'And so do I.' He won't say that Agna does, though.

Divitt's eyes bulge as they widen, the yellowy discharge stretching in the corners. His plan now appearing all the more straightforward. 'You do something for me and I won't tell anybody what your daddy's been up to,' he says slowly. 'That agreed?'

Archie hesitates, then nods his head.

'You have to say it.'

'Agreed,' says Archie, shaking.

Divitt smiles again. 'And now if you don't do it, *you'll* be the one responsible for him going to prison.'

Archie's stomach churns at the thought of what Divitt is going to ask him to do, at the thought of his father going to prison, at the thought of what would become of him, of them all. Divitt looks down at the greyhounds curled in a tight bunch around Archie's feet.

'There's guns at that house.' Divitt coughs then slowly chews whatever he has coughed up, swallows. 'Pistols, rifles,' he continues. 'Must be. He needs to protect that big house of his, so there must be guns. Rifles too, for hunting. You seen them?'

Archie knows that the display case in Edwin's study contains four ornate pistols. One of his jobs has been to fill the scuttle to the right of the fireplace with firewood. He has admired them. Has seen that the glass case is secured with locks. The pistols are obviously valuable.

'Yes, sir.'

'You bring what you find to me – tomorrow – and your daddy will stay a free man.'

'Tomorrow?'

'Is there a problem with that?' Divitt's tone shifts, becomes tighter and more sinister.

'I'm not working there 'til Thursday.'

Divitt snarls, then laughs. 'Fuckin' eejit. Ten, fifteen years your father could get, easy.'

Archie immediately nods, signalling to Divitt that he'll do as he asks.

'Bring the guns to me – tomorrow. I'll be here, wait 'til it's dark.'

Divitt pulls back, satisfied he has the boy well and truly under his thumb. Archie turns, lifting his feet from out of the huddle of dogs who begin whimpering, and walks slowly to the door of the storeroom. Divitt gives the dogs an unmerciful kick. Archie feels sick. He should have known by the way the dogs had cowered and dragged heavily on the ropes on entering the storeroom that they were afraid of the man.

Archie keeps walking forward but his insides are screaming for him to swing back around and grab the dogs and get them out of there. Screaming also to keep going in order to save his father from prison. His thoughts flying around like a blizzard in his brain.

Oliver is pleased that it is so easy. He parks the Morris Oxford van down a lane behind the farmhouse so that it won't be seen or heard and walks quietly into the yard. Divitt's mill is deserted, a whimper or two from some dogs somewhere on the premises – the storeroom, he thinks, *dogs? Thought Divitt didn't want dogs around the place –* but no one appears. He finds the cross-cut saw where Manger had said it would be, hanging on the back of the byre door. Now he walks spritely back to the van, puts the cross-cut saw in the back of it and drives off.

He catches a sullen Sydney Brown at the Empire. Two soberly dressed men are leaving Sydney Brown's office as Oliver comes in. They are taking out boxes filled with papers and files. They tell Sydney Brown that the Tax Commissioners will be in touch.

Sydney Brown sits at his desk looking more bloated than usual. He has the womanly wave to his hair which Oliver had noted that time when he had caught him off guard. His skin is greasy, he smells fetid.

'The acts are pulling out faster than you can say "breach of contract".' Sydney puffs through his fat lips.

'I need a slot on tonight's bill!' Oliver says.

'Everything's going to shit – backers pulling out—'

'I want the headline slot on tonight's bill!'

'Take whatever you want – but don't think that you're going to get paid because you're not.'

Oliver takes his cue to leave. Seeing Sydney Brown so caponised, he thinks, is payment enough.

As he passes the quick-change area backstage he sees a long black cape which someone has left there, likes the look of it, takes it with him and heads to the van.

Reaching Manger's workshop, he uses any available wood that is at hand together with segments and panels from 'The Amazing Crystals Cabinets' illusion to reassemble a box suitable for 'Sawing the Lady in Half'. The plan he has drawn on the sheet of brown paper, which the barman in The Crown had given him, is crumpled and stained but he works according to its calculations, sweat falling on the paper, on the wood. When it is finished he hauls the box out into the yard and drags and pushes it until he has it in the van.

For his new look he'll use the cape but he needs something else to reinvent himself. As he drives off at speed towards the Empire Theatre the rear doors of the van swing back and forth slapping and battering against the box.

Thirteen

A rchie stands in Edwin's study. He gawks at the objects in the room. He knows exactly where the pistols are, can see them from where he stands, but he looks everywhere else, as though to put off the moment of stealing. A jar of spills on the hearth, two vases on the mantelpiece, a clock in the centre, ten minutes to ten, a velvet mantel-valance, an ornament of a sleeping nymph in a conch candlestick, a decorative fire screen, a Staffordshire figurine, a lithograph of a horse, a watercolour of two dogs, that statue of Hercules. His eyes move methodically from one object to another.

The mirror hanging over the fireplace offers him his reflection. He is as white as a ghost. He pulls a wire from his cap and picks the locks of the display case. His hand is shaking but after working the wire for a while the locks of the case click open. In his hands the pistols feel much heavier than he had anticipated. They are beautiful, the wooden handles appear shinier now they are out of the case, the stones decorating the handles a brighter emerald and ruby. Archie places the pistols into the hessian bag he has brought with him. He hears a noise behind him and turns. Standing in the doorway is

Sadie, a pair of newly polished fire tongs in her hand. Sadie gapes at Archie, her eyes lift to the empty display case then drop to the hessian bag.

What happens next takes Archie as much by surprise as it does Sadie. Archie walks slowly towards her. Then he lifts his hand and, holding his softly opened fingers a few inches from her face, he stares intently into her eyes and begins to talk to her in a low, calm voice. He tells her she is feeling sleepy. He tells her she has not seen him lift the guns out of the case, he tells her she has not seen him in the room at all, that she is so very sleepy and wants to close her eyes. He remembers what he has seen his father do over and over again. He speaks a kind of mumbo-jumbo, makes a low churr-churring sound.

'You stealing those guns?'

Archie persists. 'Close your eyes, Sadie.' She closes her eyes. 'You will wake up when the clock on the mantelpiece strikes ten o'clock. You will have no recollection of any of this.' Then more mumbo-jumbo. Archie passes his hand in front of her face. Sadie does not flinch or make a move. She appears to be in a deep sleep. Archie calls her name. She does not respond. He calls her name again. She remains in a trance. Archie is very pleased with himself. He lowers his hand. Sadie sways from side to side. Archie lifts the bag, moves quietly past Sadie and leaves the house.

As soon as Archie is out the door Sadie opens her eyes, turns and runs straight to the kitchen to find Lily.

Archie continues speedily out to Divitt's mill. He finds Divitt in the byre at the back of the farmhouse scraping at rusted machinery. Divitt turns, reaches out to Archie for the pistols, tests their weight, is bemused by their decorative stones, points one at Archie's head, teases the trigger with his finger.

'These are worth a pretty penny. The stones alone – they're the real deal. There must be some really nice things in that house.' Divitt speaks with a flat growl, then pokes his tongue through his lips. Pointing one of the pistols at Archie, he closes one eye and looks along the sight.

'Sir?' Archie is finding it hard to concentrate on what Divitt is saying. He wants to be as far away from Divitt as he can. His knees are shaking. That twist again in his stomach, feeling he needs to use the toilet. He guesses the pistol isn't loaded, nevertheless, he wants Divitt to stop.

'You must have seen nice jewels and valuables and stuff.'

'I suppose so, sir.'

Divitt whips the pistol to the side of Archie's head and thrusts his jaw out at the boy. 'Did you or did you not?'

'I did,' Archie stammers.

Divitt drags the barrel of the pistol slowly across Archie's cheek and, prising open the boy's lips with its tip, gently pushes it into his mouth.

'You need to go back to the house and get me some more, and get me rifles too.' Divitt slides the pistol deeper into Archie's mouth. Archie wants to gag, metal seeping into his swallow. 'Bring it here to me tomorrow. Jewellery, silverware. If you don't, I'll tell on your daddy and that'll be the end of him.'

Divitt withdraws the pistol from Archie's mouth, then wipes the boy's lips, wet with saliva, with his grubby fingers. 'You're dribbling, so you are,' Divitt says in a half whisper, staring at Archie's mouth. Then he wipes the pistol on his trousers. 'You anything to say to me?'

'Yes, sir. I'll bring some.' Archie can feel tears well up but is determined not to let Divitt see that he is about to cry. He digs his fingers into the palms of his hands.

Fourteen

'What have you done?' Edith cannot believe the sight in front of her. Oliver has arrived home. His hair is a milky pearl brush of havoc, tufted as though it has been caught in an intense electrical current. The skin around his temples and his eyes is an angry red, his eyelids are swollen. A spatter of tender red risings across his forehead.

Agna comes into the sitting room, covers her mouth in alarm when she sees her father.

'What in God's name have you done?' says Edith. 'Oh – what in God's name is going on? Where have you been?'

Oliver grits his teeth, tugs at his hair. 'Improvised a nice little cocktail for myself, that's what I've done! Peroxide, ammonia, a hint of methylene blue, all mixed sweetly together and plastered all over my fucking head.'

Oliver moves straight to the mirror hanging over the fireplace – one of the few items remaining in the flat – inspects the carnage. Edith circles him cautiously, staring at his hair.

'It was supposed to work. It didn't work. Doesn't matter.'

'Where on earth did you get the peroxide . . . the methylene?'

Oliver pulls a theatre programme out of his coat pocket and shoving it in front of Edith points at an advertisement on the back page.

'*Hair Staining, our system permanent, washable, natural and harmless, satisfaction guaranteed. Will defy sea bathing, Turkish Baths etc. Absolutely harmless. Front of head – 3 pounds 3 shillings. Whole head – from 5-6 guineas.*'

'I told him I wanted *that*. I told him I wanted to look magnificent!'

'Told who?'

'Herevetz.'

'Mr Herevetz?'

'He said it would work.' Oliver drags his fingers through his hair. Tries to brush it back from his temples. Winces at the pain. 'Looks like I've been stung by a thousand bees.' He grunts into the mirror.

'Mr Herevetz sold you peroxide for your hair? And what happened to your face?'

'He sold me that too. It's the "Pepper Rub", don't you know – all the successful businessmen are using it – the latest New York craze, a solution of red pepper and water rubbed vigorously, and the key word here is – yes – vigorously! Gives that Anglo-Saxon bloom – a commercial asset they say to any entrepreneur – painful at first – oh boy, is it fucking painful – but the discomfort is worthwhile because look – look!' Oliver turns to Edith. 'On second thoughts, does my face look like it's been boiled?'

Edith stands speechless.

Oliver answers himself. 'And I wanted to look dignified, sophisticated, a man of substance. My audience can't see me like this! What am I going to do? I'm weeping fucking acid!'

'Oliver, calm down, for God's sake – calm down. What do you mean your *audience*?'

Oliver starts to move around the flat. 'I've three quarters of an hour before the evening performance – I have a slot, I have the box.

I need to get everything else in place!' He stops suddenly. 'Where are the greyhounds?' Then a moment later, 'Where's the furniture? Where's everything gone?' He circles himself, disorientated by the space.

'The bailiffs came.'

Oliver looks at her in complete bewilderment. Then remembering something he throws his hands up in the air.

'The cowboy boots! Hope to God they didn't take the cowboy boots? I need them for my new persona.' He scurries around the flat, finds the boots eventually, tucked in behind the curtains of the main room. 'Ah, yes!'

Edith and Agna stand watching as Oliver runs into the bedroom. They hear him muttering to himself, *Where's the fucking wardrobe?* He runs back out again and throws a brown dress at Edith. 'Found this on the floor. Please, God, we'll find something better at the theatre but just in case.' He runs out the main door of the flat. 'Follow me to the Empire!'

He's gone.

Edith turns to Agna. 'I'll go after him, you stay at home. Home!' She shakes her head at the very notion of it. 'Stay here for Archie and then both of you come to the theatre. All right?'

Agna nods her head and with that Edith rushes out the door.

When Archie arrives at the flat he looks so worried and shaken the first thing Agna does is put her arms around him. He rests his head a moment on her shoulder.

'Where's Daddy?' he says breathless from the running.

Agna takes his hand firmly in hers and leads him down the stairs and back out on to the street. They catch a tramcar. Make their way as fast as they can on to Bridge Street, cut down through Corn Market and towards the Empire Theatre. Pushing past the stage doorman without explaining themselves, Agna and Archie run up the back stairs of the theatre, checking each dressing room in turn, startling the performers who are getting ready for the evening show. 'Knock before you enter!'

They reach the dressing room on the top floor where they find Oliver and Edith. They are taken aback by the sight that greets them. Oliver stands in a silk embroidered dressing gown fussing with his bleached hair and dabbing his blistered face with a Leichner make-up stick. Beside him Edith is stretched out on a short divan wearing a peacock blue basque, a pink petticoat, black stockings and black high-heeled boots. Her hair is piled on top of her head. She wears bright red lipstick. She holds a cold compress against her eyes.

Oliver turns to Agna and Archie with a look of burning wonderment, his arms raised in the air. 'Look at me!' he says to them, with an almost childish glee. 'Look, I'm on in twenty minutes with the best illusion ever! What do you think?' Oliver holds out the sides of the dressing gown. 'Not the most exotic garb but it'll do, given the circumstances. That cape was all wrong, too old-fashioned . . .' the end of his sentence disintegrating as he speaks.

Agna quickly moves over to the bed and kneels beside Edith.

Oliver shakes his head as though he is the straight man and Edith is the fall guy. 'They were working on the set for next week's "Blue Beard", you see. We were standing there all ready to rehearse and, can you believe it, out of nowhere a plank falls from the flies and knocks her to the floor – she gets up, then seconds later a wooden beam swings loose from the side rig, hits her right in the face – bang! – brings her straight down again – after that – can you believe it – a bracket falls on her from the back of the flats and ends it all like a full stop. One – two – three. Horrific as it was—' Oliver turns to Edith on the divan. 'I must admit, it had a beautiful timing to it.' He resumes applying his make-up.

Agna holds her mother's hand.

'I'm all right. I'm all right,' Edith says.

Archie, unable to hold on to his panic any longer, blurts out, 'I only stole the guns like he asked but not the other things –'

Edith turns in the direction of Archie's voice. 'What's wrong, Archie? What do you mean?'

'Divitt. He wanted silverware, jewellery—'

'What?'

Oliver pulls on Edith's arm. 'Any tips on the music for this evening?'

'I stole guns from Edwin's house.' Archie is shaking.

For a brief moment Oliver stops what he is doing. He grimaces in the mirror as his brain tries to put the pieces together. He mumbles to himself. 'Divitt – what in God's name was he doing with Divitt – and at Edwin's? For Christ's sake.'

'I wanted to bring the greyhounds back to him.' Archie looks quickly at Agna, registers her distress, looks at Oliver. 'I thought it would put things right. Nobody knows it was me who stole the guns.'

Oliver swings sharply around to Edith. 'You don't happen to have any powder on you, by any chance?'

Edith puts her hands in the air in disbelief. 'Archie! What got you doing that? Stealing?' She turns her head to Oliver who is applying black pencil to his eyebrows. She flings her arm out and knocks against his hand. The pencil goes flying. 'Oliver, we need to sort this out!'

Oliver shakes his head. 'I have to get ready . . . I have to . . .' He bends down and picks up the pencil, carries on.

'He'll come after us, Daddy – he'll come after us!' Archie's face is draining of colour.

'This is ridiculous. No one's coming after us. We'll explain everything – whatever we need to explain – whatever – we'll – it'll be all right.' Edith sits upright on the divan.

'No, it won't!' Archie is getting more and more worked up. 'He said you'd go to prison for keeping the money you found in the dead man's leg—'

'What are you talking about – the dead man's leg?' Oliver is shaking his head.

Edith turns her head to Oliver to challenge him to respond. 'What is he talking about, Oliver?'

'I haven't the faintest idea.'

'But what's to be done about this?'

'What can we do? The boy is right.' Oliver nods. 'He didn't deliver so Divitt'll come after us.'

'Who?'

'Divitt.' There is a huge bubble rising in Oliver's chest ready to burst and, like when he was a child, he might just as easily dissolve into laughter as into tears. A choked sob squeezes out and slides into giddy chuckling then he gives another choked sob. He does not want to miss this opportunity to perform 'Sawing the Lady in Half' and save himself from oblivion, he does not want anything to derail him. 'Have you any idea what that man will do to me?' He mimes a throat slit, then strangulation, then a pistol to the head. He spreads his feet a little where he stands and clasps his hands behind his head, framing his peroxide crown, plucky almost. He exhales loudly. 'We're fucked.'

No one moves. Rumination before the panic. Oliver looks up at the ceiling – something is pricking him even in the midst of the fray. Then, 'How did you do it? How did you steal the guns without being caught? How come you weren't seen?' He turns to Archie in a moment of surprising calm.

Archie swallows hard.

'How did you steal the guns from that house without being seen?'

Archie aches all over. His thoughts separating, falling off. He springs on one and holds it as best he can. 'I was seen by Sadie, the housemaid. But I hypnotised her. I hypnotised her so that—'

Oliver starts laughing in a manner which suggests that if Archie doesn't stop his nonsense then he's asking for it. 'What are you blathering about? Hypnotised!'

'I hypnotised her so that she wouldn't remember she had seen me.'

Oliver says nothing only waits.

'She went under, I promise.'

Oliver looks merciless. 'Are you trying to make fun of me?'

'No, sir—'

'So, you're actually trying to tell me that you hypnotised this – this housemaid – and it worked?'

'Yes, sir.'

'Then show me.'

'What?' Archie's face drains.

'Show me how you hypnotised the housemaid. Go on!'

'Oliver, leave him alone!' Edith gets up from the divan.

'Shut up! I want to see how the boy does it. How he holds power over the unsuspecting. Isn't that right, son? Show me how you do it. Show me this great technique of yours which has landed us – right at the moment when I am to redeem myself – in the shit!'

Archie stands motionless.

'Go on!'

Archie purses his lips, determined to show his father, but his throat gurgles and only a thin paltry rasp comes out. He cannot bring his lips to make the right shape. He swallows hard. He tries again. His lips curl but this time he makes a sound like the complaining brakes of a bicycle. Crumpled and windy. He keeps his eyes lowered and goes at it again. Nothing. Then he tries again but the direness hits him. He stops. Looks at his father.

'It didn't work – boy! Did it? It didn't work. You big shot! You *thought* you *could*. But you can't, eh? You can't do it.'

'Oliver, stop it,' Edith shouts.

Oliver turns in small circles where he stands, beating his chest with his right fist. If Archie is found out by the police the consequences will not be good and he himself is in danger now because Divitt will retaliate with an immense and vicious pleasure. But strangely what overrides these terrors and sends Oliver into this fevered pitch is the fact that Archie has failed in the mechanics of the illusion, he has botched the act.

A small figure appears between Archie and Agna. 'Five minutes, Mr Fleck.'

Suddenly Oliver pushes past them and is gone.

'Oliver! Come back!' Edith shouts after him. Faces appear in the corridors at the sound of the commotion. 'Oliver! For God's sake, Oliver! Come back!'

Archie dashes after his father, pursues him backstage, finds him standing beside the newly constructed chamber for 'Sawing the Lady in Half.'

Oliver looks at Archie, his eyes beseeching him. 'I'm sorry. I'm sorry for everything.'

'Fuck you, Dad.'

'I'm sorry, son.' Oliver looks towards the stage. 'I'm desperate.'

'Was it true?'

'About what?'

'About the money in the dead man's leg, about kissing the girl?'

'No, of course it wasn't!'

'So there's no fear of you going to prison then?'

'No!'

Archie sighs with relief.

'Help me son! What'll I do?'

Archie takes his father in, sees the expression of absolute desolation growing on his face, feels pity. He needs to help him – Bertie would, Bertie would always help out when help was needed, no matter what the circumstances were. Archie turns around, pulls a costume off the quick-change rail, throws it on, yanks a blond wig from a wig stand, plopping it onto his head, and swipes a lipstick from the make-up tray on the props table, rubbing it furiously into his cheeks and onto his lips.

'Good lad,' Oliver says gratefully. 'Good lad. We're on after the plate spinners. You just need to pull your legs up in the box. Don't worry, just do what I say.'

Rouge on his cheeks, a tint of pink on his lips, dressed in a primrose yellow frock a little too big for his frame, Archie has no idea what to do. The music starts. He and Oliver step out on to the stage. The audience boo at Archie. Not what they had paid for. They holler and spit at Oliver. *Who do you think you are, giving us a runt of a boy instead of a full-blooded woman! What have we paid for?*

Having stepped onstage with purpose, Archie now feels nervous. By the time he reaches his position centre stage his hands are fluttering like brittle leaves on a morning breeze and his knees are knocking together under the pretty yellow frock. But it is only when he catches sight of the pine box, being wheeled on to the stage by his father, that the looped blond curls of his wig begin to shake. Archie lifts his head up to the endless dark of the auditorium and smiles.

'Do a circle.' Archie raises his arms up and slowly, alluringly, he presents himself to the crowd. He so badly wants things to work out for his father.

Oliver moves upstage, a lurid bull in his peony-spotted dressing gown, his head tilted to the gods, his eyes wide and burning with intent, his arms open to the crowd, his chest thrust forward. The moment has arrived, the words Oliver has been waiting to say flow at last: *Ladies and gentlemen – for the first time ever – and for your entertainment – be amazed and be horrified as I now perform for you – before your very eyes . . . Sawing a Lady in Half.* Oliver claps to summon two assistants standing stage right – jugglers or acrobats or some such, badgered into helping him. Archie jumps at the sound. The assistants come forward, one holding a coil of rope, and they grab Archie's skinny arms, hauling him towards the pine box as carelessly as they might a sack of potatoes across a dockyard. Archie gazes out into the dark. Without any rehearsal he now wonders exactly what he has to do. Does he pull his legs up into the top half of the box? Does he do that before or after the ropes are tightened? Before they are tightened surely?

When the assistants release their grip, Archie lifts up his yellow frock to step inside the box, his ankles weak and watery. The audience shout more insults at him, this time about his scrawny legs, his flat chest, his bony arms. *Don't you have a sister who could please us? Even your mother would do!*

The piano player bangs out an inappropriately jolly rendition of 'A Milkmaid Forlorn'. The lid of the box is closed and the large hasps on the lid's edge locked. Archie's head sticks out of the top of the box, his feet out of the bottom. The assistants thread ropes through holes on either side of the box. They tie the ropes around his legs, then they tighten the ropes around his arms. The crowd settle, the bait has been taken. Archie's bound hands are slotted through a hole in the front of the box and secured again with another loop of rope. The assistants lift the box and tilt it horizontally onto a basic wooden frame. The lifting is clumsy and Archie's head hits the wood, a horseshoe graze on his chin.

Archie tries to figure out exactly how much room he has to twist. He needs room enough to pull his legs up to his chest, out of the pathway of the cross-cut saw. But as he tries to manoeuvre his body he realises he cannot pull his legs up to his chest inside the box, the dimensions will not allow it. Archie calls out to his father, but Oliver cannot hear the boy over the sound of the piano, above the noise of the crowd. Oliver turns quickly and gives a nod to Archie as if to say 'doing great'. He raises his arms to the gallery: *This is it. This will be the most magnificent and lauded illusion the world has ever seen. This will deem him to be one of the greatest illusionists of all time.*

Archie wriggles frantically to free his arms but the ropes hold him fast. There is an 'oooh' from the auditorium. Oliver has finally harnessed their desires and is about to give them their money's worth. A glint of light stage right, and the double-handed cross-cut saw is in Oliver's hand. Oliver approaches the box, angles the saw to commence cutting. The saw's teeth grip the pine. Someone shouts out, *'Should've put a suffragette in there – that would soon stop their nonsense!'* Then the music soars. Once again Oliver gives an approving nod to Archie, oblivious of the difficulty the boy is in, assuming his wriggling is part of the act. Oliver thrusts the saw forward then drags it back and it hee-haws like a donkey in distress. Forward and backward, forward and backward. On and on and on it drones. The audience become increasingly uneasy. Reams of sawdust drop to the floor.

Then the saw snags.

Oliver senses the moment the clean blade drags, but his body, fuelled by adrenaline, continues its forward and backward motion twice more before he stops. On the floor by his feet a ruby pool appears, glistening in the spotlight, thick as syrup, round as a spool. Oliver stares. From the underside of the oblong pine box, through which he has already halfway worked the saw, a red droplet dislodges itself and falls onto the floor. The ruby pool shivers on the dark wood. Another droplet falls, another. Then a continuous thin runnel of red. And all the while the viscous pool on the floor holds its shape. Fills up. Stretches.

Oliver narrows his eyes – bloodshot and crazed from lack of sleep, as they are; swollen from where the peroxide has burnt his skin – and bends closer to inspect the pool. He needs to make sense of what he sees. An image of himself looms out of its centre to greet him, a pearly homunculus distended inside the perfect red bead: Oliver Fleck, Mysterious Illusionist, fifty-six years old, performing for *One Last Desperate Night Only* in a final chance to save his crumbling career, his hair bleached clownish white and rigid as frozen thatch, his eyebrows scalped and feathery, his forehead peppered with throbbing blisters, wearing a cream silk, peony-embroidered Japanese kimono which yawns around his naked stomach, and shiny black-cherry crocodile cowboy boots. *Look at me*, he thinks, bemused, as a child might react on seeing a ladybird for the first time, *Look how small I am*.

It is only when he taps the pool casually with the toe of his boot does its seal split, sending a panic of raucous red across the floor. Oliver awakes to the horror of what he has done. He quickly turns to look at his son's face. The boy's head sticking out of the top of the box like that of a doll, pretty and pale, the eyes rolling right back, the mouth a black almond giving suck to nothing.

Oliver does not move. His body emits the white hot heat of a furnace. His right hand is still tight around the handle of the saw. His body is bent forward. One half of the saw's blade is embedded in the pine box, the other is clear of the box on the far side, free and smiling, clotted bloodstained strings of sawdust hanging from red teeth.

With immense effort Oliver turns towards the audience and

stares. A plea behind the grimace: begging to be told that what he thinks has just happened hasn't, that both his son and reputation are unharmed. He wants to see the faces in the audience fired up with admiration and amazement. Instead he sees bemusement, horror.

Now, without warning, the lights go out. The blackness which descends is as solid as a wall, until someone screams, though not the boy, and releases a tumbling of sobered voices. *What has happened? What has this madman done? Why has it suddenly gone dark? Was that blood on the stage? Did something happen to the boy?*

From the stage there is nothing, an empty darkness, too still, too quiet, only, barely, what sounds like the squeaking of escaping gas. An almost inaudible thin whine. Hardly human. Then the clunk of wood against wood, the fussy rasping of ropes being undone. A massive fumbling. The heavy breath of effort and struggle. The clang of the saw falling on to the boards. That whine again as thin as a reed's edge. Shouts coming from backstage. A torchlight swinging in from the upstage entrance, catching, centre stage, what looks like the shape of a stooped beast. The audience becoming restless. Then the sound of footsteps onstage, too hurried, almost comical. The steady voice of the House Manager from the back of the stalls reassuring the audience that the electricity will be restored as soon as possible and the show will resume, everyone is to remain in their seats. The beam from a torch illuminating here and there the worried faces of the crowd, the turning heads, the women fanning their throats.

And when the floats finally go up, a vision which shocks the audience: caught in a bleach of electric light, Oliver stumbling around on the stage with the boy in his arms, tears or perspiration – *tears, of course, they must be tears* – streaming down his face. The child's limbs dangling, across his small torso a thick belt of blood, his blond wig caught on a clasp on the back of his yellow frock and hanging like a guillotined head. No one can see the boy's eyes, except Oliver, whether they are open or closed, fixed or oscillating. No one can tell if the boy is breathing, only Oliver.

Some in the audience cover their faces with their hands. Others are transfixed and cannot look away. Still others turn their heads, as though expecting an accomplice to appear from the gloom of the wings to explain everything.

Then that disembodied keen is heard again – that long, high-pitched whine the audience had heard in the darkness – slipping now through Oliver's lips. Oliver turns in a confused stagger towards the back of the stage.

A stagehand lashes the grand drapes closed. Oliver and Archie disappear.

The call boy runs as fast as he can up to Edith's dressing room. The news of the accident moving independently ahead of him, a chorus of alarm ascending up the steps, rising faster than the boy can move, eddying up to the top floor in a brisk, tight gust of perfumed air. As he reaches the top of the stairs he meets Agna.

He tries to catch his breath. 'Something's happened to the boy.'

Agna steps forward and looks down the stairwell.

There are certain images of that night, sudden flashes of the shapes their bodies had made, singularly and apart, or the way one or other of them moved in panic or with a focus reserved only for those moments in life which beggar belief, that still have a detailed robust architecture when they come back to Agna, which they frequently do: her crow's nest view as she turns quickly to look down the funnel of the stairwell is of the shape of her father coming up the stairs, the ogre-like hunch of his shoulders, the sides of his cream silk Japanese kimono flapping loosely behind him in the rush, his white hair a stiff crest, Archie a morsel in his father's arms, hanging like prey from the beak of some monstrous bird. Meeting them at the return, the sordid mirror of Danny Moss holding his ventriloquist dummy. The other performers on the bill unaware of the tragedy that has just happened, making their way down the steps to the stage now that the electricity fiasco had been sorted, anticipating an irritable crowd, or no crowd at all. Some giddy from the blackout. Others no less weary. The girls from Goodwin's Dancing Troupe, adjusting their feathered basques and headdresses as they strut and gabble down the steps, shrinking back as Oliver passes them, Archie's legs clipping their netted hips, their sequined waists, his head tapping against their corseted bosoms, a trail of syrup-red drops dotting the floor at their feet. In whatever order these images come back to Agna they always assemble into the same incomprehensible and unchangeable truth. Always accompanied by a terrible fear gripping her stomach and always with the same words that she can never alter: *Tell Edith it's the boy – something's happened to the boy – tell her it's bad – it's very bad.*

But Edith already knows that disaster has struck even before those zephyrs reach her: she feels a dull squall in her gut like melting honeycomb, she smells the blood. She is already on the top landing, has heard the pleaching of anxious voices, its female bias, rising from the stairwell. She moves stiffly, removing the compress from her eyes.

As Oliver arrives at the top of the stairs, a molten mess holding a scrag end of an ashen child, Edith's anger organises itself, in the instant, in the deep seat of her abdomen. She places both her hands upon the stair rail and breathes in slowly. Then up through her stiff body she controls the release of a precisely channelled torrent of abuse. *You whoring, filthy, pig-pissing monster! You monster!*

The Fleck family are a pitiful cluster on the top landing: the huge, dripping figure of Oliver holding the blood-soaked Archie in his arms; the waspish figure of Edith behind them yelling abuse; Agna hiding beneath her shawl, the brine of her tears eroding her.

Oliver puts his ear to Archie's mouth to see if he is breathing. Nothing. He checks for a pulse. Nothing. Then slowly tilting his head back at the awful truth, his mouth an increasing curve of tragedy, his face a gruesome mask of intensifying terror, he opens his mouth wide and releases, from the depths of some hell, a howl so full of pain that as it rises it shakes the very walls of the theatre, the city's roofs and domes, the spires and steeples of the city's churches and its night's sky beyond, splintering heaven's pan.

Fifteen

Archie lies in bed in Mrs Earwaker's flat. It is the first place Edith thinks of taking him, an approximation of home while theirs has vanished. Despite her disdainful attitude towards Oliver, despite all the trouble with the bailiffs, Mrs Earwaker's temperament has softened almost beyond recognition and she cannot do enough to help the Flecks. Archie's bleeding has stopped but he is so weak he has lost consciousness. She will call for Doctor McKnight, who lives only two streets away, to come to administer medicine and whatever else is needed. Having served as one of the few doctors in the field hospitals competent enough to use portable blood transfusion apparatus, Doctor McKnight – Mrs Earwaker assures them – will know exactly what to do. She leaves to get him.

Edith lies slumped in the armchair on the far side of the room. Oliver turns to her. He lifts a small basin which rests on the floor, empties the contents of blood and water down the stone sink, rinses the basin, half fills it with fresh water. He walks over to Edith, removes the cloth that covers her eyes. She groans. He refreshes the cloth in the basin of fresh water, wrings it out, places it upon her eyes to soothe them. Holds it gently in place for her. She tips her head back a little, takes in the comfort of the cool cloth, touches his hand. He stands quietly beside her, her fingers resting on his wrist. He waits as the cool cloth warms with her body's heat. Then he takes her hand, caressing her fingers with his, and places her hand by her side. Shock has given him the air of polite attention and he assumes a low-grade precision in his manners, inventing business, turning now to Archie and fixing his blanket which doesn't need fixing, dipping the cloth in cold water and mopping Archie's brow when Archie's skin is already cold, but he can do nothing to help Archie and he knows it, every possible fibre of him knows he is redundant. He must wait for the doctor to save his son. He sits down on the bed, then stands up again, rolls his cuffs back as though he is about to perform an important and urgent task and then unfurls his sleeves. He pats his lips hurriedly with his fingertips as though he is organising the order of some crucial information he must impart, but there is nothing to say. Suddenly a shape moves forward out of the murky corner of the room. Oliver turns to see who it is. For a brief moment he thinks it is Eurielle, though not in her usual feminine attire but in a pair of loose trousers and a shirt and without make-up or wig. He stares at the vision before him. It *is*. It *is* Eurielle. His angel. Unmistakably her. Now pale and handsome with short hair, serious, pure, disconsolate. Hovering in the corner, her arms gentle by her sides, her fingertips touching the wall behind her, a sadness about her, a grief. Strange. Why on earth is she here? How did she know to come? Then the light shifts and she is gone. Oliver looks into her absence. Realises that she was never there. Was she ever? Those other times he talked to her? Was she merely something in his head, some image of solace he had created, a fantasy of hope. Hope. Eurielle Hope. Gone? He rises slowly and walks into the space his vision of her had occupied. Empty now.

As he turns it is Agna who steps towards him and brings her face close to his. As real as anyone could be. Oliver looks at her. He has not been this physically close to his daughter since the night he found her sleepwalking and guided her back to bed. He looks at her now and a feeling of immense loss overwhelms him. His eyes begin to fill with tears, but which tears are they? he wonders. They could be tears from any number of sorrows. Tributaries of pain and regret flowing towards the estuary and out into the sea. Any number of sorrows indeed. The geography of his life has been etched with them. And this pain – this distance between them, between him and Agna – he had never reckoned on, nor understood.

Agna's body is trembling. Her fists are clenched by her sides. Even though her face is close to Oliver's she does not look at him, but looks to the side of him as though she's caught him in a dream, a glaze not only to her eyes, but to every part of her.

She opens her mouth. 'Who—?' she says quietly to him like a polite owl.

Oliver tilts his head. Did he hear something? What was that sound? Was that a draught? A rush of air? From where? He waits, drumming his fingers absent-mindedly against his chest like rainfall luring worms from the ground.

Then again, 'Who—?' The same gentle pitch.

Oliver looks at Agna's mouth, marvelling that it has borne him a fully formed word. *Him*. From out of his daughter's mouth a pearl. He waits for another one. Keeps his fingers drumming on his chest, does not want his hope to drown.

'Who—?' she says again, a kind of poised terror in her eyes now, her body rigid.

'Who,' he repeats as a reply to her question, to tell her he understands that she has something to communicate. He becalms his fingers, brings his full attention to the moment. Waits. This alien creature is speaking to him. At last.

'Who—?' she says and leans closer to him, her mouth now only a little distance from his ear.

'Agna,' he implores, turning his ear to her, looking out into the room. He feels his heart leap with happiness and his eyes brim once again.

Agna's shoulders hunch and she lifts her fists to press them against her throat. It is taking everything within her to move the sound out of her body, to speak to Oliver. Her jaw juts forward.

Oliver softly coaxes her. 'Agna, I can hear you.'

Agna's eyes widen. 'Who – are you?'

'Agna?' Oliver is puzzled.

'Who – are you?' Agna speaks in a rasping half whisper, urgent and stark, as though possessed by a voice not her own.

Oliver turns his head to look at her again. 'What are you trying to say, Agna?'

Agna swallows hard. 'Who – are you?'

'Who am I?' Oliver lets escape a bewildered sigh. 'I'm your father, Agna. I'm your father.'

Agna steels herself to continue, her knuckles blinking white under her skin.

'What kind—?' she asks.

'What kind?' Oliver shakes his head. He does not understand.

'What kind—?' she asks again, staying perfectly still, waiting for his reply.

Then Oliver finds himself finishing her question, 'What kind of a father?' its meaning burning through him. 'Agna.'

'All wasted.'

'No, Agna.'

'What kind of a father – would do that?'

'Agna.'

'Does anything matter to you?'

'Agna, please.'

'Anything?'

'Please, Agna.'

'Why?'

'Please.'

'Please what? Stop? Stop talking?'

'No, don't stop talking, please don't stop talking,' Oliver says gently, tears streaming down his face.

'The storm around you.'

'You're talking to me,' Oliver says, '*talking* to *me*. Your voice—'

'The storm around you.'

'—is beautiful. Agna.'

'Is pulling everything apart.'

'—so beautiful.'

'I have been so afraid – of that. For so long. Of what you might do.'

'Agna, I would never hurt you.'

'But you've damned yourself through me.'

'I—'

'And now Archie.'

'Oh.'

'For whatever cross you carry.'

Oliver holds his gaze on Agna, he cannot turn to look at his son.

'But what have we done to you – to deserve this?' she continues.

'Your voice—'

'You'll deny it all.'

'—your lovely voice.'

'You'll deny it.'

'No. I won't.'

'Your need to lose faith in everything. In us. In yourself.'

'Agna.'

Agna looks at her father, a seam of sweat glistening now across her forehead.

Oliver looks into his daughter's eyes. 'Oh, Agna.'

The door opens and Mrs Earwaker enters with Doctor McKnight bringing in a rush of cool air from the hallway. Doctor McKnight immediately attends to Archie's wound. Archie groans at his touch, but he's alive, Doctor McKnight says to himself, and alive is good. He signals to Mrs Earwaker to administer some whiskey to Archie. Mrs Earwaker fills a glass half full with the stuff, slips her arm under Archie's head to raise it a little then brings the glass to his lips. The whiskey spills down Archie's chin. Archie coughs, splutters, but manages to swallow some. For a second – Doctor McKnight thinks he must be imagining it as he looks into Archie's wound – he believes he sees a small rivulet of golden fluid flush across the clotted blood and knotted flesh. He cleans the wound and nods to Mrs Earwaker to give Archie more whiskey. Then placing a clean cloth swab between Archie's teeth he begins the stitching. Archie groans and squirms in pain, biting on the swab, his eyes widening, gripping Mrs Earwaker's arm. Mrs Earwaker tells him that it will all be over soon. To hold on. Everything will be fine. The stitching is mercifully quick and Doctor McKnight then busies himself assembling the transfusion apparatus, which he has brought with him. He works efficiently and calmly. Out of the corner of his eye he catches the strange configuration of who he assumes are the father and daughter in the family, their bodies leaning into one another. Is that the father? The one responsible for this aberration? How is it possible? Doctor McKnight thinks as he prepares a syringe and a regulating flask for the transfusion. What kind of an accident was it that involved the son being mutilated by a cross-cut saw? He looks sideways at Oliver, studies the man for a brief second, finds it hard to believe that a man who appears so docile, so frail, could have done such a thing.

Behind him Edith echoes the groan. He turns his head to the sound, squints in order to see better in the gloom. Another patient? She'll have to wait. He turns back to Archie.

'The donor?' he asks Mrs Earwaker, then automatically looks to Oliver.

Oliver turns, a moment of unexpected joy when he realises he can put things to right, offer his blood to his son, save him. But Agna unfurls her fists from her throat and stretches her arms out. She moves quickly towards Doctor McKnight.

'Agna's his twin,' Mrs Earwaker explains.

'Better chance of the blood being of the same type,' says Doctor McKnight.

'Better chance?' Mrs Earwaker says, her eyes holding on Agna. 'They must have the same blood type if they're twins.'

'No, not necessarily. But we take the chance and the boy may live or we don't take the chance and the boy will die.'

Agna rolls up the sleeve of her blouse and kneels by the bed. She offers her arm. Doctor McKnight signals to Mrs Earwaker to pour some antiseptic liquid he has taken out of his case on to a clean napkin. He wipes Archie's arm and inserts a needle, connects the needle to a syringe then fits the syringe into the tube from the regulating flask. He carries out the same procedure with Agna. He draws out the piston of the flask. Watches as Agna's syringe fills with her blood. He turns the stopcock halfway around and pushes the piston. Agna rests her head against the side of the bed. She glances up at Archie, listens to the sound of her blood moving into him. She imagines her blood spreading and blossoming in Archie like twists of geranium, like the unfolding ferns, like the spreading, reaching succulents in her portable garden, their blooms eagerly growing, moving through his veins, a marvellous frondescence, giving life to him, offering resurrection's sap. With the losing of blood the world now seems softer and slower to her. The voices of Mrs Earwaker and Doctor McKnight become one, their timbres melting one into the other until she can no longer tell them apart.

She shifts her gaze. She looks across the room to see her father standing by the wall, shivering as though standing in a shower of cold rain, his head tilted back and looking up like the boy she had dreamed about who had been hanged by his mother's knotted stockings from the bridge, the stockings she had gnawed at with her teeth until they had begun to fray, his skin translucent, his bones dissolving, leaving him as fragile as freshly blown glass. A fresco of despair, dimensionless, flat, airless, which could collapse any moment at the touch of a finger, or fade completely with a swift glitch in temperature or change in light. She feels she could look and look at him and still not see a human being, a mirage perhaps, a ghost, a ghost becoming ash, becoming smoke, disappearing right before her eyes.

Why all that urgency and fret? he is thinking as he stands by the wall. Why all that effort and worry? She had named it – Agna had named it. He had damned himself through those he loved. One thing to have lived a life in the shadow of his mother's death, quite another to then learn his part in it and how she had sacrificed herself for him. Had he suspected as much, somewhere deep down? Had he known the truth all along and denied it? Whichever way, with the burden of that infinite debt he is now all things evaporable. First water, a bag of water on a boat – thank God, an image for him to cling to – the sea beneath him urging up and opening down, he's rolling starboard and then to the other side of the boat – whatever that is called he cannot now remember, he knew it once but cannot find it – trusting the battered wood and rusted slats of his little boat. No stick with which to steer it – what is that called? Another word he cannot catch – he lifts his arm and moves it behind him to make it physical, his hand clenches the unseen tiller – there it is – yes – the tiller. His heart like a compass now searching out the final course, the inner disc tilting on its axis. The stream of the world in front of him flowing and catching, catching and flowing. The jelly of his eyes quivering in the wind, then startling in tiny flinches at all they see. The air quaking around him and all the words have gone out of his head, except the words I'm sorry, and now it is the emptiness of his head which is keeping him afloat at the last moment, before he himself becomes the quaking air. Yes, he would like to curl up into a ball of water before he evaporates and turns to nothing, to roll around the boat for a while, a passive occupier of his own body, peace granted, before he sails across the desert of black ice which stretches out before him and his soul's light goes out.

As they sit through the transfusion, Mrs Earwaker reassures them all that, sooner than they think, the police will lose interest. They might look for Oliver at the port over the next few days – the Belfast to Liverpool route being the most obvious one to have taken – but she doubts it'll come to anything. But she knows people in Dublin, the Molloys, who, if they want, will take them in until everything settles down. Despite, or indeed because of, the political unrest it will be safe, she reassures them, no one will think of looking for them there. Archie can recuperate for as long as he needs, and once he's strong enough you can come back to Belfast. Then, realising they have no flat to come back to, after all her busy chat, she goes quiet.

Doctor McKnight agrees it might be risky for the Flecks to stay in Belfast for the time being. Archie may be let off with a short remand at some industrial school – that's if charges are pressed of course, which they might not be. But for Oliver it's a case of grievous bodily harm, there's no question about that (his tone admonishing when he says this) and prison is a distinct possibility. Doctor McKnight soberly turns his attention back to Archie and then to Edith, passing Oliver who stands by the wall, staring out blankly into the air in front of him. He tends to Edith, whose eyes are like slit plums. He administers arnica to reduce the swelling and laudanum for the pain. He leaves medication for Archie in case of fever. As he goes he tells Mrs Earwaker to call on him if he's needed at any stage during the night. Mrs Earwaker slips money into his hand.

Over the next two days Archie's condition stabilises. Aware of some police activity at the Empire – although whether or not it has to do with Sydney Brown's dodgy tax affairs or the recent shooting of two RIC men in a city centre hotel, she isn't sure – Mrs Earwaker makes the suggestion that the Flecks head for Dublin sooner rather than later. If the police are on the lookout for them the next most obvious place to check is their old flat. So it might make sense, if they are able, to travel a little further and out of harm's way for a while. Agna listens carefully to Mrs Earwaker and nods her head in agreement.

The following morning Mrs Earwaker brings down a few bags of clothes and sundries belonging to the Flecks, which were left in their flat after the bailiffs' raid, together with Agna's portable box garden that she had left behind in the rush to the theatre with Archie. Agna checks the garden, waters it gently, puts the lid on it. She packs a few toiletry essentials, including a box of medicines which Doctor McKnight has left for them. Mrs Earwaker gives Archie a walking stick to aid his movement and then organises a cab to bring them all to the station, putting some money in Agna's hand as she climbs into the cab. 'Be careful, my dear,' she says to Agna.

While passengers board the train to Dublin, porters load cargo assigned for transportation, wooden crates containing cloth and hats, bags of hayseed, barrels of jam. As one of the bags of hayseed is being lifted on to the train it splits and spills on the platform. A porter rushes over with a brush to sweep it up. Passengers stand at the open doors of the carriages to say their goodbyes to loved ones.

Edith, Agna, Archie and Oliver sit together in a carriage to the rear of the train. They are aware of the commotion on the platform, the hollers of orders from the station hands, the movements of the porters along the train's corridors, however, they remain seated, and silent. Agna watches as the disgruntled stationmaster waves his arms at the porters to hurry them along, while an elderly man in a top hat kisses the gloved hand of a young lady – taking the opportunity which has arisen to have a few more moments together. The young lady then twists away from him with her head bent to board the train.

They had arrived at the train station without event. There was not the police presence they had expected at the entrance or in the waiting area or by the ticket offices. They had walked easily through the ticket turnstile and down the steps to the platform. Oliver followed or was led. Agna had found an empty carriage and had organised their suitcases on the luggage rack above their seats. They had sat down. They had waited. Perhaps all the worrying was for nothing.

Now, there is more shouting from the platform and then the heavy clang of a carriage door closing, then another and another. The stationmaster waves a small flag and blows his whistle. The train gives a big sigh and moves off.

They are a sorry sight. Archie is curled up on the train seat beside Edith, limp-limbed and shrunken, wearing Bertie's shoes, which are still too big for him. His eyes open occasionally as though awaking from a trance and then they close again, Agna's shawl covering his waist and knees. Edith wears a wide-brimmed felt hat, which she refuses to take off even though its brim prevents her from resting her head back on the seat. Mottled yellow-brown bruises pattern her cheekbones. Oliver sits beside Agna, staring at his feet, his hands clasped loosely between his legs. He is unshaven, his shocking white hair is oily and limp at the back and sides, dry blisters on his forehead and behind his ears. And Agna, unlikely guardian of them all, who has flinched at life at every turn, is now their witness and protector.

At Dundalk Agna unpacks some bread and cake. She gives some to Edith and Archie who eat eagerly. But Oliver refuses the bread. He refuses the water Agna offers him from a flask.

On its way to Drogheda the train slows down and unexpectedly comes to a halt. Looking out the window Agna cannot see any station nearby. She wonders if the cargo has presented another problem for the crew. Then she sees two men walking purposefully along the stony trough by the tracks towards the front of the train. The two men are in ordinary clothes so they're not railway workers, she thinks. Their hats are pulled down over the eyes just like Edith's and they have cotton rags tied around the lower part of their faces. As the men walk a little further along, Agna sees that each of them carries a rifle. Shouts come from the front of the train. The two men with the rifles stop, then turn and walk back along the track. Agna presses her head against the window to gain a better view. She sees the two men board the train, climbing into the carriage behind them. Then she sees a group of people approach the train, walking quickly across the field. Women in aprons and boots, children as young as three or four, two more men carrying rifles, a burly older man with a handcart. She gets up. Through the windows on the other side of the train she can see a similar crowd approach. A young woman pulls a donkey on a rope. Then suddenly a loud shudder and clang as the doors on the cargo carriages are thrown open. The flat thud of wooden crates on the track. Voices lift in excitement. Agna sees a stout woman trundling back across the field, weighed down by wads of material in her arms; a child follows her, carrying a pile of hats. The burly man is filling his handcart with bolts of cloth. The young woman throws bags of hayseed across the donkey's back. A boy rolls a barrel of jam along the tracks then tips it on to the dusty trough which runs alongside them, another boy helps him push it over the small ridge and down the slope into the field.

'Why has the train stopped?' Edith asks.

Agna shakes Archie by the shoulder and he lifts his head to her. She points out of the train window and, struggling a little as he turns his body, he watches the scene unfold.

'It's a raid,' he says, his voice croaking. 'They're stealing the cargo.'

'Who?' Edith sits forward.

'Just people.'

'Leave them to it. Sit tight,' Edith whispers.

'The police might come,' Archie says.

'Hardly. Where are we anyway?' Edith presses her eyelids gently with her fingers.

'I don't know.'

'Maybe we should get off the train.'

'Why?'

'If the police arrive – what'll we do then?'

'It's too dangerous to get off.'

'More dangerous to stay.'

The noise of the looters continues outside and more people are seen hurrying away with stolen goods in their arms, across their shoulders, on their backs.

'Maybe if we changed cabins, mixed in with other people, we'd be less obvious to the police.' Edith is already straining to gather their belongings, folding up the shawl which covers Archie.

'Maybe there's nothing to worry about,' Archie says, pulling the shawl from his mother's hands. 'Maybe once they've taken what they want the train will move on and that'll be that.'

'Have another look and see what other people are doing, Agna, go out into the corridor. Archie you keep your eyes on those fields in case the police are coming.'

As Agna goes to leave the carriage she brushes against her father. He has not spoken since Agna spoke to him. For a brief second Agna stops beside him, some instinct to listen to his silence perhaps, and with that he takes her hand, squeezes it tenderly, his head bowed. She turns to him, tilts his head up with her fingers, looks into his eyes, holds her gaze on him for a moment. There is a meekness to him that is shocking to her – a quality in him which she has never seen before. He holds her hand. Surrenders his right to be. And then he lets go.

Agna walks along the corridor looking into the other cabins on the train. The passengers are still in their seats, some are talking, others are looking out of the window at the fleeing looters, none seem to be panicked, merely curious. When she arrives back at her cabin only Archie and Edith are there. Oliver is gone.

'Where's Daddy?'

'I thought he went to find you?' Edith says.

Agna looks around her, then looks up and down the corridor. Her eyes frantically scour the field, for any detail, any shape in the distance that might look like her father, any familiar outline amongst the scattered shapes of the looters moving amongst the tall grass. She moves swiftly to the other window, can still see no sign of him. She swings back out on to the corridor again and begins moving through the train looking into the faces of the passengers. Oliver is not among them. Reaching the front carriage, Agna gets off the train and stands on the track, then runs down to the emptied cargo carriages at the rear of the train. Spills of hayseed mark the escape routes of the looters. There are a few crumpled hats in the dark hold as she steps in to search it. Every ounce of material has been taken. Then she begins the whole process over again, running down each side of the track and looking out across the fields, climbing back on to the train and moving through each carriage examining the faces of the passengers. Some are now moving around the corridors. She brushes past a small group discussing the whereabouts of the driver and ticket master, complaining that they will be late for the boat they plan to catch from Dun Laoghaire.

No matter how hard she looks she cannot find him. A cold panic grips her heart. Her father has disappeared.

III

words Of snow

S he believes that all she has to do is look hard enough for him in the cabins or along the corridors of the train and he will appear. She loses count of the number of times she walks through the carriages as the train sits waiting on the tracks, boldly staring into the face of each and every passenger, checking the dreary spread of land on either side of the train over and over again.

Back in the cabin her mother and Archie wait for her. He's bound to be looking for a porter, they say, or finding out when the train is due to continue its journey, look again, they say to her. But she cannot find him anywhere. And as she searches, time takes on a strange progression. It rushes away from her and then trails heavily behind her. Her breath feels solid in her throat and a huge weight grows in her stomach.

The RIC arrive, but too late to accost the looters or their spoils. Unlike some of the passengers who have been unnerved by the incident, the RIC appear unperturbed. Once they confirm that no one has been injured they set about getting the train moving again. One young policeman shouts out to the passengers who are standing hoping to catch a last glimpse of the disappearing looters to take their seats. She urgently pushes her way towards him hoping he will see her agitated state and understand her predicament. She holds back her tears as best she can and tells him – tells him with her fists at her throat to push the words out of her mouth loud and clear – that her father is missing and that the train mustn't move until he is found and back on board again. Please, she says, as clearly as any other, please wait for him, my father is in a bad way, we cannot leave without him. The policeman, a tall boy of about nineteen with large dark eyes and two beaming red cheeks, looks embarrassed by her behaviour and tells her to return to her seat, that the train is going to move off at any moment. She grabs his sleeve and pleads with him again. Please, my father has gone missing, she says, the train can't go without him. With a shrug he pulls his sleeve free of her hand and makes his way quickly into the adjoining carriage.

As the train begins to move she hurries back to her mother and Archie, her panic mounting, and with that a growing anger at her father for having abandoned them at such a time as this, which is how she is beginning to see it, a time when what they need most of all is to stay together. She tells her mother and Archie – and they hang on her every word – that she cannot find him, that there is no sign of him on the train. He is gone, she says, gritting her teeth. What do you mean, he's gone? her mother says. Gone where? Then she turns away from her mother to the window and presses her forehead on the cool glass, once again searching the stretch of empty fields beyond. Suddenly a glimpse, a dark outline against the sky, his familiar shape rising up out of the stretch of field, or perhaps she only imagines him there. Trees cut across her vision of him, wipe him out. He's gone. As the train gathers speed her eyes fill up with tears. She watches the landscape slip past her.

By the time they arrive in Dublin they are drained and confused and stand motionless on the platform at Connolly station as though waiting to be told what to do next. Archie is in a sorry state, his dressing seeps with a rill of fresh blood and his face is as pale as a stone. When she touches her mother's hands they are cold and stiff.

Now her father is gone, an energy rises within her, a faint light hope which she finds hard to explain – she becomes nurse and navigator. She clutches the piece of paper – on which Mrs Earwaker has written the address of the place they are to stay, the Molloys' house – tightly in her hand. She shows it to a porter at the station. He kindly guides them to the platform for the train that will take them to Dun Laoghaire. She imagines he thinks them an unfortunate trio – her mother dazed and cold, her brother crippled, and her wide-eyed and frightened. He offers to purchase the tickets for them and she gives him some money from her mother's purse. Eventually, they board the train to Dun Laoghaire.

Although the journey is not long, perhaps half an hour, it feels interminable. Darkness descends and she can see nothing of the geography of the landscape through which they travel. Archie is in distress, although he tries hard not to show it. She administers some laudanum to ease his pain and gives him a slug of whiskey from a small flask in one of her bags. Her mother asks for some whiskey too. She lifts the bottle to her mother's lips and her mother sips the whiskey, then asks for some more.

Outside the station at Dun Laoghaire cabmen shuffle on the pavement beside their horse-drawn cabs. The other passengers who have disembarked the train move quickly to greet family or to run for the tram, which is trundling past the clock tower. Other people head up into the town. On the far side of the road the gates of the Pavilion Gardens are firmly closed, the Pavilion building rises imposingly behind them, an elaborate scaffold of glass and wood in the gloom.

She has no idea where to go next. She holds her mother close to one side of her and supports Archie on the other as he uses his stick.

Like this they walk along the seafront. Terraced houses grace the height above the railway tracks and on the other side of the road a line of black trees hem the brightly stoned esplanade that leads down to the sea. She can hear the sea, feel the sea breeze, but when she turns to look at the inky blackness it frightens her and she turns away. She needs to believe that somehow everything will work out, that they will not be consumed by this nightmarish situation.

Only a short distance along the seafront, by a small tram shelter, Archie staggers, pulling his weight heavily down on her. Holding him as best she can, she hauls him into the shelter and pulls her mother in after them. They take refuge here, squeezing themselves inside and propping themselves up against each other on the wooden seat as though they are being asked to squash into an already crowded room, even though there is only them. Rest for a bit, she says quietly, feigning an adult kind of calm. But her throat feels as constricted as a twisted pipe. Like pilchards, her mother says after a while, we're just like pilchards in a jar. And her mother says nothing more after that.

They have few articles with them so their bags are not heavy and her box garden, its lid on tight to protect the tiny plants, has dried out a little and feels lighter because of that. They pile their bags on top of their knees and fold their hands in under their arms in an effort to trap some heat. Their feet are freezing. Stilled in every sense of the word by the cold and the unfamiliar, and by the harshness of recent events, it feels as though there is no point in trying to work out how things will be, or what will become of them. It is too cold to think.

As time passes she becomes more concerned about Archie. He is shivering and pale. Her mother is also in a bad way and that unnerves her just as much as Archie's condition. But despite her growing fear and desperation she does not move or try to do anything for them.

She feels disorientated and rudderless. Her mother had always been the one to find a way through things, had prided herself on her resourcefulness. All through the years when they were moving from place to place her mother was the one to provide some measure of consistency in their lives. But it seems as though her mother is slipping deeper into a dark trance-like state, like the one Archie had tried to induce in Sadie, to his cost.

They huddle together in the shelter in Dun Laoghaire, immobilised not only by the shock and the cold but by an imminent, unnameable threat. Their heads drop down on to their chests and they pretend not to exist.

She allows fantasies to fill her head, as is her way: stretched out on makeshift beds, like rafts on a calm sea, she is back in the theatre dressing room and snow is falling all around her. Harry is there in his frock coat and too-short trousers and his starched white shirt front sticking out under his huge jacket, telling them jokes, making them laugh and spinning fantastical stories. She is listening to Harry, her head partly covered by her shawl, which is salted with snow, and she is comforted by the softening of her mother's face and by the weather which caresses them.

Archie groans beside her, stirring her from her thoughts. She needs to get him to warmth and safety. Leaving her mother and Archie in the shelter, she asks a passer-by the way to Dalkey and how far it is to walk, trying as hard as she can to speak clearly and without hesitation. Dalkey turns out to be a short enough distance along the coast road. They have used up the last of their money on the train to Dun Laoghaire, but she approaches a cab driver and explains their situation with such openness that he takes them to the Molloys' house and asks for no payment, for which she tells him she is very grateful.

She knocks nervously on the door. It opens and a small man of about sixty stands in the doorway looking entirely confused at the shabby threesome who have appeared in front of him. She explains who they are and tells him that she is expecting her father to join them – which is her way of keeping hopeful – and his face brightens. Nora, he calls back into the house, stoke up the fire and put the kettle back on the boil, the Northerners have arrived, which she thinks a strange way to describe them. Mr Molloy helps her mother up the steps and into the house while she takes Archie's arm and follows.

They are given coddle and tea. Archie's dressing is tended to by Mrs Molloy who applies a strong-smelling ointment to help the bleeding stop and gives him spoonfuls of medicine to ease the pain. Unpacking her bag that night she is amazed to discover a ten pound note in an envelope, on the front of which is written 'This is everything I own' in her father's hand. She gives it to her mother.

It is indeed a safe house. Mr and Mrs Molloy cannot do enough to look after them. They do not ask them what happened, only wondering if they are hungry or want more bedclothes, and such things to keep them comfortable. Mrs Molloy borrows clothes for them to wear, makes eggs and fried bread in the mornings and pea and barley soup in the evenings. At night Mr Molloy lights a fire in the front parlour where they sleep. Archie stretches out in the bed over by the window, which Mr Molloy has made for him, and she and her mother lie on their small beds either side of the fireplace. Looking at them Archie jokes: 'You're like two aul ornaments, you are.' But although they are comfortable and safe they are anxious, as there is still no sign of her father.

One evening, sitting together with the grate throwing out oblongs of orange light, her mother talks to them about their father, her bruised eyes now healed, and it is clear that, despite all that has happened, she still loves him and wants everything to right itself. She tells them about their father growing up in Eden's Cross – as though by doing so she can somehow make him appear in the room, make him real to them again. She tells them how his mother died tragically when the station footbridge she crossed had collapsed, which they are saddened and surprised to hear – their father rarely if ever talked about his childhood, and certainly not about how his mother died. Her mother says that since it happened he suffered at the thought of it, and that still as a grown man had never reconciled himself to the fact. She tells them how his misfortune was compounded by a cruel father who deserted him, and, it seems, by Edwin, who he felt had forsaken him. But we were good together, she says, we were life's double-act, we were Edith and Oliver. We toured together, we gave our best, and whenever he wasn't with me, whenever we weren't working together, I missed him. And when you were born, she says, lifting her head to Agna and Archie, there was such happiness. And she says the word as though it has magically turned on a light inside her, exhaling long and slow, her eyes filling up. She says how generous he was, how he worked so hard for everything and fought so hard, and how, over the years, the qualities and talents which lifted him out of the ordinary, and made him the brilliant man and performer he was, which attracted her to him in the first instance, had somehow become eroded or subdued or spoiled or denounced by the world he found himself in, until everything vital about him was gone. There was no place left for him to be. All he wanted was to be able to provide for them and to make them proud of him, she says quietly, and to believe in his own talents, and her mother talks with a strange nostalgic strain to her voice as though she knows it is all in the past, it is all over.

As she finishes, her mother lifts her chin to the ceiling, the light from the fire flickering on her neck. Talents, she says, there's a parable about talents, about using them, if we're lucky enough to have them. Her mother breathes deeply, her throat taut. The Lord said to use your talents and you will be rewarded. She is surprised to hear her mother referencing the bible; in all the years it was never her way. She assumes that her mother might perhaps be reconsidering her relationship with God, wanting to rekindle her desire to pray and to draw strength perhaps from the religion of her childhood. Her mother keeps her head tilted as she speaks. Dear Lord, she continues, what's the use of giving us talents if when we use them they instil nothing but contempt in others – her voice peaks suddenly – contempt in those fat-bellied goats who wouldn't know or understand talent if it jumped up and bit them on the fucking arse! The air holds still. Then a strange noise comes out of her mother's throat – somewhere between a cough and a strangled yelp – and her mother struggles to hold back from weeping as best she can. Agna is shocked to hear her mother curse. She has never heard her use bad language before, only ever that once at the incident of the sawing in half. Her mother's head remains angled to the ceiling, her jaw tight, her breath a rattle of hot air.

In the silence Archie starts to laugh, then he groans and laughs at the same time because the laughter is hurting his stitches. She looks at her brother and she starts to laugh too. She can't help it and the sense of relaxation in her body surprises her. She laughs and laughs until she feels the heat welling up in her chest and her throat getting tighter and then her eyes filling with tears. Then she starts crying at the same time as she is laughing and then the crying takes over, and she can't stop her tears. She can't stop her tears for Archie and for her mother and for her father and for the anger she feels towards him and for their family being broken from all that has happened and for being apart from each other. And her tears fall and keep falling until it is as though her heart grows twice its size and her eyes harden like diamonds and her throat is bound with ribbons and she feels she wants to break into a hundred pieces.

Her mother turns to her and rests her head on her lap. Agna lets her tears fall upon her mother's face. A rain of want and sorrow. Her mother doesn't cry but borrows her tears instead. Her body shakes and her tears will not stop. And out of nothing comes this great sea, a salt lament, which flows and flows, and she cries until the earth beneath her is satisfied she has cried enough.

As can happen sometimes, a newness comes out of her in her sorrow. She sleeps that night the deepest sleep she ever had, curled under her mother's arm, her knees resting against her mother's ribs. She has no dreams of any sort. Nothing to trouble the black bliss unfolding within her or the protected emptiness around her. She is surrounded by herself and by her mother, and by Archie. All is just so. Her swollen lids are closed to the peppered dusk. Her breathing settled. She is cavity. There is no fear. There is no blame. The snow that she imagines falling is pure and free, only itself and nothing more.

Her body does not move a jot all night. Not a muscle needs stretching, or a limb repositioning. Her curled state is all that is required of her, and that is ease itself. A reprieve so sweet that she feels that she fits into the world again. So small has she made herself from crying that she feels herself to be a baby's weight. And her bones settle still and deep. She is a smooth and gentle husk in a perfect slot.

When she wakes her body feels deliciously weak and her eyelids the heaviest part of her, aching and stinging as she opens them to the early day. Her mother is not beside her but Archie is asleep in his bed. She stretches and yawns and feels a new blood course through her body as though her tears have cleansed her veins.

As she sits up she feels as though she has slept for days and she is starving. She looks around her. Listens to the sounds coming from the back kitchen.

Then her mother appears carrying some slices of bread and butter and ham on a plate. Her mother smiles at her. They sit together and eat the bread and ham and say nothing for there is no need to talk.

Over the following weeks Archie continues to heal well. His stitches hold together despite the rushed job the doctor did in Mrs Earwaker's flat the night of the accident and Mrs Molloy, who in such a short space of time has become like a mother to them, has been forever applying poultices to his wound, which seem, right enough, to have done their job.

Archie's dressing is taken off and he gets up and about. He makes the best of himself and takes to wearing Bertie's shoes around the place. The shoes prompt him to feel strong in himself because of his fondness for Bertie. He says he wants to make Bertie proud.

Whenever Mr and Mrs Molloy's young nieces and nephews come to visit, Archie is eager to show off where the saw had cut him. He pulls up his shirt and makes up stories about how he got into a political fight over the threat of partition – do you think Ireland will be sawn in half just like me? he shouts as he rubs his stomach, the scar glistening like a silvery red centipede on his white skin. The children shriek but seem to enjoy the carry-on no end.

Even though their stay with the Molloys is to be temporary, Agna takes time to learn the small pleasures of tending to domestic things, helping Mrs Molloy with housework and with cooking. There is something about working with the bits and pieces of the everyday, rather than with life's grand schemes, which makes her feel more present in the world and less at its mercy. She tends to her box garden, her constant treasure, adding snowdrop and crocus and biting stonecrop to the alpine pan, thinking perhaps her father might like the new arrangement of their tender foliage when he finally comes to be with them again.

She walks with Archie to Bullock harbour where they watch the fishermen haul in their nets and repair their boats. Archie offers his services even though he doesn't know anything about boats but he puts it across well to the fishermen and they give him work. One afternoon, as the clouds pull in over the sea and the sky becomes heavy, she watches Archie help haul in a catch. He applies himself too eagerly and the nets get tangled. One fisherman tells Archie to pull the nets back on themselves to secure the catch. It doesn't look like there are too many fish in the nets but they appear heavy nonetheless. Archie works solidly for an hour bringing the catch in and then the fishermen get him to clean and oil the winches on the boat. Archie is mercilessly bad at keeping the boat steady and when he finishes he climbs back out on to the pier and throws up. But working again has raised his spirits and he just laughs. It feels that things are backwards, he says, the colour rising once again in his cheeks – when I was in the boat the sea felt as still as a rock and now it feels as though the land is moving.

While Archie works down at Bullock harbour and her mother rests at the Molloys', she takes to walking nearby Victoria Hill. She begins to love it and is not afraid to be on her own in the open world, which makes her feel proud. She is able to see across the whole of Dublin city from one side of the hill and across Dublin bay from the other. Plenty of people walk here and she greets them as she passes. They do not know that it is new to her to speak. Reaching the top of Victoria Hill she can see the Sugar Loaf mountain push its blue into the sky.

She takes a notion, unlikely as it is, that perhaps it might be a good place to watch out for her father, to spot him when he arrives, either to see him below the hill somewhere or walking across it. So she resolves to wait for him there. It is a plan, perhaps a naive one, she thinks, but it gives her a sense of purpose and keeps hope alive for her. Every day she finds a spot on the ridge of the hill, not far from the obelisk, and sits on a rock amongst the deadened grass, with the ashy brambles beside her and the smell coming off the squat gorse as sweet as honey. She waits for him. The trees below her are still leafless and yet, covered in ivy, they give the illusion of being in leaf and flutter their green glossy coats. The black buds on the saplings are shaped like tiny birds' beaks, so much so that she feels like picking worms out from the soil and offering them to the buds as food. She watches the sea below her and soon the soft ebb and flow of her heart becomes its echo.

She waits in hope for her father to join them. That is the plan she clings to. But still he does not come. As the days pass her mother becomes more and more anxious about her father's whereabouts but even more so about the political unrest, the ambushes and the shootings between the RIC and the IRA across the counties and all sorts of people being killed. Just the month before they arrived a young man was found dead in a church field nearby in Ballybrack with five gunshot wounds to his head. Her mother is worried for Archie, that he might arouse suspicion from the wrong sort simply by being a young man out on the road and that some harm might come to him. And then there is still all the unfinished business with Edwin in Belfast. Her mother thinks he might still have an axe to grind with Archie and come after him, although to her and to Archie that doesn't seem likely. If anyone was to be pursued, she thinks, it would be her father for what he had done to Archie.

Regardless, her mother writes to Harriet and Harry in Huddersfield. She decides they will move back to stay with them and that her father will find them there. Indeed her mother has hopes that her father might have already crossed the Irish Sea and, even though he has an idea of the address of the Molloys in Dublin, that he has not written to them so as not to draw any attention to himself or to Archie. She tells the Molloys that they will be leaving by the end of the month.

But there is a tiredness to Archie which becomes increasingly apparent. Even though his wound is no longer causing him discomfort and he has healed as best as could be hoped for, he begins to lack his usual brightness. He stops going to work at Bullock harbour, sleeps late most mornings, going out only in the afternoons for some errands to the village and back and eventually even the simplest of tasks takes it out of him. Weeks pass and still Archie's strength does not return. As April closes, and with the arrival of an unexpected bout of cold weather, Archie catches pneumonia and dies.

She learns after that, with Archie's work at the harbour and on the boats, he may have contracted something from contaminated or brackish seawater and was then too weak to fight the pneumonia when he got it – there had been such a case locally two years before. But maybe, she thinks to herself, maybe if the wrong blood had been given to Archie in the first place, maybe if her blood had been the wrong blood, then perhaps that had caused his body to lose its way of working.

Her mother sits on the edge of Archie's bed as he is dying. As he draws his last breath her mother puts her arms around him and stares into him with every ounce of her being, her son, her beautiful boy.

Agna calls her Edith from then on, not mother. Locked in a distant world it is the name she responds to quickest. The name 'mother' takes too long to register, as though she has lost that role, or given it away.

On a spring day in 1922 she and Edith wait for the mail boat to depart for Holyhead, its funnels spewing rills of smoke into the early morning sky.

Standing on Carlisle Pier, Edith removes her hat to let the wind blow her hair. The light lifting off the sea makes it look as though there is a field of snow stretching before them towards Howth, not sea.

Let's go, she says to Edith, let's go.

They do not move.

She wants to lift Edith, carry her back to Archie and wipe away the tears running down her face, which Edith tells her are only caused by the wind.

The boat brings them to Holyhead. From there they travel to Huddersfield by train. They move back in with Harriet and Harry, who welcome them home with open arms. Edith and Harriet have always been close but the shared loss of their sons now brings them even closer. Harry says to Agna that he is sorry for all her sadness, but together, in their sadness, they will help each other. He remarks how tall she has grown and how long her hair is and how it is good to hear her talking.

And she wonders why she had been so afraid to speak.

She did not decide on the rules and regulations of her silence. She did not choose, for instance, who to speak to and who not to speak to. Growing up she found that she could talk to Archie and at times she could talk to Edith but she couldn't talk to anyone else and, whenever she was expected to, language failed her. Her mind became a prison of words – as she had described it once to Edith – and she would feel a grip, both hot and cold, like an iron claw around her throat. Her heart would pound and her chest would hurt and stiffen as though a metal breastplate was being pulled tighter and tighter around it and there was nothing she could do to release it. She knows it was hard for Edith and for Archie, who only wanted to understand and help her.

Hardest of all for her father, who felt her silence as a wilful rejection. She knows it infuriated him and made him feel helpless in the face of it. But it was as though her brain would flood white whenever her father addressed her, and every thought that had been flying around her head, her grievances and hurts, got all mixed up. He didn't mean to but he made her feel, in the way that he spoke to her, in the manner in which he used his words, that she was nothing and so she made herself into nothing, both to please and escape him. In his anger he always talked so clearly, as though the synapses in his brain fused together in straight lines, and his ideas and thoughts had no distance to cross before they were said. But in these instances, particularly with an amount of whiskey taken, she did not feel safe.

In all the talking about him, no one ever mentioned his drinking. Not Edith, not Harry, not Harriet. And she feels a nub of anger in her chest at their omission. To her that is just as important a part of the story as all the other parts, because when he drank, the father she loved disappeared and, like in a magic trick, someone else took his place.

But she doesn't believe he intended it to be that way. He just didn't see himself. He didn't see the anger set in his face as he talked, he didn't see how defensively he stood in the room, his feet splayed and his arms folded across his chest, he didn't see how aggressively he pointed at her, how he bared his teeth when he spoke to her, snarled at her, grimaced at her, how he would ask if she was all right in a way which implied that she had better be. It was the energy underneath his words which carried the meaning, the words themselves were merely the lick of paint.

When he would talk and behave like that she would feel herself descending into an instant, black panic where the very air she was taking in wounded her, and her own breath became a knife which flailed at her lungs. She couldn't understand why she provoked such anger in him. It made her think there was something wrong with her.

She remembers the nights on tour with his one-man show when things didn't go well, or when people let him down, or when his props got lost or broken, how the room would fill with his anger. She remembers the times when he would suddenly go missing and Edith would be beside herself with worry. She remembers the promises he never kept. She remembers his constant damning of Edwin and the arguing with Edith over her employment at his house. She remembers the uncomfortable tension around him, the darkness, the sullen chill of his presence. And how when he punched the bullock, he became a nightmarish version of himself: the sinister cast to his face, his eyes burning black, a violence within him so resolute in its intent it had shaken her to the bone. The terrible disdain with which he looked at her. And then the insults which he flung at her.

After hearing Edith talk about his childhood that night as they sat by the fire, she begins to understand that perhaps her father had learnt those ways from his own father.

But so it goes in life, within a family, like a wave following a wave on the sea.

From his place of suspicion he did not trust that she loved him. And she did love him. Does love him. Wants him to come back. And she knows that he loved her. Loves her. And does not want to be alone, and lost. That's the funny part of it. And the sad part of it too – sad that even when all the possibilities are there for love, love loses faith in itself.

Thinking about what her father did to Archie is, however, the hardest of all – she still sees the picture in her head of that night, her father carrying Archie in the blood-soaked dress up the theatre stairs – because, in truth, she feels partly responsible for Archie's fate. If she hadn't encouraged Archie to take the greyhounds back to Divitt to keep her father out of trouble, then Archie wouldn't have been forced into doing something which was so against his nature. And he probably wouldn't have got caught up in the 'Sawing the Lady in Half' disaster. And although giving her blood to Archie might have seemed a brave thing to do, being his twin did not mean they had the same type of blood. Perhaps it was her father's blood which was more suited to Archie's, but that's something she will never know.

A week after moving to Huddersfield a letter arrives from Edwin. It had been sent first to the Molloys' in Dalkey then redirected to the Gardners'. Edith reads it out to her. *Dear Oliver*, it says, *I am not sure what I have to say to you or indeed how I might say it. I know it was Archie who stole the pistols – though on that matter let me say I have no desire to press any charges, only to say that I am, as a result, concerned about what situation you – all of you – may have found yourselves in. It was Sadie who told Lily and Lily told me, but Lily added that there had been an accident at the Empire the same evening the pistols were stolen involving an illusionist and his son – and the illusionist, word had it, had been named as Oliver Fleck. So as you can imagine my concern for your welfare became all the more heated. After Edith did not turn up for work I paid a visit to your address on Joy Street to make enquiries. A Mrs Earwaker informed me that you had all gone, under rather unexpected circumstances as she put it, to Dublin. When I pressed her further, and rather reluctantly, she offered me the address to which I am now sending this letter. I apologise for not attempting to contact you on immediately receiving the address for, despite my worry, I found it hard to secure the courage to write. I feel I have treated you unfairly and hope I can make amends. Seeing your family – my family – has caused me to re-examine my behaviour towards you. Your wife, Edith, is nothing but gracious and hard-working and your son, Archie, has an earnest optimism about him, which is admirable in such a young man, and he gives without calculation. But it was seeing Agna in particular, her likeness to our mother, which affected me most deeply and is why I am writing to you now.*

I realised that night when you called at my house to take Agna home that you had a different picture in your mind of what had happened that dreadful day. That is why I had to tell you then in the hallway, clumsily I know. I am mentioning this again by way of explaining that I have always known that you could have done nothing to save Mother, but irrational as it is I kept asking myself why she did not take that moment on the footbridge to save herself from falling instead of saving you. I am afraid it is the reason why I hardened myself against you all these years and it is with a deep sense of regret that I did.

I have struggled my whole life with the longing for Mother to return on the one hand and the fearing of our father's return on the other. It has coloured my every waking hour. Perhaps you feel the same, I have no doubts now that you do. I offer you now my assistance in any regard – money, friendship, a home – but particularly if Archie needs any medical attention. I do hope it is nothing serious for the boy. The house remains at Eden's Cross by the way, as it was. I have travelled there twice in the past but on both occasions found myself unable to step inside. I did, however, leave flowers on Mother's grave. I am at your disposal and will protect you all in any way I can. I look forward to your reply. Your brother, Edwin.

She finds the letter sad, particularly Edwin's asking after her brother. That was Archie, giving without calculation, easy and gentle in the world, like a bird moving with the current or a green crab catching the ebbing tide he trusted that the world would work with him. A happy arrangement all told, was Archie.

She wonders how she will carry on in the world without him.

And she finds curious the fact that she should resemble her grandmother so, and that Edwin should comment on it.

She is also surprised at the letter's gentle and forgiving tone. For she remembers the harsh accusation which seemed to colour Edwin's voice the night she overheard the conversation, the night she stayed in his house as a sleeper. She had stood on the landing and listened. Unseen, had looked down at them. She listened until Lily appeared and then she could only hear her voice and not theirs. She remembers her father's skin was as dry as bark and as pale as ash. He hadn't shaved. He wore the button fly collared shirt and bow tie he normally reserved for the stage. The shirt was grubby, the bow tie loose and shapeless. Over the shirt he wore his greatcoat, shabby and torn at the pockets. He held his Borsalino in his hands.

Time passes. Six months now since Archie died. She helps Edith and Harriet around the house. Three days a week she works in a local clothing factory as a machinist. She gets better at knowing how to use the sewing machines in the factory. The hardest part is being among strangers, but she is getting better at that too. And Edith is determined that she attend continuation school on the days she is not working. Even though Edith always took pains to give her, and Archie, a good grounding in education on the road, and she is at least efficient in reading and writing and arithmetic, she missed out on elementary school and what that could offer her for the future. Edith believes she is able for more in life.

In the yard of the house in Huddersfield – this house where she and Archie grew up – she tends to her box garden every day. It has given her pleasure since she was a child, since her father first made it for her. She has watched the hardy plants survive, has replaced those that have had their time, renewed the soil, and along the sides and bottom of the box it is plain to see where Archie has, over the years, reinforced the casing and repaired the wood. She places it on the stone plinth in the backyard to catch the light, let the sun slip off the flat roof of the meat shed to warm it, and she thinks about how things happen. Big things and small things. And thinks that it's not only from big things that big things are learnt; all the small things play their part. Individual elements which might seem trivial at the time but in hindsight take on a significance. Like the shoes Archie was given. They had brought him to a sense of himself he hadn't known before – he said that to her, said they had made him question what he was capable of. Bertie's shoes had been too big for him but his feet had filled them nonetheless.

And if it is true that her father was in some way responsible for her withdrawal from the world, he was equally responsible for her reappearance when the moment came, the moment when she spoke out against him, and terrifying though it was, she did not disappear. She remained visible. And she has remained visible in the world and is not afraid to hear her own voice in the midst of it.

She thinks of the times when she and Archie were small and they would watch their father make coins disappear and wine magically move out of one glass and into another and make a mouse run over his fingers. He moved his hands like water. She and Archie would be held in delicious suspense and then would laugh and clap their hands and their father would smile and his eyes would be kind.

She hopes she will see him again. Then she will tell him what happened to Archie and how they did everything they could to save him.

As she twists her box garden on the stone plinth to take the light, she imagines them together up on Victoria Hill, where, protected by nature's truce, she felt unshackled from the sadness of the past and did not know the sadness which was yet to come, because Archie was still alive and with them. She felt the calmness of the blue sky, of the birds singing, of the sound of laughter rising from the lower reaches of the hill. And hope rose in her like a sweet smell on the afternoon breeze.

She sees them there now. Archie gathering strength as she and Edith – she called her *Mother* then – gather nettles for soup. Archie is . . . her mother is . . . the weather falls. Through the drift of coarse grass, as she picks the nettles, she can see tiny yellow protrusions pushing up from the soil. The bulbs are waking up. Their papery tunics peel around their rims. She bends her head to look closer and feels the gentle spread of the sun on the back of her head. Insects buzz past or scamper along the dust patch to find shelter in the undergrowth. The sea can be heard this far up. She turns to look up at the sky. And it is as though she is part of the sky and can look across at the clouds. She is as real as vapour and as shapely. Each cloud fluidly tells its story as it moves across the tender blue. As she watches the clouds she sees a boat become an island and then the island become a tree. Birds break loose from the tree and the trunk floats away like a boot down a river. A bicycle appears, then a huge head of a man with one gigantic eye. A horse leaps across a hedge then becomes the hedge, then a spongy hill, after that a sleeping cow. There's a cloud that looks just like a cloud. Now a cobweb. Spiderless. There are three miserable greyhounds. There's a cart looking for the leaping horse. Then a cloud the shape of Ireland, where memory shimmers most. And there is her father. Floating on his belly as he clasps a strange bird. He lengthens. He lets the bird go. His cloud falls upon Victoria Hill, a blue shadow deepening until it seems he becomes as real as the hill itself. Real and solid, handsome in his town coat, holding his Borsalino in his hand, at odds with nature.

And for a moment they are together again, all four of them. Agna, Archie, Edith and Oliver. And as the sun shines brightly so the snow begins to fall around them and the wind caresses them and the rain spots their shoulders. And all manner of weather comes to bless them.

Her father looks happy to see her and she is pleased that he is here. And he is easy in himself. He smiles at her and gently nods as though to say that things will be sweeter now and all the chaff will fall away and we will be a family once again. She smiles. He holds his arms out and walks towards her. She holds her arms out to him.